WHEN
SORROWS
COME

Maria Dziedzan

SilverWood

Published in 2015 by SilverWood Books

SilverWood Books Ltd
30 Queen Charlotte Street, Bristol, BS1 4HJ
www.silverwoodbooks.co.uk

ISBN 978-1-78132-343-4 (paperback)
ISBN 978-1-78132-344-1 (ebook)

British Library Cataloguing in Publication Data
A CIP catalogue record for this book is available from
the British Library

Set in Adobe Garamond Pro by SilverWood Books
Printed on responsibly sourced paper

To all the victims of oppression

'When sorrows come, they come not single spies,
But in battalions…'
HAMLET, William Shakespeare

Part One

Autumn 1939 – Spring 1941

Chapter 1

The truck screeched to a halt at the barred double gate, which protected the farm and its compound. Three soldiers jumped down from the cab and hammered on the firmly closed wooden gates. The headlights of the lorry lit up the sturdy two metre high fence and made the rest of the October night blacker beyond the circle of lights. The first snows had not yet come, but the cold froze the men's breath. They raised their heavy Tokarev rifles on the nod of their leader, fired at the centre of the gates and pushed them wide. The noise of their gunfire masked for a moment the storm of barking within the compound and, as the soldiers entered the wide circular enclosure, two dogs flew at them, teeth bared. It was difficult to know whose shots killed them as all three soldiers fired automatically at the leaping dogs, who thumped to the ground. There was a whine and some brief twitching and then they lay still. The high walls of the compound had done nothing to protect the family in the farmhouse, nor the livestock in the barns and henhouse. All was open now.

Two of the men crunched across the frozen grass with their leader, while the driver brought the vehicle into the compound to pour light onto the dark home, the fearful listening of its inhabitants palpable. Boots thumped onto the raised wooden platform which skirted the house. The leader gestured at the front door and one of the men struck it with the wooden butt of his rifle.

"Come on, come on," grumbled the leader through his moustache.

His companions shuffled their feet impatiently. This was only one of many deportations they had to attend to before morning and their ally, the darkness, would help to disorientate and make malleable their victims for only a couple more hours.

The door opened and someone peered out, holding a lantern. He saw infantrymen of the Red Army on his porch wearing crumpled greatcoats with red collar patches. On their heads, soft *ushankas*, the red star prominently displayed at the front, framing hard faces.

"Who's there?" he asked in Polish, hoping his eyes were deceiving him.

The leader nodded to one of his men, who put his boot in the opening and leaned on the door with his shoulder.

"Soldiers of the Red Army, comrade," announced the leader as he barged in. "And you are Enemies of the People!"

The Polish farmer stepped back quickly in order to avoid being knocked over. In his night-shirt he was shocked and frightened, but he looked almost as if he had been expecting them. The rumours had begun to spread of Polish families being turned off their farms and being sent God knew where. He began to gather his wits. "You can't just barge in here. This is our home…"

"Get your family dressed. Warm clothes. Pack what you'll need for a long journey. We'll be back in an hour."

"Where are we going?" asked the farmer, now speaking the soldiers' Russian.

"You'll find out when you get there," said one of the soldiers, laughing.

"You can't make us leave our home," cried a shrill voice as the *kulak's* wife entered the hallway. "You have no right."

"We have the power of the Soviet state." After a pause the leader added, "And we have the right to use our guns," pointing his pistol at the farmer's temple.

The wife drew back, her heart hammering, but still managing to say, "You wouldn't dare…" However, she stopped as the pistol was cocked and a gleam entered the eyes of all three men as the routine became more interesting.

"The Soviet state demands this land for all its citizens and not just greedy colonisers like you. So get on with your packing. We'll be back in an hour and if you're not ready, you'll go as you are. Your choice!" he said, shrugging. He nodded to the wife. "You would be wise to pack some food, and you," he turned to the husband, "take some of your tools." And with that the intruders were gone. The door was still open and the truck's motor could be heard as it went down the lane in the darkness, on its way to another Polish-held farm, leaving a stunned silence in its wake.

A couple of hours later, Anna approached the farmstead confidently, as she did every day, but drawing near to the gates, her heart began to pound at the sight of the splintered wood and bullet holes. She stepped cautiously into the compound, wondering if she would be greeted by the dogs, but they were nowhere to be seen. Looking down, she noticed two dark stains on the gravel and drag marks leading in the direction of the midden. She looked towards the shadows under the high fence, but then turned slowly towards the farmhouse. The front door stood open and a light was shining out into the breaking dawn.

She approached the open door slowly, calling out, *"Proshu Pane! Proshu Pani!"* to her masters. She paused to listen for a reply, but, receiving none, stepped over the threshold into the tiled hallway. She called out again, a little more loudly but not so loud that it would wake the sleeping children. There was still no reply. She entered the empty dayroom. Her heart began to flutter as she took in the details of the cupboard doors and drawers left open, their contents spilling out. Her scrupulously neat mistress would never have gone to bed leaving the house untidy. There were dirty bowls on the table and the cooking pot was still warm. The larder door stood ajar, the padlock hanging on its hasp, and Anna peeped into her mistresses' pride and joy, only to see the gaping holes in the well-stocked shelves. Where was their store of flour and sugar? Where was the flitch of bacon which had just been cured?

Her heart jumped in her chest again as she saw the paler shadow of the absent crucifix on the wall. She lifted the lamp. There had been talk in the villages of rich Polish farmers disappearing into the night. Anna hurried to look in the bedrooms. When she approached her mistress' room, she again called out, "*Pani?*", but this time was not surprised to receive no reply. She entered the room and was unperturbed to see the unmade bed, that would have been one of her morning tasks, but on seeing the open wardrobe, she looked for their suitcases. When she could not find them, she hastened into the children's bedrooms to be met by the same emptiness. She sank onto the little girl's bed and reached around automatically to straighten the pillow. Where was the child's beloved doll? They were inseparable. She stood up and shook out the quilt, but there was no doll. She looked into the girls' cupboard and saw that both daughters' warm clothing had been taken. She checked the son's room to find the same dishevelled state of affairs, then hurried back down to the hall to open the cloakroom door. All the warm coats and boots had gone. So they had not been shot, yet...

Chekists, she thought. The rumours of the disappearances had implied unknown destinations, although the word "Siberia" had been whispered, its dreadful susurration speaking of icy steppes and snow-filled forests, where winters lasted for eight months of the year.

She went back through the house into the kitchen, trying to assimilate what had happened to the family. And what about her? She walked into the larder again. It was well-stocked. She knew from her work just how many preserved jars there were against the coming winter, and even in spite of the gaping shelves, its store was abundant by anybody's standards. Just as she was reaching the decision that it would be a waste to leave the food on the shelves, she heard the younger serving girl arriving.

She clattered into the kitchen. "Where are the dogs?"

Anna looked at her face, red from the cold, her young body bundled into an old jacket with a scarf pinned across her chest, and knew the last wages either of them would receive from this master remained in the larder. "The family's gone," she said.

"Where?" asked the girl.

"I don't know, and it's better not to ask. I don't think they'll be coming back either."

"But the dogs…"

"I would guess that whoever did the taking, shot the dogs."

"But why?" persisted the girl.

"I don't know. We need to milk the cows and feed the hens." Anna paused and then came to a decision. "I'll make up a sack from the larder for each of us. There won't be any wages."

The girl's eyes widened, but whatever their desire to gossip and speculate, they both knew enough to do their duty by the livestock and then to get out of there quickly.

When she returned from the milking, the girl said, "I've found the dogs."

Anna looked up. "Where?"

"At the back of the barn."

They went out and across the yard. The younger girl led Anna behind the barn, where the dogs lay side by side, bloodied and limp. "Who would do such a thing?" she said, tears in her eyes.

"The soldiers who took the family," said Anna. "Perhaps *Pan* put the dogs here so that the children wouldn't have to see them."

They stared down at the brown and cream pelts of dogs who had greeted them every day.

"Shall we come back tomorrow?" asked the girl.

"Yes, we'll milk the cows, feed the hens and so on until…" Anna left the future hanging in the air. She led the way back to the house and handed the girl a sack from the larder. "Take this. It may be the last."

The girl took her sack and a pail of the foaming milk. With a brief goodbye, she set off home, her head bowed.

Anna extinguished the lamp and left through the kitchen, picking up her supplies from the larder as she went. She closed the outer doors, crossed the compound, but left the gates open. As she made her way back to the village, she wondered where her next wages might come from.

Chapter 2

The village was like any other in Halychyna, busy with the seasons. But it could be said to be different in one important regard: it rested on the last of the plain above the river Dniester and so nestled against this powerful boundary. A road came into the village, but could go no farther. Travellers would by-pass the village altogether unless they had business with its inhabitants, who tried to live their quiet lives – if only the outside world would let them. In the centre of the village, on the main street, was a low white-washed thatched cottage, its blue shutters folded back. It had two rooms, one on each side of the front door. The family spent most of their time in the room to the left since it comprised kitchen, dining room and, at night, also served as the parents' bedroom. It had the ubiquitous tiled stove – a massive rectangular affair which warmed the dwelling and where all the cooking was done. Its greatest charm, however, was the large flat space behind it where there was enough room for two people to spread a mattress and sleep comfortably.

But now, Anna's mother was seated at the kitchen table, podding the dried beans for winter. She looked up in surprise as Anna entered. "Anna, what's happened? Why aren't you at work?"

Anna placed her sack of groceries on the kitchen table with a heavy sigh. "*Pan* and *Pani*, the children, they've all been taken."

"Are you sure?" asked her mother and then shook her head at her own silly question. "How do you know?" she corrected herself.

"The gates had been broken open when I got there and the dogs had been shot."

Katerina covered her mouth with her hand and then forced herself from her own shock to deal with Anna's. She guided her daughter to sit at the bench behind the table and boiled water for camomile tea while she listened to Anna's tale.

"I think they've gone for good, Mama. They would never have left everything so open if they'd had any choice."

Katerina handed Anna her tea. "Drink this while it's warm." She did not add that it was lucky the *Chekists* worked at night and that Anna had not been a live-in servant. She, too, might have disappeared into the wastes of the east had she been there. Stalin's men were not known for their careful verification of identity. "At least you're safe, child," she could not help saying.

Anna nodded but her mind was still a kaleidoscope of the images of lives ruined. She thought of the children, the little girls and their brother, just a little older than Anna's own brother, safely at the village school. "I wonder what will happen to them."

"Or what might happen to any of us," added Katerina. The Poles had occupied their land, but had not torn families from their beds at night. She suppressed a shudder. She would talk to Anna's father about it. Mikola would be back from the farm he worked on later. Meanwhile, she needed to distract Anna from the images replaying themselves in her mind. "Help me to finish these beans and then we'll go and see if we can find any last hazelnuts."

As the evening drew in, Anna laid the table for supper, while Katerina bustled about at the stove. Anna's brother, Yuri, was shuffling the pages of a school reading-book in an impatient manner. Each appeared pre-occupied, but there was a taut stillness which belied the apparent calm.

"Where can he be?" exclaimed Anna, unable to control her anxiety any longer.

"He'll be home when he can," replied her mother.

"Is *Tato* coming home?" asked Yuri, his eyes wide with alarm.

"Now there's no need for all this," said his mother with determination. "Anna, help Yuri go over his reading passage again."

The girl sat down at the table with her younger brother, opening his school book at the passage he had struggled with earlier. "Come on, Yurchik," she said, "let's see if we can do better with this reading." She already regretted that her outburst had upset the boy and so she bent her head towards his, placing her arm around his thin shoulders in a gesture more maternal than sisterly.

The family resemblance was clear in their grey eyes and their smiles, which matched one another in their flashes of merriment. But there was no amusement in Yuri at this moment. He was simultaneously struggling with the hieroglyphics before him and all too aware of both women's attempts to hide their disquiet. It was dark, and his father should have been home by now. The table, despite Yuri's book, was set for supper. The food was ready. Both his mother and sister were twitching with ill-concealed impatience. However, there was no point in Yuri complaining and refusing to read; they would always win any argument with their determined love. So he submitted to Anna's help and to her warm arm around his shoulders. As older sisters went, she wasn't bad, he thought. At least she helped him rather than ridiculed him.

For her part, Anna led Yuri patiently through the text again, knowing he cared little for it. He would rather be running about with his friends or labouring with his father than learning to read. Anna's stomach churned at the thought of her father. He was rarely late home from the fields and never gave her mother any anxiety if he could avoid it, so his characteristic consideration made Anna more frightened for him. However, she did not allow herself to wonder what was keeping him as she knew she would only terrorise herself with her memories of that morning. So she focussed on Yuri's struggle...

The door opened suddenly and a blast of cold air accompanied Mikola into the room. All three leapt towards him with cries of "*Tatu*!" and "Mikola!" but he brushed all aside saying, "I'm ready for my supper!" He ruffled Yuri's hair and kissed both wife and daughter on the cheek. Then he strode over to the bowl of warm water beside the stove, washed his hands and with a "Come now, no fuss. Let's eat," he insisted they follow his lead, taking their seats at the table, while Katerina served their supper of potato dumplings and fried onions. They bowed their heads in a brief grace and the family ate because they were hungry, but they could all be seen to be keeping a vigilant eye on the father, knowing there would be no explanation until they had eaten.

When the dishes had been cleared away, they all sat at the table expectantly. Mikola was a little amused by their curiosity, but he was also aware of the fear caused by something as simple as a lack of punctuality. When people disappeared into the abyss with no explanation, no one could be casual about coming home. He took a breath and announced, "As you know, we elected Michaylo Dovbush to be our *starosta*, and we know that he will take our concerns seriously. Because the Polish farmers are leaving this area, the land needs to be redistributed to be worked." He paused. "I've been asked to work a parcel of land between the woods and the shrine."

Katerina smiled at her husband. "Good."

"But isn't that our old land?" asked Anna, looking from one to the other of her parents.

Mikola could not help but grin. "It is indeed. It seems we will be working our family land again."

Yuri mirrored his father's grin, eyes shining. He only knew that his beloved father was happy, and if his cautious mother was smiling too, then this must be good news.

"However," continued Mikola, "we will still have to give grain to those in the cities. We can't think only of ourselves."

His eyes met Katerina's and Anna registered the warning behind the words. This was undoubtedly a blessing, that hereditary lands were being restored, but a benign *starosta* had limited powers. The Soviet state behind him would have to make the merest of gestures and all could yet be swept away. Anna resolved to discuss this further with her father as soon as an opportunity presented itself, but for now she had to be content. She knew he would not go into detail in front of Yuri, who was still young enough to trip over the story at school. She was also familiar with her mother's caution. She would not want her children to have knowledge or opinions which might indict them.

"There we are," Mikola said smiling. "We are very fortunate. We will have our land back and be able to help others who have no land. And now Yuri, how's that reading?"

The boy groaned and fetched his book to read to his father while his mother and sister picked up their sewing. Yuri was young even for his nine years. His blond crewcut and sparkling grey eyes told of a well-loved and protected child. His merriness stemmed from the safety of his home, where there were three adults who adored and protected him. They indulged his lively humour and curiosity, only exhorting him to a greater circumspection beyond the home. But both Katerina and Mikola knew that while he might damn himself with his indiscreet talk, his charm would always save him. His ready smile and joyous response could melt most hearts. And Anna protected him as often as she could, encouraging others to see him as a child so that the armour of his infancy might protect him for a little longer. His innocence shone from him like sunlight on water; there was no duplicity in him and the adults sometimes trembled in the certain knowledge that he would have to become aware of the world's iniquity one day. He would not be able to avoid it.

Later that evening, Yuri was ushered off to bed after prayers said before the icon. He and Anna slept in the second room, but since Anna was much older than Yuri, she remained in the larger living area with her parents, listening to their murmured conversation.

"It's an ill-wind for the Poles, but many in the village will benefit."

Katerina nodded. "Somebody always has to pay."

"They will pay when they reach the North," Mikola concurred. "I heard they were driven to the station and put in cattle trucks."

"Shhh!" warned Katerina, glancing at Anna who was listening intently.

"Anna, my girl," said Mikola, his light blue eyes full of tenderness for his lovely daughter, "don't repeat what you hear here."

"You mustn't, Mikola. Don't talk like that in front of Anna."

"Mama, I need to know, too," said Anna quietly.

"She's right, Katerina. Anna needs to know what's happening. How else will she be safe?"

"Yes, but she's still so young!"

"Not so young, Mama. I'm sixteen."

Her mother smiled despite her anxiety at this younger image of herself. "I know, but we don't know what might happen."

"All the more reason to arm her," said Mikola in low, serious tones. "Anna, don't repeat anywhere what you hear at home. Trust nobody except us. Today they're deporting the Poles wholesale in cattle trucks. It could be anybody tomorrow."

"Mikola!" Katerina looked shocked.

"We've heard what they did further east," he reminded her. "Starving our people. Why would Stalin suddenly love us?"

"Hush! Hush!" whispered Katerina.

"Katerina, the whole village knows that when we heard about the *Holod*, we all contributed grain to Father Dubenko's collection for the victims in the East, but we were not allowed to send it!"

"Yes, but it's not wise to talk of it."

"I know," he reassured her. "But neither of you should ever expect anything good to come from the Bolsheviks. Just remember, they can't be trusted… ever."

"But we're lucky with our *starosta*, aren't we, *Tatu*? Michaylo Dovbush is a good man isn't he?"

"Yes, he is, he is good. But he is only one man."

They sat quietly for a few moments, each plagued by their own anxieties, all fearing a secure future was unlikely.

Michaylo Dovbush had been elected leader of the village in October 1939 and Mikola was right in his judgement that their *starosta* was a man of integrity. He would galvanize the return of the Ukrainian language in the village school and welcome its return to government and courts of law. He had long been an active and benign force in the village: organising concerts of Ukrainian song and dance, running the Reading Room where their history and literature were available to the villagers. He encouraged the women to organize "Tea Evenings" when the love of tradition could be shared over a steeped infusion of linden flowers. Now he would have considerable sway over the farming arrangements and with a member of the police force and a state procurator from the county town of Buchach, would form the *troika*, the triumvirate who had the power of life and death in their hands…but safe hands.

The villagers passed a quiet winter in the hiatus between the departure of the Polish *Pan* and the installation of Russian rule. Some breathed a sigh of relief as they returned to their land; others simply held their breath as they tiptoed towards a more overt Soviet style of government. The priests were the first to feel the steel fist tighten. They could now only travel with special passes and had to pay rent to the state for the use of their churches. Before long, they would be fleeing for their lives before the steam roller of state atheism. Others began to fear rumours of collectivisation: they felt sure Stalin would impose the *kolhoz* as a means of controlling and squeezing the people. Dovbush though, was kept busy, constantly trying to lessen the impact of new pronouncements. His gentle manoeuvring often took the edge off a dangerous situation, but even he, for all his diplomacy, reached a breaking point, in February 1940.

Michaylo was in his office at the back of the Reading Room going over the busy calendar for the approaching agricultural season. He felt confident that the men of the village knew their jobs and would do them well, as only those lucky enough to work their own soil can. So the yield might be good enough, weather permitting, for them to pay their tithe to the state and to live in relative comfort this year. His agreeable musings were shattered by the sound of footsteps tramping across the Reading Room. He looked up from his desk as the door was thrown open by two men wearing the uniforms of NKVD officers, denoted by their blue caps with red piping and their green collar patches. Michaylo stood up quickly, his features grave.

"Good evening, Michaylo Semenovich," said the portlier of the two, light glinting on his round spectacles. "We thought it was time we paid you a visit to see how things are progressing."

The thinner moustachioed man smiled smugly and reached for two chairs standing by the wall. "Sit down, comrade," he said to his companion, "while we have a chat with our good friend Dovbush."

Dovbush himself tried not to swallow. He had known the moment would come when the wolves of the NKVD would call him to account. He sat down and leaned back in his chair. "How can I help you, comrades?" he asked, smiling the smile of the damned.

"Well, let's see. I think you know your village well?"

"Yes, I think so."

"How are your farmers behaving? Ready for work are they?" asked Baranovich, the flash of his glasses a redundant warning to Michaylo.

"As usual," he replied. "Hoping for good weather."

"And your priest? Is he still saying Mass?"

"Yes."

"Well-attended?" asked Baranovich.

"Not so many as before," hedged Michaylo.

"And the intelligentsia of the village?" sneered Peskiv.

"Intelligentsia?" repeated Michaylo.

"Of course! There aren't any apart from yourself. The levels of literacy in the countryside are really frightful." He gave a high-pitched giggle.

A silence followed while the two men stared unblinkingly at Dovbush.

He sat quite still and did not allow himself to fidget as he met their gaze, apparently unperturbed by their questioning.

"And the young men…" Baranovich allowed the phrase to hang in the air for Dovbush to take the bait.

Michaylo simply looked at his opponents and waited. He would not ask their questions for them.

"Are they all preparing to defend their country tooth and nail?" asked Peskiv.

"I don't know," Michaylo replied.

"We think they are," said Baranovich. "And a good *starosta* would know, wouldn't he?"

"Perhaps."

"Don't they all go off to the woods to plot their little escapades?" snorted Peskiv.

"I don't know."

"Well now, comrade, this is how it is. We know that there are partisan rumblings here. You are a popular *starosta*, so people tell you things. We would like you to search your memory and share with us any misgivings you might have about your people."

"I can't tell you what I don't know."

"Oh Dovbush, Dovbush," commiserated Baranovich. "How short-sighted you are. You have a wife and children?"

"Yes," said Dovbush quietly.

"And how would they enjoy a change of scenery to our frozen North? I'm told the Poles are dying in quite large numbers."

Michaylo continued to sit very still.

Peskiv grinned. "Or a bullet to the head is quicker," he said stroking the leather holster which held his Nagan pistol.

"No need to be hasty," Baranovich grinned at his companion. "I'm sure that on reflection you will remember all sorts of things, won't you, Dovbush?" He rose. "We'll be back tomorrow and you can fill us in on the details then. Goodnight, comrade."

With that the two men left. Michaylo listened to their sturdy boots striking the floor of the Reading Room as they departed. He heard the engine of their car starting and waited until the tyres crunched on the gravel as their headlights were directed northwards.

He stood up from his chair and went out into the larger space of the Reading Room. He began to pace its perimeter. There was no question of his going home yet; he was too upset by the encounter, despite having anticipated it for some time. He needed to work through his turbulent emotions and reach a point of calm before speaking to anyone. He trod the familiar space and tried not to remember the glad evenings of music and plays, the happy faces… That must all belong to the past. The Bolsheviks might have allowed a resurgence of the language, but further displays of nationalism would clearly not be tolerated. And for a patriot like Michaylo, what could he do now?

To remain in the village, he would be forced to betray his own brethren and he did not need even a flicker of his mind to address this question. He would never betray the incipient partisan movement, even on pain of the death of himself and his whole family. He was utterly committed to the greater good of a liberated Ukrainian state. So could he remain in the village with impunity? He had no difficulty believing that he and his family could be deported to the wastes of Siberia; nor that he might be shot as a traitor to the Soviet state, if he did not give up the names of the young dissidents. Indeed, his corpse would serve as a warning to everyone. So to leave… He could not drag his family off to an uncertain fate: they could remain… If he disappeared without trace, they might not be punished… And where would he go? To the partisans, of course. There he could make his contribution to the stable future of Ukraine. He might be able to return one day… But to leave his family. There would be grief on all sides… At least this way they would be alive, and who knew what might happen in the future. They had to have hope. Michaylo paused in his pacing and turned back to his office. He turned out the light and closed the door.

Chapter 3

Mikola was working his garden plot, each family having at least half a hectare to grow whatever crops they wished, to feed the family and their livestock. The house stood sideways to the lane, and a smaller area was fenced, both where it bordered the lane and on the other side where it joined the cultivated ground. There was also access to the barn. Here the hens might scratch about, although Katerina and Anna took measures to protect their flowers and herbs. Beyond the inner fence was the vegetable garden which, if grassed, would have given the village boys enough room to have a football match, but where Mikola, like his neighbours, grew as many vegetables as he could. The weather was beginning to warm up and he had decided to dig over the plot in preparation for the first sowing of the year. Anna joined her father in the garden. Not only did she prefer to be outdoors, but she loved her father's company. So did Yuri and he had hurried out as soon as he had seen his father getting his spade.

"*Tatu*, I'll get the smaller spade."

Mikola and Anna grinned at one another. "Yes, a little spade for a little man," said his father.

"It won't be long before I'm as big as you," countered Yuri.

Mikola watched his son. Neither of his children resembled him. With their thick blond hair and grey eyes, they were clearly their mother's children. Mikola was dark and stocky. He had a strong peasant frame with broad shoulders and a deep chest. His face, too, was broad, although enlivened by his blue eyes, which were currently bright with amusement at Yuri's determination.

Anna fetched the wheelbarrow to gather any of the old vegetation which might have survived the winter. As she returned she heard her young brother ask: "*Tatu*, is there still no news of Starosta Dovbush?"

Anna's heart jumped in her chest and she looked quickly at her father.

"No son, but there's no need for you to worry."

She looked up at this bland reply, but caught her father's swift shake of the head and changed the subject immediately. "Some of last year's beetroots were a bit small. Are we going to plant some more this year?"

"Yes, of course. If it's a dry summer again, we'll just have to keep watering."

The dangerous moment over, Mikola directed Yuri to break up the ground behind him, intending to keep up a brisk pace so that the youngster would not have the breath to ask any more foolhardy questions outdoors. They worked in silence until they had covered a good patch of ground.

"That's good," said Mikola. "Let's go and see if that *borsch* is ready."

They went into the kitchen and washed their hands. Katerina was stirring a perfumed pot of carmine liquid. "It's ready," she announced. "Sit down and we can eat." She brought the pot over to the table, already set with bread and soured cream. As the steam rose, their mouths watered in anticipation.

"Mama, when I ate *borsch* at Vasilko's, his mother didn't make it like you. It was too thin!" announced Yuri.

"Everyone makes it differently," said Katerina.

"I prefer it with beans in it, like you make it."

"Vasilko's mother has four children to feed, Yuri. She has to stretch her *borsch*," said Anna.

"What do you mean, stretch it?"

"Make enough for all of them. Vasilko is the youngest, but the others are almost grown."

"How do you know?"

"Because Vera, Vasilko's big sister, is my friend, silly."

"I haven't seen you eating there."

"No, I haven't eaten there. But it's like that in big families."

"And your mother is a very good cook," added Mikola.

"Oh now stop!" laughed Katerina. "It's only *borsch*. Eat it while it's still hot."

When their bowls were clean, Yuri looked hesitantly at his father.

"*Tatu*…"

"Yes?" He looked up when Yuri did not continue. "What is it?"

"In the garden," Yuri began and paused again. "You didn't want me to talk about Starosta Dovbush did you?"

"No, I didn't. Yuri, it can be very dangerous to talk about grown-up things, especially outside."

"Yes, but you always said we should ask you if we want to know something," continued the boy.

"What's this?" asked Katerina, looking from one to the other.

"Alright, Yuri, I'll explain to you, but you must remember what's said in this house does not go beyond these walls. Alright?"

"Alright."

"Mikola, don't," said Katerina, putting her hand on his arm.

"I have to. It's important that the children understand." But he softened his firm words by placing his large calloused hand over his wife's smaller one.

"Yuri," he began, his voice quiet but deadly serious, "nobody knows where Michaylo Dovbush has gone. Even his family don't know."

"Doesn't his wife know?" persisted the child.

"No, even she has no idea what has happened to him."

"Then why is that such a big secret? Why couldn't you tell me in the garden?"

"Because it's better not to discuss such things. It's also none of our business."

"But…" began Yuri.

"Yuri!" exclaimed his mother. "Your father has explained to you and you should be a good boy and do as he says. Do you want to get him into trouble?"

"No!" exclaimed the horrified boy. "I just wanted to know."

"Well, now you know as much as any of us," said his mother, "and let that be an end to it. Don't let me hear you questioning your father again."

"I'm sorry."

Anna looked across at her mother. "I'm going to get some wood in for later. Give me a hand will you, Yuri?"

He scraped his chair back and followed Anna out of the cottage.

"It's alright, Yurchik," she said to him as they gathered the logs. "They're not really angry with you. It's just that it's a really difficult time for *Tato* with all of the changes. And children can get their parents into trouble very easily."

"But I wouldn't do that!"

"I know that. Mama and *Tato* do, too. It's just that they're worried for us as well as themselves."

"Will we be sent away?"

"Don't even say that! Even to say it, could bring it down on our heads. Don't say anything… Not to Vasilko, not anyone." She hugged him urgently, hoping he would keep his curiosity in check. But she understood his anxiety only too well.

Anna was sixteen that year, pretty, but not remarkable among the bevy of girls in the village, perhaps set apart by her gentle nature, her ready kindness and her sweet smile. She was regularly to be seen in the lanes bringing the cows back from pasture, the calm beasts even calmer under her care. She helped her father handle the horses for ploughing and was always able to harness them up without upsetting them. It was this tender care which drew the eyes of both men and boys to her thick honey-blonde hair and grey eyes; her straight back, high breasts and small waist. Unremarkable, but lovely. And, for Yuri, a big, protective sister.

The absence of Michaylo Dovbush did not go unnoticed in the offices of the communists in Buchach either. The authorities decided to put in their own man. There had been enough playing at democracy. Now was the time for the

25

steel of the Party to show itself. A local Party activist was chosen. A reliable man who would have no truck with either empathy or nationalism. Volodimir Ostapenko was in his forties. He was tall and broad. His belly did not yet betray his age and he worked diligently to preserve the muscular tightness of his biceps. His fists were large and hard, as many weaker mortals might have lived to testify. Even his hams bespoke a pride in physical and moral mastery. There would be no gentle touch with Ostapenko, who was known for his quick judgements and his swifter justice.

He was told to select his lieutenants to serve him in his subjugation of a community considered to have gone soft and he chose those very like himself; big men who would not hesitate to demonstrate their physical power, but unlike him, needing to be led and given their cue. His lieutenants had acquired cheap leather jackets and wore these with pride, a badge of their authority, so that when Ostapenko gave them the nod, they could beat up the victim with a grave professionalism. There would be no sloppiness in their work. If they were ordered to bludgeon someone into submission, they would do so efficiently. Anything less would be considered a failure.

In the village, their fame went before them, and suddenly eyes were lowered, heads bowed, as the populace tried to remain unremarked by these flat-headed, crew-cut monsters. However, with the sowing of wheat, the unavoidable climax came.

The snow had suddenly disappeared leaving the soil wet and cold, but within a few days, warm westerly breezes had blown it dry. Everyone was eager to begin, not only to mark the turning of the seasons, but also to begin the serious process of creating food. This spring, too, despite Ostapenko, there was an air of festivity as each family was excited and hopeful about being able to plough the land they had traditionally thought of as their own. But before the men could take matters into their own hands, authority once again took over. Ostapenko called a meeting late one afternoon. The trumpet sounded in the centre of the village for the call to a meeting and all of the adults and children hurried to the village hall. To be late was unforgivable; to be absent was not an option. Everyone took their place in the hall quickly. There was little conversation as the community waited to hear the latest announcement.

Ostapenko strode onto the small stage, flanked by his lieutenants. He leaned his massive head forward like a belligerent bear and said ominously, "Comrades, I have been told that some of you are planning to sow land which is not rightfully yours."

There was a collective intake of breath.

After a dramatic pause, he continued. "The Soviet government has announced that all land will be held communally. We are all shareholders of this land now. So I have drawn up the plan of who will work where. The map lies here on the table. Look at it carefully to find your work sector. Anyone straying from this plan will be dealt with. Work begins tomorrow, comrades."

With that, he strode from the stage, his moustache bristling the way before him as he propelled his bull-like chest through the lines of shamefaced villagers.

Some were already quietly accepting the new orders, feeling that at least they would have a share of what had previously been denied them, but there was a hesitation of movement in others who had not yet fully absorbed the sudden change from Dovbush's style. The hall did empty, albeit slowly, under the watchful eyes of Ostapenko's cronies, and just as slowly, the people walked to their homes absorbing the information they had received so summarily.

In Anna's house, there was a heavy quiet as they each waited for someone to begin. Eventually, Mikola announced: "There's been a change. I have to go to the fields just past the school."

"Why don't they put you in the lower field where you know the land really well?" asked Katerina.

"Yes, they could do that, but we mustn't be critical. Nothing belongs to any of us separately, so we must get to know all of the land around the village." And of course, if it never was mine, I can't feel any tie to it, can I? he thought but resisted saying.

In the pause which followed, Yuri went to lean against his father. He was too old to climb into his lap, but would try to comfort him as best he could.

"So we'll have a share of the crops we grow," said Mikola, putting his arm around Yuri with a sigh.

"Will it be as simple as that?"

"I don't know, Katerina. We'll have to wait and see. It will depend on how much the Russians want to siphon off for their own."

"So we won't be any better off, then?"

"Perhaps...perhaps not. We would be, if we only shared the harvest within the village."

"But will it be done justly?"

"In principle...it's only fair to share what we have. But who can say what quotas will be demanded. And then there's the sharing out within the village..."

"What if some don't want to work?" asked Anna.

"Exactly," replied her father. "Should he get as much as another who works hard each day?"

"And what about those with lots of children?" added Anna's mother. "They'll need a greater share if they're not to starve."

"We must wait and see what the new *starosta* says, but I hope he will take this opportunity for justice. There can be no justice if we who grow the food get no share of it. But we know that's happened before."

"We can't change anything at this moment," said Katerina sighing, wondering how they would manage to keep their family safe.

Anna went over to Mikola, too, and put her arm around his shoulders, resting her cheek on his head. "Never mind, *Tatu*, I'll be up there with the girls, sowing. I'll keep you company."

"I know, thank you, Anna. I'll look out for you." He patted her arm absently.

Anna withdrew from him and met her mother's glance. Both women felt his disappointment. Despite his rational approach to the new regime, he had clearly hoped that he might farm the land which his family had considered theirs. Yuri felt his father's disappointment, too, his heart aching for his beloved father. He would go with him tomorrow. He would be a man soon and must help his family.

The following morning, just after dawn, the villagers made their way to the fields. The men were to gather near the shrine on the outer edge of the village where the space between the road and the woods would allow many farm vehicles to gather. They were not calling it a revolt, but a blessing, for there was the priest in his cassock, his stole around his neck, armed only with holy water and a crucifix. He intoned a prayer, as the men bowed their bare heads and hoped for some reprieve from Ostapenko's wretched plan. Out there, amongst the fields which had been farmed by these men and their ancestors for generations, under the open sky, one could only believe that God was good and that he was going to enable them to cultivate their own land, despite the interruptions of usurpers. The dawn cast a pink glow on the congregation and the fertile earth shone blackly. The undulating land was ready to be worked and the dark woods, bordering its breadth to the west, protected it.

The women stood in a group a little way off as Father Dubenko walked among the vehicles, blessing men and machines, in their new venture. Mikola stood among the men with Yuri at his side. The boy had begged to be allowed to go to see the start of the sowing and his father had made a rare concession to Yuri missing some of the school day. Katerina and Anna should have been among the women, but they had been delayed on a mission of mercy. As they had set off up the lane with Mikola and Yuri, they had been startled by cries of distress from their neighbour's house. Nastunia was a very old lady, fiercely independent, but Anna and her mother made a habit of calling in on a variety of pretexts. Now they hurried over to her front door and Katerina called to Mikola to go on; she and Anna would join him as soon as they could.

"Fine, but don't be late," Mikola had warned.

The villagers stood shivering a little in the cold breeze, hoping they might gain some control over their lives. However, despite the weight of their longing, there was to be no miraculous change of plan.

Volodimir Ostapenko suddenly appeared among them on his horse, looking furious. He carried his customary whip in his left hand, not being a rider who cared to give his horse time to make up its mind what it might do. "Who gave you permission to gather here?" he demanded. "You know where you're to work. Get off there and do your duty."

"I have almost finished the blessing," said Father Dubenko, his calm exterior belying his inner fear.

Ostapenko pushed his horse through the crowd of men to the spot where the priest stood beside Mikola's horse-drawn plough, and with a swift flick of the wrist, cut at the priest's face with his whip.

"No you don't!" cried Mikola leaping forward. "That's no way to treat our priest."

"Back off now," bawled Ostapenko, even more angry to have been thwarted twice in one morning. "Get to work! Vasil," he called to one of his lieutenants, "get these peasants moving!"

Vasil was only too pleased to have permission to move in and he barged into Mikola, knocking him off balance. In a moment, Mikola was on his feet glaring at Vasil, who swiftly drew his gun from inside his jacket. He pointed it in Mikola's face. There was a shocked hush, but Yuri, who had been watching from the sidelines, propelled himself forward, yelling, "Don't you dare touch my father!"

Mikola glanced at his son in horror and then barged Vasil's shoulder to deflect his aim. Vasil turned immediately and fired at Mikola's head. He fell to the ground and Yuri threw himself on his father's body, screaming. Vasil took automatic aim again and fired at Yuri's head. The boy slumped over his father's lifeless body.

The crowd looked on, shocked into silence and immobility, but Ostapenko was the first to recover. "Anyone else have anything to say?"

The men shuffled away, but the women remained frozen by the spectacle of double tragedy. Ostapenko's lieutenants forced the peasants away, striding this way and that, chests puffed out, while Ostapenko himself sat on his horse, like the tyrants of old. That will do, he thought. There'll be no problem now with the rest of them doing as they're told. And he began to walk his horse between the fields, an immoveable force, visible from a great distance.

But where were Anna and her mother? They were hurrying along the lane, hoping to catch the last of the blessing, anxious at what they thought had been gunfire. Why would shots ring out at the blessing before work? As they hastened up the gentle incline towards the shrine, they saw the unusual sight of the priest, almost running towards them, holding up his cassock in one hand and his stole in the other. He was closely followed by the altar boy carrying the holy water.

"Katerina! Anna!" the priest panted. "Come away! Come with me!"

"What's happened?" asked Katerina. She had never seen a priest behaving like this.

The altar boy was about to speak when Father Dubenko turned on him. "Not a word, boy!" He took Katerina's arm and almost pulled her with him through the village to the presbytery. Anna followed, equally mystified, but carried along by the unwonted behaviour of the priest she had known all of her life.

They entered the presbytery and he shut the door, turning the key and putting it in his pocket. Pulling out two chairs for the women, he ordered them to sit and then drew a deep breath for the most difficult part of his task.

"There's been a…" he paused. It could not be described as an accident and the word disaster, while true, seemed too brutal…"a terrible incident."

Both women stared at him, fear taking over from their shock at the priest's behaviour.

"What is it, Father?" asked Katerina.

"Mikola and Yuri have been shot by one of Ostapenko's men," he said at last.

"Dead?" asked Katerina, staring at him intently.

"What?" cried Anna, almost simultaneously.

"I'm afraid so," he said, taking Katerina's hand.

She snatched it away. "Come, Anna, we must go to them."

But he stood in their way, as the women rose to go. "You can't. If you're associated with them, you, too, may be shot. If they don't shoot you, they will definitely transport you. You must wait here."

"I can't! I must go to my husband and my son. I may be able to help them."

Anna looked at him, knowing she had heard shots being fired. "Is there really no hope, Father?"

"They were both shot in the head."

Katerina set up a terrible howling. She fell to her knees, wailing and tearing at her clothing.

Anna clasped her mother's arms. "Wait, Mama. There may be some mistake. We'll go and see for ourselves."

"You can't," repeated the priest. "Didn't you hear what I said?"

"But what are we to do?" asked Anna. She turned to him in horror. "Just leave them there?"

"No. We must wait for darkness. I'll find help for you and we'll try to bring their bodies back here."

Katerina was on her knees now, weeping uncontrollably. Anna knelt beside her mother and took her in her arms to try to hold her back from the pit of grief, while her own tears fell down her cheeks and seared her young heart.

Anna held her mother's hands tightly, hoping to hold her down on the earth. Katerina had gone somewhere beyond her daughter and Anna feared she might never be able to pull her mother back. They were seated side by side on hard wooden chairs, still wearing their coats and scarves. It was chilly in the presbytery, there being no stove. She was worried about her mother's lack of movement, but feared shock and grief more than the cold. She leaned back a little and gently rubbed her mother's back in a circular motion, but she got no reaction from Katerina. The coarse wool of her mother's coat snagged on Anna's work-roughened hands, but the girl felt comforted by her own action. The scent of incense and doused candles was present and, underlying it all, a damp smell of earth and stone, of a building uninhabited by the living. Anna wondered how much longer they would be there and when the priest might return, for then she might find out what had happened to her father and Yuri. Her heart gave a little thrumming flutter as she thought of them and her breath came shortly. She stood up and walked around the room, trying to control her breathing and the fluttering of her heart, a bird trapped on the wrong side of a window, and she knew she must not break herself in futile fear... She must wait calmly to find out what must be done. She swallowed and again tried to relax her breathing, consciously controlling its pace and depth.

As darkness fell, a key turned in the lock and the priest's mother entered, carrying a basket. "Katerina, my dear," she began and stepped towards the newly-made widow. But Katerina sat as still as a granite statue, her crying over.

"Mama hasn't spoken since this morning," explained Anna.

"I've brought you some food," said the older woman. "You'll need your strength for what you have to do."

"Mama won't eat and I can't. I'm sorry."

"There's no need to apologise but I'm worried about you both. I don't know if Father Stepan has found any help for you tonight, and even if he has, what you'll have to do will require you to be strong."

"I know. But it must be done."

"Perhaps if I bring some tea..." and settling her headscarf more tightly, the priest's mother went out of the presbytery, leaving her basket behind.

Anna sat beside her mother, stroking her hand from time to time and looking at her implacable face, which seemed to have aged decades since the morning. Anna still could not believe what she had been told and hoped that when the time came to collect the bodies, they might not be those of Mikola and Yuri. Her family priest had known them all their lives, but surely he could be mistaken.

Father Dubenko returned with his mother, who offered the tea she had brought, but Anna shook her head and turned to listen to the son.

"I've managed to borrow a cart for you," he said, "but no horse, I'm afraid." He paused. "And none of the men felt able to come and help."

"But how will we manage, Father? Mama…" she gestured toward her mother, whose grief was firmly etched in every line of her body.

The priest shook his head. "I'm sorry, Anna, but people are afraid. I won't be coming either."

Anna's eyes widened and the tears began to gather.

"But I'll wait for you here and we'll bury them together."

"Will I have to dig the grave, too?"

"No, my dear, you won't. There were other graves needed today so the sexton dug an extra one. Your father and brother can be buried together."

Anna felt a sob escape, but then clamped her jaw shut and stood up, holding herself erect. "Very well. Let's get on with it."

The priest watched while she helped her mother to her feet. "Mama," she said, "come with me. We're going to find *Tato* and Yuri."

She led her mother outside and helped her to sit in the cart. Taking the handles, she pulled the cart away from the church and began to haul it towards the lane, through the dark village. It was a cold night, but Anna sweated in her scarf and warm coat as she pulled her oblivious mother the two kilometres or so, dreading what awaited them and wondering how her mother would bear it. She tried to keep the cart steady on the rutted road and as she tired, she counted her paces to manage the long, slow stretch.

When they reached the open ground, Anna hurried toward the space where the crowd had gathered only that morning, and in the moonlight, saw a heap on the ground. She gritted her teeth and pulled the cart closer. She put down the handles, then went alone to examine the bodies. They lay as they must have fallen: her father on his back and across his chest, her brother lay sprawled where the bullet had hurled him.

She let out a howl of anguish and fell to her knees, embracing them both, sobbing, making no attempt to control herself. Her cries jerked her mother back to consciousness as perhaps nothing else could have done. Katerina edged herself off the cart and stumbled across the few steps to her wrecked family. She tended to Anna first, putting her arms around her distraught daughter and rocking her with wordless murmurings until Anna quieted

32

a little. Then she drew Anna away saying, "Let me see."

The sight of her beloved boy and her husband was as bad as anything she had been imagining all day and she wept freely. Eventually, she rose, saying to Anna, "We must try to do this well, for them."

Anna nodded and they lifted Yuri gently off his father's body and laid him to one side and then they tried to lift Mikola. He was too heavy for them, but Katerina told Anna to bring the cart around to face Mikola's head. Then, taking an arm and a shoulder each, they pulled him onto the cart. They had to heave several times before his feet cleared the ground, and although undignified, they were relieved that they had been able to move him. Katerina lifted Yuri alone and laid him beside his father, then both women took a handle and set off with their terrible load, back towards the churchyard. They saw no one and if anyone had heard a cart rumbling over the stony road at that late hour, no one looked out to see who it was. Curiosity could bring death and Anna and Katerina bore their burden alone, unhelped but unmolested.

When they reached the churchyard, the priest appeared in the lighted presbytery doorway and gestured toward the far corner of the graveyard, to the space reserved for the suicides and unbaptised. They drew the cart there without pausing, but when they reached the graveside, Anna asked her mother: "Shouldn't we wash them and dress them in their *sorochki*?"

"No, Anna, let them lie. Will you help us now, Father?"

Both women kissed Mikola and the priest helped them to lift the heavy body of the man into the ground. Once again Katerina lifted her son in her arms, holding him briefly to her and kissing his cold face. His sister kissed him in her turn, but then he, too, lay with his father.

There was no help for it... Anna and her mother took up the spades and shovelled the loose earth into the grave. A sob escaped Anna as the first soil was sprinkled over their faces and her mother hushed her gently: "Shhh, Anna, it has to be done. Better they are buried than left where they were killed."

Anna tried to nod, but was holding herself too tightly, so she shovelled the black soil into the hole.

The priest muttered a short prayer over their unshriven bodies. The earth covered them as if they had never been.

Anna and Katerina murmured "*Vichnaya Pamyat*" at the graveside, Anna knowing that the eternal memory of her father and brother would only last as long as she and her mother lived.

Katerina thanked the priest for his brief obsequies, but Anna was past speaking and so the two women stumbled away together from the cemetery back to their cold, empty home.

*

Anna awoke chilled and hungry just after dawn. She fetched water from the well and washed herself, feeling as if she was beginning a dreadful period of her life. She relit the fire and set the porridge to cook, being careful to measure out only two portions. She worked quietly, hoping to give Katerina the balm of forgetful sleep. She wondered whether to say her morning prayers. Would her father and brother's souls benefit or would it be a waste of breath, since surely God could not allow such terrible things to happen? But then Anna pulled herself out of her self-indulgent reverie: why shouldn't this happen? There had already been much misery in the village. There would be more to follow, so why shouldn't she and her mother simply be the next victims in the long catalogue? She shook herself. It was more important to look after her mother. Everything else could wait, including the answer to her spiritual dilemma. She decided to let her mother sleep in blissful forgetfulness. She ate her breakfast and, leaving the fire well-tended and the pot keeping warm, she wrote a brief note to her mother: Gone to work, Anna.

Anna pinned her scarf across her chest and set off to discover if there would indeed be work for her. She and the other villagers headed towards their labour and as they reached the fields, she joined the girls who would be sowing. They glanced at her and nodded for the most part. She expected little else. Guilt by association was a favourite Bolshevik crime and the events had been so terrible, perhaps they would not know what to say.

Anna waited stoically, while the girls began to drift towards their fields and then Vera drew closer and said quietly, "Come, Anna. We're working over here," and so she had a place. She knew the risk her friend was taking for her and that her 'Thank you' was utterly inadequate.

It was cold, damp work and the pause for lunch was brief. Anna chewed on the dry bread she had brought and wondered about her mother. Had she got up yet? Had she eaten? But she could not allow herself to become anxious. She worked on blankly till dusk and then tramped back to the village with the others. Vera linked arms with her as they strode back in the cold dusk, just as she had always done. "See you tomorrow," she said as they parted and Anna nodded and turned into her own garden gate.

When she opened the door to the house, it was still warm but she could see her mother lying in bed. She went over and touched her shoulder. Katerina half-turned and said, "Is that you, Anna?"

"Yes, Mama. I've been to work."

"Good girl," murmured her mother, closing her eyes.

Anna rose to take off her scarf and jacket, then she checked the fire and built it up. She looked into the morning's porridge pot. Her mother appeared to have eaten nothing.

"Have you at least had a drink today?"

"No, I wasn't thirsty."

"I'll make us some tea," said Anna and she set about boiling the water, thinking meanwhile of something for their evening meal. She lit the lamp and the sudden brightening of the room brought tears to her eyes.

This was all there was. The long empty bench along the wall; the tidy table. There would be no Yuri bouncing in noisily and no father with his stories of work. Anna's mind briefly touched the thought that there never would be again, but like a moth closing its wings, she closed her mind to it and selected vegetables for soup. She was hungry after her work in the cold and her mother needed care.

When the soup was ready she coaxed her mother into a sitting position in bed and prepared to spoon the warm liquid into her mouth, but Katerina nodded a little shamefacedly, and getting down from the bed, took a stool at the table. They ate for necessity and with little pleasure, but both women were hungry. After they had eaten in silence, Anna tidied the room. She picked up Yuri's reader and smoothing its dog-eared corners carefully, put it into the drawer with their Bible. Then she lay on the quilt beside her mother and at last, let the tears gather in the corners of her eyes. She did not allow herself to sob; she held the waves of her grief, tightly gritting her teeth. As she turned on her side away from her mother, Katerina said, "You might as well sleep here in the warmth, Anna," and so a new era began.

The women's lives shrank to a confined stoicism. They did not discuss their plans to survive; they simply lived day by day. Anna worked in the fields and Katerina slept much of the day. The change in her mother did not shock Anna as it did others. She understood that although her mother loved her, Katerina was simply waiting to join Mikola and Yuri. She was no longer the energetic and efficient housewife she had been, but one of the old ladies of the village, quietly and graciously waiting to die, her active life being over.

Chapter 4

Spring came despite Anna and Katerina's grief. Anna continued in her straitened circumstances, but there came a day which was so lovely in its warmth and blue sky that she could not help but feel the absence of Mikola and Yuri like a sharp knife. They would have enjoyed such a day so much and Anna spent it planting the garden with vegetables. Like all of the other villagers, her family had stored the precious seed from the previous season and now she planted against the next winter. But only enough to feed two mouths rather than four.

There was some satisfaction to be had in bending to the sweet smelling earth, but Anna felt her loneliness more than ever. She tried not feel bitter, although her young heart was sore and, as she finished work, she made her excuses to Katerina and left the house to walk off her agitation without upsetting her mother.

She walked up the lane to the anachronistic memorial, celebrating as it did the end of feudalism in the region many decades before. Ironically, personal freedoms were no greater now than they had been then. But political questions were not on her mind and, at the crossroads, she turned left downhill towards the river Barish. She passed the spring where the water leapt out of the hillside and the village women did their laundry and she followed the lively stream down into the woods. The trees began just after the laundry stones and then the wood widened and thickened. At the bottom of the hill, there was a footbridge across the thirty metres of clear water of the Barish, which would flow into the mighty Dniester. However, Anna did not cross the bridge, but turned left to meander through the protective trees. Even here, in the privacy of the early evening wood, Anna could not weep openly. She held her grief within the vessel of herself. This had become such an habitual state, she often failed to notice that she was containing her sorrow carefully so as not to spill a drop, but today it did rise up and threaten to overflow.

However, the loveliness of the wood calmed her. Many of the trees were still in bud, so allowed the late sunlight to flood the floor of the wood with light, which was reflected in a golden wash by the carpet of celandines, their bright yellow petals glistening cheerfully. There seemed to be pools of standing water, but when Anna looked more closely, she saw they were groups of wood anemones in such numbers that their delicate white petals resembled still ponds. Anna paused, taken by surprise by this gift of nature. She was suddenly lifted with joy at the beauty which surrounded her. She did not feel the presence of her father or her brother, but understood that everything continues…spring inexorably follows winter and this glorious rebirth simply reaffirmed that the cycle would continue. She stood still while she bathed in the reassurance she had just stumbled upon. She looked around her, recording the beautiful vision, knowing she would use the memory of the scene again and again to restore her sense of calm.

She was reluctant to leave this balm behind and walked in another small circuit noticing now that the pools of light were interspersed with swathes of rich green, the broad leaves of wild garlic, which would have its own white flower shortly. Soothed, she began to walk home. The trickling of the water, as she climbed the hill, added its quantity of ease to her, too, before she reached the lane and turned for home, so hidden in her own thoughts that she did not notice a tall young man observing her from the shadows. But even had she seen him, she would not have been afraid. Petro would yet try to protect her.

Like the rest of the men in the village, he had witnessed the deaths of her father and brother and, like the other men, had been deeply shocked by the events of that terrible morning. But he had had his own troubles. His father had been sick and died when Petro was only fifteen and so, for the last three years, he had been living with the responsibility of caring for his mother and three younger sisters. Not that they thought they needed to be cared for. They were all lively and energetic and Petro sometimes had far more than he could manage with their boisterous enthusiasms. Now he turned down his own lane, at right angles to Anna's and followed it to the edge of the village, where the gardens merged with the fields and then fell away to the valley of the Dniester. He wondered if the girls in his family would understand his sudden empathy for the quiet Anna, and thought they probably would not. But there was no rush. He tucked the image of her bent head with its thick blonde plait into his memory, and resolved to watch over her in the coming days and weeks.

Anna had needed a guardian angel in the early days of her bereavement. Ostapenko had considered deporting her and her mother, but the shock of the unauthorised killings of father and son was so great among the community that he hesitated…long enough for the dangerous moment to pass. Besides, he observed the pair of women surreptitiously and saw that they had been broken by the deaths rather than being incited to insurrection. So he let the matter slide. A year later he would not have done so.

Nor did he look upon Michaylo Dovbush's family with the same clemency.

They were the living witnesses of a father's dissident activities and he had disappeared; the only likely conjecture being that he was continuing his opposition to the Soviet state. So one night, Ostapenko and his lieutenants arrived at Dovbush's house and bundled the terrified family into the back of a lorry, not even giving them time to pack. They were taken to Temne, the neighbouring village, and temporarily housed in the prison there, its high walls and narrow windows speaking grim warnings. Michaylo's wife was questioned repeatedly, but since she truly did not know where her husband had gone, she could tell them nothing. However, this did not encourage the authorities to mercy. She was sentenced to twenty-five years' deportation to the *gulags*, along with her four children.

The months passed. The hay had been cut; the men working their way methodically across the fields in the benign sunshine with their sharp scythes. The rows of hay lay shorn of their swaying beauty, their heads heavy with ripeness. The glistening rows of pale green no longer shifted like a silken dress, but lay as they had been dropped in discarded ribbons. The girls turned it for drying and it became pale and golden, ready to be gathered for threshing. The scent of the cut hay lay on the air, epitomising summer's harvest, its fertility belying the graver life beyond the fields. Only the butterflies were currently dispossessed. They had gathered in a thickening cloud as the corn was cut and when the final swathe fell, they had nowhere else to go. But the watching birds were happy to swoop down on the cut corn before it was gathered, taking advantage of the fallen seed.

The good July weather held firm and the following day Anna and the lines of girls flowed from one edge of the field to the other, raking the pale tresses into tidy rows, which they would turn once more before gathering the hay. The scene was timeless as they sang to help the work along; always songs of love and Cossacks, usually of grief and loss. And although their songs were sad, most of the girls shared the dreams of young women and were optimistic about their futures, despite what was going on around them. They swung away from their work, flinging their rakes onto their shoulders and allowing their hips to sway as they made their way, in a group, back to the village. Even Anna felt the invincibility of youth as she, too, lifted her chin and opened her throat to swell their singing.

The young men could not resist and came to the lane to see the girls in their summer glory and to speculate on partners. Petro stood among the boys, taller than most and with a ready smile. He was easy to identify with his long curly hair and several of the girls gave him their special glances. But Anna seemed to notice no one in particular, simply enjoying the sunshine at the end of a satisfying day. The edge which had been there in other people's attitudes to her shortly after Mikola's death had become blunted as other families were touched by tragedy, and Anna was now simply one of many whose life had been trimmed.

Petro found himself being nudged by Ivan, who was much smaller in stature, but handsome. "You could have your pick there, Petro."

"And so could you. Every time your name is mentioned in our house, it's coupled with a different girl!"

Ivan chuckled. "Well, it's good to keep them guessing."

"I don't know about guessing. Queueing up more like."

The boys laughed good-naturedly and slowly followed the girls back to the village.

The feeling of contentment stayed with Anna as the sun began to dip in the late evening. The light was golden as it flowed through the gaps in the trees in molten bars, highlighting the grasses and leaves. It coursed across the field beyond her garden in an exuberant display of prodigious extravagance, leaving the unlit areas dull. Shortly, the light began to take on fiery hues and the trunks of the trees glowed red while their leaves flamed in the breeze. The melting magenta was sieved across the grass through the fretwork of the hedge, whose gaps were edged with a deeper red. The swallows set up a last skirling shriek, as they hunted down their final meal of the day and the magpies chattered from the cherry trees. It was cooler now and the light only gave the illusion of warmth, as the sky darkened and the scarlet glare retreated to the tipping corner of the west, where it flooded the horizon gloriously and briefly. Even as the last light trickled away, the bats appeared, as busy as their predecessors. The great snowy barn owl glided silently on outstretched wings, preparing to feed its young. Anna turned to go indoors with the benevolence of her landscape held against her hollow heart.

The hollowness persisted, marked especially by Anna's name day. Tradition dictated that babies should be named after saints and their name day was cause for the greatest celebration each year, rather than a birth day. Anna's was 26th July, the feast of St Anne, mother of the Virgin Mary. Her father had always found her something special for this day and her mother would bake something particularly delicious. But the day dawned as any other, in the beige quilt of days since her father's death, and Anna rose to go to work, not allowing herself to be disappointed that there was no vase of flowers on the table and no pancakes filled with poppy seed and honey for breakfast. She washed herself, ate her *kasha* and set off to work with her rake, squaring her shoulders for the day ahead. There could be no room for self-pity or she would be lost. She still had her mother to love and care for. In that she was lucky. The thought made her consciously count the rest of her blessings: she had a roof over her head, food in her belly and the sun was shining.

She worked mechanically all morning and sat at lunchtime beside Vera and the rest of the girls under the chestnut tree at the wooded edge of the field. She listened to the trilling gossip as she ate her sandwich, smiling now and then at the more outrageous snippets. But she was almost moved to tears when she saw Vera produce some cake from her bundle.

"For your name day, Anna. We couldn't let it pass…" and Vera passed Anna a moist piece of plum cake.

Vera gave the girls a quick signal and they sang "*Mnohaya lita*", while Anna smiled and swallowed her tears.

"Dear Vera," she said and hugged her friend, whose undemonstrative person had the happy knack of knowing when a kind gesture was needed. Anna enjoyed her cake, spiced as it was with love and thoughtfulness, and was borne through the afternoon by Vera's sweet remembrance. But Vera had good reason to remember Anna's loss. She had not lost her younger brother, Vasilko, to the bullying hand of Ostapenko and, despite a nine-year-old brother's ability to be a nuisance, she was grateful for him every day. Yuri's untimely death had made her count her blessings, too.

As Anna returned home she resolved to take control of her own celebrations and she picked a posy of poppies from the garden before entering the house. Then she set about making pancakes.

"This is nice, Anna," commented her mother, as she sat down to a more festive meal than usual.

"Yes, I thought we deserved a treat," and she served her mother first to the delicious *nalesnyky*.

Ivan, too, was sixteen that summer and the apple of his uncle's eye. He had helped him bring in the first part of the harvest from the fields to the east of the village and they were returning on Danylo's cart. The field swept away to the deceptive horizon, beyond which the ground fell away sharply to the river valley. Ivan held the reins as the horses pulled their load of gathered corn to the barns. Danylo encouraged Ivan in the driving of the team, despite his own pleasure in the horses. He liked Ivan's liveliness and favoured him above the rest of his sister's children. His pride also extended itself to the broad field which had just been harvested.

"Look, Ivashu, this is all ours now."

Ivan's faith in the Russian regime was less firm and he was more cynical than his years warranted. "Maybe…but there's no knowing yet how things might turn out."

"Shh!" hissed his uncle. "Don't let anyone, not anyone, hear you speak like that!"

Ivan shrugged, but knew that it was unwise to speak so freely. Even this innocuous remark could have cost him his freedom. Danylo might keep Ivan's secret because of his fondness for him, but Ivan needed to keep an adult's control over his words.

As they swayed over the ruts, Ivan saw the village girls ahead of them, singing as they walked.

His uncle chuckled, "You see, Ivash, lots of choice for a young man like you."

The girls parted on either side of the lane to let the cart through, creating two rows of smiling faces.

Danylo at least had the decency to wait until they had passed the girls. "What about that last one?"

"Anna?" asked Ivan. "Yes, she's lovely, but she doesn't seem to notice any of us boys. Still mourning her father and brother, I think."

"What? Oh, that one... Well, maybe you're right. There are lots of others."

Ivan saw Anna later, drawing water at the well for her evening chores. Many houses had wells in their own gardens, but Anna and her mother used the well at the branch in the road almost opposite their gate. Ivan watched her confidently turning the wheeled handle and lifting the heavy bucket herself.

"I'm not going to offer you any help," he grinned.

"I wouldn't expect it," she laughed. "A *parubok* like you hasn't got time to help a girl with her chores. Who is it tonight?"

"I haven't decided yet." But he thought it worth risking a throw here. "My uncle thinks it should be you."

Her sad smile told him he had been right to tell Danylo she was impervious to him. "Goodnight, Ivan. Have fun!" and she turned away from him, walking towards her house in the gathering dusk.

He shivered a little, feeling oddly unsettled and set off down the lane towards Sofia's house. She was lively and always ready for some fun, he thought. She would do...

After some rain in early September, Anna waited a week or two for the mushroom season to begin. In the past, she had gone with her mother and Yuri to collect as many as possible to be dried for the winter. The thrill of finding a large group of mushrooms had been exciting for all three of them and so she approached her mother, hoping the project might interest her and lift her spirits.

41

"Mama, I'm going to pick mushrooms tomorrow morning. Would you like to come?"

"No, Anna, I don't think so."

"Are you sure, Mama? The fresh air would do you good."

"No, thank you, dear Anna. You go alone. You'll be able to walk more quickly by yourself."

"I won't be in a hurry. I don't mind walking slowly with you. We might find more that way."

Katerina sighed. "No, Anna, you go."

Anna tried not to show her disappointment, nor her grief. Surely her mother could remember the laughter they had shared as Yuri pounced on another group of mushrooms in their competitive desire to come home with the fullest basket. But, Anna chided herself, perhaps she could remember only too well, and that was why she was unwilling to go.

So Anna rose alone the next morning and, taking her mother's larger basket, set off. She began along the route they usually took, knowing the mushrooms would show themselves again, but also keeping a sharp lookout for new groups. She picked efficiently, rejecting any dark, moist fungi which had already gone over and filling her basket with fresh specimens. The lovely pale brown *pidpenky* were clustered around the stumps of felled trees, sometimes camouflaged by the leaves which were beginning to fall. She followed a promising new trail and was bending to pick a patch of mushrooms when she heard voices and laughter. She straightened to see several figures approaching through the trees.

They were led by a young girl of nine or ten years with fair curly hair erupting from her plait. She was calling to the rest of her party: "Come on! I'm going to beat you all. My basket's nearly full."

"Of course it is," said an older female voice. "It's smaller than ours."

"That's not true!" The child came to a halt and almost stamped her foot. "Petro, tell them my basket's as big as theirs."

Anna hesitated, not knowing whether to continue. Generally, families had their own secret places which they always searched first and she did not know if she had stumbled on what they would consider their territory. The figures came forward and Anna saw not only the young girl, but her older twin sisters and their brother, Petro. They saw her, too, the child turning an enquiring face to her sisters.

"Good morning," said Anna. "I hope I'm not taking your…"

"No, no," said Petro. "It's our first time trying this stretch of the woods. Nina can't find them quickly enough," he laughed, "so we thought we'd try up here where there are some felled trees."

The twins exchanged glances at this, in their opinion, overlong explanation, but then turned to Anna with polite smiles.

"Have you found many?" one of them asked.

"Yes, a few," said Anna, holding out her basket for them to see.

"Are you on your own?" Nina asked, only to be nudged violently by one of her older sisters.

"You've done well, Anna," said Irina.

Despite their closeness in age, Anna had never been friends with these confident, self-sufficient twins.

"We're going over that way," indicated the second twin, Natalia, drawing the encounter to a close and staking out their projected search area.

"Of course. Good luck," said Anna, moving off in the opposite direction.

"Good luck to you, too, Anna," added Petro, following his sisters' imperious backs with a rather shame-faced smile.

"So why is she on her own? And why can't I ask?" asked Nina, as the gap between them widened.

"Shh," warned Petro, "she'll hear you."

The twins glanced back to see Anna moving away out of earshot.

"Because her father and brother were killed and her mother's no use to her," snapped Natalia.

"Well, I didn't know," protested Nina.

"There was no reason why you should," said Petro. "But, Nina, you're old enough to know that you can't just say what's in your head. That poor girl is unhappy enough without you pointing out that she has no family to gather mushrooms with."

The twins raised their eyebrows at each other, but Petro caught their telepathic criticism. "And?"

"You seem very concerned about her welfare," murmured Irina.

"Don't be so unkind! You have two sisters, a brother and a mother, while Anna might as well be alone in the world. Have a thought for others, for goodness sake!"

"Alright, alright. There's no need to get angry," Irina replied.

"She was doing alright," added Natalia. "You saw how full her basket was," and the twins moved away together, leaving Petro to shake his head. He had felt hurt on Anna's behalf that she should carry out this happy autumn task on her own and had felt the cut she had received when Nina had unwittingly exacerbated Anna's awareness of her solitude.

A small hand insinuated itself into Petro's larger one. "Are you still cross with me?"

"No, of course not," replied Petro, smiling down at his pretty sister. "I know you didn't mean to be unkind."

Happy to be back in her beloved brother's favour, Nina returned to her earlier enthusiasm. "Come on, be quick! We have to get more mushrooms than Irina and Natalia!"

Anna had no more desire for her work after the meeting with Petro and his sisters. She had girded her loins to perform this task alone, but the girls' insouciance had punctured her resolve. She felt her determined energy wither suddenly and she made her way home, not bothering to look for more mushrooms.

When she entered the house, her mother was still in bed and Anna could not bring herself to speak. If she had had to say a word, she would have broken into sobs. So she sat at the kitchen table, slicing and stringing the mushrooms to hang over the stove for drying. As she worked, she selected some to eat fresh, but mostly she stored the mushrooms for her own bleak future. How easy it would be, she thought, to lay her head on the table and howl with grief. Instead she made herself finish the chore.

As she did so, her mother stirred and got out of bed. She tidied herself and made some tea for the two of them. "You've done well, Anna," she said, but hesitated to stroke her girl's silken head as she saw the tears threatening to brim over. "I'll fry some potatoes to go with them." She knew she had failed Anna again today, remembering her earlier failure to celebrate her child's name day and she resolved to try harder, at least to be a companion to her solitary daughter.

One Sunday, as autumn became more established, Anna led her mother to church. Katerina, despite her resolve, leaned heavily on Anna's arm, hunched over with grief, her steps uncertain. She saw no one and nothing except the ground ahead of her. Anna helped her into one of the few seats reserved for the old and infirm and her mother struggled to her knees with the faith of childhood, that a merciful God would watch over her and hers. Anna did not know whether her mother's bowed head signified a continued belief in God and it did not really matter in any case. Her mother had nodded when Anna asked her if she wanted to observe the Sabbath and so Anna had brought her down the lane to the church. They knelt side by side, their faces bearing witness to the months of strain. Katerina's was no longer that of a woman in her prime with her drawn cheeks and her thinning hair scraped back under her dark headscarf. Anna's face was more complex, and yet simpler. She had become tanned by her work in the fields and she looked healthy. But her eyes were ringed with the dark circles of broken nights, wondering what might have happened had she and her mother gone with Mikola and Yuri instead of helping old Nastunia.

The worshippers went through the rites of Mass and the priest's sermon erred on the side of the bland. He had seen too many deportations and worse in his shrinking congregation to be a firebrand bucking the Bolshevik system. He knew he was there on sufferance and that the country's new masters would not hesitate to shoot or deport him. His collar would not save his neck. Many of the former faithful now kept away from the old rituals in fear of the communist oppressor, so instead of exhorting his flock to fight against the godlessness of the Muscovites, Father Dubenko suggested gently that people might turn to prayer when in need.

Despite her bowed head, Anna paid little attention to his words. Her world had shrunk to survival for her mother and herself. And if God wanted to help, he was welcome to do so.

As Mass ended and the villagers emerged, Anna felt the coldness of some of their neighbours, who were too afraid for themselves to help anyone who might be tainted in any way, and so there were some who hurried past them on their slow progress up the path from the church and along the short distance along the lane to their home. Although she was grateful to those few who did speak to her, she bore no grudge against those who failed to acknowledge them. She knew better than most how dangerous life had become.

So she was doubly surprised later that afternoon to hear a knock at the door of her cottage. Opening the door cautiously, she saw Petro standing there with an axe in his hand.

"Hello," she said.

"Hello. I see your father managed to cut some wood, but it needs to be split and stacked. I wondered if I could do it for you."

Anna looked at this handsome young man and wondered what she had done to deserve this offer of help. "Thank you, but I plan to do it bit by bit. I have begun."

"Yes, I've seen you working at it, but as we both know, once we're in the depths of winter, it just needs to be ready to be brought in, and it's getting colder and wetter every day."

"Yes, I know, but I'm sure you must have work of your own to do."

"I do, that's why I've come to help you on a Sunday. Look, if your mother doesn't mind you working, why don't I split the logs and you stack them?"

"I'm sure she won't mind." Anna made up her mind. "Alright, I'll just get my jacket."

She disappeared into the cottage and Petro went over to the untidy pile of cut logs. He gathered the nearest beside the chopping block and began to split them. Anna came out of the house and started to stack them beneath the overhanging eves on the narrow end of the house.

She was kept busy supplying Petro with fresh logs and tidying away those he had split. They both worked hard, without pause, for a couple of hours, making serious inroads into the work Anna's father would normally have done.

As it began to get dark, Anna said, "We should stop soon. I'm really grateful for your help. Thank you."

"It's nothing. I'm glad I could help."

"I thought I'd manage it, but looking at how much we've done this afternoon, I realise I couldn't really have done it all alone."

"I'll come by one evening in the week if I can, to finish this lot off. If I can't, I'll come again next Sunday."

Anna looked at him in surprise. "You don't have to."

"I know, but I'd like to," and with a smile and a wave he was gone.

Anna looked at the fresh stacks of winter logs still feeling puzzled, but surprised and relieved that so much had been done. She had not dared to admit to herself that she might not have the time or the energy to cut enough wood in advance of the winter.

The following Sunday Petro appeared again. They both set to with a will, as if they had been working together for years. Again, he split the logs and she stacked them, collecting the smaller pieces for kindling and generally making a tidy job of what had threatened to look like neglect. As they finished their work, Anna said shyly, "Can I bring you a cup of tea out? I've baked a honey cake."

He grinned at her. "When have you heard a man turn down food?"

She smiled back and disappeared into the cottage, emerging a short time later with their tea sweetened with honey, and two slices of cake. "I'm sorry we have to sit out here, but my mother's napping."

"That's fine. I wouldn't want to disturb her."

They ate their cake companionably and then Petro licked his fingers clean. "That was a delicious piece of cake."

Anna blushed. "Thank you."

They sat on for some time in the dwindling autumn light, neither of them quite wanting to break the silence which had fallen over them.

Chapter 5

The winter blew in, reducing the temperature of relations with the Russians as the benign mask fell. The villagers fell into three distinct categories: the Communist sympathisers, often in the Militia; the nationalists trying to pursue their aims in secret; and those who simply wanted to be left alone to live their quiet lives. Disaster could strike anywhere. No one was safe in a regime built on suspicion. The liars distrusted the liars and the spies betrayed the spies.

One family, who fell victim to the chill, were living in a newly built house across the lane from Anna and her mother. It was a monument to an independent spirit, as Hrich Terblenko had not only constructed it himself, but he had also quarried and dressed the stone in the valley behind his house. He had carried every piece back to the building site to create a home for a family of six. But Communist dogma dictated that all citizens were equal, so the builder of such a dwelling might be setting himself above others. After all, there were Communists in the village who did not have a comfortable place to live...

Anna woke suddenly, trying to identify the noise which had disturbed her. She sat up in bed listening intently and then she heard it again: a door being struck by a heavy object.

"Open up, you bourgeois scum!" shouted a voice.

Katerina sat up, too. "What is it, Anna?"

"I don't know, but it sounds like the Militia at the Terblenko's," she whispered. The women sat without moving, straining to hear, not daring to light the lamp.

There were sounds of a door being unbolted and hurried footsteps on gravel which faded indoors. There followed the cries of people being struck. The voices of a man and a woman were raised in protest and then came a shriller cry after ominous thuds.

Anna's heart was pounding and she felt her mother's hand creep into her own. She squeezed Katerina's bony fingers, but kept listening.

Within moments there were shuffled footsteps and a gruff shout of "Get in!" A vehicle door was slammed and an engine started. The sound of the truck driving away left only darkness and silence behind it.

"What do you think it was?" whispered Katerina.

"I don't know, Mama, but we should try and get some sleep."

So the two women lay down on their backs, eyes wide open in the terrifying dark. Anna tried to relax, focussing on her heartbeat and her breathing, but it was some time before her pulse slowed. Just as she was about to turn on her side to try to sleep, she heard a scratching on the lower part of the cottage door. Her heart began to pound again as she listened for the repetition. When it came, she slid out of bed.

"What are you doing?" asked Katerina in alarm.

"There's someone scratching at the door. I'm going to look."

"No, Anna, don't! It's too dangerous."

"Mama, I must." Anna edged forward in the darkness, feeling her way to the door. "Who is it?" she hissed.

The scratching came again, more urgently.

Anna slid the bolt back, careful not to make a sound and opened the door a fraction. "Who…"

"Let me in," muttered a low voice.

Anna opened the door wide enough for a shadow to glide in and then she shut the door swiftly, sliding the bolt home. She reached out to touch the shadow and encountered a boy's short hair. "Who…"

"It's me, Hrichko."

"But I thought I just heard your family…"

"You did." The boy paused. "I ran away."

"Come in," said Anna, feeling for the boy's arm and guiding him to the bench by the wall. "What happened?"

She could hear Katerina moving in bed. "It's alright, Mama, it's Hrichko from over the road."

"I know. I can hear him."

Hrichko, at twelve, was a little older than their own Yuri. Old enough to associate a knock at the door during the night with fearful danger, and to react instinctively; but young enough, on reflection, to be appalled by his actions.

"What happened to you?" asked Katerina.

"I heard banging and *Tato* shouting, so I jumped out of the back window. I didn't think about it."

"No one would," agreed Anna.

"Then I hid in our garden, you know, the dark corner by the bread oven."

"Yes," said Anna.

"I saw the Militia truck and I heard the men banging to be let in. *Tato* had to let them in."

"Yes, he did."

"*Tato* didn't want any of us to be shot." The boy swallowed a sob.

Anna stroked his arm. "I didn't hear any shots."

"No. No one was shot. They just told Mama and *Tato* that they were Enemies of the People and made them all get in the lorry. All of them. The girls, too." Hrichko leaned forward into Anna and sobbed.

She held him, stroking the rough fabric of his shirt. "Hush, you did the right thing."

The boy tried again to hold back his sobs, but could not. Anna simply rocked him until they ceased.

"Anna," Katerina breathed. "What are we going to do with him?"

"We'll keep him here until we can find a way out for him."

They could hear Hrichko snuffling and trying to tidy away his tears. "I shouldn't have come."

"You did the right thing," said Anna. "You can sleep in Yuri's bed tonight and tomorrow I'll find out where you might be able to go."

"*Tato* said that was all..." and he began to sob again.

"I'm sorry, I don't understand."

"When the Militia asked if that was the whole family, *Tato* said that was all of them."

"Well, of course he did. He wanted to protect you."

"But I should have gone with them!"

"Your father didn't think so. Come. I know you might not sleep, but at least you can lie down." Anna led him into the next room and unrolled the mattress and eiderdown on Yuri's old bed. She settled him as best she could, then slipped back into bed beside her mother.

Katerina turned towards her daughter and whispered in her ear: "Anna, we could be killed for taking him in."

"I know, Mama, but no one helped us. I won't turn my back on anyone who needs help." She put her arm around her mother. "Let's try to sleep. There's nothing else we can do now."

In the morning, after feeding Hrichko *kasha*, Anna gathered some eggs from her hens and placing them in a straw-filled basket, told Katerina she would be back shortly. Katerina nodded.

Anna took her eggs to a house where she knew the wife would be busy with her morning chores. The husband's work often took him from home. Anna was greeted politely and invited in.

"What can I do for you, Anna?" asked the woman.

"I need to find a place," Anna began.

"A place?" the woman prompted, indicating a chair for Anna to sit on.

"Yes." Anna paused not knowing how to continue.

The woman waited patiently.

"I'm sorry. I'm not thinking very clearly. I didn't sleep much last night."

The woman nodded and returned to preparing her vegetables for soup. There was a silence and then with a sigh, the woman asked, "And how is your mother?"

"Sometimes she seems a little better, thank you."

"But not at the moment," the woman prompted.

"No, she slept badly last night, too. She was reminded of my brother, Yuri."

"I'm sorry to hear that."

Anna swallowed. "If my brother had ever needed shelter in the forest, he would not have known how to find it."

"Not many do."

"Especially being so young. And on his own."

"Indeed."

"It would have been very hard for him. Without the rest of his family."

"Yes, I suppose it would."

"I wouldn't know how to advise him to remain hidden," said Anna in a small voice.

The woman glanced briefly at Anna. There was another pause. "It was good of you to bring me some extra eggs for my baking. If you come back tomorrow, I'll let you have some of the cake."

"Thank you," said Anna, with some relief.

The woman turned to her store cupboard. "But take this cherry cordial I made in the summer. It might make your mother feel better."

Anna rose. "Thank you so much."

"There's nothing to thank me for. Come back tomorrow afternoon for the baking."

"I will. Thank you." Anna left the house, the jar visible in her basket, as if her bartering request with a neighbour had been successful.

When she arrived at her own house, Katerina got up quickly from her chair. "Well?"

"I'm to go back tomorrow afternoon."

"Not till then? How will we manage?"

"By carrying on as normal, Mama."

A little later, Anna entered the second room and began to turn out the cupboards. Under the noise of her work, she said, "Don't worry. We'll know more tomorrow. Just keep very quiet till then."

*

The following afternoon Anna returned to the woman's house, to collect some baking from a neighbour. She knocked at the door, half afraid of having her request rejected, but once again she was invited in. She stood inside the door as the woman gestured to the baking on the table.

"It all turned out well," she said.

"Good. I was hoping it would," said Anna and then she waited for the woman to take the lead.

"Which would you like?" She pointed to the cakes.

"My brother's favourite was the honey cake," said Anna swallowing.

"Then take that one," nodded the woman. "Did he used to play in the woods, down near the Barish?"

Anna looked into the woman's eyes.

"Mind you, perhaps he didn't. It can be swampy in the spring."

"Mama used to worry about him going there," nodded Anna.

"But boys will be boys. Even young ones. Coming home after midnight."

"Yes, dreadful." Anna nodded again.

"Well, take your cake, and give my best wishes to your mother."

"Thank you. I will." She wanted to embrace the woman, but dared not, so she left with her neighbourly gift.

When Anna returned home, Katerina looked up from her sewing.

"Tonight," Anna murmured and then went into the second bedroom. "I'm going to sort through these old things," she called to Katerina and then she took Mikola and Yuri's clothes from the cupboard. She hummed as she worked and then murmured, "I'll leave some warm clothes here. Put them on later. We leave tonight."

"Where to?" came the quiet question.

"Somewhere safe. I think we can trust them."

"Are they our people?"

"Yes, our boys in the forest." Anna felt his anxiety and added, "I'll take you part of the way. Try not to worry."

Then she followed her own advice and continued with her afternoon chores in the garden. She dug up enough leeks to flavour a pot of soup and passing her three pole fence to the field beyond, she casually slid the middle pole to one side, creating a gap large enough to slip through easily in the dark. The field which bordered Anna's garden rolled away gently downhill to the wooded valley below and to the river Barish.

Later, as Anna knelt with Katerina before the icon to say their evening prayers, she was aware of her mother's nervousness.

"Anna?"

"Yes, Mama."

"What will you do?"

"There's no need for you to worry, Mama. You just get a good night's sleep."

Katerina turned sharply to look at her daughter. "No!"

"I must. He's too young to go on his own," whispered Anna. "Think how Yuri would have felt."

Katerina bowed her head.

"Please, Mama. Let's finish our prayers."

Katerina tried to comfort herself with the idea that someone might have helped her son in similar circumstances, but she dared not think of the risks Anna would be taking. She prayed to the Virgin to guide and guard her remaining child and as they prepared for bed, Katerina held Anna a moment longer than their customary embrace, then Anna went to tend the fire.

A little before midnight, Anna rose and put on her outer clothing. She felt her way over to the bedroom door and opened it quietly. "Come," she said under her breath. She felt the air move as someone joined her in the dark and she took the boy's hand. They moved to the outer door, which Anna had left unbolted. Once outside, she led Hrichko round to the woodpile, where they went through the gap in the fence to Anna's vegetable garden. They hurried along its edge to the border with the field, where she tucked his head down to slip under the space she had created into the open land beyond. The ground was bare now, but the cloudy night helped obscure them. They followed the hedgerow down to the woods. Anna gave a small sigh of relief as they went under the sparse cover of the winter trees and she led the boy diagonally downhill, avoiding the path. Occasionally, she squeezed his hand to alert him to an obstacle, but they were able to make smooth progress to where the hill dropped down to the Barish. Anna made the boy pause before they began the descent, but they heard nothing. They reached the bottom of the wood where the swamp stood in summer, but all was frozen now. Anna led Hrichko to a thick stand of bushes where they crouched and waited, peering into the darkness, their eyes wide for any sign of movement. However, there was none, nor any sound as they continued to wait, while Anna hoped she had not misunderstood the cloaked message.

She started when she felt a hand on her shoulder and heard one word muttered in her ear. "Go!" She stood and returned home up the hill through the trees. She wanted desperately to turn and check on Hrichko, but dared not jeopardise his chance of rescue. She gained the top of the hill and hurried along the field and garden into the safety of her house. She bolted the door, slipped off her warm clothing and slid into bed beside her mother. Katerina squeezed her arm and the two women lay on their backs in the darkness, their eyes wide open, brimming with tears.

The women carried those tears in their hearts across the intervening days to the first anniversary of the deaths of Mikola and Yuri, which dawned grey and overcast. The rain came down unremittingly all day, but despite that, Anna and Katerina would have liked to visit the unmarked grave to pray over their dead. However, they could not be seen to be paying any respect to those who were perceived to have defied the state. Ostapenko not only had his vile lieutenants, but any number of spies who would be happy to inform him of the women's activities. So Anna and Katerina knelt before the icon in their home, and said their prayers for the souls of father and son. Nor could they have a memorial Mass said, as the church doors had been locked against worshippers, a faithful few gathering quietly in Father Dubenko's house. Neither of the women allowed themselves to wonder how many more such anniversaries might pass. They simply tried to contain their pain to avoid their sorrow spilling and overwhelming them.

When the rain ceased, Anna told her mother she would walk a little. She took the route she had taken with Hrichko. The sun was beginning to set behind the trees and Anna tried to see its red glow pouring towards the village as a blessing, rather than an omen of things to come. Apprehension crept from the corners of her mind, despite her attempts to hold it back. Where would it all end? Deaths and disappearances had become commonplace and Anna tried not to fear the disaster she felt was looming. The optimism which had accompanied the use of the Ukrainian language in schools and government institutions had faded as, inexorably, the tide of the Russian language flowed into Western Ukraine.

Easter should have arrived full of promise. The villagers would normally whitewash their cottages, but this time many homes were left with winter debris splashing their skirts. However, the cemetery could receive its annual transformation. This was the responsibility of the children, who tidied the graves of their relatives, putting fresh spring flowers on them. The older ones snipped the grass between, in preparation for the celebration of Christ rising from the dead on Easter Sunday. It was an energetic and happy affair, part of the year's renewal.

Anna thought that under cover of so much activity, she might be able to trim the corner where Mikola and Yuri were buried, thinking it might assuage her ache a little to know the spot where their corpses lay had not been abandoned. So she took her scythe and cut the grass in a wide area over and around Mikola and Yuri's grave. She raked the grass away toward the hedge and lifted her face to the spring sunshine. Then she turned to watch the youngsters in their noisy busyness, calling to one another, and felt cheered by the scene's gaiety.

Suddenly, there was the shrill peal of a whistle as a young woman appeared at the top of the cemetery beside the church. Anna peered to see who it was and caught sight of the new school teacher. She was clapping her hands together and calling the children.

"Come along, come along, children," she said in Russian. "Gather round."

The youngsters did as they were told, the habits of the schoolroom easily translating themselves into the open, although some of the children raised their eyebrows at one another, wondering why their teacher had appeared here.

"Come along, you stragglers," she called again and then waited until all of the children were in front of her. "Now then children," she began, again in Russian, "this is a very primitive thing that you are doing. This is a place of death. There is no one living here and so you do not need to do anything for them." She paused and looked around the expectant faces. Satisfied she had their attention, she continued. "When we die, that is the end. There is nothing more." Noticing the odd flicker of objection, she pressed her point home. "Our dear Father, Comrade Stalin, has told us that God is dead. And that is true, children. You must not waste your time here, but should go to your homes. You can help with the creation of bread for our beloved country. Go home and tell your parents: God is dead." And with that she ushered the children to the gate of the graveyard and out onto the lane.

The children seemed stunned by what had just taken place, some still holding flowers or tools in their hands, but they walked like automata. There was no chatter, merely a shocked silence, snapped as one or two youngsters broke into a run for home. When she was certain the last child had left the cemetery, the teacher closed and locked the gate.

Petro was painting their cottage when his youngest sister, Nina, ran sobbing along the garden path and into the house.

"Mama! Mama!"

"What is it?" her mother exclaimed, as she left the stove to tend to the child.

Being safely home with four adults to comfort her, Nina's sobs became inconsolable. She clung to her mother's firm frame, while Halia tried not to become either impatient or afraid. "There, there," she soothed. "Let's wipe your face. Natalia, pass me the flannel."

Natalia cooled the cloth first in cold water and then passed it to her mother. Halia sat down and brought Nina, who was really too old for this sort of attention, onto her lap. Then she wiped the child's face clean. "There, that's better. Now try to tell me what happened."

"She said *Tato* was dead."

"Nina, you know *Tato* is dead. He died three years ago," said Halia.

"But she said that was the end."

"Who did?"

"Valentina Fedorovna."

Halia looked questioningly at her daughters.

Irina said drily, "The new Russian teacher."

"But I still don't understand…" began Halia as Irina went outside.

"Petro," she called. "Can you help us with this please?"

Petro put down his brush and approached the house. "I can't come in now. I'm dirty."

Irina glanced at him and murmured, "We need you."

He barely nodded and stepping out of his shoes at the door, entered the kitchen. "What's happened?" he asked, crouching beside Nina.

"I'm not sure," replied his mother. "Nina's upset at something the new teacher said to her."

"Not just me. To all of us!"

"But it's Saturday," said Petro. "Why was she speaking to all of you?"

"She sent us out of the cemetery."

The four adults exchanged glances.

"Were there any other grown ups there?" asked Petro.

"Only the mushroom girl."

Petro looked puzzled and Irina said, "She must mean Anna."

"Yes, her. The one with the mushrooms."

"What was she doing there?" asked Petro.

"She was at the bare bit at the bottom of the cemetery."

"I still don't understand any of this," said Petro. "God knows what's going on."

"God's dead," announced Nina.

"Nina!" exclaimed her mother.

"That's what Valentina Fedorovna said."

Petro stood up. "I think I'll walk to Anna's to see if she can throw any light on this."

"Alright," said Halia. "But be careful."

"I will," he sighed. "I'll try not to be long. That lime wash won't wait."

He made his way along the lane to the monument at the centre of the village and then turned left towards Anna's cottage. He was not sure what he was going to say, nor what her role in all of this had been. But Nina's distress and confusion needed to be addressed.

Anna was nowhere to be seen when he arrived at her home. He had hoped to find her in the garden, but at least the cottage door was open. He knocked, beginning to feel a little foolish and wondering if his family had over-reacted to a child's distorted sense of proportion.

Anna came to the door, wiping her hands on her apron. "Hello, Petro. What can I do for you?"

He hesitated, embarrassed. "Erm, Nina has just come home in floods of tears..."

"Just a moment."

Petro waited until she came out of the cottage, having removed her apron. "Let's go this way."

He followed her across her vegetable garden to the field and down to the woods where they walked side by side.

Anna paused and looked round. There was no one in sight. "Nina..." she prompted.

"Yes. She came home very distressed and told us some garbled tale about the teacher in the cemetery."

"Valentina Fedorovna ordered them out of the cemetery."

"Why?"

"Because she said there was no after-life and that they were wasting their time."

"I see," he said. "And you..."

"I was there, too."

"Why?"

Anna hesitated and then made herself meet his eyes. "I was scything the grass at the bottom of the cemetery."

"Oh I see." He stopped, annoyed at himself for his blunder. "I'm sorry. I should have realised."

"I was doing it then, while the cemetery was busy."

"Of course. Anna, I'm sorry," he said again.

"There's no need. It's better that people don't think about what I'm doing. But as for the children... They were all shocked I think. Valentina Fedorovna told them that God is dead."

"That's what Nina repeated. We couldn't understand any of it. And she's upset about *Tato*, too."

"Yes, she would be. The children weren't allowed to finish brightening up the graves. She ordered them to leave and saw them out of the cemetery."

"It seems so stupid to upset the little ones over a few flowers," he mused.

"They're determined. The church is locked and I don't know how much longer Father Dubenko will last – if he's still here..." Anna made herself stop. It was a relief to talk openly, but Anna knew she should not be expressing her opinion to Petro, despite his kindness to her. "You should be getting back to your painting," she said, nodding at his paint-spattered clothes. "Unless Irina and Natalia have taken over."

He grinned. "You must be joking. Those two! No, the job's all mine."

They turned to climb out of the woods and at their border, he said, "I'm going to go this way. Thanks for your help."

She waved and strode up the path to the back of her cottage.

But the misery did not end with children being ushered out of a graveyard. As one side hardened their efforts, so did the other. Very little was said overtly, but it was generally known that the partisans were becoming more active. They were also becoming more aggressive in the western regions, where they were recruiting. Even a child like Hrichko could be a valuable and ostensibly innocent messenger. Some of the young men of the village found themselves joining "the boys in the forest", especially if they were due to receive their Red Army call-up. They had seen some of their peers having to join the military, Vera's older brother being one of those who had already left the village for an uncertain future in their ranks.

But at least one boy of nineteen had slipped away from the village after having had his Army medical, the choice of being a homeless partisan being more attractive than being one of Stalin's recruits. It was hard on his parents, but Boris knew his mother's anguish and being a loving boy, he called in to see her one cloudy night. He approached the cottage stealthily and agreed to his mother's plea of supper and a good night's sleep. His father promised to wake him early so that Boris could withdraw to the woods again. But they were all woken at dawn by the Militia, who had received a tip-off from an observant and unsympathetic neighbour.

The Militia leader of this particular operation was one of Ostapenko's favoured lieutenants, Prutko, a man as hard as his master could wish. "Come on. Let's be having you," he shouted, shouldering the door as soon as he heard the bolt being drawn. "Where have you been, my lad?" he barked.

"He's been visiting my cousin. There's been some illness over there and he's been helping with the work," said the boy's father.

"Oh really? There can be a lot of illness in the forest if you're not careful."

"He was helping the family," repeated Boris's father.

"I'm sure," said Prutko. "But just so we don't get a rash of boys helping their distant families, we'll take your lad with us." Nodding to his subordinates, he turned away out of the house.

Boris's wrists were quickly bound with wire. He was tethered with a rope around his throat and led from the house.

"Wait!" called his father, as Boris's mother clung to her husband's arm in shocked disbelief.

But the men simply pulled Boris hard enough for him to cry out.

It was light now and people were beginning to attend to their livestock and their early morning tasks. Any attention was grist to the Militia men's mill and they drove Boris with sharp sticks, like a calf to the slaughter. Their purpose was to take him along the main lane, past the monument and the church, to the quarry at the southern edge of the village, where they would shoot him. And if his distraught parents should accompany them, all the better for delivering a message to those with foolish ideas of fighting for an independent state.

They succeeded in passing the monument, but as they drew towards the branching lane and the well opposite Anna's house, Boris's father realised that there was no hope. He pushed the Militia men out of his way and stood between his son and Prutko. "Look, he truly was helping my cousin. If you need to take someone, take me. Leave him here to help his mother. Please."

"Alright then," said Prutko, taking his gun from its holster. He raised the pistol, aimed at the father's throat and fired. Boris's father fell to the ground.

There were gasps and shouts from the watching villagers but there had also been a heart-rending cry of "No!".

Katerina had come out of the cottage to see what all the commotion was about in time to witness the cold-blooded shooting. She did not see Boris and his father, but her own Mikola. As did Anna. But she was the first to realise her mother's danger and, dropping the bowl from which she had been feeding the hens, she ran over to her mother, clamped her hand over Katerina's mouth and pushed her into the cottage, slamming the door behind them. They both dropped on their haunches against the door, but Anna continued to keep her hand clamped over Katerina's mouth.

"No, Mama," she hissed. "No!" She riveted Katerina with her eyes. "Don't make a sound!"

They remained thus while outside in the lane shouts could be heard as Boris was dragged to his fate in the quarry, his father's corpse lying in the dusty lane, his mother howling in agony.

Anna felt a moment's pity for the woman, knowing her anguish had only just begun, but then she turned her attention back to her own mother. "Mama, it wasn't *Tato*."

Katerina's eyes were no longer focussed on Anna, who rocked her mother in her arms. Katerina wept inconsolably. Anna shared her mother's grief, but even she was shocked at the well of despair she now peered into. It was as if Katerina had never felt a moment's grief before, nor cried a single tear, as her misery poured from her. Anna felt afraid as she tried to soothe her mother, wondering if Katerina would ever find her way back from the sorrow into which she had disappeared.

Another shot rang out and Katerina shuddered in a paroxysm which threatened to drown her entirely, while Anna rocked and chanted, "Mama, Mama" as she tried to anchor her mother to the present. Eventually, Katerina calmed a little and Anna drew her towards the bed. She sat her mother on the side of the bed, removed her boots and headscarf and helped her to lie down. Then she made a strong infusion of vervain and holding her mother up to drink, she hoped it would give her the blessed unconsciousness of sleep.

Chapter 6

But cruelty did not hold complete sway. Some days later, Petro returned from the fields to find Nina jigging up and down with excitement.

"The kittens are here!" she announced. "Come and look!"

He followed his youngest sister into the barn with an indulgent smile. Only she would be excited about a litter of creatures about to be drowned.

"Look! There are six. I counted them."

Petro shook his head. "You know she can't keep them all. She won't be able to feed them and we won't be able to find homes for them."

Nina's bottom lip trembled and her eyes filled with tears. "But they're..." she hiccupped, "they're babies..."

"All the better to take them away now, while they know nothing about it."

As the tears threatened to spill over Nina's lashes, Petro said quickly, "We'll let her keep two. I know someone who wants a kitten and I suppose we could find room for another cat here."

Nina beamed up at him and for a moment he wondered how much of an actress his little sister might be, but he took her hand and led her into the kitchen. His mother was cooking the evening meal and he bent to greet her with a kiss on the cheek.

"Haven't you even washed yet?" she said, pretending to scrub at her face with a towel.

He laughed, and then Nina tugged at his trousers.

"Oh yes. Nina and I have decided to leave two of the kittens. Is that alright?"

"Two?" Halia asked.

"Yes, I have a home for one of them."

"Alright," she said and nodded to him above the child's head. "Nina, set the table and Petro, get washed for supper for goodness sake!"

Petro pretended to grumble as he left the kitchen and before washing himself, disposed efficiently of four kittens.

Later, as the girls cleared the table, Natalia asked, "So who wants our kitten?"

"I'm not allowed to say for the moment," he replied. "I'll tell you when the kitten is in its new home." He did not say that he had chosen an extremely handsome tabby, with whose help he planned to encourage the girl fall in love – both with the cat, and with him.

The corn was ripening and in mid-June the fields were almost ready for harvesting. There would be work from dawn till dusk once they started cutting, but for now, on a beautiful balmy evening, Petro strolled down the lane, his shirt tucked into the band of his trousers. He reached Anna's house feeling a twinge of nervousness, but then he thought of her beauty and her loss, and knocked.

Anna opened the door.

"Good evening," he began.

"Oh, it's you…" she said and let out a sigh of relief as she put her hand to her throat.

"I'm sorry if I frightened you."

"It's alright. I just wasn't expecting anyone." She gathered herself and smiled politely, saying, "What can I do for you?"

"I have something to show you. Could you step out into the garden?"

She followed him, wondering what he could want. Petro led her to the bench beneath the walnut tree and motioned for her to sit. He joined her and she was very surprised to see him reach inside his shirt to extract a plump, mewling creature. He stroked the kitten's fur smooth and let it sit on his lap to show itself off. It was a beautiful grey tabby whose wide face wore the customary look of surprise. The kitten looked around and would have hopped down to the ground had Petro not made a circle of his arms to hold it in view.

"What do you think?" he asked.

She laughed a little and said, "Well, I think it's a kitten."

"Obviously. Don't you think he's handsome?"

"He's lovely, but I wouldn't have expected you to come here to show me your kitten."

"He's not mine. He's yours."

Anna became more serious. "I don't have a kitten."

"You didn't. But you can have this one. I saved him for you from our last litter."

"Why did you do that?"

"Because I thought you might enjoy watching him grow up. I think he's going to be a very entertaining character." Petro removed his arms from around the kitten and it walked over to Anna's lap.

She stroked its head tentatively with one finger. "What's his name?"

"He hasn't got one. I thought you might want to name him."

She stroked the kitten again and a loud purr erupted from his throat. He hopped off her knees to explore the grass, where he attacked and killed a twig and then bounced after a leaf before stopping to lick his paw.

"I didn't know you were so clever," she said, "nor so kind," and she bent to stroke the kitten so that he would not see her sudden tears.

"Well, now you know," he said to this lovely girl, knowing he could begin to approach cautiously.

They watched the kitten for a few moments longer and then Petro said, "If you give him some milk indoors and maybe a soft bed, I'm sure he'll happily stay with you."

Anna rose and picked up the kitten. Holding it to her, she said, "I'm not sure if Mama is still dressed…"

"Oh, that's alright. I won't trouble her. You take him in and get him settled. I can always come and see him another time."

"Yes, you can," she smiled. "And thank you."

"You're welcome." He made his way across the garden and out into the lane.

Anna hugged the kitten and put her face into its fur as she watched Petro's receding back, taking in his long fair curls and his broad shoulders.

It was the custom in the village for neighbours to share taking the cows to pasture. Most families had at least one cow and to spend several hours every day pasturing it was impracticable, so there was a rota. Anna was often paired with Ivan, and his conversation enlivened what could be a long day. They simply walked their section of the lane, gradually gathering a herd of twenty or so obedient beasts and drove them past the church, towards the quarry, and along the track to the Dniester. They could be pastured either along the hillside above the river, or down in the river bottom, depending on the season. It being summer, they allowed the cows to pause and graze on the grassy hillside just below the tree line. Ivan and Anna could now relax as long as they kept an eye on the animals.

Ivan instantly returned to the moment of their meeting that morning, when Anna had seemed flustered as she left the house, calling to her mother to close the door quickly. He was not a young man troubled by diplomacy so he asked outright: "What was the problem at the door of your cottage, Anna?"

"When?"

"This morning when I called for you."

"Oh, we have a new kitten and I wanted him to stay in the house today with Mama."

"When did you get him?"

"A few days ago."

"Where from?"

Anna was annoyed to find herself blushing. "Someone gave him to me."

Ivan instantly scented something interesting. "Who was that then?"

"Petro."

"Aha!"

"What? 'Aha'?"

"And he had the nerve to suggest I was playing the field."

"What do you mean? 'Playing the field'?"

"Well, I don't mean he is…with you. He was commenting on my love life, that's all."

"Well there's plenty to comment on there," laughed Anna.

They strolled a few metres to be standing above the cows, which were now scattered in a black and white patchwork across the green sward. The peacefulness of the scene lulled them both with the sun sparkling on the broad stretch of the Dniester below them. There were the plaintive cries of buzzards above, as a pair hunted over the vibrant woods. In the meadows, bees buzzed among the wild flowers, the poppies, cow parsley and ragged robin attracting their attention. A stork rose into the air, flapping its great wings as it worked to gain height over the rich flood plain. For a moment, Anna held her breath, feeling as if the great bird would not gather enough momentum, but then, as if by magic, the ungainly bird glided above them gracefully on strong wide wings, its long legs trailing behind. Anna felt calmed and allowed herself to relax. However, her mind went back to Ivan's phrase, "playing the field", and she could not help but ask, "Is Petro playing the field?"

Ivan grinned that she had taken the bait. "Why are you interested?"

"I'm not. I'm just passing the time," she smiled.

"Hmm." He paused to see if she would ask again and then decided to be kind to her. "Alright. I don't think he has a girlfriend at the moment."

"Oh."

"Yes, oh. You don't need to play the innocent with me. I've known you all my life."

"I'm not playing innocent," she blushed. "You started it."

"Well, maybe, but why is he bringing you presents?"

"Not presents. Just a kitten."

"Yes, but why?"

"If you really want to know… I think he felt sorry for me."

"Oh Anna! That trick always works."

"He's not playing tricks," retorted Anna, feeling disappointed at the same time that Petro might be.

"No. You're right. He's not that type. And besides," he grinned at her again, "why shouldn't he simply be attracted to a beautiful girl like you?"

"Oh stop it!" said Anna laughing and blushed again. She set off to walk around the herd to escape Ivan's sharp eyes and to examine her own feelings for Petro. There was every reason to be cautious, but she was also young enough to be fluttered with excitement at the thought of handsome Petro seeking her out.

But the subject had also caused interest elsewhere.

"So where has our kitten gone?" Irina had asked on the day of its disappearance.

"The mushroom girl's got it," said Nina.

"Anna's got it," corrected Petro.

The twins glanced at one another.

"Anna has it?" asked Natalia. "Why her?"

"I thought she might like it."

"That was thoughtful of you," said Irina.

"Yes, I thought so, too," said Petro. "Living alone with a mother driven almost mad with grief can't be easy," and he was unable to stop himself from striding from the house.

"Well," commented Natalia. "Now we know."

"Know what?" asked Nina.

"Where the kitten went," answered Irina, flicking a sharp look at her twin.

June should have been a lovely month full of summer activities and the anticipation of a good harvest, but rumours were rampant about Germany's invasion of the USSR. Not only was Stalin taken by surprise, the whole country was. But once again, people were reluctant to wonder out loud what it might mean for Western Ukraine. Anna missed her father badly at this time. Not only would she have been glad of his protection, but she would have been able to discuss her anxieties openly with him. He would have known the current thinking among the menfolk.

When, at the end of the month the terrifying news came that the NKVD had summarily executed all of the hundreds of prisoners being held at the jail in Temne, the feeling of walking on eggshells spiralled up into a fierce dread of what their Russian masters might do next.

Anna was hoeing her vegetables when she was joined by Petro.

"Have you got five minutes?" he asked.

She rested her hoe against the fence. "Yes, of course."

He gestured towards the woods.

"I'll just tell Mama."

He nodded and waited until she hurried back, then he led the way to the path beyond the fence down to the woods. When they were among the trees, she waited for him to speak. He was in too serious a mood for this conversation to be anything other than grave, but she was confused by his first question.

"Have you harvested much of your garden yet?"

"Not really. We're eating as I pick things, but there hasn't been any need yet. Why?"

"I don't want to frighten you, but I'm worried about what might happen next." He took a breath. "Look, you know they think the Germans are coming, don't you?"

Anna nodded.

"And the Communists shot the people they were holding in Temne… God knows what they might do to the rest of us."

Anna looked at him with wide eyes.

"And our livestock," he struggled to add, cursing himself for his lack of tact and wondering whether she would not be better left in ignorance.

"So what are you advising me to do?"

"I'm not sure myself, Anna. At home, we're trying to prepare for any disaster – as far as we can without frightening Nina. And with your father… you might not know what the men are saying."

"What are they saying?"

"If it comes to a violent attack, we might have to hide."

"Where?"

"In the woods towards Petryn. They're quite close to reach, especially from your side of the village, and they're the deepest. You could come down through these trees and slip across the bottom of the valley. You wouldn't be in the open for long."

"Yes, I can see that's a good idea," said Anna, busy calculating how she might save her cow, hens and kitten while dealing with her mother.

"Anna, I'm sorry to worry you."

"It's alright, I'm just thinking about how it might be done. Thank you for warning me. I'll need to give it some more thought…"

"I'll get word to you as soon as I can, if I need to."

"You have your own family to protect. I'll manage."

"Yes, but as soon as I know anything, I will get word to you," he repeated.

"Thank you, Petro. My greatest worry is Mama of course. I honestly don't know whether to try to prepare her for whatever is coming or whether it's better not to worry her."

"I wish I could advise you, Anna. How has she been?"

"Very quiet…since poor Boris…"

"Hmm."

They both stood in silence, remembering the brutal morning of Boris's death. Anna's mother was not the only traumatised woman living in the close community.

"I'd better get back. I'll think about it while I'm weeding. And thanks again for telling me." She made herself walk away. He had enough problems without taking on hers, Anna told herself, and anyway, she had to be self-sufficient. Who else would save her and Mama?

She returned to her garden, calling her mother to tell her she was back, then continued the soothing task of hoeing her peas. If danger came suddenly, she thought, all that truly mattered was that she and her mother escaped with their lives. But if there was warning…she would try to save the cow simply by taking her with them. She mused about the hens…they were more problematic…and the kitten? She would tuck him in her blouse. And Mama… She chopped at the fresh young weeds and turned the bed black again, as she tried to decide how to minimise her mother's distress.

That evening, after supper and prayers, Anna and her mother lay down to sleep, but before extinguishing the lamp, Anna said, "Mama, I have to talk to you about something Petro told me today."

"What is it, Anna?"

"There are rumours that the German Army is moving west," said Anna.

Katerina stiffened a little. Anna took her mother's hand. "They might not come through here, Mama, but if they do, I want us to be safe."

Katerina nodded.

"I don't know what we might have to do, Mama, and I don't want you to be frightened. But I think it's important that you know that there might come a moment when I will have to ask you to do something quickly. I need you to trust me and to know that you must do as I ask. Can you do that, Mama?"

"I'll try. When will it be?"

"I don't know. Maybe not at all. But it's better for us to be prepared. Just in case." Anna looked carefully at her mother. "Are you alright, Mama?"

"Yes, Anna. I'll do as you ask."

"I know you will," said Anna. She stroked the stray hair back from her mother's forehead. "Shall we try to sleep now?"

"Yes."

Anna turned out the lamp and lay down beside her mother, trying to relax into sleep. But thoughts and plans jostled one another in the tight space of her mind. Eventually, Murchik jumped onto the bed and curled his warmth beside Anna and stroking his silken coat, she fell asleep to his loud purr.

*

The war with Germany touched the village first in a way that none of its inhabitants might have imagined. Quite early one morning, the trumpet sounded and the adults of the village hurried to the hall to obey its summons. Anna left her mother at home and joined the women as they entered the hall in a quiver of expectation. The men also filed in and people stood in rough rows looking up at the stage where Ostapenko, burlier than ever, strode back and forth in his highly polished boots. He was flanked by his hulking lieutenants, but on this occasion, there were also a dozen or so Red Army soldiers around the edges of the hall. The community waited anxiously for the latest pronouncement.

When the hall was almost full, Ostapenko bawled, "Close the doors. Shoot any stragglers."

The men and women kept their eyes on Ostapenko and fervently hoped no stragglers would appear.

"Comrades," Ostapenko began, "it is our great privilege to make an airfield for our brave pilots to continue the war against the Germans. We have been especially chosen by our leaders to create a large enough space for take-off and landing in our region. So work begins today. You are to return to your homes now to fetch your scythes and we will meet again in half an hour at the school. For this part of our work, we will not need the women. You should stay at home. But I expect to see all of the men thirty minutes from now. You may go." He walked from the platform, head erect, whip held firmly in his hand.

The villagers were astounded by the announcement, but they simply poured from the hall and hurried to fetch their scythes, those who lived further away doing so on the run.

As Anna left the hall, she came face to face with Petro and was able to mouth, "Take care!" to him. He nodded and hastened away. Anna walked up the lane with the women, deciding to check her garden for vegetables which were ready to be picked and preserved. Jars could be buried…

Meanwhile, Petro joined the flow of men and boys, who gathered promptly at the doors of the school on the north end of the village where the fields began. Suspicions had begun to enter their minds: scythes and fields could only mean one thing. But those to whom the unthinkable had occurred, tried to ignore the terrible preposterousness of the idea… However, they were not wrong.

Ostapenko, mounted on his horse, was waiting for them beside the steps of the school, and this time he was accompanied by a unit of Red Army soldiers, guns at the ready. "The airfield will begin here, comrades," he announced, pointing to the fields full of fat green wheat, which needed only two or three more weeks of sunshine to be ready for harvesting. "You will form one row and

67

begin to cut from this end of the field, working towards the shrine."

This confirmation of their fears horrified the men.

"But Comrade Ostapenko," called one brave soul, "we only need a couple more weeks before we harvest this wheat. It will feed the village all winter…" He did not have time to finish his plea as a shot rang out from Prutko on Ostapenko's nod. The man fell in that second where he had stood, and no more words were needed to persuade good farmers to cut their wheat too early for it to be of any use to anyone.

The men walked towards the edge of the field and reluctantly spread out in a long line from one end to the other. They did not dare to look at one another, as they saw they were not only followed by Red Army soldiers, but that the field was bordered on both sides by more soldiers, armed with their self-loading Tokarev rifles. They all knew that the rifles could fire ten shots without the soldier pausing to re-load, so Petro and the others bent their backs to their work and it did not matter that everything they had learned from their forefathers cried out against this violation of the countryside. Without speaking, the row of men moved slowly forward across the field, cutting the strong green stalks, the only sounds being the swish of blades and swathes falling uselessly. There was none of the gaiety which often accompanied the harvest, the brightly dressed girls, the singing…only a harrowing ache in the hearts of men emasculated by those better armed than they.

The terrible cutting went on all day and as the exhausted labourers longed for the reprieve of dusk, Ostapenko rode up and shouted from the saddle, "Stop work now. We meet at the school again tomorrow morning at seven." He wheeled his horse about and trotted off, leaving the men to unbend their aching limbs.

There was none of the balm of satisfaction at a job well done, nor the soothing knowledge of storing grain for the winter – only the vision of loathsome waste. The men set off for their homes, exhaustion and shame clamping their tongues.

The work continued the following day. Teams of men were sent to work towards Temne and Petryn in a broad sweep of devastation. The younger men had been sent the furthest and that evening they walked home at twilight, their muscles sore. They were spread out along the lanes, walking with their heads down, dreading the talk at home of just how far they had been to destroy perfectly good crops.

Petro reached the shrine, and glancing back, saw Ivan trailing behind. He waited for him to catch up. They walked side by side for several strides.

"I just can't bear the waste!" Ivan burst out.

"I know."

"You know Danylo, my uncle?"

Petro nodded.

"He thought collectivisation meant that the land belonged to us. Couldn't have been more wrong, could he?"

Petro grunted.

"Ours! As if we'd cut down our own wheat like this!"

"I don't want to think of the winter," said Petro. "We've got our vegetable garden, but I don't know what we'll do for bread. And there are four of us."

"There are six of us and my sister's pregnant, but the Bolsheviks don't care," muttered Ivan. "If they're prepared to shoot and deport us, they'll certainly let us starve."

"Your sister's pregnant? Has her husband had his Red Army call-up?"

"No, and we're hoping Nestor doesn't get it."

"Well, at least you won't be going. You're still too young, aren't you?"

"Yes, thank goodness. And Pavlo's only fourteen, so that means plenty of mouths to feed this winter."

"God knows what's going to happen."

"Have you had your call-up yet?" asked Ivan.

"Not yet. I've had the medical though."

"Will you go and fight for the bastards?"

"What choice will I have?"

"Some have gone to the woods."

Petro glanced at him. "Ivan, you need to be careful who you're saying such things to."

"I know. I trust you though."

"Why? Any of us could be traitors."

"One reason."

"What's that?"

"Anna." Ivan looked at Petro to observe his reaction.

Petro met his eyes and smiled slightly. "She needs someone to look after her."

"And she's beautiful."

"Yes, she's that," sighed Petro.

"Take your time with her," advised Ivan. "She won't run away."

Petro looked at Ivan in surprise, then nodded.

Ivan grinned and shrugged.

They walked on together until they reached the monument at the centre of the village, where they went their separate ways.

The cutting continued until it seemed that there could not be a field left with its crop standing, but no more was said about the projected airfield. The green wheat rotted where it had fallen and the women realised why they had not

69

been needed…the crop was not to be cleared away.

One evening, Ivan was closing up his family's stable for the night when he heard a horse and cart in the lane. He glanced up and saw his neighbour, Timko, returning home. "You're late," he called.

"I am. I had to go to Buchach with a load."

"You must be shattered."

"I am and so is this poor horse. Oats and bed, I think," he added with a weary smile.

"See you tomorrow," called Ivan and the older man slowly drove his horse further along the lane and into the yard. He was untacking the grateful animal, when there was a crunch of several pairs of boots on gravel. Timko looked up from the leather straps and saw Red Army soldiers entering his yard.

"Stop that work," ordered one of them.

"I'm just untacking her," said Timko.

"I said stop. We need some transport to Buchach."

"Look, I've just come from there. It's a fair distance for this horse. She's tired…I'm tired."

"Enough of this nonsense," said one of the soldiers striding forward. "We've told you. We need to get to Buchach. Put that tack back on and let's get going."

"And I told you, this horse can't do anymore today. You'll have to find another one."

The soldier took another step forward and struck Timko a blow to the head with the butt of his rifle. Timko fell to his knees, his head ringing.

"Take him over there with a spade," he ordered the youngest soldier. "Make him dig a hole and when it's big enough, shoot him." He jerked his head at the rest of the group. "Come on, there'll be more carts in the village," and with that they stomped away up the lane.

Timko was dazed, but understood what had been said. The young soldier looked uncertain for a moment and then commanded him to get a spade. Timko staggered to his feet and lurched towards the barn door. He picked up his spade which was leaning against the wall, wondering whether to risk taking a swing at the soldier, but was still not sure enough of his aim against the soldier's nervously held rifle. He turned away from the comforting smell of dry hay and manure and, as he passed his horse which he had had from a foal, could not help patting her in a gesture of thanks.

The soldier motioned with the barrel of his rifle towards the orchard beside the yard. Timko stumbled through the gateway. The birds were chittering as they prepared for darkness and he turned his face up to the apple and pear trees, heavy with their loads of ripening fruit. He had courted his wife under these trees and for a moment, remembered the heady scent of their blossom, and her young body. He shook his head and heard the soldier bark, "That's far enough. Dig here!"

The order was easily given, but Timko was able to respond slowly as the ground was covered with closely growing grass and the first layer was difficult to remove. Even as the work became easier, he did not hurry. He tried not to be seduced by the lovely smell of the earth being turned and he knew he wanted to live.

The hole was still only a shallow rectangular depression when the quiet of the evening was shattered by the sound of an engine flying above them. Both men looked up in the greying light, but were able to discern the black crosses on the wings and fuselage, the swastika on the tailfin, as the plane passed overhead. Timko opened his mouth in shock, but the soldier, after a swift cry of fear, took to his heels. Timko rested on his spade. "So that's why they needed transport in a hurry!"

When he woke the following morning, Timko's first thought was one of relief. He had been spared being shot over his own grave. He decided that one of the first things he would do that day would be to fill in the wretched hole. He breakfasted, kissed his surprised wife and went out to the barn to fetch his spade again. As he did so, he saw Ivan and his father passing down the lane.

"Morning! What are you doing?" called Ihor.

"Come and see," said Timko. Ivan and Ihor followed him into the orchard and stopped by a shallow hole.

"Looks like a grave," commented Ihor.

"That's exactly what it is."

"Whose?"

"Mine."

"What?" exclaimed Ihor, as both father and son gaped at Timko.

"Yes, the Bolsheviks came for my cart yesterday, just after I'd seen you." He nodded at Ivan. "They wanted me to turn round and go back to Buchach again. I told them I wouldn't. The horse was done in."

"So they threatened to kill you," said Ihor.

"I think digging my own grave was more than a threat," replied Timko. "But the Germans saved me."

"How could they? They're not here yet."

"A plane flew over with black crosses on its wings."

"You were lucky," said Ivan.

"I certainly was. The sooner they get here to save us from those Red devils the better!"

"You're right," agreed Ihor. "The NKVD have been seen much less often this last week."

"And that arm of Satan, Ostapenko, has been keeping quiet, too," added Timko.

"You realise that even a week ago, for three of us to be talking together would have made us Enemies of the People. We could have been deported."

"It didn't even need that. They've been sending anyone and everyone to Siberia."

"Well, maybe the Germans will help us get rid of that fiend in Moscow," said Ihor.

"Fiend is right," agreed Timko. "There were whispers yesterday in Buchach that all of the prisoners there had been shot."

"If they're slaughtering the evidence, Hitler must be closer than we think."

"We'll see," said Timko. "But it won't bring that wheat back."

"No, but the Germans won't get it now, will they?"

There was an air of optimism in the village at the thought that this might be the end of Bolshevik subjugation, which touched most of the adults over the coming days. There was no sign of the Red Army, who disappeared eastwards, taking whatever equipment they could carry and destroying the rest. The German advance was rapid. Hitler had invaded the USSR in June and it took the Divisions fighting in Western Ukraine only weeks to oust the badly prepared Russians, who fled, leaving a legacy of death in Lviv, Ternopil, Ivano-Frankivksk and other towns, where they had emptied the prisons of thousands of suspected nationalists by the simple expedient of shooting them. Battles flew across the land, but some villages remained unscathed, including Anna's. She and many of her neighbours watched all of one sunny afternoon as great plumes of black smoke appeared on the horizon north of them. They could hear the thump of mortar fire, but it passed them by. It seemed inconceivable that they should remain untouched by tanks or planes, but this time they had escaped.

However, several days later, the village received a visit from a couple of *Stabsgefreiter*. They arrived on motorcycles, which drove slowly past the ruined fields to the centre of the village, where they were greeted by several men, who had been alerted by excited young boys. The Germans stopped their motorcycles and dismounted, wondering if they would need their pistols, but they saw that these villagers were happy to greet them. One of the men stepped forward to tell them that they were welcome here, where previously the presence of those wearing military uniforms had meant death or deportation. One of the Lance-Corporals spoke some Russian, so was able to make himself understood on the vital subject of supplies for the rapidly advancing German troops.

"Tell me – what happened to your crops?"

Ivan's father, Ihor, spoke up. "The Russians ordered us to cut them down."

"When?"

"Two weeks ago."

"Didn't you think it was a terrible waste to do this?"

"Of course."

"Then why do it? You're farmers!"

"Yes, we are."

"I ask again – why do it?"

"We had no choice. The Red Army stood over us while we cut it down."

"So you did it at gunpoint?"

There were several cries of "Yes!" as the men spoke up, hoping their loss might somehow be compensated.

"Who gave the order for this?"

"Ostapenko!" they cried.

"And where will I find him?" asked the *Stabsgefreiter*.

"He has a house in Temne," said one.

"Who will show me?"

Several men stepped forward. The sweetness of the possibility of retribution being served on Ostapenko appealed to many. The soldier pointed at two of the volunteers to mount pillion on the motorcycles and the powerful machines roared away.

In a complete contrast to the crises of the last two years, the villagers stood about in groups, talking of this latest development. Women and children gathered, too, and many wondered aloud what would happen to Ostapenko and whether any of his abhorrent lieutenants might share his fate. They did not have very long to wait for the answer. They watched as an armoured car and a lorry drove towards them, coming to a halt beside the memorial. A Second Lieutenant got out of the car, the two bars of his rank clearly visible on the collar of his jacket and his officer's sidecap setting him apart from the helmeted infantrymen, who swarmed from the back of the lorry on his brusque command. There was a pause and several men in civilian clothing, their hands tied, descended from the lorry under the watchful eyes of the officer. The villagers sighed with satisfaction as they recognised Ostapenko, Prutko and others who had been happy to do their leader's cruel bidding. Ostapenko was tall enough to make some of the German soldiers have to look up to him and his taut bulk still made him a force to be reckoned with, but there was a significant change. Whereas only a few days ago he would have glared whole villages into submission, now his eyes met no one else's. He looked at the ground or shifted his gaze from time to time to the unfamiliar weapons of his captors. His lieutenants tried to make themselves less visible behind him, watching both the grey-clad soldiers and their leader closely.

The officer gestured to his men and the wrongdoers were lined up against a garden wall opposite the monument. He turned to the villagers.

"Which of these men gave the order to destroy the crops?" he asked in Russian.

Many shouted and pointed at Ostapenko, but then others called out, "They were all there. They're all guilty."

The *Leutnant* drew closer to Ostapenko. "Is it true? Did you order the destruction of the wheat?"

Ostapenko met the officer's eyes and then spat on the ground, narrowly missing the German's boots. The officer shrugged, stepped back and gave the orders for the infantrymen to make two lines, one kneeling in front, the other standing behind.

Anna stood towards the back of the throng of onlookers and, as the orders were carried out, she turned away and walked towards her home. Petro saw her go from the other side of the crowd, but he did not have long to wait before he could leave the assembled witnesses and join her. The *Leutnant* gave the order: "*Feuer!*" and the tyrant and his comrades dropped to the ground, their strings cut. They would no longer act for the Master Puppeteer in Moscow. But there was no cheering, just quiet relief.

Petro walked away towards Anna's house. He was not able to see her in the garden, so he approached the house and knocked. Katerina came to the door.

"Good afternoon. I'm sorry to disturb you, but I was looking for Anna."

"She's not here. Is it over?" asked Katerina in low tones.

"Yes," said Petro, not knowing how to help this woman.

"I think Anna may have gone to the cemetery," said Katerina and she turned away into the darkness of her house.

Petro walked further up the lane and took the side entrance to the cemetery, walking among the overgrown graves across to the bare lower corner. He saw Anna standing in the long grass and, wondering whether he had the right to disturb her, walked down to the last of the graves and waited. She stood, head bowed, hands clasped and it was some moments before she looked up towards him. Then he joined her and took her hand in his. "Are you alright, Anna?"

She nodded and leaned against him a little.

"You didn't want to stay?"

"No. I'm glad my father's killers are dead, but I couldn't watch it."

"No," he agreed. "Maybe we'll get some peace now."

"Too late for them," said Anna nodding towards the ground beneath which her father and brother lay.

They stood for a few minutes in silence and then Anna looked up at Petro and said, "Shall we go?"

They walked hand in hand towards Anna's garden, taking the quiet route along the bottom of the cemetery.

Part Two

Summer 1941 – Spring 1944

Chapter 7

The villagers did have peace for a time. The German troops were kept busy in their advance across the wide river Dnipro, driving the enemy eastwards. They left only small groups of personnel in the vanguard, as in the nearby town of Temne. They supervised supplies and communications, and kept an eye on the local population, despite their tractability with the new occupying force. The unhampered villagers spent the late summer preparing for the fierceness of winter, thinking themselves free of the fear of random deportations and executions.

It had been a gloriously hot day in September. In the early evening, Anna and Petro sat on the hillside above the Dniester in blissful coolness. He had simply appeared at her cottage and asked her to go for a walk with him. No pretext; simply a walk. She had acquiesced easily and now they sat under a blue sky, watching the clouds, which bore a blush of rose pink as sunset approached. The leaves on the cherry trees, bordering the small fields to their right, were changing to their autumn colours and the golden pink light from the west set them further ablaze. The woods below took on a deeper green against the paleness of the sky and all was peaceful apart from the late twittering of sparrows and the odd bark of an unsettled dog. In a few minutes, the gold faded from the sky and the smokiness of the lilac deepened on the horizon. The clouds faded from pink to grey and the stillness seemed benign. Even the broad Dniester sparkled gently in the deceptive stillness.

Anna pulled up her knees and encircled them with her arms. She felt happy at this moment and, as the sky faded further and the evening deepened, she sensed Petro watching her. She turned to look at him and her heart snagged on his blue eyes and long lashes. As his mouth sought hers, she sighed and moved into his arms.

One sunny morning several days later, Anna gathered the linen off the bed, the towels and the rest of the laundry. Her cat, Murchik, enjoyed this game, as he leapt on the fabric, attacking and killing enemies large and small. Anna dangled some string to distract him and then bundled all of the washing together. Leaving Katerina sitting in the sunshine preparing vegetables for their lunch and Murchik cleaning his paws beside her, she called on her old neighbour, Nastunia.

"Good morning," she said, crossing the garden towards Nastunia, busy among her vegetables.

"Good morning, Anna. It's a lovely morning for laundry," commented the old woman.

"That's why I'm here. Would you like me to take any of your larger pieces to do with mine and Mama's?"

"That's very kind of you, but no, I'll manage. Thank you."

"It's really no trouble. Let me at least take your sheets. They're so heavy when they're wet and you know the girls all help each other."

"If you're sure."

"Of course," replied Anna. "I'll just wait here while you get them."

Several minutes later, Nastunia returned with her bed linen and Anna added the sheets to her bundle. "See you later," she called and she set off up the lane to the memorial and then down the hill to the laundry area.

The vibrant spring burst out of the hillside. The men had made a stone trough for the water to flow into, with stone slabs laid on either side for the women to pound their washing. There was enough room for ten laundresses at a time and their chatter made the work go more lightly. The broad area was sheltered by mature trees, the sunlight dappling on the water, giving them shade while they slapped and scrubbed. Then they stretched out their linen further uphill on the rocks, to dry in the sun.

Anna chose a spot between her friends Vera and Marusia, and set about the washing. Marusia was a blonde beauty with thick golden hair and very bright blues eyes. She was often sought out by the young men of the village, but despite her liveliness and love of gossip, she had given little encouragement to prospective suitors. Inevitably, it was she who began the conversation. "They were up in the top copse again yesterday."

"Who were?" asked Vera.

"Ivan and Olena."

"But I thought he was going with Sofia," said Anna.

"Not anymore."

"Unless he's with both of them," giggled Vera.

"Does Sofia know?"

"I don't know. We'll see when she arrives. But he's been seen several times with Olena."

"That's going to cause some problems when Sofia finds out."

"Poor Sofia!" said Anna. "There's just no privacy."

Vera and Marusia smiled at one another, but refrained from teasing Anna about the rumours of her walking out with Petro. She was happier than she had been for a long time, but she was perhaps not ready yet for their banter.

The women helped one another to carry the larger pieces of linen to dry and bleach in the sunshine. Anna and Vera began the strenuous handling of wet linen, meeting and parting in the dance of folding; carrying the heavy linen up to the rocks to dry and then returning to what remained in their bundles.

Marusia began again. "There's been talk of a new leader being chosen for the village."

"Oh, Marusia, don't start on politics," moaned Vera. "It's too dull."

"Yes, but it'll affect us all, won't it, Anna?" persisted Marusia.

"It will, but we'll just have to wait and see. Anyway, here comes Sofia."

"Much more interesting," laughed Vera as Sofia joined them with a small bundle. "You've not got much to do," she commented.

"No, I told Mama I wouldn't bring the rest of it. I'm sick of washing everybody's things," retorted Sofia.

"Your poor mother," commented Anna.

"Well, Olha could do her own," said Sofia.

Vera pursed her lips as she continued her own and her brothers' laundry. "And who would do Levko's?" she asked.

Sofia had two siblings, Olha was fourteen and Levko ten, but she baulked at the duties of an older sister. Her appearance defied her speech though. She had abundant black curls, framing a pretty pink-cheeked face with a rosebud mouth, which at that moment was tight with annoyance.

"So how are things with you?" asked Marusia.

"Very good, thank you for asking."

"Been doing anything interesting?" persisted Marusia.

"Like what?"

"I don't know. Maybe taking some nice walks?"

"Marusia, you're hopeless at this!" cried Sofia. "Just ask what you want to know."

"Ivan?" prompted Marusia.

"What about him?"

"Have you seen him lately?" asked Vera.

"Yes, I have. Why?"

"We just wondered," said Marusia.

Sofia screwed up her lips even tighter. "He can do as he pleases."

"He usually does," said Anna, making Vera and Marusia shout with surprised laughter. She looked up. "You forget I know him very well. He talks a lot when we take the cows to pasture."

Marusia and Vera grinned at Anna.

"And what does he say about Sofia?" asked Marusia.

Anna laughed. "It would be more than my life's worth to tell you right now," and she nodded towards the figure of Olena, coming down the path to join them.

Later, as Vera helped Anna wring the water from Nastunia's sheets, she muttered to Anna, "I don't know who to feel sorry for – Sofia or Olena."

"Maybe for Ivan. They could both make him pay."

"You're right. He's never serious with anyone."

"Not yet, anyway," replied Anna, and they carried the sheets upstream to dry.

Marusia, too, had rinsed her laundry and called to Anna, "Please come and give me a hand."

"Of course," replied Anna. When she reached Marusia, she asked, "Where's Rachel today?"

Rachel and Marusia had been close friends since they were little girls, running away from cross mothers to each other's houses, and although they were completely different in character, they stood by one another. Rachel was far more serious and studious than Marusia and had little time for gossip, but it seemed that the girls compensated for each other in the balance of their friendship.

"She's afraid to leave home at the moment," said Marusia, as she came closer to Anna in the folding. "Her father has kept them all at home. They haven't been to Temne for weeks."

"Why?" asked Anna.

"The Germans."

"But they've left us alone."

"Only the Christians."

"What do you mean?"

"Rachel's family know that they've been killing Jews."

"But that's only a rumour. The Germans have been around for three months now and we've barely had any contact with them."

"Yes, but you might still be cautious."

"What does the rabbi say?"

"Rachel says that he doesn't seem to think they have anything to fear yet, but Rachel's father's anxious. He thinks they could easily be rounded up at the synagogue in Temne."

"Oh Marusia! I hope nothing comes of this. We've had enough suffering in this village."

"You know that better than most," said Marusia, putting her arm around Anna's waist, as they walked back down towards the washing trough.

"Let's hope it comes to nothing."

Anna tried to finish her laundry with a light heart, but realised that over the last few weeks, she had been too quick to let her guard down. Everyone had. In the euphoria following Ostapenko's execution, there had been a joyous feeling of release. Perhaps they had all been unwise to relax so swiftly, and before many more leaves had had a chance to fall that autumn, everyone in the village had to reassess their attitude to their apparent liberators. It began with another order to dig, although this time the order was issued to several men.

Timko and Ihor were among the dozen or so men ordered one morning to assemble at the monument with their spades.

"What for?" wondered Timko aloud.

"Who knows. But can a spade destroy crops?" answered Ihor.

"No, but these buggers might still be as bad as the last lot."

"Difficult but possible..." agreed Ihor, as a mounted *Feldwebel* approached the men.

"*Kommen Sie mit*," was the brief order.

They set off at the sharp pace set by the *Feldwebel's* horse, down towards the Barish. They reached the end of the lane and went past the last of the houses and the duck pond, crossing the river on its plank bridge. Then they turned south-west and followed the meadow downhill for about half a kilometre until they reached the edge of the wood which ran from the Dniester to Petryn and beyond. The men exchanged anxious glances as they hurried along. They entered the wood and took the path for another ten minutes until they reached a small clearing, containing, ominously, one of Hitler's SS *Einsatzgruppen*.

The men came to a bedraggled halt and the sergeant ordered them to dig a pit. They saw a rough rectangle had been marked out, so they set to, spreading out around its edges and beginning to mark out the shape more clearly. The hole was about three metres wide and ten metres long and the men were required to dig until it was more than three metres deep.

They dug for much of the morning. There was no respite as the villagers worked in silence, watched over by the SS infantrymen with their Mausers ready. When the *Feldwebel* was satisfied with the results, they were ordered out of the hole and sent to wait a couple of hundred metres away. Two soldiers stood watching them with their guns at the ready.

"What now?" muttered one of the men, but before anyone could answer, one of the soldiers called sharply, "*Ruhe!*" and pointed his gun at the speaker.

The villagers stood in nervous silence, but they did not have long to wait. They could hear people approaching and they all craned to see who it might be.

"It's the rabbi!" whispered Ihor.

"And his whole congregation!"

The men looked on, shocked to see the whole Jewish community of their village, and that of Temne and Petryn, being led by the rabbi.

"Why are the women and children there?" breathed Timko, but the agitated men were quickly silenced again by their German guards. "*Halt's Maul!*" one of them ordered and they both took a firing stance, aiming at the unlucky diggers.

However, they were to have more luck that day than their Jewish neighbours, who were ordered to stop and the men were told to disrobe completely. This caused consternation among both the men and the women, who looked to their rabbi for confirmation of what they had to do.

"Just do as they ask," he said. "They have promised me they will not harm us, as long as we do what they ask."

So, slowly, the men undressed and then they were ordered forward in single file. They walked towards the pit, hands covering their genitalia, and were halted just before it.

"The first ten, stand on the edge of this hole," barked the *Feldwebel*.

The men did as they were ordered. They were then instructed to kneel facing the pit, the SS standing behind them, rifles raised.

"*Feuer!*"

Shots rang out and ten bodies slumped forward into the purpose-built mass grave.

"*Weitermachen!*" snapped the *Feldwebel*.

The men hesitated, but heads bowed, the next ten moved forward to their deaths. This time their movements were accompanied by the sharp cries of the women and hysterical crying from the children.

The *Feldwebel* fired a shot into the air. "*Ruhig! Setzen!*"

The women did as they were told, but they continued to sob quietly and those who had children held them to their fearful breasts. Shortly, the women and children were ordered to undress, too. They did so, the mothers helping their children to take off their clothes, hoping desperately that the madness might end before they or their children were murdered. But it was not to be. The mechanical horror continued until all of the Jews of the *shtetl* were shot and the hole filled with the dead and the dying.

And the diggers…they stood sweating and trembling as they watched and listened to the blunt reports of the guns followed by thuds and cries of agony, unable to believe what was happening. But their ordeal was not yet over. When the lines of naked people came to an end, the villagers were ordered to fill in the hole. None dared protest that the earth was thrown over both the quick and the dead, and none dared ask what might become of them when they had completed their task. But they were sent back to the village with no more than a brief command of "*Raus!*" and with shaking legs, they hurried away to their families, knowing that one devil had been replaced by another and that their village had not been left unscathed.

They returned to their homes forever altered. Shaken to the core by what they had witnessed, they would never be the same again and in tremulous tones, they told their wives a little of what they had seen. The horror rippled through the village and many, who had welcomed the Germans, were stunned into silence, wondering what other monstrous acts they might perpetrate.

In the forest, a silence fell. No birds sang and even the leaves on the trees failed to rustle in the shocked stillness. Nature herself seemed struck dumb and the earth lay motionless, mute in the misery she held to her breast. A hush descended, too, over everyday life as people withdrew into places of fear and mourning, knowing now that the German army was nobody's saviour, but an implacable enemy.

Although the villagers knew of the executions, they only spoke about them in whispers to those they trusted. They were too well-acquainted with the fear of being suddenly wrenched from their lives to hope for any mercy, so they behaved towards the Germans with caution. But the question of the killing ground remained.

Why had the Germans taken their victims to such a remote spot and then covered up the evidence in a way that would make the mass grave difficult for anyone who was not there to find it again? Ihor had told Ivan and Pavlo the whole gruesome tale in a vain hope that knowledge might protect his sons, although he and his wife had tried to shelter Halyna, Ivan's pregnant sister, from the knowledge.

"But *Tatu*, why there do you think? Why choose that spot?"

"To hide it. When we had filled the hole in, they made us brush twigs and leaves over the ground."

"But you'd still be able to see it?"

"Yes, but not as clearly as if the earth was bare. And it'll soon be invisible after the autumn and winter."

"Why did they want to hide it though?" asked Pavlo.

"Maybe because they know there might be an outcry against the killings. Looked at how they called in the Geneva Convention at Vinnitsa to make sure people knew the Russians had killed those prisoners there."

"Yes, but that could only have been the NKVD. When they emptied the jails, they slaughtered the prisoners in the yards and left the bodies there. They didn't care who knew," said Ivan.

"Or were in too much of a hurry to save themselves."

"This looks more planned to me," said Ihor. "They were so organised. And they took away all the evidence afterwards."

"All the clothing you mean?"

"Yes, everything. Timko sneaked down there afterwards and he says everything's gone."

"It doesn't make sense," said Ivan. "If they want to keep it so secret, why didn't they kill those of you who had dug the hole?"

"They know when men are afraid. And they may know the NKVD taught everyone a very good lesson in keeping silent."

"That's true enough."

There was a pause as father and sons tried to assimilate the ghastly knowledge and then Ivan asked, "Do you think that's the end of it?"

"Not for one minute. Apparently they're still hunting for any Jews who managed to escape the shooting."

"God help them if they're found."

"If they're found, they'll be shot…as will anybody harbouring them."

Anna had taken a walk to gather hazelnuts. They grew prolifically in the woods downriver of the village near the Dniester and along the edges of fields, so she gave some time to gathering what would be a valuable food source for the winter. She picked up the nuts from where they had fallen and rubbed off their bedraggled brown caps, which had once been a gay serrated green. Anna heard a buzzard's cry and looked up into the blue autumnal sky to see first a single bird, then its partner, wheeling and crying. She drew in the earthy scent of the changing season. It did not seem to evoke endings, but was rich and full of promise. Anna began to walk back to the village with her heavy basket and decided to call at Marusia's house.

She had not seen the girl for several days, since she had heard of the slaughter of the Jewish families and knew Marusia would be mourning her friend.

She came to Marusia's cottage and, seeing no one in the garden, approached the door and knocked.

There was a clatter and a rustle indoors as Marusia called out, "I'm coming! I'm just getting dressed."

"It's alright. It's only me…Anna."

There was a pause and then Marusia opened the door a little way and her blonde head peeped out. "Oh, it is you, Anna," she said breathlessly and then she slid out into the garden, closing the door behind her.

"I'm sorry if I startled you."

"Oh no. Not at all. I was cleaning and hadn't got properly dressed."

"Well, I won't keep you. I've been gathering hazelnuts and found so many, I thought you might like some of them."

Marusia looked at Anna carefully and her bright blue eyes suddenly filled with tears. "Anna, you are kind. Thank you."

"That's alright. Do you want to take the basket indoors and take what you want?"

"I will." Marusia took the basket and turned to go, but then stopped and looked again at Anna. In a whisper she said, "I can't ask you in. I'm sorry."

Anna shook her head. "That's alright. I'll just wait here."

Marusia nodded and, only opening the door a little, slipped into her cottage.

Anna walked down the garden, turning her back to give Marusia the privacy she needed, trying not to wonder what secret Marusia was clearly keeping. She made herself look over the cabbages fattening up for winter and hoped the villagers would be allowed to keep their produce to feed themselves.

Marusia returned with Anna's basket, now half-full of nuts, and thanked her for her generous thought once again.

"It's fine," responded Anna. "If you need anything, just let me know," and she set off towards her own house, keeping her own counsel.

There was one last promising day when Anna decided to take advantage of the sunshine and do her laundry. As she walked down to the spring, she saw Marusia hurrying to catch her up. She looked a little dishevelled and her laundry bundle seemed larger than usual.

Anna waited for her and called, "Don't rush. I'm not in a hurry."

Marusia joined her, a little out of breath. "I'm in such a muddle this morning." She clamped her lips together and Anna covered the moment for her.

"Never mind. Washing's always soothing."

The girls set themselves up side by side and Anna discreetly placed her own laundry close enough to Marusia's for the separate loads to be muddled at a casual glance. They took their wet laundry to dry on the rocks and again, Anna deliberately mixed hers with Marusia's. Her friend only glanced at Anna once in surprise, but then continued arranging the wet linen in the most ordinary way. The girls sat on a bench nearby and watched the other women, who were also glad of the late sunshine.

"How's your mother now?" asked Marusia.

Anna was startled at her friend's question, for although all knew that Katerina had been enfeebled by the losses of Mikola and Yuri, it was rare that anyone spoke of it to Anna. "She's a little better, thank you." Anna said nothing further for a few moments then relented. "She's started cooking again and sometimes will come into the garden."

"It must have been very hard."

"Yes, it was." Anna drew a breath. "And is. But I just deal with one thing at a time," and she smiled at her friend.

"Yes...one thing at a time..."

"I don't get so flustered then." Again Anna looked at her friend's serious profile. "And I plan things carefully. Mama doesn't like surprises."

"No. I can see that's a good idea."

And there Anna left it for now. She had an inkling of her friend's secret, but knew better than to voice it. She also knew that if she continued to support Marusia discreetly, she might ask if she ever needed Anna's help. Later, as Anna made her way home with her load of clean laundry, she found herself wondering where Hrichko was now...and if he was safe.

Inside Marusia's house, there was still the hollow terror of discovery. On the day of the round-up of the Jews, Rachel had gone to Temne with some of her father's books hoping to exchange them for different ones. She had gone alone despite her father's repeated exhortations that she should remain safely at home, but Rachel had been adamant. She desperately needed a new supply of books and would not be persuaded to be content with the few she had. "I need to study, *Tatu*," she had said and so she had gone on her errand, leaving her parents and two younger brothers behind. It was only as she began her homeward journey that she learned of the arrival of the SS and their round-up of the Jewish families. And she learned it from her friend Marusia...

She had been walking along the road from Temne, about a kilometre outside of the town, when she saw a figure running towards her. It was a young blonde woman and Rachel was not at first sure whether it was Marusia, so distressed did the figure seem to be. Soon Rachel could hear incoherent cries, too. She drew nearer to the wild creature and saw it was Marusia. Her heart thumped painfully as she realised her friend must have had a terrible shock and she ran towards her, arms outstretched, books forgotten in the dust of the road.

"Oh, Rachel! Rachel!" sobbed Marusia as they reached one another, and Marusia flung her arms around her friend. "Thank God I've found you!"

Rachel held Marusia tightly for a few moments, hoping her sobs might calm a little. "Whatever's happened?"

"You must hide," said Marusia shrilly, tugging at Rachel's sleeve. "Come on, into the ditch!"

Rachel looked up and down the deserted road and, fearing for her friend's sanity, crossed the brown and brittle autumnal verge into the ditch beside the empty field. Marusia held her hand so tightly, Rachel could not let go and, for now, decided to humour her friend, terribly afraid of what she would say. She could only assume that for some reason, the Germans had taken Marusia's loved ones.

The girls crouched in the ditch, shoulder to shoulder, peering out onto the road, one blonde and blue-eyed, the other with her dark hair and brown eyes. After some minutes, Rachel whispered, "My books."

"What?"

"I dropped my books in the road. I'm going to get them."

"No!" shrieked Marusia in a whisper. "Stay here," and she began to climb out of the ditch, but then seemed to remember something. Taking off her flowered headscarf which had fallen around her neck, she tied it on her friend's head, covering as much of the black hair as possible. Then she took off the cross and chain she wore and placed it around Rachel's neck.

"What are you doing?" asked Rachel, thinking her friend was going too far in her madness.

"Wait here. I'll explain in a moment," and with that Marusia jumped up from the ditch, skittered into the road and, gathering up Rachel's books as quickly as she could, hurried back to the poor cover of the ditch. "We have to move from here," she said and before Rachel could frame anymore questions, Marusia took her friend's face in her hands and with a piercing look into her dark eyes said, "You must not be found by the Germans. I don't know what they were planning, but they rounded up all of the Jews today and put them on a lorry."

Rachel stared at Marusia for a moment. "My family?"

"They were on the lorry," admitted Marusia, "but you must move, Rachel. That's why I came to find you."

Rachel seemed paralysed by the news and Marusia added, "I'll take you to my house for now, but we can't go by the road. Then we'll try to find out where your family were taken."

Rachel nodded automatically and the young women stepped up out of the ditch into the field beyond. They hurried towards the woods, which would bring them almost all of the way to the east side of the village where Marusia's house lay. The wide arc they made to bypass any traffic took them some time, but eventually they slipped into the safety of Marusia's house.

Marusia's mother was busy in the kitchen, drying what would probably be the last of the autumn's mushrooms when the two young women entered, thoroughly out of breath.

"What have you been doing, Marusia?"

"We've got to hide Rachel, Mama. Haven't you heard?"

"No, I've been here all day. Busy. With no help." She shot a meaningful glance at her daughter.

"Mama, the Germans took all the Jewish families away today," said Marusia.

"Then, Rachel, you must go into the storeroom now…until we find out what's happening."

"Thank you," said Rachel, "but I must go and find out what's happened to my family. I need to go home."

"No, you mustn't," said Marusia. "Rachel, I saw them. They weren't playing games. They came here with a large group of SS soldiers and they gathered the people at gunpoint."

Rachel's eyes filled with tears of frustration and anxiety. "But I can't just hide in your storeroom while Mama and *Tato* are in danger. And what about my brothers?" Her voice rose into what threatened to be a wail and Marusia's mother took the girl into her arms.

"Shhh," she soothed as she rocked her a little. "We don't know anything yet. Marusia will sit with you and I'll go and see what I can find out." Keeping her arm around her shoulders, she took Rachel to the storeroom, saying to her daughter, "Bring a couple of stools, Marusia, and I'll just make some strong tea before I go."

They made Rachel sit down and then Maria turned to Marusia's younger sisters, who had been watching with wide eyes. "I want you two to stay here. You are not to leave this house until I return. Is that clear?"

The two youngsters nodded, overawed, and as Maria set off for the centre of the village, Marusia whispered, "Be careful, Mama."

It was some time before Maria returned with her husband, their faces grim.

"Well?" asked Marusia, her arm around Rachel's waist.

"I'm not sure," said her father. "But there have been shots coming from the woods towards Petryn this afternoon."

Rachel would have fallen had not Marusia been holding her up.

"She must lie down, Mama."

"Put her in your bed and stay with her. If anyone comes, I'll tell them you're unwell."

Marusia led Rachel from the room.

As the door closed behind them, Maria and her husband looked at one another despairingly. "What are we going to do?" asked Maria.

Andriy shook his head. "I don't know, but we can't put her out. They'll kill her."

"And they'll kill us if they find her here."

"Then we'd better make sure they don't find her."

"How can we do that?" asked Maria, thinking of how easily their cottage could be searched.

"I'll change things around in the loft above Marusia's room. It won't be pleasant for Rachel, but it will be safer than anywhere else."

The following day, Andriy returned from the village. He walked home feeling like an old man, dreading the tale he must tell his daughter's best friend. First, he took his wife into the garden where they walked down to the end of their plot.

"Is it true, then?" asked Maria.

Andriy nodded. "They shot them all."

"Even the children?"

Her husband nodded dumbly.

Maria crossed herself. "May God rest their souls." She struggled with her tears for a few moments and then said, "How are we going to tell Rachel?"

"I don't know. I really wish I didn't have to."

"Dear God, that poor girl." Maria put her shoulders back. "Well, we'll just have to keep her here."

"Yes, and we must be open with the girls. They need to know how serious a secret they'll be keeping."

Maria knew he was right and wished she could protect Marusia's younger sisters from the terrible knowledge. But thirteen-year-old Oksana and eleven-year-old Odarka needed to be warned of the terrible consequences of gossip.

"Have they been anywhere today?" asked Andriy, worrying that a slip might already have been made.

"No. I kept them busy here and they're with Marusia now."

"Alright. After supper," said Andriy. "We'll do it then."

As darkness fell, Andriy closed up his livestock and barred the door of his home. He called his daughters into the kitchen, where they all sat at the table and then he asked Marusia to fetch Rachel down. The solemnity of the gathered group in the candlelight told Rachel what she had longed to know – the fate of her family. She had almost been prepared to be told they were dead, but she had not been prepared to hear the means of their deaths.

"Rachel dear," began Andriy, "what I have to tell you is dreadful, but I cannot avoid it… Though I would if I could." He swallowed. "The Germans shot everyone they took yesterday."

Rachel swayed a little against Marusia, but mother and daughter held her between them. The younger girls looked on wide-eyed and Andriy could have wept at the sight of the dark-haired Rachel among his blonde daughters. His heart ached for the girl, but he knew it was better that she be told the worst in this relatively safe environment. So he faced the question in her deep brown eyes.

"All of them?"

"Yes, all of them."

"Even my little brothers?"

"Yes, even them. They shot everyone."

Rachel wanted to howl, but could not gather enough breath to do so. She felt stifled and wanted to run and keep running until she collapsed with exhaustion. Marusia's family watched her agony helplessly.

Andriy turned to his younger daughters. "We're going to hide Rachel here. You can't tell anyone of this. Do you understand?"

The girls nodded, still awestruck.

Their mother added emphatically, "We can't tell anyone. Not even our closest friends."

"No. No whispering just to this person or that special one," said Marusia. "Tell them what will happen, *Tatu*."

"If we are found to have helped Rachel, the Germans will shoot her first and then they will shoot every one of us." He stared at the girls. "Mama, Marusia, me and each of you."

The youngest's eyes filled with frightened tears and their mother said, "There's no need to cry. We can't let them have Rachel and she has nowhere else to go. You must be more grown up now. Think before you speak and tell no one anything."

The girls nodded solemnly.

"There's no need to be upset or frightened. As long as we're very careful, we will all be safe," said Maria rising from the table and, putting an arm around each of her younger daughters, kissed them both.

So Marusia's family accommodated the orphan, moving some of the stored hay to make a small space for her to live. Marusia, for the first time, was glad of the disorder in her room caused by the younger girls. If Rachel should leave something behind, when she came down from the loft, it was easily camouflaged. And Rachel...she would spend her time in hiding thinking of how she might repay those who had taken all of her beloved family.

Chapter 8

On a blustery day, when the wind was ripping the last of the leaves from the trees in the wood below Anna's cottage, Petro led her to their scant shelter. His hair was whipped about and Anna's scarf snapped in the gusts. They held hands tightly as they made their way downhill and Anna revelled in her happiness, which had come to her with all the joy of an unexpected gift. They paused under the trees and Petro said, "There was a lovely spot I saw you in, once in spring."

Anna blushed, shy again. "When?"

"Oh, not this year. Last year."

She looked at him, surprised. "Last year?"

It was his turn to blush. "Yes, last year." There was a pause as he studied the toe of his boot. "It was the first time I noticed you properly."

Anna looked at his face in profile. Already the way the long lashes rested on his cheek was so dear to her that she could not resist stroking his face. "Petro."

He looked at her and then folded her into his arms, holding her tight for a moment.

The luxury of the warmth of his neck against her cheek and the strength of his embrace was a healing balm to Anna. Day after day, it seemed, someone lost a loved one and everything could be snatched away. She took his hand and led him down through the wood towards the stream and into the glade that in spring would be awash with wood anemones. "Here?" she asked when they reached the broad, flat rocks.

He nodded.

"Where were you?"

"I was coming from the houses in the bottom and I thought I saw a woman on her own…but when I saw it was you…you looked so unhappy, I felt I couldn't intrude."

"I used to come here to be alone. I couldn't cry in front of Mama – she was struggling enough as it was. I couldn't cry here either, but at least I didn't have to pretend to be strong."

"You are strong," he said, putting his arm around her shoulders.

"If only you knew."

"I know we can all put on an act, but you kept your mother alive when she might have died otherwise. And I see you in the village, always quiet, but always there when you're needed."

She turned her cheek into his shoulder, glad of his approval.

"Just as you're helping Marusia now."

Anna drew back.

"What have I said?"

"What do you mean – helping Marusia?"

Petro looked non-plussed, but carried on. "Well, she must be so upset at the death of Rachel and I've seen you giving her a helping hand. That's all."

"Yes, it's been hard for her." This seemed both lame and abrupt, but Anna was not sure whether she could confide her suspicions to him.

"It's alright, Anna. You only need to tell me what you're happy to."

She instantly felt guilty, but did not want her trust in him to be forced. For that matter, neither did he. He realised there was something Anna had observed, that was unknown to him, and did not want to push her for the knowledge, so he changed the subject. "I spent some time with Roman Shumenko yesterday."

"How does he like being the new *starosta*?" asked Anna, relieved to be talking of something else.

"He wants to do a good job for us, but we'll have to wait and see if the Germans will let him."

"Well, at least he's not married."

"No. He is aware that the lack of a wife and children, as potential hostages, is one of the main reasons he was elected."

"How does he feel about it?"

"He knows it's a risky job, but he really does want the best for us. Like the new quotas."

"What quotas? We have no wheat yet."

"No – people."

"People?"

"Yes. The Nazis are asking for a number of people from each village to be sent to Germany to work."

"Work where?"

"The men on farms, the women as servants."

Anna looked surprised. "Why do they want to take our men from their own land and put them to work on German land?"

"To replace their young men who've gone to war."

"Oh, of course. But the women haven't gone to fight."

"Maybe Hitler thinks German women shouldn't be doing domestic work, whereas our women can."

"How will the quotas work? Will we all have to go?"

"I don't think so. Roman says we only have to send so many in the first batch."

"So it will continue?"

"It looks like it." He paused. "You won't be expected to go. You have your mother to look after."

She looked relieved. "She can't be left you know. She's better than she was, but I can't leave her."

"Of course you can't. Anyway, Roman thinks people might volunteer as they'll receive wages."

There were those who were attracted by the opportunity to earn hard cash, so Roman Shumenko's job was not too difficult on this first occasion. Nevertheless, there were those who chose to go against the wishes and advice of their loved ones. In Petro's house the argument raged. His twin sisters, Irina and Natalia had announced their departure to Halia, Petro and Nina in their usual pragmatic way. They were all seated at the table having eaten the midday meal when Natalia declared, "Irina and I will be leaving this Thursday."

Halia looked confused. "What do you mean, leaving?"

"We're going to Germany," said Irina.

"To work," added Natalia.

"And to earn money."

Their mother continued to look at them open-mouthed.

Petro was the first to gather his wits. "Why are you going? You don't have to, you know. They're only asking for volunteers."

"We know. We volunteered."

Halia found her tongue. "Have you gone crazy? These are the people who took whole families into the woods and shot them."

"Mama," Petro put his hand on his mother's arm and glanced at Nina.

Halia struggled to rein in her fear in front of her youngest daughter, but the thought of the loss of the twins almost overwhelmed any sense of discretion. "Natalia! Irina! You can't go. There's no need. Petro says so."

"Mama, there is a need," declared Irina. "There are five mouths to feed here and no bread this winter. If we go, there'll only be three mouths to feed and we can send money home to make things easier."

"We'll manage," said Halia. "I have always managed to feed all of us, even after your father died. You can't go."

"We can, Mama," said Natalia. "And besides, it might be fun to see Germany."

Halia blenched and swayed against Petro.

"Think again, girls," he begged. "Mama's right. It's safer to stay together."

"Not necessarily," remarked Irina. "This village has seen plenty of death."

Petro glared at his sister as Nina's shock gave way to sorrow. Fat tears bounced down her cheeks as she drew breath and then released it in a wail of protest. "Don't go," she bawled and she threw herself at her sisters, hitting them with her fists.

"Don't be silly," ordered Natalia, trying to hold Nina's arms still.

"Stop it!" commanded Irina more sharply. "Don't be so spoiled, Nina. The world doesn't revolve around you."

"Nor you neither," declared Petro. "Think about Mama."

"We have," said Natalia. "And it's best for all of us if we go."

"Anyway, we could come back after a year," added Irina.

Halia shook her head. "Look at how much has happened over the last couple of years. No one can be certain what will happen today, let alone in a year's time."

"No one can be certain anyway," maintained Natalia.

"Don't go, girls," begged Halia. "Don't make my life harder, please."

"No, Mama, we've made up our minds. We're going."

Irina and Natalia spent the intervening days before their departure making energetic preparations. They seemed unaware of the cuts they dealt their family as they packed their clothing. They deigned to allow Halia to bake bread for the journey, but were unmoved either by her tears or by Nina's, and Petro felt unable to say anything else which might move them to remain.

"At least write to Mama," he begged. "You know she'll worry until she hears from you."

"We'll write if we have time," said Natalia.

The day of their departure arrived much sooner than those being left behind would have liked and the twins set forth to join the other volunteers at the Reading Room in the centre of the village. The green beside the hall was already crowded with the young men and women loaded with boxes and bundles, ready to embark on their German adventure. Their tearful families had come to see them off on the assembled carts, which were to take them to Buchach for the train.

The twins would have mounted the wagons without a proper farewell if Petro had not held them back. "There's no rush. You won't be left behind. Give Mama and Nina a kiss at least."

The sisters hugged their mother and kissed Nina's cheek.

"What about me?" demanded Petro, giving them both a fierce hug. "Take care of yourselves and write to us."

Halia could not speak for her tears and despite the distractions of so many family farewells, Nina, too, cried that her protectors and tormentors were leaving. The twins climbed up into one of the carts and placed their bundles beneath their feet, then they looked out at the other villagers with a touch of impatience. Soon enough, the carts were fully loaded and their drivers clicked the horses to a brisk trot along the lane towards the shrine, leaving the village behind.

Petro took his mother's arm and led her home, knowing she would find it hard to accustom herself to the quiet of the house. Nina would fill the gap to some extent, but Halia would miss her self-sufficient young women. He wondered how long he would be able to remain in the village. He had been lucky to miss his Red Army call-up when the Germans had swept east, but who knew when he might be expected to play a role in the huge conflict. He knew, too, that there were already those who had taken to the woods and joined the partisans, determined to fight whichever opponent presented itself to Ukraine's independence.

Later that day when he met Anna, he was finally able to reflect on his reaction to the twins' departure.

"Are you alright?" she asked, looking closely into his face.

"Yes, I am," he replied with a weary smile. "I know those two will be fine. In fact, I feel sorry for any German housewife who has to tell them what to do!"

"How's your mother taken it?"

"Hard. She'll worry about them all the time and I think she'll miss them. They often did their work together and Mama had begun to rely on them."

"And Nina?"

"She's been tearful and I think she'll miss them, but she might enjoy being more important at home."

Nina did enjoy having her mother spoil her a little more and for a time she regressed into sitting on her mother's lap for a hug, which comforted them both.

The first mail came from the twins within weeks of their leaving. They had written separate postcards given to them for the purpose of contacting their families. On the face of the card, the address was on the right and there was room for a message on the left which could be continued on the blank reverse of the card. Above the written text, there was a blue ink stamp of the *Ostarbeiterlager* the writer was living in. Irina and Natalia wrote that they were alive and well and that they were working in separate houses for employers who were taking care of them. Halia read and re-read the few words, trying to hear the girls' voices behind the automatic phrases, but they were not there, and each time she saw almost identical postcards in other homes, she felt more anxious for her daughters.

When a second batch of volunteers left for Germany, information of a different kind began to filter back; of hard work and very long hours; of poor food and little of it. Some wrote of the badges they had been obliged to sew to their coats, a blue and white square of fabric with the letters OST clearly denoting their status as Germany's Eastern European slave labourers. The pain and humiliation being experienced by their loved ones was evident to those who had been left behind, and the growing unease was accompanied by a growing reluctance to be part of the workforce being sent West by the trainload. So the "volunteers" began to be encouraged to take part in the migration at gunpoint and tales reached the village early in 1942 that round-ups of the able-bodied were taking place in the cities and towns as German soldiers forced anyone and everyone – in a market, at worship, at school – onto transport bound for Germany and Hitler's over-stretched war machine. The illusion of an opportunity to earn hard cash had long been shattered as almost nothing was sent home in the form of wages and those who had blithely gone "for a year", even leaving behind their young children with relatives, found themselves unable to return.

The quotas began to bite, but some, like Anna, who were the only providers in their households, were safe for now. The homes from which no one had yet gone became increasingly challenged to make the same sort of sacrifices as their neighbours, and the wave reached Marusia's house as winter turned to spring. It was Andriy who brought the dreaded news to his family. "They're saying almost everyone who can, has sent someone to Germany, except us."

Maria looked up sharply. "We're not the only ones."

"No," added Marusia. "Sofia's family hasn't been touched yet."

"Well, they're looking at us," said Andriy. He felt an enormous dread of his beloved daughter suffering the same fate as those who had already left as *Ostarbeiter*, but he also worried about how easily they might continue to hide Rachel, without Marusia's presence to camouflage her.

The women looked at one another. Marusia's chin went up at the thought of being forced from her home, but for her mother, there was the instant fear of her child being sent out alone in a dangerous world. There was a coded tap on the ceiling above them and at Marusia's, "It's fine," Rachel appeared in the bedroom doorway.

"If Marusia has to go, I'll go, too. I should be moving on anyway. Especially now it's almost spring."

"There's no question of you leaving. Where will you go? You can't go to Germany. And besides, we've managed all winter. We can continue to hide you whether Marusia's here or not."

"I can't thank you enough for what you've done for me, but I feel cooped up. I need to get out."

Marusia turned to her friend. "We both do. When's the next quota going, *Tatu*?"

"I'm not sure, but soon."

"Then I'll think about what we must do," said Marusia. "I might be able to come up with something."

Her parents looked doubtful, but Rachel looked less surprised. The girls had had plenty of time over the winter to consider ways of escaping their quandary and, while some ideas had seemed fanciful when they were snowed in, they became more realistic now.

"I'm going out," announced Marusia. "There's something I can try."

"No, Marusia. Don't think of doing something dangerous."

"I won't, Mama. But I do need to think."

She left the house to pursue a long-held suspicion that if Anna had kept Marusia's secret without either being told or asked, then she might have been keeping other secrets, too.

When Marusia arrived at Anna's house, she was pleased to find her alone, turning the soil in her vegetable garden. "Hello, Anna, I'll just get another spade."

Anna smiled in surprise. "I can stop, you know, if you've called for something special."

"No, no," replied Marusia coming towards her, armed with a spade. "I'll keep you company in your work."

"Alright," said Anna. "You can begin a new row opposite me if you like."

The young women set to work, digging the black soil. They worked in silence for a few minutes.

"So how are things?" asked Anna.

"Not too bad. Although *Tato* came home today and said it looks like I'm expected to be one of those going to Germany next time."

"I assume you don't want to go."

"No, I don't. The rumours are very worrying aren't they?"

"Yes, they are. The girls seem to work from dawn till dusk with little to show for it. Petro's sisters are really angry about how they're being treated, but they can't do anything about it."

"Have they written as openly as that to their mother?"

"Oh yes," said Anna. "They haven't given much thought to the distress they might be causing Halia."

"I would have thought those two might be able to find ways of fighting back."

"Perhaps, but both the German families and the authorities are very strict."

Anna stopped herself. "I'm sorry – none of this makes your problem any easier, does it?"

"No, but I'm not going."

"How will you avoid it?"

Marusia dug quietly for a moment and Anna straightened her back to look at her.

"There are other options," she announced at last.

"Yes," agreed Anna.

"I would rather be fighting the Germans than cleaning for them."

Now it was out in the open, Anna did not feel surprised. "Wouldn't you be afraid?"

"No," answered Marusia. "Who knows what will happen with the Germans. They're murderers. We've seen that."

"Of course. But you seem so strong despite those killings…"

"You know why those executions didn't destroy me, don't you, Anna? You've known a long time."

"I guessed."

"So you'll understand why I can't go to Germany."

Anna nodded. Rachel, if found in the village, would be shot and a future for her in Germany was unthinkable.

"So the partisans would have their numbers boosted by two?" Anna asked.

"Yes."

"When will you go?"

"Well, that's just it. I don't know how to go about it. Or who to make contact with…"

"I do."

"I thought you might."

"How did you know?"

"I just have this feeling about your ability to keep secrets."

Anna smiled sadly. "Yes, there are always secrets." She was thoughtful for a moment. "I'll look into it for you."

"The next quota goes soon," added Marusia.

"I know. I won't waste any time, but we'll probably have to wait for a reply."

"I realise that."

They dug thoughtfully for a few moments.

"What will you tell your parents?"

"The truth. They deserve that after the last winter."

Anna nodded, thinking of the strain Marusia's whole family must have been living under, and it was about to get worse. "I'll do what I can, and I'll let you know as soon as I know anything."

Carrying a small stock of beans for planting, Anna made her way to the house which she had visited a year ago, when Hrichko had needed a haven. She knocked on the door and was invited in by the same discreet woman. They exchanged polite pleasantries and Anna offered the beans as a gift for her garden.

"Thank you. Did you get a good crop from these last year?"

"Yes. I'm hoping they'll do as well as last time."

"Hmmm. Sometimes they grow well – they become sturdy and useful."

Anna could not help smiling. If young Hrichko could be described as sturdy, then he was not only surviving, but thriving. "It's such a pleasure when things grow well."

"Yes it is." The woman waited.

Despite the good news about Hrichko, Anna felt awkward that her new request could endanger so many people. But she had promised to help Marusia, so she forced herself to say, "I'll begin planting again soon. I'm lucky – I don't have to go to Germany because I can't leave Mama alone. But others aren't going to be given a choice."

"No, that's true. But sometimes girls have to go where they're sent."

"Yes they do…unless they can't."

"What's 'can't'? Women have left babies to go."

In a rare moment of impatience, Anna burst out: "But they can't leave Jewish friends to go."

The woman looked sharply at Anna and as Anna opened her mouth to speak again, she shook her head quickly. She turned to remove a dish of *holubchi* from the oven. The cabbage parcels smelled delicious, as the woman lifted the lid off the dish. "They're done."

"They smell good," said Anna, feeling dismayed that she had made such a mess of her mission. "I'd better go."

"Just a moment." The woman replaced the lid on the dish. "Two?"

"Yes."

"Like you?"

Anna guessed she was referring to age, so nodded.

"Come back tomorrow."

Anna left feeling immense relief that she had not been rejected out of hand, but was annoyed at what she felt was her clumsy handling of the situation. However, she had had to make matters clear somehow. She returned home and felt so unsettled, she returned to her digging to calm herself. She focussed on lifting and breaking up the soil, trying to take pleasure in the simple task and after a short time, the clean black rows and their lovely scent soothed her.

The next day, Anna returned to the woman's house, hoping to receive an answer. The woman was as brusque as ever, but she told Anna what she had been hoping to hear. Marusia and Rachel would be met that night. They were to follow the Barish down to where it met the Dniester and were to turn west in those woods. There was a stand of willows where they should wait.

"Should I go, too?" asked Anna.

The woman shook her head. "There's no need."

"Alright. I'll make sure they know."

"Don't go straight there from here," cautioned the woman.

"No, of course not. Thank you again."

"There's no need."

Anna left the house, relieved that Marusia and Rachel had been offered a lifeline, but afraid for them, too.

Anna gathered some empty jars in a basket and taking her sharp knife, she set off for the birch stand in the woods beyond Marusia's home. She called in on her friend, ostensibly to invite her to collect birch sap.

Marusia invited Anna into the deserted kitchen. "It's alright. They're all out."

"It's on for tonight," Anna announced.

"That was quick!"

"Yes, it was. After dark, you need to go to that triangle of woods the other side of the Barish, beside the Dniester. You know the stand of willows?"

Marusia nodded.

"You'll be met there."

"Who by?"

"I don't know, but I think it's safe. You'll have to trust that it is."

Marusia looked uncertain, her rosy cheeks had paled at Anna's news.

Anna laid her hand on Marusia's arm. "If it was safe for a child, it will be safe for you."

Marusia's eyes widened and filled with tears as she embraced Anna. "Goodbye, dear Anna. Thank you for this."

Anna hugged Marusia tightly. "Take care of yourself and don't take any unnecessary risks. It would be good to see you again one day."

There was the tiniest of taps and Marusia said, "Just come into the bedroom, Anna."

Anna followed Marusia, closing the door behind her. She looked up as Rachel slid down from the trapdoor in the ceiling and smiled with relief that she had guessed correctly – Rachel lived, despite her indoor pallor. The young women hugged one another and Anna said, "The same goes for you,

Rachel. Be careful and come back one day."

Rachel shook her head. "I'll be glad to be living in the open again, but who can say what will happen, Anna. I thank you for myself and Marusia. She's been the best of friends and doesn't deserve any of this."

"None of us do," replied Anna. She embraced both girls again and let herself out of the cottage. She walked up the lane, determined to look more cheerful than she felt.

After Anna had closed the door behind her, Marusia and Rachel shared a moment of jubilation, grinning at one another with shining eyes.

"At last!"

"We're going!"

"Aren't you afraid?" asked Marusia.

"Not a bit. We'll be able to do something useful at last."

"Yes. We need to think carefully about what we should take."

They gathered what they imagined they might need, warm clothing, a blanket each. As they began to fold their packs, Maria returned. Rachel did not bother to withdraw to the attic, but waited, her dark head bowed, as Marusia told her mother they would be leaving after dark.

Maria looked stricken. "So soon."

"Yes, Mama. The message is that we must meet them there tonight."

"Meet who? And where?"

"All I know is, they once took a child in trouble and that child is safe."

"How do you know?"

"I shouldn't say, Mama. I'll tell you, but don't tell the girls. It could be dangerous for everyone."

"Of course I won't tell them. They'll have enough secrets to keep."

"Anna is my contact."

Maria looked confused. "Anna? But she seems such a good girl."

"Yes, she is. I trust her, Mama."

"So do I," said Rachel, at last taking part in the conversation, but feeling a guilty bystander.

Maria stepped forward and embraced both young women. "Oh, my dears." She forced herself to step back. "What else are you going to need?"

"What can you spare?"

"A small cooking pot, some spoons..."

"And a good sharp knife," said Andriy, coming in from the cold garden. "It's lucky it was only me coming in!" He held out the knife to Marusia. "I have no other weapon to give you," he said. The sharp blade twinkled in the light and Andriy took it back to show both girls how to use it. "It's difficult to stab a man," he began, ignoring Maria's sob, "so try to put the knife here under the ribs and push it upwards as hard as you can."

Marusia and Rachel nodded and swallowed.

"If you don't have time for the knife, or if you haven't got it, chop the side of your hand hard against his windpipe. Here." He pressed his hand against the throat of each girl in turn. "That's not pleasant is it? Just pressing gently. So if you hit someone hard there, you'll slow them down. Failing that, a sharp kick between his legs will do the trick."

"Andriyu!" cried Maria.

"They need to be able to look after themselves." And then turning to Marusia and Rachel, "Trust no one, only each other. You've lived here as sisters. Now you must look after each other as sisters." And he took them in his arms one at a time to kiss them a blessing. "So when do you go?"

"After dark," said Rachel, giving Marusia time to swallow her tears.

"And where are you going?" he asked.

The girls looked at each other and then at Maria, who said, "They thought they should keep that secret."

"Yes, from everyone else. But I don't want you to be caught before you've even left the village."

Marusia told her father.

"Have you thought how you'll get there? Your problem is crossing the Barish, which is pretty high at the moment."

"So we'll have to use the footbridge?"

"Yes, you can't risk being trapped in the marshy ground lower down."

"No, and you can't risk the depth of the Barish at the moment either," added Maria.

Marusia paused to imagine their route. "It seems we have two options. Risk going through the middle of the village to get to the bridge by that short route or…"

"Going all the way around," said Rachel. "But that's a long way."

They were quiet for a moment as they pondered the dilemma. If the girls took the longer route, they could be sheltered by trees for most of the way, but it would require them to circle more than a third of the village, crossing the open quarry and regaining the woods to cross the Barish. Then they would still have over a kilometre's walk to the banks of the Dniester. Anna had not mentioned a time and both girls looked at one another nervously as they thought of the distance they must cover. It could take them almost an hour to reach the Barish alone… But if they went through the village…there was no curfew, but it would be considered odd for two young women to be out after dark. And if Rachel were recognised…

Andriy sighed. "It's too dangerous to go through the village. There are too many houses and no one really knows where people's sympathies lie."

The young women agreed. To Rachel's relief, Marusia said, "Can we eat soon, Mama, and then we can get off as soon as it's fully dark."

Maria nodded and they spent their last moments together being pragmatic. She went into her storeroom and returned with the last flitch of bacon and some butter. "You'd better have something to give them when you arrive."

"Mama!" protested Marusia.

"We'll manage."

Marusia took the food to put in her pack, making it much heavier with this burden of her mother's love.

Marusia's sisters returned from school and detected the tense atmosphere as soon as they entered the house.

"What's going on?" asked Oksana.

"Nothing. We're just eating a bit early today. Take your coats off and let's eat."

As usual, Rachel sat alone in the attic. Even on this momentous occasion, they could not risk her presence in the living room. But after darkness fell, they all gathered in a crush in the girls' bedroom. By now Oksana and Odarka had guessed that a dramatic event was imminent and so were not very surprised when Andriy told them to take their leave of Marusia. "We're not sure when we'll meet again, but if God's willing, it will be soon and safely."

The younger girls looked as if they might cry, but Maria pre-empted their tears. "Let's be cheerful. Marusia and Rachel are going to do important things. We're proud of them and their courage."

So the danger of noisy distress passed and they all embraced the young women and then the lights were extinguished in the house, so that Marusia and Rachel could slip out into the night.

The first part of their journey was the most nerve-wracking as they hurried past their neighbours' houses. They could not risk slipping through gardens, where household dogs would announce any intruders. However, when they reached the junction with Petro's lane, they did slip through the garden of an old couple to reach the pine wood beyond. They paused for a moment beneath the soughing trees to listen, but all seemed quiet. There was some moonlight, but the breeze was sending clouds scudding across the face of the moon. The tricks of light would help the girls to ghost their way, just below the brow of the hill, between the dark trunks. They had to be careful of their footing, as the hill descended steeply to the plain of the Dniester below and, although they could see the woods in which they had to meet their contact, they could not approach them directly.

They hurried around the southern outskirts of the village as far as the quarry, where the patchy moonlight helped them to negotiate the rocks and stones. They tried to cling to what cover there was between the dips and hollows and quickly gained the wood behind Anna's house. As they hurried down to the Barish between the trees, Marusia's thoughts touched on Anna and she hoped that all of the appropriate messages had been passed on. The girls reached the footbridge and slowed their pace to step quietly on its boards, as they crossed the swiftly flowing river. Under the trees again, they paused to listen, but only heard an owl hooting higher up in the wood.

They set off on the last part of their journey more slowly, as the ground was rougher in this denser part of the wood. Rachel did not worry about the time or missing their contact. For her, the feeling of fresh air on her face was exhilarating and her dark eyes glittered with the pleasure of being outdoors after so many months. She took the lead from Marusia and they made their way toward the stand of willows beside the Dniester, reaching their shelter with some relief. There was no one to be seen and afraid to speak, the girls held hands, reassuring one another with a squeeze of the fingers.

They had stood long enough in the thin embrace of the willow's bare branches to become cold and to worry that no one was coming, when Marusia felt a tug on her sleeve and turning, saw the figure of a boy, beckoning them to follow him. She gasped at the touch of someone come back from the dead – or worse than that, Siberia – thirteen-year-old Hrichko grinned at her in the moonlight and beckoned again. Marusia and Rachel picked up their bundles and followed the soundless youth through the trees, both deeply impressed by this emissary from Anna's secret world. Marusia wanted to laugh aloud at the discovery of the child who had survived thanks to Anna, who had had the courage to save him. She blessed Anna's determination, hoping to meet her one day to thank her from the bottom of her heart.

Chapter 9

Anna reached the end of Marusia's lane and turned the corner to pass Petro's house. Nina was in the garden teasing her young cat, but looked up as Anna went past.

"Hello," she called. "You're Anna, aren't you?"

"Yes," Anna smiled. "And you're Nina."

"How do you know?"

"Petro told me."

Nina approached the fence and looked over into Anna's basket. "What are you doing with those jars?"

"I'm going to collect birch sap."

"Can I come?"

"Yes, I suppose so, but," she put out her hand as Nina approached the gate, "you must ask your mother first."

Nina turned and sped into the house, calling "Mama, Mama!"

Anna waited in the lane feeling awkward. She had had little contact with Halia in the past, and none since she and Petro had begun their courtship. She did not want Halia, or Petro, to misinterpret Nina's actions.

But Nina was inside the cottage gabbling: "Mama, Anna, the mushroom girl, Petro's girlfriend, has asked me to collect birch sap with her. Can I go?"

"Just a moment. What girlfriend?" She peered out of the kitchen window into the lane.

"Come on, Mama, she's waiting," and Nina hurried out again.

Halia followed her, wiping her hands on her apron. She stood on the path for a moment, a sturdy figure with her legs planted firmly on the earth. Her arms were muscular and tanned. She had a round face with high cheekbones and a generous mouth. Her hair was smooth and straight, unlike Petro's curls, but her direct blue gaze was the same. She looked at Anna now, examining the girl.

"Hello," said Anna. "I'm sorry to trouble you. I was passing and Nina asked me where I was going."

Halia nodded at Nina, "And you invited yourself to go with Anna?"

"She said I could."

Halia turned to Anna.

"It's alright…if you don't mind. She's welcome to come with me."

"That's very kind of you," said Halia, still standing on her dignity. "Don't let her be a nuisance," she said, as Nina let herself out of the garden.

"I won't and I'll bring her back safely. I'm not sure how long we'll be."

Halia nodded. "Before dusk though."

"Of course," replied Anna and Nina took her free hand to lead her along the lane.

They walked, or Anna walked and Nina skipped, towards the woods and the biggest birch trees.

"So what are we going to do?" asked Nina.

"We're going to collect sap from the birch trees," explained Anna.

"What for?"

"It makes a tasty drink and it's very good for you."

"How is it good for you?"

"It helps keep our insides clean and it kills bad things in our bodies."

"How do you know?"

"My mother told me."

Nina looked at Anna in disbelief.

Anna read her look. "My mother used to be a strong woman and she taught me lots of things as I was growing up. She's very sad now and that makes her seem frail."

Nina was quiet for a moment. "Alright." Her exuberance soon returned. "So what do we do?"

"Well," said Anna, putting down her basket, "I'll show you."

She reached for one of her jars, wound some thin wire around its brim and made sure the remaining wire would encompass the tree's trunk. Then she picked up her knife and placing its point against the tree, she tapped it firmly upwards under the bark. She took a small stick, flattened on its upper side, and inserted the stick into the hole so that it pointed downwards, directing the tree's sap along its length. Fixing the jar just below the stick, she watched as the sap began to fill the vessel. "That's it. If we come back in an hour, the jar will be almost full."

"And then can we drink it?"

"Yes, you can taste it then."

"Do you do this all the time?"

Anna could not help smiling. "No, look at the trees, Nina. What do you see?"

Nina looked around her. "Trees, branches."

"Look again, especially upwards."

"The sky?"

"Yes. Why can we see the sky?"

"No leaves?"

"That's right."

"But they're starting," said Nina. "Look," and she pointed to the buds just beginning to show themselves in a purple veil over the slender branches.

"Good. That's when we can take the sap. Just when the trees are about to go into leaf."

They approached another tree. "Do you want to do this one?" asked Anna. Nina nodded. "Yes. Give me the knife."

"Wait. First get the jar and the stick ready and then you won't waste too much of the sap."

They continued to set the jars and as they returned to the first one, Anna said, "We might have to wait if it's not quite full." She watched Nina hurrying towards the tree, her eyes glistening with interest as she gauged the level of sap in the jar. Anna was struck by the vividness in her heart-shaped face, haloed by her fair curls.

"Is it full?"

"Almost. Shall we wait?"

Anna glanced at the sky. "Yes, we've a little time, but we mustn't be too long. It'll be dark soon and we've the other jars to collect."

The work went quickly with Nina's deft enthusiasm and they collected their haul of sap as the sun was beginning to redden above the trees on the opposite side of the Dniester.

"We'd better be going back," said Anna. "I don't want your mother to worry."

"Alright," said Nina. "It's been fun, hasn't it? Can I come out with you again?"

"Yes, you can come with me again sometime."

"Tomorrow?"

"Maybe not tomorrow. I still have some digging to finish."

"You should get Petro to do it for you. He does it for Mama."

"Then I'm sure he has enough to do," laughed Anna. "And besides, I'm strong enough to do my own."

As they approached the house, Nina would not let go of Anna's hand, so she found herself being pulled into Halia's kitchen.

"Mama, look how much we got!" announced Nina.

Halia turned to look in the basket. "You did do well. Did your mother teach you Anna?"

"Yes, she did. We used to go together."

"And how is she?"

"She's quite well, thank you. I should be getting back to her now."

"Yes, of course," said Halia. "Thank you for taking Nina."

"She was very good. I'm going to leave you her share of the collecting, if I may," said Anna taking half of the jars out of her basket.

"No, Anna, there's no need," said Halia.

"But there is. Nina worked very hard. She's a quick learner."

Halia laughed and stroked Nina's head. "Yes, she's certainly that."

"Anna says I can go with her again," announced Nina.

The women smiled at one another over her head and with a last goodbye, Anna left the cottage.

As she walked home, she felt pleased that Petro's mother had thawed a little, but felt there was something daunting about strong women like Halia, who had survived the death of her husband and looked after her four children. Anna thought that the destruction of her own mother's strength had come from the terrible shock she had experienced. She also wondered if the death of Yuri had been a greater blow to her than the death of her husband. Katerina had loved them both, but the loss of a child… Anna could only try to imagine how harrowing that would be. However, in the end, it mattered little that her mother had been so debilitated. She was fragile and Anna accepted her lot philosophically. She would care for her mother for as long as she was needed. Anna knew, too, that despite the gradual loss of friends in the village, as the war took them in one way or another, she was strong enough to survive. Petro was right, she could endure. She might not like it, but she could go on.

The rumours of Marusia's disappearance began to filter out. Her mother looked terribly drawn and her father defeated when Anna saw them in the village and she felt for them. The next time she passed their cottage, she called in with some marigold seeds.

"Come in, Anna. It's good to see you."

"Thank you. I wasn't sure whether I'd be welcome or not."

"Yes, you're welcome, Anna. We're very afraid for Marusia, but the alternative just wasn't possible."

"Well, I'm sorry she had to go at all and I'm sorry, too, for your trouble."

"Thank you." Maria sighed, but tried to smile, despite the tears gathering in her eyes.

"How are Oksana and Odarka?"

"Better and worse. They have more freedom and more space in the house, but they miss Marusia. I hope this is all over before they have to go."

"They're too young, surely?"

"Yes, thirteen and eleven. Perhaps people will leave us alone for a while, now we've lost Marusia."

"Not 'lost'. You might hear news of her from time to time."

"Yes, perhaps. I'll let you know." Maria paused and then, with an effort, added, "Perhaps you could let me know, if you hear anything."

"Of course I will," said Anna, guilty that Marusia's perilous course had been made possible through her efforts. "I brought you some seeds from my garden," she said. "They're marigolds. Marusia always admired them – they're so bright and cheerful. I thought you might like some."

"That was thoughtful of you. I won't need reminding of her, but I will need to remember to look on the bright side."

Later as Anna walked home along the lane, she saw Vera returning from the village shop. Her heart lifted at the sight of her tall, slender friend, the familiar dark brown hair drawn back to reveal her widow's peak and her hazel eyes all concern.

"Have you been to Marusia's?" she asked.

"Yes. Her mother's very upset."

"I'm not surprised," said Vera. "I don't know why Marusia took such a difficult route. Going to Germany would have been much easier."

"But not for her."

"Do you know why she joined the partisans? I assume that's where she's gone."

"Who knows why people do things. It must have felt like the right thing to do. Marusia was never silly."

"No, but I'm surprised. I wouldn't have thought it of her."

"No, me neither. Anyway, how are you?" asked Anna.

"Oh, I'm fine. Same as usual."

"Have you heard anything from Evhen?" Vera's older brother had been called up for the Red Army early in 1941.

"No, not for a while. We have no idea where he might be."

"That must be very hard for all of you."

"It is. We just hope he's so busy fighting, he has no time to write."

"And the post can't be relied on," added Anna, hoping to comfort Vera.

"I don't know what it's all about, Anna. I hate politics. It just seems to drag us all this way and that."

"Yes, there's a great temptation to concentrate on surviving each day."

"I know. I just do my work and help my mother and the boys and hope to be left alone."

"Well, there's enough to do there. Mama and I get along well enough now. She does a bit of work in the house, but more importantly, she will talk to me sometimes."

Vera put a sympathetic arm around Anna's waist. "I shouldn't complain, Anna. You've had a terrible time."

"We all have," said Anna, returning her friend's gesture. "We should just be happy for each day."

"Yes, we should be. We'll have a pact, Anna. To be happy every day!"

Anna kissed her friend's cheek. "Till tomorrow."

"See you tomorrow," called Vera as she went further up the lane to her own house.

Anna returned to her depleted home and said a small prayer of thanks that she still had her mother. Katerina was boiling up the birch sap and adding sugar, so that it would keep until it was needed in the hot summer months. She looked up as Anna entered. "How is everyone?"

"Just as you'd expect. Marusia's mother's upset and there are rumours about where Marusia's gone."

As she took off her coat, Anna caught her mother's anxious glance. "Don't worry. I'm not going anywhere."

"Not yet."

"No, Mama, and who knows what will happen," she said, scooping up Murchik from the chair and stroking him.

Katerina sighed.

"I'm sorry, Mama," said Anna. "I meant that I take each day as it comes, and I'm glad to get through it with at least one thing to be thankful for."

"Yes, you're right."

"And we're lucky to have each other," she said, leaning over to kiss her mother's withered cheek.

The demand for labourers became more intense, as Germany threw all its forces East in Russia and West in Europe. Young men were taken off in droves and more young women were being taken, as they proved themselves useful in the factories of the *Wehrmacht*. But news filtered back of Nazi complaisance; strong youngsters were literally being worked to death.

On a lovely day in May, Anna took the cows to pasture with Ivan. The cows huffed their way up the incline and settled to graze, tearing at the fresh green grass. Seeing that they were happily settled, Anna turned to Ivan. "What's wrong?"

"Oh, bloody Germany, that's what."

"Have you got to go?"

"I don't know. None of us have gone yet from our house, but someone will have to."

"Will it have to be you?"

"Perhaps. Nestor's older than me, but as Halyna's pregnant he might be protected."

"When's her baby due?"

"Soon." He sighed. "I feel for Nestor. He's a good brother-in-law and he's excited about the baby, but, to be honest, Anna, I'm not ready to go."

"Not many are."

"I know it's daft to say so, but I don't feel old enough."

"At eighteen. Others of that age have gone, haven't they?" she asked.

"Yes, they have, but you know me."

"Hmm. I've lost track. Is it Sofia or Olena now?"

He grinned. "It's still both."

"Oh Ivan! You're a disgrace!"

"I know, but Sofia's so lively."

"And Olena?"

"Oh she's lovely! So kind and cheerful."

Anna shook her head at him. "You are such a boy! You can't have them both!"

"I know. I'll have to make a decision soon."

"Unless it's made for you."

And it was, but not as anyone had anticipated. Sofia and her younger sister, Olha, hurried home, clutching the laundry, their mouths dry. The pounding of their hearts made it difficult to breathe. Their reactions to the sight of the Nazi uniforms had been exactly the same: the enormous fear of being taken to Germany to work. Sofia and Olha's feet skittered on the gravelly road and their shoes were covered in dust. The hens were busy pecking at the grass at the front of the house, as the girls hastened into the sudden darkness of the kitchen.

"They're here!" panted Sofia.

Their mother turned from the oven, lifting out the freshly baked bread, putting it down carefully on the table, despite the lurch her heart had given. She wiped her forearm over her hot brow and sank into a chair. "Who's here?"

"The Germans!"

"What for?"

"They think Starosta Shumenko hasn't been honest with them about numbers," said Sofia.

"He came to the laundry and told us which families have got to send someone today," added Olha, appalled by the drama of her sister's imminent departure.

"And he pointed at us?" their mother asked.

Both girls nodded.

The widow sighed again. Why they could not be left alone, she did not know. The Nazis had been leeching the young from the villages for months and she had known that her family would not be safe this time. They would take one of her girls. Her girls... Sofia was now eighteen, the roundness of her figure attesting to her being a fully grown woman. She was buxom and strong, while Olha, at fourteen, had yet to grow into her strength. She was small for her age, but with a sweet smile which always reached her bright blue eyes. Those eyes were fixed on her older sister with concern. "I'm sure it'll be alright. Lots of the others have gone. You might meet up with them."

"What do you mean – you?" countered Sofia. "I'm not going. Mama couldn't manage without me. You'll have to go."

"But I'm younger than you. The oldest always goes first."

"Not necessarily. Irina and Natalya weren't the oldest."

"But they wanted to go."

"And I don't... Anyway, Mama needs me here," retorted Sofia.

Olha saw her sister as if for the first time: her black curls escaping from her headscarf, her direct blue eyes and most of all, her jutting chin. She has thought this through and planned it, she thought. She never intended to go. She always knew she would be able to manipulate Mama and bully me, so that she could stay here. Olha felt sick, not only at the thought of leaving everything she knew, but at the thought of her sister's betrayal. She appealed to her mother.

"Mama, you know I can't go. I'm only fourteen."

"I know, darling, but they'll make one of you go. Sofia is right – she helps me more than you do."

"That's because she's bigger and stronger than me. And I do help you."

"I know you do, so I know you'll manage. Besides it might not be for long."

"For long?" wailed Olha. "Who has come back? They've been taking people for months and who has come back?" But she could not continue as she broke into sobs. It was not the sound of a hurt child wailing, but a girl, suddenly faced with the burden of being a woman and crying at the enormity of the task. How could she leave her home; her end of the bed; the warmth around the blue stove; her mother's arm around her shoulders; her little brother... Levko... He was only ten. She would not see him grow up. She looked in horror at her mother who turned away saying, "You must take a spare set of clothes and I can let you have this old cloth for a towel. You can wrap your blouse and underwear in it."

Olha tried to understand that her mother was resolved and seeing Sofia's smirk, she correctly suspected that the ground for this decision had already been laid. The two older women had discussed it and Olha had been chosen. She felt herself teetering on this cliff-edge of knowledge and could not speak. She turned away from both of them, taking the clean laundry into the bedroom she had shared with Sofia for as long as she could remember. She sat down on the large bed and stroked the quilt, which was so comforting on cold nights. She looked out of the window, through which came the sounds of birds oblivious to her misery. But there was no more time for tears. She must deal with what was coming to her. Olha gathered her clean clothes and her embroidered blouse. It was becoming too small for her, but she and her mother would not sew a new one together. She would have to take it and make do.

Parania came in cautiously. "You must take your winter coat, too," she said and, handing Olha a coarse sack, "Put all your things in here. It's clean."

"Thank you, Mama."

The tears welled up again in Olha's eyes as she thought of passing several seasons away from home. She reached into the bottom of the cupboard for her boots. She packed them into the sack and followed her mother into the kitchen. The homely smell of the freshly baked bread almost undid Olha, but she hardened her heart as her mother cut her off a hunk and, wrapping it in a small cloth, placed it in Olha's pitiful bundle. She looked at Sofia, standing beside the cooking range and could not resist saying, "Do you think it will do you any good with Ivan to stay? He'll have to go soon anyway."

Sofia reddened. "Don't be such a fool. I'm thinking of Mama."

"Of course you are." She turned away and put out her hand for her meagre luggage, as Levko, her ten-year-old brother, rushed into the house.

"The *starosta's* waiting at the carts with those German soldiers..." but he paused as he saw Olha standing with the bundle in her hand. "No!" he cried. "Why isn't Sofia going?"

Sofia took his arm firmly. "Not all this again. It's been decided. Be quiet!"

"Let go of me. You're not my mother. Mama..."

"I know Levko. It's terrible, but Olha has to go."

"I do," said Olha. "Come and give me a hug now," and she took the boy in her arms. He was hot from running home and Olha could feel his heart palpitating in his bony chest. They drew apart and Olha took a good look at her brother. "Be good."

He threw himself back into her arms and sobbed like the child he still was, but she withdrew after a moment saying, "I must go now, Levko."

She turned to her mother and they embraced, the older woman forcing her tears down until later; Olha holding hers in fiercely while her mother kissed her and murmured a blessing over her. Then Olha turned to Sofia. The sisters embraced cursorily, Olha no longer allowing herself to think about what Sofia had done to her. As she went out of the door into the blinding light of the early afternoon, they made to follow her.

"No, please don't," she said. "It'll be easier for all of us if you stay here." She turned away and set off along the stony road.

Olha found herself beside Olena as they hastened towards the green beside the Reading Room.

Olena looked at her. "No Sofia?"

"No," said Olha and saw that Olena knew her sister better than she did.

"Well, never mind. We'll stick together shall we?" said the older girl, linking arms with Olha.

"Does Ivan know you're going?" asked Olha, feeling that Olena's friendliness allowed her to ask the question.

"No. This has been really sudden, hasn't it?"

"Yes, you could say that."

The girls reached the crowds at the carts. Already some had climbed onto them, while others made their farewells.

"*Schnell! Schnell!*" snapped the soldiers.

The departing young men and women mounted the wagons. They crowded along the benches on either side, placing their bundles and boxes at their feet. It would be a hot journey with the sun blazing down. The carters mounted up and taking the reins, clicked their horses into a walk. Once the soldiers were satisfied that the carts had begun to lumber towards the town, they mounted their motorcycles and sped off to supervise the round-up at the next village, leaving a cloud of dust behind them.

As the carts drew into Buchach three hours later, Olha felt her nervousness rise again. Where would they be sent? But she had had time to think and she felt a rising anger, not just with Sofia, but with the power which was forcing her from her home. She glanced at the older girl and saw that she, too, was searching for clues to their destination.

The travellers were hot and dusty. They climbed down, hoping for a drink of water and found they were in luck. There was a water pump at the station, so a crowd formed around it. Olena and Olha were well behind the others and realised it might be some time before they could get a drink in this jostling melee.

"Never mind," said Olena. "Let's go over to those houses. There's sure to be another pump. We'll be fine, as long as we're quick."

Olha looked along the platform. There were soldiers in the distance, but no train. "Yes, let's go."

The two girls slipped away from the busy platform and hurried along an alley between the houses. There was a communal pump at the end of the shared yard and they hastened towards it. After slaking their thirst, they washed their faces and arms and wrung out their headscarves, feeling much calmer now that they were cooler.

Another alley led away towards an open area. Olha looked towards apparent freedom. The idea that she did not have to board the train came to her like a sudden revelation. Sofia has done what she wanted to do, why shouldn't I, she thought to herself. "Let's not go back," said Olha.

"What?" asked Olena.

"No one's missed us. Let's go down here and see where it leads to."

"Alright, but it's very risky…"

"Be quick," urged Olha, setting off at a trot down the alley. It opened out into a broad street with a church and a cemetery. Ignoring the thudding of her heart, Olha said, "We can hide in there. No one's likely to be passing by."

Olena hesitated, but Olha ran across the road and was soon hidden among the gravestones, so Olena had little choice but to join her amongst the raucous cawing set up by the crows, disturbed from their perches high in the trees. The girls squatted behind neighbouring headstones facing the street, keeping watch, although they had still heard no alarm being raised. They tried to quieten their breathing, but anxiety churned in their stomachs.

"You know we've burnt our bridges, don't you?" said Olena.

"Yes, but if I've got to leave home, I want to know where I'm going," said Olha, sounding much more determined than she felt.

"Where are we going?"

"There's only one place now – the forest."

"The partisans? What experience can we offer them?"

"I don't know – our youth maybe. Our patriotism. I shouldn't think Marusia had much to offer in the way of experience," said Olha.

Olena stared at this young girl, who seemed suddenly possessed of a knowledge and determination beyond her years. "Sounds better than a factory or a laundry, I suppose."

"Exactly! How many of them have come back? None. At least we'll be with our own."

"Sleeping rough, nowhere to…" Olena stopped.

"What?" whispered Olha, her blood thudding in her ears.

There was the click of a safety catch being taken off behind them. The girls turned in unison. A dark figure towered above them, silhouetted against the light. The girls raised their eyes, taking in the black boots over the grey infantryman's trousers to his jacket with its *Wehrmacht* insignia. His soft cap looked less threatening, but his rifle was aimed directly at them. "*Raus!*" he ordered, gesticulating with his gun.

The girls stood up, barely able to breathe.

"Thought you'd run away did you?" he barked. "Thought we couldn't count?"

"No, of course not, officer," said Olena. "My friend felt ill and we were trying to find her some shade."

This sounded hollow even to Olena's ears and the private wasted no time on the tale. Nor did he correct her gift of a rank. He had his orders: shoot all runaways. He motioned with his gun again, herding the pair towards an open grave.

"Kneel and say your last prayers."

The girls looked at him and then at each other, their eyes as wide as their mouths.

"No, please..."

"Oh no..." they howled.

"Kneel!"

The girls did so, sobbing loudly.

"*Was geht's?*" a loud voice demanded.

The infantryman looked up to see the peaked cap of his senior officer. "*Heil Hitler!* Two runaways, Captain," he said, leaping to attention.

"*Heil Hitler!* Where from?" demanded the Captain.

"The group just brought in by cart."

"So what are you doing with them?"

"Our orders were to shoot all runaways, Captain."

"A waste of good slaves, man. Don't be stupid. Just march them back to the train and make sure they get on it."

"*Sieg heil!*"

The girls got to their feet, not sure whether they had been lucky or not. They were alive, but being marched at gunpoint to board a train for a fate the captain had described as slavery. They walked ahead of their guard, back towards the square where he barked, "*Nach rechts!*"

They joined a huge crowd of young men and women carrying their few possessions in bundles and cardboard boxes. None of these people was from their village.

"There are hundreds of them," whispered Olha. "Where have they all come from?"

"Villages like ours," muttered Olena and the girls quickly took each other's hands, their fingers gripping their only ally. There would be no one else to turn to now, and who knew how long they might have each other.

Chapter 10

For those remaining in the village, the workload increased as Hitler made greater demands on the fertile land. German quartermasters came to inspect the work and to estimate yields. They had no concern for the farmers other than their ability to produce grain for Germany, and so the remaining villagers found themselves slaving at home, under the rigid eye of authority, straining from dawn till dusk.

Petro and Ivan, once again, found themselves side by side, returning from the fields at twilight.

"It's not much of a choice is it?" began Ivan.

"What isn't?"

"Whether to work for the Nazis here, or in Germany."

"No…but as you said before, there's another way."

"Will you go?"

"Go where?" asked Petro, forcing Ivan to return to his earlier fantasy.

"To our boys in the forest?"

"They're fighting back. At least you can say that for them."

"Risky though."

"You've changed your tune! It was you suggesting it not long ago."

"I know."

"What's wrong with you? At least one of your problems has been solved," laughed Petro.

"What do you mean?"

"Olena left with the last quota, didn't she?"

"Yes, but Sofia didn't."

"Oh I see…"

"She's become so demanding! She thinks she's caught me now."

"Has she?"

"Maybe not. But I need a better reason for risking my neck with the partisans."

"We may all be pushed to making a stand."

When Petro talked to Anna later of Ivan's apparent change of heart, her view remained the same. "He hasn't grown up yet. He doesn't really know what he wants."

But Sofia did. Regardless of any help her mother might need, she saw Ivan frequently and was always available when he sought her out. The closeness she hoped might spring from their greater contact did not blossom...but something else did.

One evening, she sent Levko to tell Ivan she needed to see him and so he came, having washed cursorily after work. They sat in the orchard, which ran behind her house and, despite its lovely promise in the balmy evening, Ivan felt uncomfortable.

"So what was so urgent?"

Sofia ducked her head in what she hoped might convey shyness, but it did not charm Ivan. He simply waited.

"Aren't you going to ask me?" she said in hurt tones.

"I just did."

"Ask me again."

"Sofia, I've been working since it was light and I'm tired out. Tell me what you have to say, so I can get some sleep before tomorrow's work."

"You are cross! I've never known you so cross." And what she hoped were pretty tears overflowed down her cheeks.

"Oh, stop it. Did you cry when Olha left?"

"Is that what's upsetting you? That I didn't leave?"

"Only that it shows your selfishness so well."

"Mama wanted me to stay."

"Yes, but it was your duty to go before your younger sister."

"Don't talk to me about duty. We'll see if you do yours!"

"What do you mean?" he asked stung, wondering if she, too, thought he should have left for Germany by now.

"I mean your duty to me." She paused dramatically. "And to the baby." The look she gave him was so triumphant that Ivan quailed before her.

"You aren't!"

"I am!" she crowed. "Aren't you delighted?"

Ivan nodded and took her in his arms so that she could not see his face. Why had fate dealt him this blow? Why couldn't Sofia have been on that cart instead of Olha; and certainly instead of Olena? But he also knew that she had every right to demand that he did his duty. He had no doubt that the child was his. What would they say at home, he thought, as his mind tumbled through the need for a swift wedding.

"How long?" he asked, drawing away from her.

"Oh, about two months I think."

"So it's due in the spring?"

"Yes, I suppose so."

"What has your mother said?"

"I haven't told her yet."

"Alright. But we must. And soon." He paused. "Let's do it on Sunday, when there'll be more time."

"Yes, that's a good idea," she said, blue eyes sparkling, but their brightness was wasted on Ivan, whose head was bowed.

"You'd better go in," he said at last. "We don't want you catching a chill."

She stood up, delighted with his attention, and let him lead her to her door. She held up her mouth to be kissed. Where was her delightful liveliness now, he wondered as he looked at her smug face, but he bent to kiss her nevertheless. He hardly knew how his feet carried him to his own door. He could only think of his stupidity in falling into this old, old trap.

His mother was still tidying up as he came in. One look told her he was upset and her heart ached for him. He had been such a sickly baby she had almost lost him, so she had never given up the habit of checking him more carefully than her other children.

"What is it?" she asked, coming towards him.

He hung his head. "Sofia's pregnant."

She drew him to her, putting her arm around him.

"You don't seem surprised."

"I'm not."

He looked at her sweet face. "I'm sorry, Mama."

She shook her head. "Don't apologise to me. You must do the right thing for Sofia and the baby."

He nodded. He would have liked to unburden himself to his mother, who had been more philosophical and sympathetic than he had expected and he realised, suddenly, that she may have seen the rest, too: his dalliances, his expectation that he could have it all with no consequences and worse, that his infatuation for Sofia had withered. He would not love his wife. He wanted to lay his head on his mother's breast and weep, but knew he could not. He shook himself like a dog. "I think I'll go to bed."

"Yes, you need your sleep. We'll talk about it again tomorrow with *Tato*."

The arrangements were made for the marriage, and despite the suddenness and haste, many of the traditional customs were carried out. Ivan's father accompanied him to Sofia's house to ask formally, and belatedly, for permission for the youngsters to marry. They were accompanied by Roman Shumenko, who had been asked to act as the Master of Ceremonies at the wedding, and they took the traditional gift of bread, freshly baked by Ivan's mother. Sofia's mother gave her permission and it was agreed that after the wedding the youngsters would live at her house. Sofia and Ivan exchanged embroidered *rushnyky* as symbols of their engagement, the long, rectangular pieces of fabric that were small works of art.

The customary lapse of time between the engagement of the young couple and the wedding, during which the bride's family helped her to gather her linen, could not take place, but since Sofia and Ivan would be living with Parania, there was less need for such preparations. The families' closer friends and neighbours selected the livestock to feed the wedding guests for several days of celebrations. Since Sofia's mother was a widow, people helped her with their contributions of a goose, or duck or hen; and Ivan's parents provided the pig for the feast. For several days before the wedding, the young couple's houses resounded with the sounds of the culinary preparations. The pig was slaughtered; the meat roasted; and salamis and jellies were made. The poultry were stripped of their feathers and roasted. There was no shortage of volunteers to bake cakes and pastries for the guests, the centrepiece, the *korovai*, being made with great care. The tower of sweet bread was decorated with pastry curls and birds adorned its high top. It would have its blue and yellow ribbons added at the last moment.

Sofia revelled in all the excitement and rituals, although she did have difficulty with one task. As the bride-to-be, she had to send a headscarf to her fiancé, so that he could carry it on his belt on their wedding day. It would be used to symbolise her passage from girl to woman during the reception. Ordinarily, an older brother or male cousin would take the token, but Sofia only had ten-year-old Levko. He did not feel it was a job for him.

"Come on, Levko. You only have to take this to Ivan's house and give it to him."

"What do I have to say?" asked the boy.

"Just tell him it's from me, for tomorrow."

"Why can't someone else do it?"

Sofia gripped Levko's upper arm tightly and hissed through gritted teeth, "Because there is no one else."

"Come, Levko, help your sister," admonished their mother.

"She would have more people to help her if she didn't send them away!" he burst out.

"Oh, you little..." Sofia shook him. "Olha couldn't have done this anyway."

He pulled away from her. "Alright. Stop hurting me. I'm going." And he stomped from the house, his face clouded with anger.

Moments later, Anna and Vera appeared in the doorway. Sofia had asked them to be her bridesmaids, so according to custom, they had already walked the village, inviting the guests in person, and had come to spend the eve of the wedding with Sofia.

"Whatever's wrong with Levko?" asked Vera as they entered.

"I sent him to Ivan's with my headscarf."

Vera giggled. "He didn't look as if he liked the errand."

"Too bad. I couldn't do it myself!"

"Of course not," said Anna. "Come and look at the lovely guelder rose we picked for you."

The three young women went into the garden to inspect the materials for Sofia's wedding crown. Anna and Vera would make it from the emerald foliage and ensure that the green halo was studded with ripe red berries. Not only would it identify the bride as the centrepiece of the wedding celebrations, but the berries of the *kalyna* also symbolised fertility.

"You certainly picked a lot, girls," said Parania, coming out to look.

"Yes, we wanted to be able to select the best bits here as we worked," explained Anna.

"Mama, fetch me a stool and then we can get started."

Anna and Vera exchanged a quick glance at Sofia's order, but bent to their task, selecting and trimming the foliage and beginning to weave it onto a wire base before fitting it to Sofia's head. As they worked, they sang and female friends and neighbours gathered to watch and join in the singing. Sofia sat flushed with pleasure, her cheeks pink with the attention.

The benches outside the house filled up with village girls and older women, brightly dressed in their embroidered blouses, but also wearing their most decoratively embroidered aprons. The older women wore coloured kerchiefs, while the young women were adorned with crowns of field flowers. The musicians arrived and the violin, mandolin and drum accompanied songs of love and promises. Not all of the songs were serious; some referred to the couple's future in coy terms. But all took the jokes in good part and Sofia avidly played her role as the blushing bride.

Later, as the girls took the crown indoors to keep it safe for the next day, Vera asked Sofia, "How do you feel? Are you nervous?"

Sofia looked surprised. "No. I'm excited. What do I have to be nervous about?"

"It's a big step," said Vera. "You're making promises for the rest of your life."

"That's alright. I want to spend the rest of my life with Ivan. It'll be fine. We love each other."

"He's good at bottom," said Anna.

"What do you mean, '...at bottom'?"

"He's grown up a lot recently," said Anna quickly.

"He's had to, and he'll have to even more once the baby's here." She looked at their surprised faces. "Surely you guessed?"

"Perhaps. But no one has spoken of it," said Vera.

"It's none of their business."

"No, you're quite right," said Anna. "Anyway, I'm sure you'll both try to be happy."

"Yes," agreed Vera. "You'll be fine."

"We will," said Sofia.

Anna and Vera linked arms as they walked back through the noisy village, the sounds of the groom's celebrations reaching them from Ivan's house.

"Well, that's that!" announced Vera.

"Not quite. There's the ceremony yet."

"Ivan won't back out though, will he?"

"Oh no. He knows it's too late for that."

"He must be sorry she didn't go."

"Yes. It's no way to start a marriage, is it? But they might still be happy."

Vera turned to Anna with a wry smile. "You're such an optimist. Can you see Ivan bending under her yoke?"

"It won't be as bad as that."

"Don't you think so? Sofia's not known for her consideration of anybody, except Sofia."

"No, she certainly thinks of herself first."

"Well, I wouldn't want such a life."

Anna smiled at her friend, looking into her honest, heart-shaped face. "What sort of a life do you want?"

"A quiet one!" laughed Vera.

"With no love?"

"What's love? I look at the young men in this village and none of them excite me."

"There are men in other villages…"

"Oh, I'm not desperate. I'm happy as I am. And what about you, Anna? When are you and Petro going to make an announcement?"

Anna smiled and blushed. "We're not at that stage yet."

"No, but you'll get there."

"Perhaps."

"No perhaps about it. It's obvious that you love one another."

Anna blushed even more deeply. "Yes, I do love him, but there's Mama… and Halia would be on her own with Nina. We can wait."

Vera patted Anna's arm. "Don't think of everyone else for too long. You and Petro deserve your own lives, you know."

"Yes, we do…and we will when the time's right." Anna was glad to be able to talk frankly to Vera, but wished her dearest friend had a lover, too. "We'll find you someone tomorrow."

"No need. Don't you go setting me up with some boy!"

"Only with someone who deserves you!"

"That sounds worse!" and with that, the girls said their merry goodnights.

Sofia's smile could not have been more self-satisfied as she processed with Ivan through the village the next day. They made a colourful spectacle with the bridesmaids and grooms, the guests arrayed in their embroidered blouses and shirts. The procession was announced by the musicians playing loudly at the front of the column. There was even a priest available again to marry the couple in the church, for although the Germans wanted Ukrainian wheat, unlike the Russians, they did not care about hearts and minds. The priest was not from the village – there had not been a resident priest since Father Dubenko's disappearance – so the presiding cleric had come from Temne.

The church had been made to look as lovely as possible, despite its dereliction, and Sofia's mother and her friends had cleaned and bedecked it with flowers. The couple stood before the small altar on the congregation's side of the *iconostas* and went through the ceremony with the exchange of rings and vows to love one another and to be faithful till death. Sofia also promised to obey her husband. The couple stepped around the small altar with their laurel crowns, as they were bound to one another for life. The ceremony was lifted by the singing from the balcony of the choir…whose voices were raised again in the less ecclesiastical singing which accompanied the noisy reception, held beside the Reading Room in a temporary barn raised especially for the nuptials.

It was crowded with the men on one side, the women on the other, until the dancing could begin. The tables were groaning with food and during the feast, the younger guests frequently interrupted the proceedings with calls of "*Hirke!*", suggesting the drinks were too bitter and could only be sweetened by the young couple exchanging a kiss before their guests, which they duly did, Sophia looking jubilant, Ivan more serious.

Anna and Vera waited upon Sofia during her special day and had one more duty to perform in a break in the dancing. Sofia had to exchange her lovely crown for the headscarf, which symbolised her status as a wife. Ivan removed the object from his belt and handed it over to his wife's bridesmaids. This was a bitter-sweet moment for Sofia, because, although she was delighted to be Ivan's wife, she did not yet want to relinquish her role as the most important and the most beautiful woman in the gathering. However, she followed the dictates of custom and then waltzed with her husband, who tried to hide the gloom he felt.

"You're very quiet," commented Sofia. "You're not ill, are you?"

"No, I'm fine. It's a big day for us, that's all."

"Good," Sofia grinned. "I don't want you to be ill on our wedding night."

"No, I'm not ill," repeated Ivan, forcing his lips into a smile. But he confided his despondency to Petro a little later. "I don't know how this is all going to work out."

"Well, no one really knows how a marriage will turn out. And Sofia loves you."

"As much as she loves anybody."

"So be positive then. You've made your vows, now try and make a good job of it."

"That's easy for you to say. Anna's beautiful and sensible."

"And Sofia is lively and attractive. Cheer up! It's your wedding day. Have some fun!"

Ivan did smile and dance through the evening and there were some moments of lightness, but he carried the dark weight of disappointment in the pit of his stomach nevertheless.

Petro and Anna were delighted with the opportunity to dance together. As the band began to play a waltz, Petro turned to Anna and drew her towards him. She met his smile and, placing one hand on his shoulder and the other in his, they struck off in three-four time in an exuberant circular waltz. They held one another tightly enough to be able to lean out from their figure as they circled: one, two, three, one, two, three; whirling outwards in the bliss of their balance against one another. They saw no one as they turned with the round music, their eyes locked, their smiles broad. Little wonder that older guests nodded indulgently and younger guests longed to be in that special circle. Sofia pursed her lips at what she saw as Anna deliberately upstaging her on her wedding day. Anna herself was in love with the handsomest man in the room and unaware that their shared joy was being witnessed by the other guests, including Halia and Katerina.

Halia had taken advantage of a space on the women's bench beside Katerina. "How are you, Katerina? It's good to see you here."

"I'm well enough, thank you. I take it all slowly, you know."

"Yes, you're right. That's the best way."

"And how are you, Halia? Is Nina with you?"

"Oh yes. She's running around somewhere with the other youngsters. I'm fine, too – learning to live without my girls to help me."

"That must be hard. I'm so grateful for Anna. She helps me so much."

There was a pause as the women observed the dancers, not least the radiant couple their children made. The two older women turned and smiled at one another and then both sighed.

"Let them be happy while they can," commented Katerina.

"Yes, there'll be little enough of that in life for them," agreed Halia, although feeling the dip in her stomach at her son's delight in his beloved. Would she lose him, too? But she shook herself sternly. He might have to go and fight. It would be the least of her worries to have him besotted with a girl of Anna's worth. She made herself relax into a welcoming smile, as the young couple joined them at the end of the waltz.

"Are you alright, Mama?" asked Anna.

"I am, dear. But I'm going home soon. I'm beginning to feel tired."

"Alright. I'll walk you up the lane."

"No, there's no need. You stay here and enjoy yourself."

"I'll come back when I know you're comfortable," said Anna.

The two older women said their goodnights and Petro turned to Anna. "I'll walk down for you in a little while."

"Alright. I'll just get Mama settled."

Anna took her mother's arm and they made a slow progress away from the wedding party, Katerina taking her leave of neighbours, who had been pleasantly surprised to see her at the reception.

"You didn't need to walk me home, Anna," she said, once they were in the comparative quiet of the lane.

"I prefer to, Mama. I'll be happier if I know you're safely home."

"You're a good girl," said Katerina, squeezing her daughter's arm.

"And you're a good mother."

"That Petro is so handsome," continued Katerina.

"He is. But you have nothing to fear. I won't leave you."

"I don't fear that at all. You'll have your own life, Anna, and I would be glad for you to have the happiness I had when I was younger."

Anna felt the tears gather and thought how far her mother had come. There was a time when she could not have spoken at all of Mikola, even as obliquely as she had just done, and she appreciated her mother giving, not only her own approval, but that of Anna's father, too. She knew he would have liked Petro's honesty and kindness. But she stopped her thoughts there. She would not have both of her parents at a large wedding and there was no point in dwelling on it. She had her mother, walking home after having braved a big social gathering and she had Petro coming to meet her, to walk her back for more dancing…she would be happy with that. It was more than she had thought she might have.

She settled Katerina carefully for the night and, leaving her cottage to return to the reception, she saw Petro's white shirt in the gathering dusk, waiting for her at her gate. As she rejoined him, she stroked her hand across his broad back and drew in the warm scent of him. He put his arm tightly around her waist and thus they returned to the dancing. Her happiness was only increased when she saw Vera pass them, dancing in the arms of Roman Shumenko.

The *starosta* was unusual in that he had reached his thirties without marrying and it was for this reason that he held the post of leader of the village. His fairness over the quotas of labourers sent to Germany had shown he was a good and just man. He had also arranged for all the men remaining in the village to be responsible for their ancestral lands. So while the Germans had quickly taken up where the Russians had left off, with the collectivisation of land as the most efficient means of production, Roman had followed their instructions in the most benign way to suit his neighbours. He had been responsible for smoothing the villagers' paths to growing enough food for themselves for the coming winter and so the popularity and respect he commanded had grown. And here he was, the same height as Vera, short brown hair smoothed back and lively blue eyes smiling into Vera's hazel ones.

Anna grinned at her friend, as they danced past one another, mouthing "Not a boy!" while Vera tried to look innocent.

The dancing and drinking continued through the night and Ivan's uncle, Danylo, did not resist the opportunity to drink deeply and dispense advice. He had his arm around his nephew's shoulders, breathing vodka-soaked philosophy into Ivan's ears, when Petro came to find refreshments for himself and Anna.

Danylo turned to look at Petro blearily and said, "Isn't that right, young man?"

Petro and Ivan raised their eyebrows at one another.

"I'm sorry. I didn't hear what you were saying," replied Petro.

"Dance with them and enjoy them while you can. Before they turn old and start nagging."

Petro laughed. "Yes, yes. Good advice."

"That's what I've been telling Ivan here. And you," he stabbed his forefinger into Petro's chest, "with that lovely Anna, you're the same."

Ivan laughed, pleased that Danylo's attention had found another victim, but Petro took pity on Ivan nevertheless. "Come on, Ivan. Let's dance with our lovely girls while we can."

They left Danylo swaying alone and beginning to look around for another conversationalist.

Much later, the bridesmaids and the grooms accompanied Sofia and Ivan to their marital home, singing raucously of love. Tonight, the couple would have the house to themselves. Anna and Vera deposited the plate, on which the wedding gifts of money had been placed, in the kitchen and then withdrew to renewed dancing, which would go on till dawn.

Chapter 11

On a hot and sunny afternoon, several days after the wedding, those youngsters who could, made their way down to the river. As usual, they chose the broad sweep of the flat valley bottom, where the lush grass created a perfect beach for swimmers and loungers alike. The sky was a flawless blue and the wooded hills on the opposite bank spoke of a deep shade, the peace of which was to be shattered by the joyous cries of the young, who could forget, briefly, that they would all soon be called to account. The younger boys leapt in and out of the water, showering any hapless victims, and the girls joined in the shrieking and splashing. Many of the young women, Anna among them, took off their skirts and blouses and stepped into the water in their shifts. They giggled and paused as the water lapped around their ankles and then their knees, their toes wriggling in the silt below. In ones and twos, they dived in to swim in the silky luxury of the river, washing away the dust of roads and fields.

Anna struck out and swam with powerful strokes, delighting in the strength of her muscles. She swam right across to the opposite bank, away from the play, enjoying the knowledge that she was a strong enough swimmer to cope with the current.

She swam back, smiling at the boisterous nonsense around her, retrieved her clothes and took them a little way along the bank, before spreading them on the ground beside Vera. Anna sat down on her skirt, squeezing the water from her long plait, the sun warming her arms and shoulders.

"Aren't you afraid of the current, Anna? It's very strong."

"It's alright as long as you know which route to take. I wouldn't swim lower down, near the bend."

"No. It's far too dangerous."

They looked up at the noisy cries.

"The boys are going to have a race."

"Can you see Vasilko?" asked Vera anxiously.

"Do you think he'll race, too?"

"Oh yes. He wouldn't be left out!"

They scanned the gathering boys for twelve-year-old Vasilko and when

Vera caught sight of him, she hurried over to him. Anna saw Petro had joined the swimmers and, as she rose to stand with the spectators, she felt proud of his wide shoulders. She did not have long to admire him before the competitors leapt into the water and began to swim across to the other side of the Dniester, where a stand of willows grew. Tradition dictated that they mount the bank, run around the trunk of the largest willow and swim back to the home shore further downriver, where the girls would be standing in a colourful row, cheering on their chosen heroes.

Petro was one of the first to race up the opposite bank, circle the tree and rush headlong into the water, where his stamina told on his opponents, as he swam for home with strong strokes. Anna, too, was cheering, girl again. She clapped as he emerged first, his golden curls a sparkling halo. He came across to her, grinning. "Still able to beat the littl'uns."

They walked back to her picnic spot, his wet arm around her shoulders, she smiling up into his face, a gaggle of small boys around their legs. He shook them off, whispering that he wanted to talk to Anna of love and they ran off groaning at the awful nature of being almost grown up.

He sat down on the grass beside Anna, leaning back on his elbows, grinning at the scene before him, the jostling mock fights, the flirting. He looked at Anna, her full lips turned up in a delighted smile, eyes shining and could not help stroking her shoulder. She returned his smile and blessed this moment of happiness.

"Anna! Anna!" shouted Vasilko, running up to her. "I did it, too! I crossed the river," and he threw himself down beside them.

"I'm sorry," called Vera, hurrying after him. "I tried to stop him from disturbing you, but he was desperate to tell you!"

Anna turned to the boy, whose hazel eyes were sparkling with pride and glee. Water dripped from his hair onto his narrow face and his thin chest rose and fell as he caught his breath. "That's wonderful. It shows how much stronger you're getting."

"I'm almost a man!" he exclaimed. "I might be able to beat you next year," he added, turning to Petro.

Petro laughed, too. "You'd be welcome, Vasilko. We need strong ones like you."

Anna and Vera smiled at one another, but their pleasure was tinged with sadness. Vera feared that her young brother might only grow up to be killed, while Anna…she could almost see Yuri beside his friend, delighting in the fun and competition of the race. Anna felt the lump in her throat as she thought of her brother. He would have loved Petro…

*

The days continued close and hot. The intense work of the harvest had been completed in a battle against the heat, but now that the wheat was safely in, everyone longed for the weather to break. It came one afternoon as Nina was returning home from an errand on the other side of the village. She had almost reached the first crossroads on the outskirts, when a deep rumble of thunder rolled up from behind her and seemed to lurch over her right shoulder. She was so startled that she leapt to her left, but the ominous noise was almost immediately followed by a flash of lightning, which lit up the field and the trees beyond in a stark spotlight. Nina's heart pounded in her chest. She was so far from home. It was almost two kilometres to her house and the thought of this made her young legs buckle under her as another roll of thunder growled its bass notes over her head.

She sank to her knees on the grass verge beside the dusty lane, trembling and beginning to sob. The lightning followed swiftly and Nina knew she must be in the centre of the storm. She curled forward on her knees and covered her head with her arms, hoping that if she could not see it, the storm would not be able to harm her. She felt pinned to the ground, her back terribly exposed to the twin blows of the thunder and the lightning. Her sobs became louder and she gave no more thought to where she was. She was alone in the world, and at the mercy of whatever the sky might do to her.

The next clatter of thunder seemed to rattle the earth beneath her, as if an angry god wanted to shake her off the surface of the planet and fling her into the outer darkness. It was followed by the shimmering rain, striking the dust of the road up into little puffs, until there were so many large drops that the whole road darkened with water. The rain struck Nina's back in malicious jabs as it pattered up and down her body, soaking through her thin summer dress. It became heavier and poured down in relentless rods, flattening Nina into the ground. Her sobs continued, but the rain poured down undeterred.

Anna, too, had been caught in the rain. She had walked out further than Nina, along the lane towards the shrine, to glean any remaining ears of corn in the fields. She had received her share of the harvest in payment for her work, but she had been at a loose end and decided a walk might do her good. However, once in the fields, alone, she had suddenly been struck by the memory of her father and Yuri. Her breath caught in her throat as she looked towards the spot where they had died, a spot which had less power to wound when she was busy with her work in a crowd of other villagers. But such a sense of loss had swept Anna that she had stood helpless with grief.

The thunder, when it arrived, had shocked her into action and she had tried to outrun it. She was hastening towards the village when the rain came, its force making her slow to a hurried walk. She almost missed Nina, the darkness of her soaked clothes camouflaging her against the earth, but as Anna drew closer to the small bulk, she realised it was a child crying. She hurried over and kneeling beside it, put a hand on its shoulder. "Are you hurt?"

The figure shook its head and as Anna lifted the child up towards her, she saw Nina's terrified face.

"Nina!" she cried as the girl recognised her saviour and leapt up, clinging to Anna with all four limbs. Anna held her close for a moment or two and then said, "We must find some shelter." She was calculating whether to take the girl to Anna's house which was nearer, or to her own home where Halia could be reassured. She tried to get up, but Nina continued to hold on to her like a limpet.

"Come, Nina. I'm going to take you home, but I can't carry you. You're too heavy." Again she tried to stand and this time succeeded, with Nina still clinging to her. "Let's try and run to the monument," but Nina was shaking so much that Anna had to carry her.

So with Nina's arms around her neck, her face hidden in Anna's shoulder, they staggered towards the monument. Anna gritted her teeth and counted her steps to encourage herself to keep going, but when they reached the left turning towards Nina's house, Anna put the child down, saying, "Nina, you have to help me. I can't carry you the whole way home. Do you think you can walk a little?"

Nina had stopped crying, but she still looked terrified. However, she nodded.

"Let's see if we can run together a bit," said Anna, "and then you'll be home sooner."

Holding hands tightly, they jogged through the driving rain, splashing through the puddles, depending on their knowledge of the road as they ran on blindly through the dark downpour. As they passed Marusia's house, Nina stumbled and Anna knew she would have to carry her the rest of the way home. She lifted the girl up again and half walking, half staggering, she reached Nina's gate.

Petro was coming down the path towards them and, flinging open the gate, he took Nina from Anna's arms and turned towards Halia who stood in the doorway. They hurried indoors and Petro drew Anna towards the lit stove and gave her a towel.

"Just hold Nina, please, Petro, while I get some dry clothes for these two," said Halia and she disappeared into what had been the girls' bedroom.

"She was terrified when I found her," said Anna.

"I can see. Are you alright?"

"Just wet." She moved towards Nina and stroked the girl's wet hair away from her face. "The storm was well underway…" Their eyes met.

"But knowing Nina, she would try to be brave," said Petro.

Halia returned with an armful of dry clothing. "Make yourself scarce, Petro, while these girls get dry."

While Halia tended to Nina, Anna changed into some old clothes belonging to the twins. When Petro returned, they were both sitting beside the stove and Halia was warming some soup for them.

"Will your mother be worried about you, Anna?" asked Halia.

"She can't go yet, Mama, it's still raining," said Petro.

"She might worry a little, but she'll probably think I've taken shelter somewhere." Anna looked about her. "I think I must have left my basket where I found Nina."

"We'll go and look for it later," said Petro.

Having eaten, Nina revived enough to look a little shame-faced, but as Anna retold their story, she held firmly to the belief that Anna had been a heroine in saving her. "I don't know what I'd have done if she hadn't come along," she announced. "Anna saved me."

"Of course she did," said Halia, "and we're very grateful to her."

The storm passed and, in the brightly washed landscape, Anna and Petro retrieved her basket from the roadside.

"Weren't we lucky to get the harvest in?"

"Oh yes. I'm very relieved to have got all the wheat in for Hitler."

Anna looked up sharply at Petro. "But we'll get our share, too?"

"Yes, but if we had kept all we grew, we could have sold some of it, instead of just surviving another winter."

Anna took his hand. "I didn't realise you felt as angry as this."

"I do, Anna. It seems that I haven't stopped labouring for someone since my father died. First it was the Poles, then the Bolsheviks and now the Fascists. It would be good to work for ourselves. Think how strong we could be, if we only had that to do."

Anna knew that, like all of the men in the village, Petro had resented being someone else's forced labour, but she could also see that he was being pushed too far. "I know it's hard," she said, "but this war isn't over yet. Who knows which way it will go."

"As it stands, we can only end up being the losers again. The Germans want this land as much as the Russians. We have to help ourselves more."

"But we're too small to fight them off," she said, her heart in her throat, knowing where his thoughts were turning.

"We have to try though. Look at how many of our young people have been taken away to work in Germany. I know my sisters went voluntarily, but that was in the beginning. No one wants to go, now that they know the truth." He could not stop himself from continuing. "And we thought we'd got our schools back, but we haven't. Four years! I'm sure German children get more than four years of education."

"Things might change."

"And they might not. There's talk of our boys rising up against the Nazis, and we know there will be reprisals. Did you know that further north in Volyn, they've razed whole villages?"

Anna looked shocked. "No, I didn't know it had got as bad as that."

"It has, Anna. We're in their way. They want our land, but not us, and as soon as Hitler has got time, he'll start wiping us out. Or at least, those of us he doesn't need." He stopped for a moment and then, almost as if he had suddenly remembered that she was not the enemy, he said, "Don't worry. I'm not going yet."

But you will, she thought. She guessed he would be struggling to balance his desire for a free country and the needs of Halia and Nina, but she realised it would only be a matter of time before he went to join the partisans. She felt almost annoyed at herself that she had not anticipated this conversation, but knew he had brooded while working so hard to bring in a heavy harvest, especially after last summer's destruction.

"If you go..." she began, "I'll help your mother keep an eye on Nina."

"Anna!" He stopped in the middle of the lane and kissed her, holding her close for a moment. "I know you will. But who will keep an eye on you?"

"You know I can do that perfectly well." She swallowed and made the leap. "I must stay here with Mama, but I will always be ready to do what you need me to do. I promise."

"I don't need you to promise. I know you. You'll always be the rock that others hold on to. And I will come back."

It seemed to Anna too short a time later, that she and Petro met at the memorial at dusk. It was a calm, still evening, the sky like milk in the gathering gloom. The geese and ducks waddled back to their roosts from the communal ponds and streams, their orderly files simultaneously comic and tender. The boys had already returned with the cows from the rich pastures by the river and, as they passed every gate, the herd diminished as each cow returned to the warmth of her own stall. Anna thought that only the human beings were dislocated from their routines and their homes; the livestock knew exactly where they belonged. Even the horses were sometimes left unhobbled, cropping the verges.

They turned from the memorial and walked slowly down the rough lane beside the stream, past the laundry stones and into the comforting depths of the wood. They reached the footbridge and walked to the flat rocks beside the Barish. They sat in their usual place and Anna leaned back on the rock to search for the stars above the canopy of the woods and, at the sight of her bare throat, Petro sighed deeply.

"What is it?" she asked, keeping her voice light.

"I'm going soon."

Anna felt the tears rise, but she held them back. She leaned forward and stroked his shoulder, then took him into her arms, breathing in the scent of his long curly hair as he laid his head on her breast. He passed his arms around her and held her tight. They held onto each other for a few moments longer, each fighting their sorrow and their fear. An owl hooted as Anna withdrew from his arms first. "When?"

"In the next few days."

"Do you know where to go?"

"Yes, I have a contact." He looked at her shame-faced, but in the same moment realised that she was offering him a contact with the Insurgent Army. His surprise was short-lived as he remembered how reticent Anna had been just before Marusia's departure. "You would have been able to find me one, wouldn't you?"

"Yes," she admitted, "but only because others were desperate."

"So I might meet Marusia again?"

"And Rachel."

His eyes widened. "You really know how to keep a secret!"

"I didn't know about Rachel for certain until they went. But I'd guessed."

He continued to stare at her as if he did not really know her. "You're marvellous! I thought I knew you, but you continue to surprise me."

"I'm sorry I couldn't tell you before."

"No, don't be. You did the right thing. Nina's right. You are a heroine."

She blushed. "No, I'm not. Don't forget, I know what it is to be desperate."

"I know you do and I'm sorry. You cope so well that sometimes I forget how harshly you've been treated."

"Don't feel sorry for me. I manage. But you help me, too."

"Even though I'm going away."

"Even so. I know you'll be doing something worthwhile."

"It's no boyish dream, Anna. You know I think we should fight back. I want to be ready for a free country which we've created ourselves, and I want to be part of this fight. You know what it says on the UPA flag – for liberty and a better life."

She looked at his handsome young face, shining with idealism and hope.

Why shouldn't he go and use his goodness in the best cause? "I know you do. And you're right – we shouldn't just allow others to trample over us."

He looked relieved, as if she had permitted him to take this terrible risk. "I was dreading telling you."

"There was no need. Just promise me that you'll tell me when you're going."

"I will," he vowed, breathing the words into the warmth of her neck. He slipped his hand under her blouse and stroked her warm, smooth back, committing her to memory, folding away the softness of her skin, the smell of her. He would keep these remembrances of her and later would unwrap them as talismans against the dark. She groaned softly as he kissed the hollow of her throat and she reached around his waist to tug his shirt free. She returned his kisses on the soft skin of his neck and breathed in the sweet smell of hay on him. Their hands explored the unknown other as they lay themselves down on the soft forest floor...

Later, they walked back up to the village, their arms around each other's waists, too full to speak, knowing that they were now more deeply committed than ever before, no longer sweethearts, but lovers.

Anna let herself into the house. Her mother appeared to sleep on, as Anna slipped off her blouse and skirt and slid under the quilt, where she lay, her heart in turmoil. She had avoided thinking about this moment, but she had known for months that Petro would have to leave one way or another. For as long as the conflict lasted, boys would go. Her stomach churned with anxiety – to join the UPA, the Ukrainian Insurgent Army, or *Ukrayinska Povstanska Armiya*. There could be no good outcome for the foreseeable future. If Petro was not killed in the fighting, he might be captured and tortured. Unless freedom for the country was secured, he would never be able to come back to the village. She realised that she felt not only enormous anxiety for him, but that she was grieving for their lost selves; the young couple who might have reared a family of their own. She had had so little time with him, and now? Her mind churned with unanswerable questions. Would she see him again? Her mother turned in her sleep, snorting as she rolled over. Anna knew she could not go with him, but perhaps she could help him. She turned on her side and closed her eyes, trying to relax, but already feeling hollow.

Her first thought on waking was, he is going. She did her morning chores automatically. She fed the hens, made the porridge for herself and her mother, swept the floor, watched by plump Murchik seated on the windowsill. Then she went out into the garden and hoed the vegetables. She kept their garden very efficiently. The food they grew would be needed to keep them alive in the winter, just as it had the previous year, so crops which could be hidden and stored were invaluable. The task was a mindless one, although Anna wished it was a day when she could have joined the hurly-burly of village activity, not only to see Petro, but to stop herself from thinking too much.

She concentrated on the beetroots, hoeing between the rows, breaking up the small green weeds. She looked up as she heard the chattering of her pair of magpies. At least, she thought of them as hers, nesting as they did each year in the walnut tree, which marked the corner of Anna's ground. Anna loved the swift flash of black and white plumage, their confident pouncing on any available food and she had watched the protective way they fed their young each year that they nested with her. She found their bold company and the intelligent way they eyed her work comforting, feeling that she could not be quite so alone, while these lovely birds frequented her garden. She would have to take in her ripened sunflower heads soon, before the birds got too many of the seeds. Anna always grew a row of them between the two parts of her garden, so they would smile at her in the morning as she came out of the cottage. By evening, they would be gazing at the woods across her vegetable garden.

She worked hard through the morning, moving on to the onions and potatoes. Her crops looked promising and she felt some satisfaction in her work. She returned to the house towards midday to eat with her mother and, as she walked up the path to their door, relaxed her shoulders and prepared a smile for Katerina.

Petro and Anna met again that evening and walked down into the darkening woods, their arms wound around each other's waists. They felt as if they were actors in a play they had had no hand in writing. The next scene was already written and they had only to go through the lines.

They reached the footbridge and turned towards their own secluded spot, but Anna did not go to sit on their rock as before, she turned into his arms instead. "So when are you going?"

"Tonight."

They seemed to hold themselves as still as the night around them, awkward with each other for the first time.

"I'm sorry…" he began, but Anna interrupted him.

"There's nothing for you to be sorry for. We've agreed you have to go."

"I will try to come back."

"I don't want you to take any risks coming here. If you can come, then do. But don't put yourself in danger."

They both thought about the difficulties he might face, returning to the village only at night, unable to risk friends knowing where he was, let alone those openly in favour of the German yoke. They held each other a little longer, thinking about the trials to come and the possibility of meeting secretly.

"Do what you can," she said at last. "I'll be waiting."

"I don't know how long it might be..."

"I know and we shouldn't worry about that now. Let's deal with one day at a time. All you need to know is that I love you and I'll be here. They can't take me as long as Mama is alive."

"Alright," he let out a long breath. "But I will come and find you when I can. I love you, Anna."

And then there were few words, as they took their leave of one another as lovers. Afterwards, as they returned to the village, they both seemed heavy with loss, even though still within touching distance. Anna stroked the rough cotton of Petro's shirt, feeling the warmth and strength of her lover's young body. She, like Petro, packed the sensation away like a miser, to take it out for comfort later when the loneliness became unbearable. They reached the memorial and he offered to walk her the rest of the way home, but she refused.

"Leave me here as normal," she cautioned, more adept at secrecy. They kissed briefly and turned away from one another.

Anna had no idea when or how he would go tonight, only that tomorrow, he would no longer be a member of the village. There would be no casual encounters in the fields, by the well, or by the river...and no more evening walks. She fought back the tears. This was what she had to deal with and crying would help neither of them. She made herself count her blessings as she had learned to do. He was alive, he was going to fight for their future, and they both had the energy of youth. That was an abundance of riches for which, she admonished herself, she must be grateful. But as she lay down to sleep, she did utter a prayer for him stepping out alone into the dark.

The days passed slowly for Anna as news of Petro's departure filtered out into the village. She continued all of her usual tasks and tried hard to maintain a cheerful demeanour. To those who asked outright where Petro had gone, she told the truth: "I don't know where he is..." and she confided in no one.

Her mother became quieter than ever and seemed to try to make even fewer demands on her dutiful daughter, although she found more opportunities to stroke her girl's arm as they passed one another in the house. When Anna did not leave the garden at dusk, but found herself a desultory task among the remaining flowers, her heart ached for Anna's troubles. Katerina knew that if Anna had had both parents, or neither, she would have been free to go, too. She called to Anna's silhouette across the darkening garden, "Come in now, child. It's getting cold."

Anna responded automatically. "Coming."

She entered their living room, made cosy by an evening fire and sat on the bench beneath the *kilim*-lined wall, where the cat swiftly found her lap. It purred and circled before sitting down to knead Anna's legs in an ecstasy of affection for the kind girl who had always spoilt him with milk.

"I thought we should do something with *Tato's* old shirts," Katerina began.

"What do you mean? They're too good to be cut up into rags."

"I know. I thought you might want to look through them and perhaps re-work the best one."

"Are you sure you don't mind me altering them?" asked Anna.

"No, of course not," replied her mother. "It's a waste if they're not re-used. Look, this one is very good." She drew out a shirt and held it up for Anna's inspection. "This one is almost new. I had not long made it for *Tato*…" The words hung in the air, the memory almost palpable in the warm room. "Take it, Anna, and do something useful with it." She passed the shirt to her daughter and then leaned across to kiss her forehead. "I think I'll get into bed now," she said, busying herself with her own clothes.

Anna held up the shirt to the light of the oil lamp and saw that while the shoulders would fit Petro, the girth was that of an older man and so she took up the task her mother had chosen for her lonely hands, unpicking the stitches of the side seams and thinking of her absent men as they might have been at this moment, her beloved father stroking her hair, her lover's smile.

Chapter 12

Anna worked energetically every day, approaching each task with vigour, trying to tire herself, so she would sleep. There were nights of blessed exhaustion, but there were also those when she woke suddenly, listening for a repetition of what had woken her. Sometimes she woke confused, wondering where the wave of loss had come from, until she recovered consciousness sufficiently to remember, "He's gone." But with the morning, she would chide herself.

The mist lay in the hollows and filled the river valley, announcing the onset of autumn, so Anna decided to carry out one of the season's most rewarding chores. "Mama, I'm going to pick mushrooms tomorrow morning. Would you like to come or shall I leave you with Murchik?"

"No, you leave us here, Anna. We'll be fine together."

Anna glanced at her mother, but, satisfied that she was simply unwilling to make the effort to walk to the woods, she laid her basket and knife aside ready for the morning.

"I should think Nina will find this autumn strange."

Anna looked at Katerina in surprise. "Yes, she will."

"Do you think she's too young to collect mushrooms alone?"

"She probably remembers where to go, but I'm not sure if Halia would like her going alone."

"Perhaps you should check…"

Anna walked up the lane to Petro's house, startled by her mother's greater empathy for Nina. She realised guiltily that she had been so engrossed in her own loss, that she had forgotten her promise to Petro regarding his young sister. She reached Petro's gate and let herself into the garden, which was as carefully maintained as her own. Halia had been working hard to prepare to feed herself and her remaining child that winter. She knocked on the door and it was flung open by a tousled looking Nina.

"Oh, it's you. Come in. Have you come to ask me to do something interesting?"

Anna smiled at Nina's perspicacity, and her honest revelation of her needs. "Yes, I have, as a matter of fact."

"What is it?"

"Let Anna into the house before you start pestering her," said Halia, coming forward, drying her hands on her apron. "Come in, Anna. You're very welcome," and she kissed Anna's cheek in greeting. Anna felt a quick warmth at Halia's acceptance of her.

"Well?" repeated Nina.

"I wondered if Nina would like to gather mushrooms with me tomorrow?" Anna addressed her question to Halia.

"Yes, I would. Can I go, Mama?"

"That is, if you hadn't already planned to go together…"

"No, we hadn't, Anna. I'd like to go, but there's so much to do. It would be a great help if Nina could go with you. She tells me she's a very good gatherer of mushrooms," added Halia with a wry smile.

"Then we should return with a good harvest. I'll call for you early tomorrow," she warned Nina.

"I know. I'll be ready."

They set off in good time the following morning, armed with their knives and baskets, and their knowledge of where to find thick clumps of *pidpenky* on the stumps of trees, sometimes following the drifts of pale brown caps to where the scattered spores had taken them. Nina's picking was often erratic, but Anna followed her, patiently completing the gathering. Their baskets filled steadily as the morning sun broke through the mist.

"We'll just do this section, shall we," suggested Anna, "and then we'll make our way back."

"Can we do the same tomorrow?"

"Yes, let's. There are a couple of really good places which we haven't tried."

As they paused in their work, they looked across to where the hillside fell away among the trees, busy shedding their golden leaves. Anna felt overwhelmed by the transient beauty all around her. Slivers of topaz spiralled and floated between dark bronze trunks painted copper by the sunlight. The layers of trees and their individual dramas went on as far as the eye could see. The lemon leaves of the silver birches shimmered and fell, lightly as butterflies. The grand serrated ovals of the sweet chestnuts made a more regal journey to the ground, adding to the carpet of damp red and brown leaves, which exuded a strong scent of delicious decay. The whole wood seemed to be full of precious light as the spaces broadened between the trunks where the undergrowth had died back.

Nina's hand crept into Anna's. "Do you miss him, too?"

"I do. Very much." She squeezed Nina's fingers, resolving not to forget the girl's needs in future. She also gave a thought for Halia, for whom the house must often be unbearably quiet.

142

Anna was a little late shutting up her hens for the night. She stepped down the path to the pen, where her hens had been busy all day, and counted them into the hen-house, closing the door securely on this precious supply of food. As she turned to go back to the house, she noticed a loose pole from her fence lying in the grass. Puzzled, she picked it up. There had been no one but herself in the garden that day. Anna looked at the piece of wood again. It could not have fallen from its supports and she was certain she had not moved it. She reached out to touch the fence and there was a movement in the shrubs beyond. Her heart leapt with fear, so she raised the pole to defend herself, but heard a low voice utter her name: "Anna…"

She thought her heart would burst out of her chest. Despite her shocked state, she looked around quickly to check no one was passing her garden along the lane.

"Wait," she murmured. "I'll be back."

She hurried into the house and picked up her shawl. "I'm going for a walk, Mama," she said, relieved to see her mother making herself comfortable in bed. "I'll be back later. Don't worry." She kissed her mother's cheek and left the house. She walked to the bottom of her vegetable garden as if taking the air and when she reached the corner, she slipped out between the fence and the hedge. A hand reached for hers and she and Petro hurried along the path at the edge of the field across to the cemetery, to the derelict mausoleum of the Polish *Pan*, who had once ruled the region. They went around to the darkest side of the building, where it was sheltered and overgrown, and at last were able to embrace, their movements flurried and urgent.

Later, as they sat in the moonlight, they shared their news.

"Hrichko sends his greetings," began Petro, with a half-smile.

"I'm so glad. How is he?"

"Very well…considering the life. And full of energy."

"Good."

"He was sent to meet Marusia and Rachel, you know."

"Was he? He would have enjoyed that."

Petro kissed her forehead. "How many more secrets, Anna?"

"Oh that's pretty much it." She paused. "Your mother and Nina seem well. Nina and I have been mushrooming."

"I feel guilty about leaving them," he said, thinking of the irony of "the mushroom girl" and his noisy little sister keeping each other company.

"I don't think you need to feel guilty. They miss you, of course, but your mother seems to have everything under control."

He took her hand. "I'm not allowed to tell you where I'm based at the moment, nor where I'm going…I'm to be sent southwards for training very soon. I might not see you for some months."

Anna held in her sigh. "I hope it goes well."

"I know it's hard for you…to be left behind."

"It's hard for all of us."

"There is something you could do…" Petro hesitated. "We're always short of food. Do you think you could put something together?"

"Now?"

"It would be good to take something back. But I was told to ask you if you'd be willing to bring food to us on a more regular basis."

"Of course. I'll try. What does 'regular' mean?"

"Every couple of weeks…" he suggested.

"There are some people I could ask, but you know it will get harder during the winter."

"I know. Do what you can. There are others who help us, too. And there are only about a dozen of us in this group at the moment."

"Alright. I'll get you some things to take back tonight, but I'll give some more thought to future supplies. How will I get them to you?"

He looked a little embarrassed. "Hrichko will come a week from now."

"And where should I meet him? We should vary our meeting places."

"Not here then?"

"No. Tell him to meet me where I left him."

Petro smiled. "Good."

"And then I can arrange the next one with him." Anna stroked Petro's hand. "Can I tell your mother you're well?"

"Yes. Tell her I was only here briefly. I don't know how well Nina would cope with me visiting and then leaving again."

"You're right. She might find it very hard." Anna sat quietly for a moment. "And Marusia's parents?"

"Yes. She sends her love to them. Do tell them not to worry. They're going to begin their proper nursing training soon. It seems to me that she and Rachel are thriving on the excitement."

Anna put from her mind the reasons why the UPA would need trained nurses and said instead, "Good. I might be able to get help with the food from Maria and Andriy. I'll try anyway."

There was the rustle of a breeze through the trees and Anna shivered a little. "You'd better wait here while I go and get you some food."

"Don't worry if you can't spare much this time."

Anna slipped among the shadows back to the cottage. She ran through her winter stores in her mind, as she hurried home and decided on salamis and root vegetables, adding, at the last moment, some of her jam and the last of the baked bread. She bundled the items into a clean sack and crept out to rejoin Petro.

They took their leave of one another almost as soon as she returned, holding one another tightly.

"Take care of yourself, even in training."

"You, too. I know I don't have to tell you how to be discreet, but be especially careful of who knows what you're doing."

"I'll be careful."

"I'll get in touch with you whenever I can."

"I know."

With a final embrace, they made themselves turn away to their own paths.

The following morning, Anna walked to Petro's house. She knew Halia would be relieved that her son was safe, but she might be hurt that he had not been to see her. Nina, as ever, was delighted to see Anna and, after some preliminary chatter, was sent to let out the hens. When the girl had gone, Halia turned to Anna, "So what is it, Anna?"

Anna blushed a little. "I saw Petro last night, but I wasn't sure whether to tell you in front of Nina."

"That was thoughtful of you. I think Nina would like to have news of her brother and it might help her to be more grown up."

"Shall I tell the whole story when she comes back?"

"Yes, please."

They waited a few moments until Nina returned.

As soon as she came through the cottage door, she glanced at the two women. "What's wrong?"

"Nothing's wrong," replied her mother. "Anna saw Petro last night and we were waiting for you, so she could tell us all about it."

Nina stared at Anna. "Why didn't he come here?"

"He came to my house after dark to ask me to help with supplies for his group. He came secretly, Nina, to the field at the end of my garden."

"Which woods had he come from?" asked Halia.

"From beyond the Barish. He didn't tell me exactly where."

"There you are then, Nina," said Halia. "It would have been too dangerous for him to come here through the village."

Nina nodded sadly. "I know, Mama. But I would like to have seen him."

"So would I, but his safety is more important than what we want. Now let's listen to what Anna has to say."

Anna described much of her meeting with Petro.

Nina remained silent throughout Anna's recital, only asking at the end, "So we won't see him through the winter, while he's in training?"

"No," said Anna, "but he wants us to help provide food for his group."

"And that's something we can do," said Halia. "Can't we, Nina?"

"Yes. I'll pick more mushrooms for them."

Anna and Halia could not help smiling at this most indulged youngest child.

"But we must be careful to keep all of this secret," cautioned Anna, wondering how well Nina might be able to control her impetuous nature.

"That's right," agreed Halia. "Nina, you can't speak to anyone of this, except me or Anna. Do you understand?"

The girl nodded.

"I'm serious, Nina. If the Nazis find out that we're helping our boys, they'll shoot you, me and Anna, and probably Anna's mother, too."

Nina nodded again, more solemnly this time. "But can I talk to you two about him?" she asked, the tears rising in her eyes.

"Of course," said Halia, taking her girl in her arms. "Of course you can."

Anna, too, felt the tears rise and joined Halia and Nina in their embrace, the three women who loved him best, mourning Petro's absence.

Later, Anna called at Marusia's, thinking that, in future, she would not link these two visits. Maria was gathering leeks from her vegetable plot in the cold air. She straightened up from her work. "Good morning, Anna."

"Good morning. I've brought you something for your winter garden," she said approaching Maria. "It's some of my good garlic."

Maria looked at Anna rather than the proffered cloves and said, "Let's go inside and have some tea to warm us up."

They entered the cottage and Anna felt her friend's absence sharply.

"Sit down, Anna."

"Will you sit down, too?"

Maria paled and sat down opposite Anna.

"It's alright." Anna smiled. "I've had news of Marusia. She's well."

"Oh, thank God!" Maria gripped Anna's hand and tears of relief poured down her cheeks.

"I can't tell you how I know," continued Anna, "but I can tell you my source is completely reliable. She's well and sends her love to you and her father and sisters. In fact, they're both well."

Maria nodded, unable to speak, as Anna talked of the nursing skills they were to be taught and then turned to the question of food.

"I'll let you have what I can in the next few days," said Maria. "We'll have trouble stopping Andriy from sending everything we have."

"Tell him they're going for training soon and the group left behind will be small."

"I will, but it won't make any difference."

"Will you tell the girls?"

"Oh yes. They'll be glad to know she's safe."

"How are they?"

"They seem fine. Oksana has accepted the changes more quickly than her father and I have."

"Perhaps because there've been so many young people leaving the village."

"Yes, and things were much more fraught over the winter, especially for Odarka. She's still only eleven."

"I can imagine how terrifying that time must have been."

"They've become such serious girls, though. They've had to grow up too quickly."

"That's true. There are so many who've had to do that."

"Oh Anna, of course you did, too..." said Maria putting her hand on Anna's arm.

"Yes, I did, although I wasn't thinking of myself. It's hard on all of us." She rose from the table. "I'll leave you the garlic anyway."

"Thank you, and I'll see you soon with our contribution. Andriy and I will discuss the best way to get it to you."

"Thank you."

Anna felt a return of the gloom which had threatened to overwhelm her earlier that morning. She missed her friends, but more than that, she knew Petro had been right about the hardening of German attitudes and she felt sure that a greater struggle was yet to come.

As the autumn days darkened into winter, Anna not only missed Petro, but realised she was seeing very little of Vera. She missed their intuitive conversations, so late one afternoon, she went along to the Reading Room, where she had heard that Vera could be found. As she entered the hall, she could see Vera's dark head in a pool of light, bent over an account book in the office. Anna made her way over to the office doorway and peered in, tapping on the door frame as she did so. Vera looked up, her eyes full of the concentration of her work.

"I'm sorry," said Anna. "Did I disturb you?"

"No," replied Vera and then shaking herself, "no, Anna. What can I do for you?"

Anna smiled. "Be available for some conversation."

Vera glanced up to her left and moving forward slightly, Anna saw Roman Shumenko standing at the bookcase, an open volume in his hands. He turned to look at Anna. "I'm sorry. Have I been depriving you of your friend?" His tone was warm and teasing, making Anna feel childish, but she stood her ground.

"Yes, I think you have. I haven't seen her for ages."

"Then we must change that immediately," he said with a twinkle in his eye. He came forward and picking up Vera's jacket from the back of her chair, said, "Come along, Vera. Finish early for once and catch up on the gossip with Anna."

Both women blushed, Vera as Roman helped her into her jacket, and Anna at the loftiness in his manner.

"I wouldn't want to take Vera from her work."

"I'm only teasing," he smiled. "She works too hard and deserves to finish early. Vera's such a help to me that I've been monopolising her."

Vera smiled at Roman's compliments and, in the moment that their eyes met, Anna understood that they not only loved one another, but had talked of their feelings, too. She stepped out of the office, turning away to cross the hall in order to give them some brief privacy. She heard Vera's footsteps following her across the bare boards and Roman calling goodnight to them both. They shivered a little as they went out into the cold and Vera linked arms with Anna.

Anna turned to speak to Vera, but, as the girls' eyes met, they burst into peals of laughter.

"No boy for you then!"

Vera's eyes sparkled. "No. I told you I didn't want one!" and they giggled again.

"How long…" began Anna and they both gave the answer simultaneously. "Since the wedding!"

Anna squeezed Vera's arm. "I'm so pleased for you."

"So am I," said Vera. "But there's to be no wedding for us."

"Why not? There's nothing to stop you."

"He won't have me become a hostage."

"Ah."

"We're not going to let it be a problem."

"How can you do that?" asked Anna, thinking of the difficulty of a partnership outside marriage in such a village as theirs.

"We can love one another and work together. I'm not worried, Anna. Who knows what the future might bring."

"But…"

"I know. He's a lot older than me, so we have less time than most."

"I don't know whether that's your common sense or your courage speaking. But I think you're brave to love him."

"Oh I'm not. You know bravery has nothing to do with love."

Anna glanced at her friend.

"Petro's gone. Have you stopped loving him because it's become harder?"

Anna shook her head.

"Of course you haven't. How could you? We all find our paths as best we can."

"We do."

"So how have you been managing without him?" Vera looked in Anna's face. "By working yourself into exhaustion, while keeping an eye on everyone else!"

"You know I find it easier that way. If I take care of those who depend on me, I feel less sorry for myself." Anna was thoughtful for a moment. "And he's doing a good thing. I couldn't possibly complain."

"No, but that doesn't mean you don't miss him."

"No, it doesn't. But we made our promises, too…and I know he'll keep them."

"Yes, he will."

Anna felt her tears threatening again so shaking herself, she returned to teasing her friend. "Such a man as Roman!"

Vera smiled. "Yes, such a man…"

Anna had received substantial contributions of food during the days leading up to her meeting with Hrichko. She realised that there would be too much for the boy to carry, so she selected a sackful of useful items, knowing she would have to talk to him about logistics. On the appointed night, she waited until Katerina was asleep and then she crept from the house. There was not a sound from her door, because she had treated the hinges, the latch and bolt with grease. She collected the sack from its hiding place behind the woodpile and slid through the new gap she had made in her fence in the darkest corner behind the cottage. She walked quickly down the path alongside the hedgerow with its bare hazelnut bushes and into the woods, where she slipped among the trees to the Barish. She reached the spot where she had waited so anxiously with Hrichko, almost two years previously and leaned against a tree to make herself a little less visible to the casual eye.

She had not waited long when she felt a cold hand slip into hers. She turned and found herself reflecting Hrichko's delighted grin.

Anna hugged him. "I'm so glad to see you," she whispered.

"Me, too. I wanted to surprise you. You didn't hear me coming, did you?"

"Not a sound."

"I've been practising."

"I can tell. You've got good at it."

Hrichko grinned more widely and then seemed to remember himself. "And I wanted to thank you."

"Seeing you well is thanks enough." Anna lifted the sack towards him. "I'm a bit worried about this. I don't know how much food to bring or when. I'm not sure how much you can carry. And I don't know how often we'll be able to do it."

"I know."

"Can you talk to someone? Perhaps it would be better if I delivered it somewhere nearer for you."

"I don't know, but I think you're right."

"See what they say and let me know."

"I will."

"I don't want to endanger you," said Anna. "And I think doing it this way, puts us both at risk. I'm already taking a risk, so it doesn't matter if I meet you here, or further away. But it does matter to you." She paused. "Tell them I want to help, Hrichko."

"I'll tell them." There was a rustling of leaves on the ground, whether from a breath of wind or footsteps was difficult to discern. "I'd better go."

"Good luck," whispered Anna as they parted.

Anna mounted the path to the cottage, and looked up towards the night sky. She felt relieved she had made the decision to help the insurgents. Petro was right. They could not be slaves forever.

Chapter 13

Anna hurried home from Buchach on foot. She pushed back her headscarf and pulled it from her neck to wipe the sweat off her face. She moderated the pace of her walk and tried to slow her breathing. Her concentration on the physical seemed to calm her flurried mind, which was full of violent impressions and wild conjectures. She had gone to Buchach market for supplies, taking some of her own produce for barter. She had hoped for the opportunity to buy some sugar and perhaps exchange a little gossip. She had not bargained for the public execution of five partisans.

As soon as she had arrived in the town, she had realised that something was different. At the Militia post, there had been half a dozen soldiers posted instead of the usual two, and they had been accompanied by Alsatian dogs, ready to obey their masters' commands with their teeth. The town had been more crowded than usual, even for a market day, and as Anna had approached the centre, she had seen a wooden structure, which had struck cold into her heart. A platform stood between two tripods, with a horizontal pole about three metres above. The platform itself did not seem secure, as it lay loose across a couple of sawhorses. As Anna stared at the structure, hoping against hope that its purpose was not what she dreaded, a German infantryman mounted the platform and began to fling several ropes over the horizontal pole. Then he looped and allowed the nooses to dangle empty.

She turned to others in the gathering crowd. "Who…"

"Partisans!"

Anna swallowed and turned again to look at the platform. Her heart was pounding so hard that she thought she might fall to the ground under its hammer. She felt someone take her arm firmly and looking around, saw an aged *babushka*, her scarf tied tightly around her wrinkled face, and heard her say, "Calm yourself."

Anna stared at the woman.

"They'll think you know the victims. Straighten your face."

Anna seemed to come to her senses. She knew she must present a bland expression and that she must control herself. But the anguish she felt was almost overwhelming. She felt her sight darken, as the band of tension tightened around her skull. Nevertheless, she took the old woman's advice and breathed more deeply, trying to flatten her body's reactions. She felt herself begin to relax and, as she stood a little straighter, the old woman patted her arm. "Good girl."

They waited in silence like the rest of the gathering crowd. It did not occur to Anna to leave. She had to know who was to be hung. She did not have long to wait. Helmeted soldiers marched five young men out at gunpoint. All were bareheaded. None wore any kind of uniform or insignia. But the crowd knew well enough who they were – members of the Ukrainian Insurgent Army, the UPA. The oldest of them might have been thirty, while the youngest looked no more than eighteen. They stepped up onto the unstable platform and stood quietly, their hands at their sides, while the nooses were placed around their necks.

The officer in charge addressed the crowd. "For the crime of attacking a collection point and taking the labourers away from their dutiful service to the Fatherland, these men will die. *Heil Hitler!*" He turned to warn his men, "*Achtung!*"

The prisoners looked out at the gathered crowd and began to sing the national anthem. "*Shche ne vmerla Ukraina…*"

The *Stabsfeldwebel* gestured to the waiting infantrymen. The platform was swiftly tilted forward and the men's feet slid from under them, leaving them dangling from the nooses, their patriotism choked off.

The suddenness of motion from life to death seemed to choke Anna, too, but her guardian gripped her arm, saying, "Quietly, quietly…"

Anna reached for some control of herself, telling herself over and over, "It wasn't him. It wasn't Petro."

As the crowd began to disperse, there was a hubbub and Anna overheard some of the resentful muttering that Hitler had given his officers in Halychyna the power to perform executions without trial.

"I must go home," Anna murmured, turning to the old woman, who still held her by the arm.

"Go then, but be careful."

Anna nodded and turned south, towards home. She walked through the quietening streets and passed unmolested through the Militia post.

The long walk calmed her. She no longer felt the need to scream or run, but she felt anger replacing the panic. So they were determined then. The Nazis had no sympathy for her countrymen's desire for independence. They were simply pawns in the game being played out between two evil giants. Well then, let them reap what they had sown. They had to be defeated and driven out, as surely as those occupiers who had preceded them. Anna's gait became a march as she worked through the logic of refusing to be a victim again. She welcomed the role of active resistance and looked forward to her next meeting with Hrichko.

That night, Anna woke suddenly with the vision of five dangling bodies before her. She lay completely still and breathed evenly until her heart slowed its racing. She examined the self who, twice in one day, had lost control to fear. She had buried her father and her brother with her own hands. She had cared for and protected her broken mother for almost three years... Now she felt both curiosity and shame. Why was she losing control of herself in this way? Surely her love for Petro could not have weakened her? Anna admonished herself. She had known when Petro left that he might be embracing an early death, but she realised that, for her at least, that possibility had been theoretical. Seeing those young men today had startled her into reality. She thought again of Boris's death, which had evoked her sympathy, but had not shocked her as today's events had. When Boris was shot, her only thought had been to protect her distraught mother.

Anna remembered Vera's words, that she coped by caring for others. Then that would have to be the road she would take. She would continue to care for Katerina and she would give more time to Halia and Nina, while helping to supply the partisans...and she would try to be prepared for the fact that Petro's death would probably be untimely. As she turned onto her side, she resolved to love him for any moments she might still have with him. She hoped that he would withstand the conflict, but she knew she would have to be strong. There was no other way forward.

Anna waited motionless among the dark pines for Hrichko. She concentrated on the sounds beyond their soughing, but could hear nothing. The boy approached her silently again on the forgiving quiet of the pine needles, so that Anna's first awareness of him was the touch of his cold hand on her wrist. She turned to him and picked up the sack of food, as he jerked his head in an instruction to follow him.

He led her towards the Barish, where they crossed the wooden footbridge and then passed the scattered houses in the hollow of the valley on its far bank, before regaining the cover of the trees towards the west. Anna felt her heart constrict when she realised they would pass close by the mass grave of Rachel's people and hoped fervently that the insurgent camp was not near this spot. But they continued through the forest and she offered up a prayer for the souls of the dead.

Half an hour later, Hrichko put out his arm to warn Anna to stop. He hooted a signal and receiving a reply, gestured to her to move forward. They walked at a measured pace and Anna still could not see their destination, until, abruptly, she found herself face to face with a man in his thirties, wearing a khaki jacket and his trousers tucked into his boots. His cap seemed to be from the Red Army, but its insignia had been replaced with a *tryzub*. Was he a deserter then? He was old enough to be one of those forcibly signed up by the Bolsheviks before the Germans had come. Whatever he had been, his grim face told her that now he was determined to do whatever it took to gain independence for his country.

"This is Anna," Hrichko began.

"I can see. Take that to the quartermaster," he said, gesturing at Anna's sack.

Hrichko picked up the supplies and hurried away.

Anna waited for the man to speak.

"So you want to help."

"Yes, I do," she replied, determined not to be cowed by his cold attitude.

"This isn't a game."

"I know that."

"Nor can you decide that you've had enough after a week or two."

Anna remained silent.

"Do you understand?"

"Yes. Do you want my credentials?"

"No. Others have vouched for you."

"Then you must tell me what you need from me."

"At the moment, food. You'll be told if that changes."

"Alright," she said and after a moment's pause, "I suppose you know about the executions in Buchach."

"Yes, we do." He seemed to examine her again and then he gave a low whistle. Two men appeared from among the trees within several feet of Anna. "These are our witnesses," he said.

Anna stared at him and then at the two men, wondering, and fearing, what they might be about to witness.

"Are you willing to take the oath?" he asked her.

She looked about her.

"Well?"

"Yes. Yes, of course."

"Then repeat after me. I promise to attain a Ukrainian state or die in battle for it."

Anna blinked at him and repeated the oath. The suddenness of her initiation should not have surprised her, but in any case, she was willing.

The witnesses melted away after hearing her repeat the oath and the man said, "Come back in a week's time with more supplies."

She nodded, unwilling to ask for clarification of what they might need. She knew the lives the insurgents had chosen were difficult and dangerous and she knew everyone had a tragic tale to tell, but she still felt alienated by this man's antagonism. However, it would not prevent her from playing her part. She turned to go and was surprised to hear him say, "Take care."

"I will."

"Orlan," he said quietly.

She nodded. "Orlan," and took the trail eastwards and home. As she walked, she realised that the position they had chosen was in an ox-bow of the Dniester, so their part of the forest was protected on three sides by the mighty river. But she also conceded to herself that it could trap them, too.

Anna walked along the edge of the field above the tree line and was heartened to see the silver birches taking on a dusky pink veil over their outspread skeletal arms. It was too soon to look for buds, but the insubstantial promise of spring was there. The clouds reflected the pink hues of the setting sun, despite the moon already being visible and sailing above the trees. She felt a stirring of happiness at the thought of the end of winter and wondered what spring and summer might bring now that the Germans had been defeated at Stalingrad and wondered, too, when Petro might return. Would 1943 bring them closer to a successful resolution for Western Ukraine, or would they still be an occupied country this time next year? Whatever might come, she thought she should not deny the hope she felt.

She had spent the winter working by day to care for herself and Katerina, punctuating the nights with the life she would have chosen if she could. She would wait till her mother's head nodded forward onto her chest and then she helped her from her seat by the stove to their shared bed, the down-filled quilt tucked in around her bony shoulders. Extinguishing the light and collecting the hidden sack of food, Anna would creep from the house. Whether there was a moon or not, she could easily find her way, although she preferred the moonless nights, which gave her a greater illusion of safety. Recently the growing group she had been helping to supply had moved to the deeper woods on the southern bank of the Dniester and Anna had had to become adept at borrowing the fishermen's coracles to cross the river.

She slipped through her fence into the field and down the path past the wrought-iron fence, protecting the derelict mausoleum and its dead inhabitants, and across the quarry. She climbed its shallow bowl and, crouching, ran over its lip towards the steep path down to the river, where she was finally able to take advantage of the protection of the trees. She paused to listen. Only the whisper of a breeze disturbed the silence, but she could hear the persistent thump of her blood. If she was seen at this hour… The path led down, steeply at first, and then levelled out into more marshy ground as she made for the coracle. No one would know that she had used it, for she intended to return it well before dawn. The boat lay upturned, but she was strong from her work in the fields and she easily manoeuvred it into the water, flinging in her sack and stepping in at the last moment. She had to row hard against the current, but reached the opposite bank, as she had intended, about half a kilometre further downstream.

Her routine helped to sustain her on the eastern bank of the river. She pulled in the boat and hid it, took the sack of bread and potatoes, butter and *kovbasa* over her shoulder, and began the climb up the wooded bank, the group of silver birches at the top of the cliffside a beacon for her. Halfway up she paused, held her breath and listened. Nothing stirred, so she continued up to the birches, where a low hoot stopped her in her tracks. She waited, expecting to be invisibly checked, but was astonished to feel a large hand clamp itself over her mouth. She knew better than to scream or struggle and waited the long moment until the man's arms encircled her body and a quiet kiss was planted on her bare neck. She turned, not daring to breathe and, recognising his beloved face, relaxed against Petro's body. They held one another tightly for a few moments and then, in silence, continued deeper into the trees to the camp.

As Petro escorted her through the checkpoints, she barely saw the guards, posted at intervals, to protect their comrades seated around the fire. The vast majority of the group were busy about their disruptive night time raids on enemy vehicles and supply lines. The quartermaster checked Anna's latest contribution to the stores, as she brought Orlan and the others up-to-date on activity in and around the village, although there was much they already knew.

Later, as Petro took her back towards the river, she examined him more closely. His hair had been neatly cut, although a stray curl flopped over onto his forehead beneath his cap, his *petliurivka* with its *tryzub*. He wore a greatcoat from which the Nazi insignia had been unstitched and now bore the badge of a rifleman. She felt the cold of the night and stroked his sleeve. "I'm glad you've got a good coat to keep you warm."

"Most of us have one now. It was part of our booty."

"Booty?"

"A supply train."

Anna listened as he told her the tale of his first real action…

Petro had completed ten weeks of training. He had spent some time with the squad closest to his village, ranging more widely with the nearest platoon, and even further afield with the one hundred and twenty insurgents in his company. In his first encounter with the enemy, it was deemed sufficient by their leaders to send a platoon to ambush one of the many German supply trains heading for the Eastern Front. These trains usually travelled within sight of at least one other for greater security, but as the partisans prepared to go into action, they received intelligence of a solitary train. German personnel were so far stretched running their railways, that they had to employ locals, too, and, in this case, the information for Petro's platoon came from a nationalist insider.

As they prepared to move out, Orlan and the other two squad leaders assigned tasks to their own men. They were to be accompanied by horses and carts borrowed from sympathetic villagers.

Orlan glanced at the skinny thirteen-year-old boy, who was watching him longingly. "Hrichko, you can come with us, but you must stay with the horses."

"Can't I help in the action?"

"No. You haven't got a gun."

"I could win one tonight."

"No. If you look after the horses well, I'll get you a gun."

The boy nodded, trying not to be too disappointed and trying to comfort himself with the thought that after this night's work, he might be allowed a more adult role.

Orlan turned to Petro. "I want you to accompany Yakiv and Dmitro in setting the charges on the lines. I know you've done it in training, and I want you to do it tonight."

Petro nodded.

Orlan continued appointing tasks until the thirty-odd men each knew what he had to do. They were almost all armed, albeit with an odd mixture of weapons handed down from conflicts as old as the First World War and with more recently acquired armaments. Everyone hoped for a significant increase of weapons and ammunition from this night's foray.

As the men turned to depart, Petro murmured to Hrichko, "You've got a big responsibility tonight. Without you, we wouldn't be able to move any goods."

Hrichko tried to smile and Petro slapped his shoulder. "Do your best."

"I will."

They set off in small groups just after dusk, their rendezvous just above the point where the train line was edged by woods on either side. The Germans had cleared a three hundred metre border on each side of the main supply lines, but since there had been few partisan attacks in this area, the woods came within fifty metres of the line, enabling the men to wait under cover. As they reached their destination, Hrichko and the other boys tucked themselves and the carts under the trees beside the road. The men deployed themselves on both sides of the line and Petro and the two explosives experts stepped up to blow the track.

Orlan was right that Petro had been shown how to lay a charge, but that was under supervision and with no pressure of an actual attack. He felt nervous as Yakiv took out the dynamite and fuse wire from his knapsack, but as soon as he was handed the materials, with a "Here you go, boy!" he found his hands were steady. He chose his point well, placing the charge tightly where the rail was pinned to the ground, and then he rolled away the fuse wire. Yakiv and Dmitro watched him and followed him into the trees to allow Petro to blow the line.

The thump of the explosion was felt by the waiting men. The horses flinched and shifted nervously, but Hrichko and the other boys soothed them again.

Yakiv and Dmitro went to inspect Petro's work. There was a satisfying gap in the long straight section of line which might invite the train driver to go at some speed. Petro and his colleagues cleared away some of the debris, so that the driver would not have too much advance warning of danger. And then they waited.

The night was bright with a clear sky and a gibbous moon. Although crisp, it was not cripplingly cold. The men hunkered down, some smoking, others merely waiting until the silence was broken by the rhythmical thunking of an approaching train. The men became alert as the train rattled along the straight towards them. The locomotive engine was in front, another suggestion that no attack was anticipated. The engines could be protected mid-train in more dangerous regions, but Orlan's insurgents were not expected. As the train hit the damaged part of the line, there was a terrible squealing of metal against metal as first the locomotive was derailed, and then the cargo-carrying trucks followed suit.

The attackers waited for the train to come to a halt and then opened fire with the two machineguns they had, firing at the Nazis protecting the roof of the train. Then they blasted open the doors of the trucks which had remained intact, killing each of the guards. They took a quick inventory of goods to prioritise what they would seize and reported back to Orlan and the other two squad leaders, who deployed the men to gather what was most urgently needed. They were in luck. The train had been carrying munitions, but had also been carrying quantities of greatcoats, blankets, tents, boots and other items necessary for German soldiers fighting the Russians much further east.

Meanwhile, Hrichko waited, quietening the horses until the shots became less frequent, then he and the others led them and their carts to the trainline.

Yakiv and Petro approached the crippled train together. "Stay close, young'un," muttered the older man and Petro felt grateful for his perception. He was both excited and afraid, his stomach churning. He was acutely conscious of his exposed chest and head, offering inviting targets. Both men were ready to fire shots at the guards as they slid back the door of a truck. They walked forward and Yakiv hopped into the truck. He glanced around the interior and nodded to Petro, who also now entered the dark space. "Let's get rid of these." He rolled the German corpses aside and then went to check the crates stacked in neat piles. "These are worth taking," he said. "Looks like grenades."

They began to drag the crates to the entrance and then Petro lowered them to Yakiv, who had jumped down onto the track and was gesticulating to one of the boys approaching with a wagon. They were joined by a couple more pairs of hands and they made swift work of unloading the truck.

As their wagon filled up, Yakiv called, "That'll do." He turned to Petro, "Strip those two of anything useful, including their uniforms and their boots."

Petro was startled, but as he turned towards the corpses, he made himself ignore their faces and he remembered their insignia. They were the enemy carrying valuable arms, so he took their Mauser pistols and the holsters, too, rolling the dead men back and forth to undo the buckles. He picked up their rifles and ammunition belts and laid this part of his haul on one side. He forced himself to pull off their boots, ignoring the intimacy of their feet in badly fitting socks and thinking only of boys like Hrichko, who had no boots. Some of the partisans still wore civilian clothes, Petro reminded himself, as he removed trousers and jackets from the dead men. He jumped down from the truck and, gathering up his spoils, he took them to one of the wagons, which Orlan was ordering out.

"Go with this one, Petro, and keep those guns handy. Look out for any patrols."

Petro jumped up onto the wagon and the young driver flicked the reins and clicked his tongue to the horses. Both sat tensely as they made their way along deserted roads, aware that the sound of the horses' hooves would carry. The rhythmic clopping might at any moment be fractured by the roar of German vehicles. But they reached their base safely, where the work continued. The wagons were unloaded and returned to the farmers who would need them that day.

Petro was able to lie down for some rest shortly before dawn. He felt restless, but made himself lie quietly on his side, reasoning that if he had not fired on the enemy, he would have been killed. They had gained vital equipment this night. The UPA was growing faster than it could equip itself, so he knew he had done good work.

"And did Hrichko win a gun?" asked Anna, as Petro came to the end of his story.

"Yes, he did. Orlan let us each have a Walther."

"So the odds have been evened a little?"

"A little," agreed Petro.

Chapter 14

Roman Shumenko called a meeting, and Anna joined Vera and the other villagers in the Reading Room. The hall buzzed with conjecture until Roman took the platform with a sheaf of leaflets in his hand. "Dear neighbours, if I may begin…"

The villagers settled themselves and turned their faces to him, with a curious mixture of hope and disillusion.

"As some of you know, I attended a ceremony in Lviv recently. Not only was it attended by the Governor of Western Ukraine, Dr Otto Waechter and his staff, but by some of our glorious heroes of 1914. There was only one purpose to the ceremony – to announce the creation of a Ukrainian fighting unit within the German Army."

There was a flurry of noise at this as the men sat up straighter, and all listened with far more concentration and vested interest.

"It is to be known as the *Waffen-Grenadier Division der SS Galizien…* they would not allow the word "Ukraine" or "Ukrainian" in the title, but, nonetheless, it will be a unit made up of volunteers from Halychyna. These soldiers will be trained and armed by the Germans to fight the Bolsheviks on the Eastern Front. They plan to begin recruiting next month." Roman paused and looked around the gathering. He raised the hand holding the documents. "I am told that recruitment will begin in May, with the training following quickly afterwards. I have some leaflets here which I have been asked to distribute. If anyone is interested, they should come and take one."

"Just a minute!" called a gruff voice from the back of the hall. Heads turned to look at Timko as he continued. "This is all very well, but where does it leave our boys?"

Roman looked at the older man. "I assume you mean the UPA. To be honest, I don't know what they think of this yet."

"And can we trust the Nazis?" called Ihor.

Roman shrugged. "I don't know that either. The Germans have made these announcements publicly, in front of some of our priests, too. But we're adults. We know there are no guarantees. I've simply reported to you what I know. I'm not telling anyone to go…or not to go."

There was a general commotion and the villagers began to break up into groups, discussing the possibilities.

Anna did not know what to think of this development. She, too, had no idea where it left Petro, nor any notion of its possible effect on Ukraine's future. She looked around and saw Ivan in a lively argument with his uncle.

"What have you got one of those for?" asked Danylo.

"I might go," said Ivan, looking at the leaflet.

"What for?"

"What for? We're being given a chance to fight the Muscovites and you ask what for?"

"But what if you lose and the Russians come back?" persisted Danylo.

"I might be dead by then…and if not, I'll have tried."

"Ivashu, I beg you, don't go. It's not the best way for us."

"I'm sorry, uncle, but I think it might be."

They made their way out of the hall and as they went outside, they encountered Ivan's father.

"Ihor!" cried Danylo, "this young fool's thinking of going."

Ihor looked at his eldest son and said, "Walk up to your mother's with me."

The three men walked to Ihor's home, Ivan worrying now about what his mother would say. She had always been staunchly against him joining the UPA, fearing for his safety.

Once indoors, Ihor asked, "Are you sure this is right for you?"

Ivan nodded. "I've thought about the UPA, but I think this way might be better. I'll be trained. I'll get a uniform and a weapon. It'll be more organised." Ivan turned to look at his mother. "It might be safer, Mama, and anyway, I can't just sit here and do nothing."

Ihor turned to his wife. "They'll all go, one way or another."

"I know. Ivashu, have you discussed this with Sofia?"

He shook his head.

"You should. She's your wife."

"Mama…" Ivan began.

"I know you think she might have deceived you, but you owe it to her to be honest with her."

Ivan looked glum. "She lied to me, Mama."

"She may have thought she was pregnant and later realised she wasn't," said his mother carefully.

Ivan shook his head. "No, I don't think so. She wanted us to marry and so she chose a way to persuade me."

"But she is pregnant now," his mother said.

"Yes, she is." Ivan looked no happier. He had bitterly resented Sofia's "mistake".

"And she and the baby will need looking after," continued Lesia.

"I know, but she has her own mother to help. And you could help, too."

"Of course I will. But it's not the same as having your husband nearby."

"No, but lots of women have had to manage without their husbands. Even you, Mama, when *Tato* was away fighting in the First World War."

"Yes, and it's not easy," said his mother remembering the five-year-old son, whom Ihor had left behind in 1914, and who was dead before his father's return four years later. She knew Ivan was familiar with this story, too, but did not press the point.

Ivan returned slowly to Sofia's house. It was now his home, but he did not consider it as that. Nor did he belong anymore at his mother's house. Neither of these uncomfortable facts explained his eagerness to take a leaflet on the new Division. He knew that he had to fight for his country and, despite his parents' natural fears and Danylo's more politically motivated choice, he knew this was the route for him. He could not spend his life living in a bunker, hiding from everyone but one's comrades and taking the terrible risks of the UPA. He wanted to fight out in the open, with some sense of order…although he knew that life in the Division would not be easy either.

He entered the house to see Sofia in her habitual pose of resting "for the sake of the baby" and her mother cooking at the stove. There was no sign of Levko. He frequently took himself off, heaven knew where, to avoid Sofia's interminable orders.

"So what was so important?" demanded Sofia.

Ivan simply passed her the leaflet and on glancing at the supply of wood in the kitchen, went outdoors to bring in more logs.

"Thank you, Ivan," said Sofia's mother.

"You're surely not thinking of going, are you?" asked Sofia.

"Yes, I am."

"Look, Mama. He's planning to leave us. With me in this state." Sofia handed her mother the leaflet.

She read it carefully and looked up at Ivan.

"See!" cried Sofia. "Mama doesn't think you should go either."

"She hasn't said anything yet, Sofia."

"You agree with me, don't you, Mama? Ivan shouldn't go."

"I know it's difficult, Sofia, but Ivan might think he has to go."

"Has to go? What about the baby?"

"You'll manage, Sofia. You always do. You have your mother and mine to help you."

Sofia's eyes filled with fat tears. "I need you here."

"Yes, but I am also needed elsewhere. I must help to fight for our future."

"Mama!" Sofia's voice rose in a howl.

"Sofia, calm yourself. Think of the baby," said Parania.

"Why should I? He isn't!"

"I am. I don't want him to be anyone's slave."

"Him? What if it's a girl?"

"Her neither."

Sofia looked at Ivan from under her lashes, wondering where the charming boy had gone. He had been sullen and resentful all winter. Ivan had clearly made up his mind to leave and part of her, she admitted to herself, would not be sorry to see the grim young man go.

Anna had left the Reading Room with Vera and when the two were alone, walking towards home, Anna said very quietly, "I couldn't take a leaflet. Can you get one for me?"

Vera glanced at Anna quickly. "You want to show it to them?"

"Yes," said Anna. So…it had been said. Vera now knew she took messages, but Anna had to trust her friend.

"I'll just go back now. Don't wait for me. I'll call in later. Here, put this in your pocket," and she handed Anna one of her gloves.

"Thank you."

Vera walked briskly back to the hall, feigning a search for a lost glove, as she disappeared through the doorway.

Katerina looked up anxiously as Anna entered the house.

"It's alright, Mama."

She relaxed as Anna took off her headscarf and jacket and set about making some tea.

"The Germans are making up a new Division for our men to fight the Bolsheviks. Roman Shumenko was telling us all about it."

"Where will they fight them?" Katerina looked bewildered.

"Wherever they're needed in the east. You remember I told you that the Germans lost Stalingrad."

Katerina looked dazed. "So those devils will come back again?"

"Maybe not. Not if this Division gets off the ground."

The water boiled and Anna poured it over some dried linden flowers. She sat down to allow it to infuse, but moments later, rose again impatiently. She picked up her sewing and made herself sit down to finish off some final stitches. She had only been seated a few moments, when there was a knock at the door.

"It's alright, Mama. It's only Vera."

The young woman entered and, as Anna took her jacket, she slipped a folded piece of paper into Anna's hand.

"Sit down and have some tea with us," said Anna.

Vera thanked her friend and turned to Katerina. "How are you? Are you well?"

Katerina nodded once slowly. "I'm not too bad. How's your mother?"

"Oh, busy with the boys. As ever."

"Have you heard from Evhen?"

"No. Still no word. But it's not surprising. They're hard-pressed in the east."

"Yes, it was a pity he had to go with the Bolsheviks."

"He had no choice. He was the right age, so he had to go."

Katerina nodded sadly. "It must be very hard for your mother."

"It is." Vera sighed and turned to Anna. "What's that you're sewing?"

Anna gladly helped her friend to change the subject. "I'm altering a shirt of *Tato's*."

Vera picked up the garment and examined its neat stitches. "You're doing a good job," she commented and smiled as she noticed the white thread of embroidered kisses hidden in the seam on the white fabric of the shirt. "Lovely."

Anna smiled back. She knew it was childish, but she had enjoyed sewing in her love for Petro. She poured the tea and handed a cup to Vera.

"Thank you." Vera breathed in the scent of the infusion. "Are these still your linden flowers?"

"Yes, but the last of the ones we gathered last summer."

"I'm honoured then."

"We'll pick them again in summer and dry them. I've promised to show Nina how to do it."

Anna handed her mother a cup and the three women enjoyed the scent of summer, although none of them dared venture too far ahead in their thoughts.

On hearing Katerina's gentle snoring, Anna got up and dressed to go out. Her father's clothes served more than one purpose. She had taken an old pair of his trousers for her night-time activities. She moved quietly, even though she had helped her mother sleep with a cup of vervain before bedtime. She did not like to leave Katerina alone at night, so she salved her conscience by doing everything she could to avoid her mother lying awake and worrying. She opened the door, pausing in the covered doorway to listen for any movement and then hurried behind the house to retrieve the sack of food she had hidden earlier. She placed the finished shirt in the sack and taking a length of rope, wound it around her waist. She set off along the edge of the field towards the cemetery, since she had to cross the Dniester, slowing as she walked through the bottom of the graveyard, past the spot where she had buried her father and Yuri.

"Goodnight *Tato*, goodnight Yuri," she said under her breath as she passed. "Watch over Mama while I'm gone." She hurried across the open ground of the quarry into the relative cover of the pines and then made her way downhill to the banks of the wide river and the coracles.

As she approached the river, a momentary dread churned in her stomach. The water was running high and fast. Nevertheless, she sought out a little boat to borrow and, stowing her sack in the bottom of it, she pushed out into the water and stepped aboard. She put all of her effort into crossing the river's powerful force, concentrating on every stroke, knowing that to look across the expanse of water would dishearten her. At last she felt the flow begin to diminish, as she approached the far shore. She had travelled downriver further than she would have liked, so, after jumping onto the bank, she tied the rope to the coracle and dragged it upstream, before hiding it for the return journey.

Anna climbed up the hillside to the stand of birches. She heard the crack of a twig and paused to hoot a signal. She did not know tonight's password and hoped those on guard would recognise her. Letting out her breath with relief when she received another hoot in reply, she advanced over the brow of the hill and descended to the hollow, where the partisans' dug-outs were. There Orlan awaited her.

His determined features no longer looked hostile to Anna, but there was nothing gentle in the firm set of his mouth. "We weren't expecting you tonight. What's happened?"

Anna handed him the leaflet. "They're giving these out in the villages."

"Come with me," and he led her into the dug-out, pulling down the sacking screen and then lighting an oil lamp. He glanced at her before reading the leaflet. "Petro's not here tonight."

Anna tried to hide her disappointment. She had, after all, come for a more important reason than simply to see the man she loved.

Orlan read the leaflet and Anna related all that Roman Shumenko had told the villagers.

"You have no man at home, do you?" Orlan asked.

"No."

"Is there someone who will be able to tell you more as the Germans begin to recruit?"

Anna thought of Ivan. "Yes, there is."

"Be discreet, but find out all you can."

"Of course." Anna forced herself to ask the question that was worrying her. "Where will it leave us?"

"Us? Or you? Or Ukraine?"

"All of us…"

"Who knows. We're all fighting the same enemy in the long run. We don't want the Bolsheviks back, but neither do we want these Nazis running the country. We'll have to see."

"But how will it affect the men who join up?"

"They'll get weapons and training, which might help us, too." He relented a little. "Don't worry. We're all working hard. So are you. Now let me empty your sack and you can set off back."

Anna blushed. "I brought a shirt for Petro…"

"I'll see that he gets it. Let's leave that here," and he took the bag from Anna. Telling her to wait where she was, he disappeared out of the dug-out. Anna did not want to leave the shirt for Petro without speaking to him, but she had little choice. She hoped he would understand the message she wanted to send with it.

Some moments later Hrichko appeared with Anna's empty sack. He grinned at her. "Hello, Anna."

"Hello," she said, relieved to see a friendly face.

"Good food again. I like it when you come over."

"Glad to be of service, but I'd better be going. I've a fast river to cross."

"Is it bad?"

She nodded. "It's very high."

"Want me to help you?"

Anna looked at the skinny teenager with a slight smile.

"I'll help you pull the boat upriver a bit."

"That would be good. I did that when I landed, but I think I need to start higher up. I don't want to end up on the bend when I'm crossing."

"No, you definitely don't."

They both knew of the drownings which had taken place downriver of the village, where the mighty Dniester disappeared from view around a tight bend. The current there was stronger, more unpredictable and with the spring melt adding to the volume of water, would be a very dangerous place in a small boat.

Just as Hrichko went to extinguish the lamp, Anna said, "Could you do one other thing for me, too?"

"Of course. Anything."

She felt shy, but ploughed on. "I brought this shirt over for Petro. Orlan says he'll give it to him. Will you make sure Petro knows about it?"

"Don't worry. Orlan likes Petro. He'll give it to him. But I'll make sure Petro knows."

They left the dug-out and climbed up out of the clearing. Hrichko gave a brief signal and they crossed the summit of the hill and began their descent to the river. The ground was damp and slippery, but they reached the bank without incident, finding the coracle where Anna had left it. It was light enough for the two of them to lift and so they set off, walking almost a quarter of a mile west before setting it down.

"Will you be alright to start from here?" asked Hrichko.

"Yes, I think so. You get back now and thanks for your help."

"Alright. Take care, Anna."

"You take care, too."

She stepped into the coracle and Hrichko pushed her away from the bank. She began to paddle hard as soon as she was away, re-crossing the river with the same trepidation at the power of the water that she had had earlier that night.

Chapter 15

Anna planted her vegetable garden as April warmed the earth, knowing she was not catering only for herself and her mother. She planted her staple crops of potatoes, onions and beetroot, carrots and cabbages. She also put in squashes, cucumbers and tomatoes, and beans to climb the lower fence of her garden where it bordered the field. She sowed maize at the top of the vegetable plot to provide a screen from the lane, and tried to make it look less conspicuous by taking the rows of the tall crop along the southern edge of her half hectare plot, as if it were a windbreak. Nearer the house, she encouraged thyme, rosemary and marjoram to flourish while the mint took care of itself. She scattered the poppy seed she had saved from the previous year's harvest, the bulk of which had given character to her bread and cakes over the winter. She kept a close eye on the bushes of currants, planning to defend them from the birds. She would also forage, as she had always done, but she was well aware of the need for an efficient garden.

April moved into May and she became anxious to talk to Ivan. She had heard rumours that many of the village's young men planned to join the *Divizia*, but she had not been able to get any detailed information. Ivan rarely took the cows to pasture now. His place was often taken by his younger brother, Pavlo, or by Sofia's brother, Levko. But one bright morning, Anna was feeding her hens when she saw Ivan coming down the lane, collecting the cows for pasture. Anna flung the last of the feed to the poultry, ran indoors to tell Katerina where she was going and hurried out into the lane to importune the girl partnering Ivan to let her take her place.

"Please swap days with me. I have to take Mama to Temne tomorrow."

The girl hesitated. "Why didn't you ask me sooner?"

"I didn't know myself until late yesterday."

"Oh, alright," said the girl.

Ivan continued to gather the cows and Anna brought up the rear, until they had them contentedly browsing the lush green pasture beside the Dniester.

"Why have you got to take your mother to Temne?"

"She's not been well again. She has trouble sleeping. We're going to see a woman who might be able to help." Anna felt guilty lying to her old friend, but she knew she had to be discreet. "How have you been?"

"Oh you know…" he shrugged. "Sofia…the baby…"

"Is she well?"

"Oh yes! She makes sure of that!"

"Ivan, it's not so bad, surely?"

He looked at her gloomily. "It is…and worse."

"I'm sorry. I'd hoped things might improve for you."

"They will. I've volunteered for the *Divizia* you know," and he proceeded, with little encouragement from Anna, to describe joining the new force.

He had gone from the village to Buchach to join up, since even Temne was not deemed large enough by the Germans to warrant a call-up centre. When he arrived on the outskirts of the town, he was directed by German infantrymen to the temporary centre. A banner above its entrance proclaimed the date and was decorated in the centre with the shield of the lion rampant, the coat of arms of Halychyna.

"I thought they'd use the *tryzub*," commented Anna, the trident being the symbol of Ukraine.

"Yes, they said they would in April, but they seem to have changed their minds."

The German military had set the red Nazi flag with its swastika above the banner, alongside the blue and yellow flag of Ukraine.

"Were there many men there?"

"I've never seen so many. But if you think how far we are from Buchach and draw a circle around, that's a huge area for volunteers to come from." Ivan was quiet for a moment as he remembered the long lines of men, two or three deep, smoking and discussing what they might achieve with the Germans, whose presence was visible but discreet, as the Militia kept order. He remembered the occasional member of the Gestapo hovering, watching the proceedings.

"What was it like?"

"Businesslike. People seemed to accept that the Germans have been in trouble since Stalingrad, but there's a strong feeling that this Division might be able to fight off the Russians."

"Do you think they will?"

"Perhaps. I'll have a better idea once training begins."

"When's that?"

"Twenty-eighth of July."

"Will you have to go to Buchach?"

"To meet the train, but then we'll go to Heidelager…in Germany."

"So the Germans are going to ship you all off?"

"Yes. That's what they said."

"Are you scared?"

"No. I'm ready. And not because of Sofia. We have to protect ourselves and when the Nazis lose, we'll have the beginnings of a Ukrainian army."

"I hope so."

"We will, Anna. They were already dividing us up for officer training and those who'll go into the ranks. So it's not just about uniforms and rifles. We'll have our own leaders, too."

"That would be wonderful. If we all fought in our own way, we might hold the Bolsheviks off."

Ivan looked at her. "How's Petro?"

She smiled slightly and nodded.

"Is that it? Aren't you going to tell me more?"

She shook her head.

"Alright…I miss him, Anna. I would have liked to talk to him over these last months. Give him my best, if you can."

She looked away, trying not to let her eyes rest on the opposite bank of the river and then she turned her face up to the sunlight. Ivan gazed at this pretty, serious girl with her well of secrets and wondered why he had been so badly led astray by black curls and a giggling mouth. But it was too late now. He sighed.

"Would it help if I called in on Sofia from time to time?"

He laughed. "It would help her. I don't know about helping you!"

"Then I will. And you take care of yourself when you go. We'll want you back again, you know."

"We'll see," and despite the warmth of the day, they both shivered a little at the thought of the dangers to come.

Sofia's baby was due in August, so without any fanfare, Anna stepped up her collecting and drying of chamomile. It grew in such profusion, it was easy to gather as she went about her usual business and it was another of her habitual summer tasks. She not only made infusions for Katerina to help her to relax, but she drank it herself, too, especially on the nights when she did not need to go out. The women of Anna's village believed in its efficacy when bathing newborn babies and they used it in the baby's bath for up to six months. Anna guessed that Sofia would not be planning ahead and so she did this small task for her. She also trawled through Yuri's undershirts to find some soft cotton still worthy of use. As she packed the pieces of fabric in her basket she could not resist lifting the cloth to her face, but there was no scent of her brother. Anna put her shoulders back and set off for Sofia's house, which lay not far from Petro's, although along the more populated end of the lane.

She thought she might visit Nina and Halia after seeing Sofia, but Nina pre-empted her by meeting her in the lane. "Hello, Anna. What are you bringing us?"

"Hello, Nina. I'm on my way to Sofia's, but I'll call on you later."

"Can I come with you?"

Anna was not sure that this was wise, but then relented. "Alright, but be polite. Don't ask too many questions," laughed Anna.

Nina shook her curls at Anna. "Of course I won't!" and then had the grace to giggle at herself. "No, I won't, as long as you explain everything to me afterwards."

"You're incorrigible!"

As they approached Sofia's house with its well-tended green rows of vegetables, Sofia's mother was hanging out washing, her firm figure attesting to the years of manual labour she had been used to as a widow. Her muscular forearms were beginning to tan from her outdoor work and she stood firmly on the earth in her bare feet.

"Good morning, Parania. We've come to call on Sofia."

"Good morning, girls. She's inside. Go in and see her."

The door stood open and, as they passed from the sunlit yard into the cool dark interior, Anna felt a slight tremor in her heart. She was surprised, but had no time to examine the feeling as Sofia greeted them. "Well, aren't you lucky? Being able to walk around in the sunshine."

Anna looked at Sofia in surprise. "Has something happened to your legs?"

"Don't be sarcastic. You know how heavy I am with the baby."

"Oh Sofia! I wasn't being critical. Let me put a chair in the garden for you. It's a beautiful morning."

"I don't want to be in the sun."

"I'll put your chair in the shade of the walnut tree. It'll be lovely."

"Shall I take this chair, Anna?" asked Nina, pointing to a wicker chair by the door.

"Yes, and I'll help Sofia."

Anna put down her basket and gave Sofia her arm. She heaved herself up and Anna noticed that she had put on weight, not only for her baby, but Sofia was becoming plumper and rounder generally.

The young women made their slow progress into the garden, Sofia exclaiming at the brightness as they went out of the kitchen, but even she could not remain disgruntled for long. The garden was bathed in yellow light and there seemed to be a conspiracy among the flowers and the birds to sing the praises of early summer. Sofia seated herself in the dappled shade and Parania joined them.

"We should leave that chair there for you, Sofia, so that you can sit outdoors whenever you like."

"Yes, but I'm not always well enough."

"The fresh air will do you and the baby good," said Anna.

"And when did you gain all this knowledge of midwifery?" asked Sofia.

"Sofia! There's no need to be rude to Anna. She's come to see you when I'm sure she has plenty of work of her own," admonished Parania.

"I'm sorry," said Sofia huffily, "but I don't get many visitors."

"Never mind. I'm here now so let me show you what I brought." Anna went to retrieve her basket, while Parania passed Nina some chairs to take outside and then prepared a cold drink for the young women. Anna wondered how Parania's resilience had not been passed onto Sofia. Perhaps Olha had been the stronger character and Anna reflected that Sofia was always the indulged child, perhaps the only indulgence Parania allowed herself.

Anna took the pieces of cotton fabric from her basket. "I don't know how far you've got with your sewing, but I wondered if you'd like some of this material for the baby."

Sofia looked languidly at the light fabric. "I'm not very good at sewing. Olha was the one who was good with a needle."

"Well, perhaps I can help," said Anna. "Do you like this fabric? Will it be alright for the baby?"

"I suppose so."

"Then shall I make a couple of little nightgowns for you?"

"If you want to."

Anna put a gentle hand on Nina's arm. "Nina can help me cut them out. Can't you, Nina?" She nodded meaningfully at the girl, who now swallowed the anger Anna had felt rising up in her.

"Of course. I'd love to."

"We've some time yet," continued Anna. "When's the baby due?"

"Not till August. I'll have to deal with all the heat while I get fatter and fatter."

Parania joined them with the drinks. "You only need to relax and look after the baby. There are lots of us to help you."

"Yes, but Ivan won't be here."

"He's here for a few more weeks," soothed her mother. "And we'll still be here after he's gone."

Later, as Nina and Anna returned up the lane to Nina's house, Anna had to hush the girl again.

"Well!" she exploded.

"Wait till we're at your house."

As they entered Nina's garden, her indignation overflowed. "How ungrateful can you be? When you'd bothered to visit her."

"Never mind. She might be feeling unwell at the moment."

"Unwell! She should get off her fat backside and do something."

"Nina!" Halia came to the door, wiping her hands on her apron. "Who are you talking about? No, don't tell me yet. Come indoors. Hello, Anna, come in."

Anna smiled apologetically. "I'm afraid it's my fault. I took her to Sofia's with me."

"Oh dear."

"Mama, that woman is so selfish. She treated us all like servants, even when Anna offered to make some baby clothes for her."

"Calm down, Nina. It's not easy for a woman in her condition."

"She's only pregnant, Mama. She's not dying."

Halia and Anna looked at Nina in surprise, both realising that "the child" was now thirteen and seemed to have inherited some of her twin sisters' sharpness of tongue. They burst out laughing.

"What are you laughing at? Don't laugh at me!" Nina protested as Halia put her arm around her remaining child and kissed her forehead.

"Thank God for your strength, Nina!"

Anna noticed that Nina was now as tall as Halia's shoulder. She was outgrowing her young self in more ways than one. She tucked the memory away to tell Petro the next time she saw him.

"That Sofia!" Nina muttered.

"Everyone's different. Sofia always wants to feel cared for," said Halia.

"She treats her mother really badly, Mama. Even when she's doing everything for her."

"They'll both miss Ivan when he goes." Anna paused. "He's done a really good job on their garden."

"Yes, it'll be harder for them when he's gone…" and all three women ached with the absence of Petro.

"Come," said Halia. "He was well last time we heard, wasn't he, Anna?"

She nodded. "Yes. So I was told." She shook herself. "I must go. I've got work to do in the garden." She turned to Nina. "It'll soon be time to collect cherries. Want to come with me?"

"Of course," said Nina.

The women kissed one another and Halia held Anna tightly for a moment longer than usual. They parted and exchanged a brief nod, Anna knowing that she was to pass his mother's love on to Petro the next time she saw him.

It was not long until she did see him. The next time she crossed the river, he was at the dugouts. It seemed to Anna that there was a greater sense of urgency about the camp as he drew her away to speak privately. They walked deeper into the forest, their eyes becoming accustomed to the dark.

"What is it?"

"We're going north to Volyn."

She looked up at him with wide eyes. "All of you?"

"Most of us. The commanders want us up there in force. We'll leave a few hereabouts."

Anna leaned against him, her forehead resting on his chest. She could not speak. There was too much and too little to say.

He embraced her. "Try not to be sad. I have to go."

"I know. I understand."

"The commanders want us to challenge the Nazis on a much bigger scale. They've been more brutal with our people, so we can't just do nothing."

She swallowed her grief and fear. "I'd come with you if I could."

"I know. But there's work for you here. And not just with your mother."

"I know."

"There'll be more work, Anna. Those Muscovite devils are driving the Germans west. They'll get here, too, at some stage and then we'll need to hit them hard."

She slipped her arms around him and stroked his back. They stood sombrely for a few moments.

"It's a lovely shirt," he said in a lighter tone.

"I'm glad you like it."

"And I found the kisses."

"Good. They're to keep you safe."

"They will," and he leaned forward to kiss her.

As they returned to the encampment, Petro said, "Just wait here a moment. I need to get something."

When he reappeared, they made their way over the brow of the hill and down towards the river. As they reached the bank, he took something from his pocket. "Put this somewhere safe."

Anna looked down into his hand to see a Luger pistol. She looked up at him in alarm.

"Take it, Anna. Things are going to get bad and I'd feel better knowing you had this." He reached into his other pocket and brought out ammunition for the gun. "Take these, too."

"Petro…"

"It's a good weapon. It's semi-automatic and is good up to fifty metres. Be careful when you fire it as it does recoil."

"I might not need it."

"No, you might not…but if you do, it's a good thing to have."

"Alright." She took the weapon and the cartridges from him and leaned against his chest one last time. "You take care, too."

"I will. Will you take a message to my mother?"

"Of course."

"Warn her that I will come to them soon, at night. To say goodbye."

Her tears threatened to betray her again, but she nodded. "I'll tell her."

They parted. There were no more words to say and he had work to do. Anna turned the coracle onto its hull and crossed the dark river alone.

Petro had said goodbye to Halia and Nina the previous autumn when he had joined the UPA, but faced with the prospect of large scale fighting in the north, he wanted to speak to them once more. So the next night, he swam across the river he knew so well. He had bundled his clothes inside a waxed canvas bag and as he stood dripping and dressing himself on his home shore, he found he could smile at the boy he had been a year earlier, winning the swimming competition. Then, he had been the centre of attention, now, he came like a thief in the night.

He crossed the plain towards the track and then began to mount the wooded hillside to reach his house from its quietest vantage point. The moon lit his way, but even without it, Petro could have found his way home. He reached the end of the vegetable garden and climbed over the fence, skirting the rustling maize, and noticing with relief that Anna's reports that his mother was managing the garden were correct. He reached the house, felt for the latch and finding the door unbolted, let himself in.

He heard his mother sit up in bed. "Mama, it's me."

She came towards him in her pale nightgown, her long plait down her back, and took his dear face in her work-hardened hands. "Petryk!" She kissed him and despite having to reach up to his cheek, she hugged her child to her.

"Me too," said Nina, joining them and the three stood embracing one another for a few precious moments.

"Are you hungry?" asked Halia, drawing away and lighting a lamp.

"Not really," said Petro, not wanting his mother to worry that he always felt hungry.

"I saved you some *varenyky*," she said, bustling to boil the potato dumplings which he loved.

"We were hoping you'd come tonight," said Nina. "We had these ready for you."

"Come here and let me look at you," said Petro. "You've grown." And he observed her height and the changes which had begun to show in her figure. Anna had been right. The child was disappearing before their eyes. "You'll soon be a woman."

Nina blushed, her pretty face haloed by her dishevelled curls.

"So have you heard from Irina and Natalia?"

"Yes, there's the occasional letter."

Nina hurried to fetch them from the shelf and handed them to Petro, who read the short scripts quickly. "They don't really tell you much, do they?"

"I can only assume that they really are well and busy." Halia sighed. "I hope they are."

"They probably are, Mama. They'd soon let you know if things were going badly."

"Yes, they probably would." She drained the *varenyky* and placed them in a bowl for Petro with the onions she had fried in butter. Nina passed him some soured cream from the cold store and he tucked into the delicious meal. No one mentioned the fact that it might be many more months before he ate such homely food again.

He cleaned his plate and smiled at his mother and sister. "I wasn't desperately hungry, but they were so good."

The women smiled back at him and Nina sat closer.

"So have you been helping Mama, Nina?"

"Yes, of course I have."

"She's been very good. She helped me dig and plant the garden."

"I can see what a good job you've done," he said.

"And she goes collecting with Anna."

"Oh yes. We've gathered lots of things. We're keeping an eye on the cherries now. They're almost ready."

"The ones on the way to the shrine?"

"Yes, but we've got to beat the birds."

"And any thunderstorms."

"Oh!" Nina slapped her brother playfully, her shyness forgotten. "That's mean. I was only little."

Petro met his mother's eyes. It was barely a year since a distraught Nina had been brought home by Anna. "She's growing up, Mama."

"She certainly is."

"Well, I'm glad. The two of you can look after each other till I get back."

The illusion of safety burst like a bubble, as all three of them remembered why this meeting was taking place.

Petro rose. "I'd better be making my way back."

Halia approached her son. She was determined this parting would be as easy for him as possible. "Take care of yourself. Do your best to honour your country and try to come back to us."

Petro gripped his mother in a fierce hug, and then hugged Nina, too. "Will you keep an eye on Anna for me?"

"Of course we will," said Halia, knowing perfectly well that he would have made the same request of the girl he loved, to guard his mother and sister.

Nina could not quite hold back her tears and a sob escaped her. She pressed her face into his chest and he stroked her unruly hair.

"It's alright," he said. "It helps me to know you two are managing well. I'll think of you often."

"Just come back," begged Nina.

"I will." He turned to leave, knowing that the quicker he left, the less painful it might be.

The women stood in the doorway, their arms around one another's waists, as Petro disappeared down the path, into the darkness beyond.

As July progressed, Ivan, too, felt under pressure to leave Sofia as well provided for as possible. He began to prepare enough wood to last his new family for the winter. "Levko, come with me today," he said at breakfast. "We'll gather some wood to add to the woodpile."

Levko hesitated.

"Or I can leave it for you to do when I'm gone, if you'd rather…"

The boy looked at Ivan, indecision in his eyes.

"Coming?"

"Yes, alright," he muttered.

"We'll take the handcart. It'll be easier," said Ivan, ignoring Levko's reluctance.

They set off for the woods to the north-east of the village, armed with a saw and a couple of axes, Ivan pulling the cart. A little way up the lane, Levko trotted up to join Ivan at the front of the handcart.

"Shall I take the cart while it's light?"

Ivan nodded and handed it over to the skinny eleven-year-old.

They kept up a brisk pace and on reaching the woods, Ivan took one of the handles as they pulled the cart towards some dry fallen timber.

"Let's start here. We'll cut this up into pieces to fit on the cart and then chop it up smaller at home," said Ivan.

They worked at separating and chopping the wood into more easily transportable segments until the cart was full, Ivan lifting the heavier pieces while Levko worked hard to keep up.

"Let's take this back and then we'll need to return with a two-handed saw for this thick branch. Is there one at your house? I don't remember seeing one."

"I don't know," replied the boy.

"Well, it doesn't really matter. I can borrow my father's. I'll see if Pavlo can come back with me to help me cut that biggest piece."

Levko ducked his head and a slight blush spread up his boyish cheek.

Ivan glanced at his young brother-in-law. "But we probably won't need him, will we? You and I could manage it ourselves."

"Yes…probably."

"Let's give it a go first on our own then."

And they pulled the heavy handcart home. They unloaded and Levko ran around into the barn to check the old tools there. Ivan followed him.

"Any luck?"

"No, I can't see one."

"Alright. I'm going to call at my father's to get one."

Levko, still bearing some resemblance to a beaten dog, waited.

"Come on, then," said Ivan. "You can help me carry it back."

As they hurried along the lane towards the monument, Ivan noticed Levko's returning energy and regretted not thinking about the boy before. Ivan knew better than most what a time Levko would have of it once the baby arrived.

"Hello, Mama!" Ivan called as he entered the family's steep yard. They walked up to the house, where Lesia was drawing water from the well.

"Wait, Mama. I'll do that for you."

"There's no need. Who do you think usually does it?"

"Don't be stubborn. Let me help you."

Lesia gave over the task to her son and she turned to the boy. "How are you, Levko? Is he bossy with you, too?"

"No, he's not…" emphasising the word "he".

Ivan winked at his mother and so the name went unmentioned.

"Have you got time for cake?" asked Lesia.

She and Ivan glanced at the boy, his dark hair seeming to emphasise the thinness of his face. Ivan said, "Yes, I'm sure we have. I've come to borrow *Tato's* two-handed saw."

"Well, come inside. Your father will be in in a moment."

And he was. Ihor came bustling into the kitchen. "What's all this? Cake in the middle of the day!"

Ivan explained their errand and Ihor, ruffling Levko's short hair said, "Alright. You catch up with your mother and I'll take this young man to help me."

"Doesn't he get fed at home?" asked Lesia.

Ivan looked glum. "I feel bad, Mama. I should have been looking after him."

"He's not your child."

"No, but he's not a bad boy. I've been too busy feeling sorry for myself."

"Never mind. Bring him here again, then he might feel able to visit us after you've gone."

"Thank you, Mama." He kissed her cheek and noticed it was not as apple-plump as it used to be. But before he could give way to regret at leaving her too, Ihor returned and called from the yard, "Come on, Ivashu. This young man tells me there's work to be done."

Ivan hurried out to see that his father had hitched the horse to his wagon. "We have the handcart, *Tatu*."

"Poo! That's no use. You need to take a big load home."

"Alright," conceded Ivan, acknowledging his father as the foreman on this job.

They made their way back to the winter-damaged tree and Ihor circled the branches, as he and Ivan debated where best to cut.

"Come on, my lad," said Ihor to Levko. "Let's me and you take this end of the saw and see if Ivan can keep up with us on the other end." He drew the boy in front of him and placed his calloused hand over the boy's on the saw's handle. "Now, no pulling, just keep it cutting steady and smooth."

Levko leaned into the job, strangely comforted by Ihor's chest at his back and the three fell into an even rhythm as they sawed through the dense wood.

They worked on into the dusk of the summer evening, sawing and transferring the wood to Sofia's yard, ready for the next task of cutting it into logs for the winter.

As Ihor was about to set off home, Ivan thanked his father. "I'd never have got all that done without you."

"I've got to keep my grandchild warm this winter, haven't I?" he said and clicked his tongue to the horse to walk on.

Ivan and Levko washed themselves in the yard and went indoors to eat the supper Parania had prepared for them.

"You must be exhausted. Come and eat."

"I couldn't have done it without Levko," said Ivan. "He's worked really hard."

"It's about time," grumbled Sofia.

"Well done, Levko," said his mother. "I'm proud of you."

"Yes, he's done a man's work today."

Levko was too tired to bask in the unaccustomed glory being heaped on his head as he tucked into his supper.

Over the following days, Ivan and Levko spent some time each day increasing the woodpile, Ivan showing Levko how to split stubborn wood with a metal splinter under the axe. Ivan would be gone before the harvest, but he talked to Levko of the work he could do. "They'll need you boys this year more than

179

ever. All the lads my age will have gone and Sofia won't be able to work. Go with my father. I'll have a word with him before I leave. He'll get you some work, so you can earn a share of the wheat."

Levko looked uncertain.

"You'll be alright. *Tato's* a good man. He'll make sure they don't give you too much to do."

Ivan bustled about over the next few days, packing his things and fussing around the home he was leaving.

"There's no need to worry, Ivan," Parania reassured him. "We'll manage."

"I know. I just feel a bit anxious."

"Don't. I'm still strong and I looked after my family before you joined us."

"I'm sorry. I didn't mean…"

"I know you didn't. When you go, you must concentrate on your own safety. Don't worry about us."

Ivan nodded, liking his mother-in-law more, but remaining bemused about the way she seemed to be held in thrall to Sofia's whims.

Her reaction was predictable when one evening, he announced, "I'm going to see my mother."

"That's right. Leave me on my own."

"You're welcome to come with me."

"You know I can't walk that far."

"I'll walk slowly with you."

She snorted derisively.

"I'm sorry you won't come, but I will spend this evening with my mother. I'll see you later," and with that he left the house, his jaw set.

As he walked up the lane busy with the sound of birdsong, he realised he had acquired a young shadow. He turned to Levko, who looked at him hopefully. "Come on then. I'm sure my mother will have something good for us to eat."

Levko gave the ghost of a grin and fell into step beside Ivan.

"No Sofia?" asked Ivan's mother as they entered the house.

He shook his head. "She was feeling too tired for the walk," and he nodded slightly towards Levko.

"Hello, Levko," said Lesia. "I'm glad you've come. I'll need a verdict on these biscuits later."

Levko smiled shyly at Ivan's mother and Ivan felt his conscience salved a little. His family would try to keep an eye on the boy.

"Do you think she'd like to see the baby?" asked Ivan's sister, Luba, the "baby" now being eighteen months old.

Ivan looked bleakly at his sister. "She might. It would be nice for our children to know one another."

"I'll come up tomorrow," said Luba. "I'm sure there are some clothes this one's grown out of, which she could use."

"That would help. Thanks."

"Come and sit," said his mother. "You must be hungry. Come, Levko. I'm sure Ivan has been working you hard again."

Levko looked as if he might say something in defence of Ivan, but then gave it up as too complicated.

Ihor turned to him. "Come and sit by me, my lad. He's a good workman, this one," he announced to his wife and daughter. "Feed him up, mother."

Levko sat at the table, happy to be encouraged to eat by these kind people and glad he was not expected to say anything further. He was tucking into pickled herrings, with cucumbers and tomatoes dressed with dill when Pavlo and Nestor came in.

"Oh ho!" announced Pavlo. "The soldier's here."

Ivan grinned at his younger brother. "They're still not taking boys then?"

"It won't be long," retorted sixteen-year-old Pavlo, as Lesia turned to the stove, busying herself with the food.

Luba shook her head slightly at her brothers and they changed the subject quickly.

"Where've you been?" asked Ivan.

"Over to Temne," replied Nestor.

Ivan looked at his serious brother-in-law. He was three years older than Ivan, but had managed to avoid the Red Army draft through ill-health. He worked in the village office as an assistant to Roman Shumenko and so had not yet been put under pressure to leave. It was a relief to Ivan that these two young men would remain in the village. His father was still a force to be reckoned with, but he was now in his fifties.

Lesia and Luba busily filled dishes and placed them on the table, as the talk moved to the harvest which would soon be upon them.

"Levko wants to help out."

Ihor looked at the boy. "Of course he does. You come with me and I'll find you some work."

Levko nodded up at him.

"Everyone will have to help," said Nestor, "or we'll not get it all in."

The time passed quickly for Ivan in the comfort of home and as he took his leave, he saw his mother's lip tremble. "Don't worry. I'll be back," he said, taking her in his arms.

"It's easy to leave," Lesia replied, "but very hard to come home again." She hugged her child tight, knowing she had lost the battle to keep him safe.

"Where's *Tato*?" Ivan looked around.

Ihor came in from the barn with a small sack. "Take this, Ivashu."

"What is it?"

"Tobacco."

"But I don't smoke."

"No, but other soldiers do. You'll find it useful for barter. Take it."

"Thank you," and Ivan embraced his father. He felt the brief tightness of his clasp and there passed between them the warning of an old soldier to a raw recruit, to take care in the multitude of dangers to come. Ivan looked into his father's eyes and gave a slight nod. He would do his best to come home alive.

He took his leave of each of the others and hurried out into the darkening night, young Levko at his side, knowing he would see them all one last time on the day of his departure.

"Do you think Olha will ever come back?" asked Levko.

Ivan was torn from his own thoughts. He turned to the boy and putting his arm around Levko's narrow shoulders, said, "Yes, I'm sure she will when she can. It might take a while though."

Levko nodded and found himself wishing that this stern young man was not leaving.

On Ivan's last morning, he turned to his wife in the seclusion of their bedroom. "Come, Sofia. Kiss me properly and let's take a good leave of each other."

She was seated on the edge of the bed, so he sat beside her. She turned her face away from him, saying, "Why should I? You don't even have to go."

"The sooner I go, the sooner I'll be back."

"How do you work that out?"

"The sooner we'll win the fight for our own country."

"Oh rubbish! I can't see that happening."

"Please don't make me leave you on a quarrel," he said, lifting a stray curl from her cheek.

"You know how I feel."

He put his arm around her shoulders, but she shrugged him off. "Please, Sofia. I don't know when I'll see you or the baby again."

"You should have thought of that before you joined up then, shouldn't you?"

He sighed and leaned forward to kiss her cheek. "Take care of yourself and the baby. I'll write and let you know where I am, so that you'll know where to send a reply."

"I might not have time to write letters."

"Just a short note will do," he said, rising from the bed. "I have to go," and he bent to kiss her again. This time she kept still for the kiss, but did not return it. He sighed again and turned to leave the room. "Will you come to the door to see me off?"

"I suppose so."

Ivan picked up his pack and gave Parania a quick hug.

"God bless you, Ivan," she said, and then he bent to hug Levko.

"Can I help you carry your pack to the village hall?" the boy asked.

"Come on then, but we'll have to be quick. Those wagons won't wait."

And he was gone. Sofia turned into the kitchen from the doorway, the tears welling up in her eyes as she wished she had hugged him properly. But she comforted herself with her list of grudges.

Ivan and Levko hurried up the lane, joining other young men on the same road. At the green, several carts stood ready to take the men to Buchach to board their trains for the training camps in Germany. It was thronged with families ready to wave their men away. They were all wearing their embroidered shirts and blouses, making a gala day for their brave youngsters. Ivan felt proud to be part of the swelling movement to take control of their own fate and he was glad to see his family there in full force to see him off. He kissed each of them goodbye again.

"I'll be back," he reassured his mother for a second time.

"God keep you safe, my son," was all her reply, as Ihor blessed him, too.

Pavlo thumped his shoulder and Nestor shook hands, while Luba handed him the baby to kiss. "I'll visit Sofia and help her with the baby. And I'll write to you."

"Thank you. I don't know if she will."

"Don't worry. I'll let you know what happens. Take care of yourself," and she gave her brother a final hug.

Ivan took his pack off a struggling Levko. The boy went to stand beside Ihor, who put his arm around the boy's shoulders. As Ivan went to mount the wagon, Anna appeared before him.

"I couldn't let you go without saying goodbye," she said.

"Oh, Anna, thank you."

She held the friend of her childhood tight for a moment and he felt himself soften against her dear breast.

"Be safe!"

With a final, "I must go," he climbed up into the wagon.

Anna stood with Ivan's family as the carts drew away. The villagers waved until the wagons topped the slight rise as the road disappeared north, past the shrine, towards Temne and Buchach.

Chapter 16

Anna and Nina set out armed with a white sheet and their baskets. They made their way to the linden trees, which were full of the sweetness of white blossom. Spreading the sheet on the ground and using their scissors, they snipped off the fully open flowers. The headiness of the scent surrounded them and soon their feet were encircled by fallen blossoms. They filled their baskets and snipped again, this time bringing the corners of the sheet together to carry their bounty home.

They went first to Nina's, where Anna shared their harvest out and showed the girl how to spread the flowers on wicker panels. "Leave them in the sun for a few days and they'll soon be dry. You'll need to turn them from time to time so that they dry underneath, too."

"What about at night?"

"Take them in before the dew falls and put them out again in the morning."

Halia came out to join them.

"Look, Mama. The makings of lots of tea."

"That's good," said Halia, examining their haul. She looked at one another with a glance which asked, "Any news?" but with a slight shake of Anna's head, they shared their disappointment. It was still too early to hear much, thought Anna as she returned home to dry her own flowers.

She was drawn from her reverie by Vera, hurrying to catch her up. As she caught sight of Anna's load, she cried, "Oh, you went without me!"

"I'm sorry," said Anna, "but I'd promised Nina I'd show her how to dry them."

"How are they?"

"Quiet. Calm, I think. Although I know Halia worries all the time."

"And you…"

"The same…every waking moment."

Vera put her arm around her friend's waist. "I wish I could avoid adding to your worries."

"What is it?"

"Roman was talking of a huge German defeat."

"Where?"

"At Kursk."

"But that's in the east. Beyond Dnipro even. How can that affect us?"

"Roman says that it was such a massive defeat for the Nazis, the Russians will chase them all the way west, back to Germany."

"So they'll come through here."

"Eventually."

"But the Front bypassed us last time."

"I don't know, Anna. The men were talking and I listened."

"What about the *Divizia*? Won't they help?"

"They're not ready yet. They've only just begun their training."

Anna looked thoughtful. Petro and the insurgents would be harrying the Germans in Volyn only to let the Russians in…and then they too would have to be fought off…

"Don't look so worried," said Vera, wishing she had been able to keep the news from Anna.

"No, I was just thinking. It's going to be a long time before we're clear of all of this."

"Yes, I think it is."

Anna sighed, but lifted her chin. "Well, there's no choice. We'll just have to keep on, taking one day at a time."

Vera smiled, relieved at her friend's resilience.

"And does Roman talk of anything but the war?"

Vera blushed. "Occasionally."

"Good. Enjoy it while you can."

"I do," said Vera and the laughter pealed from both of them, girls again.

Roman Shumenko called a meeting several days later to address the problems of the coming harvest. "We're lacking many of our strong young men who've gone to fight with the Galician Division, so we'll have to share the work of the harvest differently this year," he told the gathering, knowing how vital their food supply would be in the uncertainty of the coming months; and knowing, too, how an enemy on the run might fight to feed its army. "I'd like to suggest, since we still have to send a quota of grain to Germany, that the heads of households who own land, create their teams of workers now, while we're gathered here."

There was a hum as people got up from their chairs and teams of family groups and their neighbours began to form.

Pavlo looked around and, seeing Anna, said to Ihor, "*Tatu*, we should include Anna in our group. She's a good worker and she might not have anyone else to join."

Ihor nodded. "You're right. Go and ask her."

185

So Anna joined Ihor's team, glad to work with such a strong family. As they crowded around, Anna asked Ivan's sister, Luba, if they'd had news of Ivan.

"Just a short note so far. He's in Heidelager and he says there are thousands of them! From all over Halychyna."

"Is he well?"

"Yes. He sounded enthusiastic even in the little he said. Didn't he, Levko?" she said, turning to her young brother-in-law.

"Yes," replied the boy.

Anna smiled at the dark youth. "How's Sofia?"

He rolled his eyes and shrugged a shoulder.

"Busy, I don't doubt," Anna said. "Are you working with us?"

"He certainly is," said Ihor, turning to them. "He's one of my best workers."

Anna warmed again to the bluff old man, still hale despite his years and as she walked home, she thought of the painful absences in the families of the village.

The days of the harvest were dry and the sun beat down out of a brassy blue sky. Every field was alive with the workforce of older men doing the jobs they had begun to give up to their sons. The women were promoted to these jobs, too, and the children took over the work of their mothers and sisters in the general re-shuffle. Anna returned home each evening, hot, thirsty and covered in dust, but curiously satisfied with the work she had done.

On the morning of the third day, Anna arrived at the fields to see Levko and Luba deep in conversation. They looked up as she approached.

"Sofia has had the baby!" announced Ivan's sister.

"Wonderful! Are they both well?"

"Apparently so. Levko spent much of yesterday evening with us, but was able to go home to sleep."

"Is she alright, Levko?"

"Yes, she's fine."

"And the baby?"

He nodded. "Yes. It's a boy."

"Lovely," smiled Anna.

She did not visit Sofia that day, but gave her a couple of days to settle into motherhood, before venturing along the lane with her basket of dried chamomile. She found Sofia ensconced in bed, surrounded by pillows, her baby at the breast.

"Shall I come back later?"

"No, come in."

Anna entered, almost shyly, realising she had last been in this room on the eve of Sofia's wedding. There seemed to be no trace of Ivan…except the baby, who gurgled at the breast, kneading Sofia with one tiny hand. Sofia herself was pink with health. She smiled smugly at Anna.

"Sit down, Anna. I'll let you look at him when he's finished."

Anna perched on the edge of the bed. "How're you feeling?"

"Oh, I'm fine. Couldn't be better."

"Good. I brought you some dried camomile for bathing the baby."

"Thanks." Sofia stroked the baby's glossy black hair.

"What are you going to call him?"

"Antin."

"Oh. Not Ivan then?"

"No." She smiled sweetly. "After my father."

"Oh, of course."

Sofia removed the sleepy baby from her nipple and handed him over to Anna. "Hold him against your shoulder so that he can bring up his wind."

Anna took the tender bundle gently and placed him against her cheek. His warm milky smell made his smooth cheek irresistible and she kissed his little head. "Oh Sofia! He's lovely."

"Yes, he is."

"You are so lucky."

"Well, perhaps if Petro comes back…"

Anna shook her head. "Oh, no. That's been over for a long time."

"He only went just after our wedding."

"Yes, since then."

"And you haven't seen him since?"

"No," said Anna, meeting Sofia's eyes. She crooned to the baby and rocked him.

"Oh well, there'll be other men."

Anna laughed shortly. "Or boys…they're all that's left."

"There are plenty of soldiers."

"The Germans?" asked Anna, surprised.

"Why not? Some of them are quite good-looking."

Anna gave a little laugh and shook her head. She was saved from replying by Parania offering them some tea.

Later as she walked home, Anna decided to call in on Halia and Nina.

"Come in, Anna. I wasn't expecting you," called Halia from under the shade of the walnut tree.

"Isn't Nina at home?"

"No, she's gone to see Oksana and Odarka. Did you want her?"

Anna shook her head. "No, I only called in because I've been to Sofia's."

Halia patted the space on the bench beside her and Anna joined her. "How are they?"

"Sofia's blooming and the baby is delicious."

Halia glanced at her. "There's no need to be sad, Anna. You've plenty of time for a baby yet."

Anna looked up in surprise, but realised, as she felt the tears in her throat, that Halia saw her more clearly at this moment than she saw herself. She swallowed. "I know."

Halia put her hand on Anna's arm. "It's hard bringing a child up on your own."

"I know," she repeated. "I can wait."

"Of course you can."

There was a pause as the women looked at the garden and then Anna blurted out, "I lied to her."

"To whom?"

"Sofia."

"What about?"

"I told her Petro and I had broken up when he left."

"Why did you do that?" asked Halia.

"I don't know. It just came out."

Halia was thoughtful for a moment. "I think you did a wise thing. Sofia isn't generous and it's better that she has no knowledge which could hurt you."

It was Anna's turn to look puzzled.

"He hasn't gone to join an official group like the Division," said Petro's mother carefully. "And besides, no one knows how any of this will turn out. You were right to be cautious."

"But I feel as if I've betrayed him."

"By keeping his secrets safe? You know better than that, Anna. You've never been the sort of woman who had to announce everything."

They sat quietly for a few moments while Anna struggled to understand why she had denied Petro. She knew Halia was right. The less that was known about his activities, the safer he was. And before he had left, they had both acknowledged that their uncertain future could not yet contain a child. But still…the scent of the baby and its warm shape in her arms had made Anna long for Petro. She sighed and turned to Halia, "I'm sorry. I didn't mean to bring my troubles to you."

"You can come here whenever you like," and Halia leaned over to kiss Anna's cheek.

"Thank you. I'd better be going home to see how Mama is," she said standing up.

"Good girl," said Halia and stood up to hug Anna. She watched the solitary girl go, her trim figure erect, the sun glinting on her smooth head. Halia sighed, too, and went to find an occupation in the garden to take her mind off the implacable absences in her own life.

Roman Shumenko was scrupulous in his monitoring of the village's yield of wheat and he was at great pains to ensure that the Germans took no more than had been previously agreed. He also ensured that each family group was able to store their grain safely and securely. He was determined that the villagers would not be hungry in the coming winter, when it was probable that German defeats would continue to mount up. Kharkiv had been bitterly fought over and the Russians were moving west, bent on revenge against the Germans and armed now with American tanks and planes. And throughout the work that late summer, Vera was by Roman's side, acting as his secretary, as she carefully noted the weights of the crops in the village ledger.

Roman had always known that the dangerous elements of his role as village leader would need to be faced and as reports from further north came through, he called a small meeting of men he thought he could trust. They squeezed into his office and when they were seated, Roman looked around the group. "I assume you've heard the stories from Hubkiv and other villages in Volyn…"

These villages to the north had recently been completely destroyed. Whole populations, including all the women and children had been driven into wooden churches and had been burnt alive by Nazi forces.

"Are you suggesting that's going to happen here?" asked Timko.

"I don't know. The Nazis tried to do the same in Lityn, but our boys fought them off."

"I heard that, too," said Ihor. "Apparently they killed about a hundred Germans."

"So what about us?" persisted Timko.

"To be honest, I don't think we're in immediate danger, but I think we need to be ready. I'm going to suggest that we mount a guard on the village."

"What? Every day? Every night?" demanded Andriy.

"Yes."

"But we're short of young men as it is."

"It doesn't just have to be men. Any able-bodied person with eyes and ears could do it," said Ihor.

"That's right," agreed Roman.

"So how will it work?" asked Timko.

"We should mount a guard at the shrine to watch the road," began Roman. This would be an efficient use of personnel, as the road forked at the shrine, the right hand lane being the only road in and out of the village.

"We could do that, but that's still a couple of kilometres from here," objected Timko.

"Whoever is on guard there, rings the bell at the shrine."

"Will everyone be able to hear that?"

"We need to test it," suggested Ihor.

"And then what?"

"If it can be heard in the village, we could have someone on duty in the bell-tower by the church and the alarm could be rung there."

"And then what?" Andriy demanded again.

"Everyone takes to the woods."

"In a mad panic?"

"No. We need to talk to about how best to go about this. To prepare everyone."

"We have a lot of families with no man to help them," Timko reminded them.

"Our women are strong. They'll manage. We've already seen that. We got the harvest in."

"And look how many have coped with their own tragedies," added Ihor.

"I agree. I think we'll be able to do this, but I want us to be prepared," said Roman.

"You're right. But we do have to be sure of the warning system first," cautioned Ihor.

"Alright. Let's do that tomorrow. And then once we know how we're going to raise the alarm, then we can hold a meeting and tell everyone."

"Everyone?" asked Andriy.

"Yes, it's safer that way."

"Safer? What if the Nazis object?"

"We'll tell them we're defending ourselves against Russian partisans."

"Which is true enough," said Ihor.

"Andriy, you seem to be very hostile to this idea."

"No, I'm not. But I think it could be seen as aggressive by the Germans so we need to be clear about this. And you have to remember that there are some people here who don't have strong feelings against the Nazis."

"You think they'd betray us? After the deportations of slave labour? And the executions?"

"Possibly. We have to make it clear that we're all in this together. Remind them of what happened to the Jews," said Andriy sombrely.

190

"Yes, if they think they'll be victims, they're more likely to stand together," agreed Ihor.

"So are we agreed?"

The following day, Roman and Timko set off for the shrine on horseback, while Ihor and Andriy walked to the bell tower, which stood beside the church. The tower was unusual in that its narrow rectangular construction was completely separate from the church, which was about fifteen metres away. Ihor unlocked the door and they mounted the steps to the bell itself. They satisfied themselves that all was in working order and descended again to wait for the signal from the shrine. In a little while, they heard, clearly on the breeze, the continuous sound of bells ringing in the direction of the shrine.

"That's it. Now we can have that meeting…"

But before Roman was able to send out the announcement, he received a visit from Anna. He looked up as she knocked on his office door. "Good morning, Anna. I'm afraid we're busy today. I can't spare Vera."

"No, that's not why I came," she said in a low voice.

"What is it then?" he asked.

Anna looked behind her and checked that no one had entered the hall and she moved into the office, ascertaining that here, too, there were only Roman and Vera present.

"I've received a letter from Petro. He's up in Volyn, but I thought you would want to know what he has to say." She took the precious package from her pocket.

Roman's expression softened a little. "Would you like to read the relevant passages to me?"

Anna blushed and nodded. "If I may…" She opened the letter and apart from giving Roman the date, twentieth of August, she skipped the first paragraph.

"And so here is the reason why I have not had time to write to you, my beloved…"

She looked up with another blush. Roman nodded her on.

"…we have had two major engagements with the enemy. The first took place several days ago when we received intelligence that the Germans were heading for the villages with thirty-eight carts to claim the harvest. This would have left our people with no supplies for the winter so we hit them hard. We fought for more than three hours to defeat them and were successful in the end. But it was a bitter battle. Their losses were

high – over ninety soldiers our Commander said – but we lost three good men. When the Nazis sent in reinforcements – planes, tanks and motorised vehicles – we managed to slip away into the forest with our booty. We'll re-distribute it to our villagers as soon as we can.

"But we also ambushed a base for German soldiers and the Gestapo. They have been carrying out massive arrests in Volyn of teachers, doctors, priests…anyone with any education…and they shot all of them. Of course, we took revenge for this atrocity. They keep sending in more tanks and planes to back up their infantry, but it doesn't help them. We don't advertise our whereabouts, and their bases are easy to surround being so close to the forest.

"I don't send you this news to alarm you, my love, but to give you information so that you can defend yourself. Tell Roman Shumenko all of this. He is a good starosta *and will do his best to defend you all. Tell him, too, that we are very amused by the new road signs the Germans have been putting up – "Beware of Partisans!" You can be sure these are no help to them.*

"Kiss Mama and Nina for me…"

Anna paused. "That's all except some more lines for me."

Roman thanked her. "I'm calling a meeting today about defending ourselves. Anna, may I relay this news – without revealing its source, of course. It might convince some people that we must protect ourselves."

"Yes. Do you want to read the letter again?" She held it out to him.

"If I may." He smiled. "I won't read it all."

As Roman re-read Petro's missive, Anna glanced towards Vera.

"He sounds well, Anna."

"Yes…"

Vera watched her friend's large grey eyes fill with tears, which Anna hurriedly blinked back as Roman turned to her again.

"I'll tell our neighbours our defence plans this afternoon, but you might hear them through now." He outlined the actions they would take and then added, "It would be helpful if our friends in the forest knew."

"It would," said Anna. "I'd better go now. I'd like Halia and Nina to have this news from him, too."

"Of course. Thank you for bringing it to me."

Anna turned to leave.

"See you later," said Vera.

"Yes, I'll be at the meeting." She crossed the hall, her footsteps reverberating on the hollow wooden floor.

192

So throughout the autumn, the villagers took turns to keep watch, but although the Germans still controlled the area, little was seen of them, as they continued to be harried in the north and east.

Christmas came and for Anna and her mother, it was the third time they had marked the coming of Christ in their shrunken family, but for many other families in the village, it was the first. In Ihor's house, his daughter, Luba, set the table for the meal on Christmas Eve, laying some straw beneath the cloth as a reminder of the manger in which the infant Jesus had been laid. She added an extra place setting for the absent guest and put the specially baked bread, the *kolach* with its blessed candle, in the centre of the table. There was another candle in the window, to light the way home for the son who had left.

The men, Ihor, Pavlo and Nestor, returned from their work and, while they were washing and changing into their embroidered shirts, Luba stood with her child in her arms, watching the evening sky for the first star to appear. This would signal that it was time to begin their holy meal.

Lesia stirred the first course, a mixture of wheatgrain, poppy seeds, walnuts and honey and then at Luba's signal, called the rest of the family to the table. They stood behind their chairs for grace, in their usual places, with Ihor at the head of the table, and then he solemnly passed the *prosfora*, the blessed unleavened bread, around the family group, saying, "May God bless us on the birth of Christ and may he keep Ivan safe and bring him home to us." They each made the sign of the cross as they joined in the prayer for his safe return.

Lesia swallowed her tears with her *prosfora*, and said, "Come, let's eat. Let's try this *kutya* Luba and I made." She ladled a spoonful into small bowls, including that of the absent Ivan, wishing them, "*Smachnoho.*" Of course, Ivan wasn't here last year either, she admonished herself. He had been with his new wife, Sofia…but at least he was only down the lane and had walked over after the meal to join in the carols with his own family. They might have some sort of Christmas meal in his training camp, she comforted herself. She thought of the thousands of young men in their barracks far from home…

"Mama!" repeated Pavlo. "Did you hear me? Can I have a little more, please?"

Lesia shook herself and smiled at her youngest son's appetite as she took his bowl from him.

There was a place set, too, for Ivan at Sofia's house, who had the infant in her arms, as her mother poured the second course of *borsch* into bowls for herself, Levko and Sofia. Each region of Ukraine had its own variations of this special meal and in this village, at Christmas, the *borsch* was served as a clear consommé over mushroom dumplings. Levko looked hopefully at his mother as she put three of the delicious mouthfuls into his bowl. He was gratified that

Sofia also only got three and was glad of the distraction of the baby, who might not let her see that she had been treated equally with her unworthy brother. He tried to savour the deep flavour of the dried *pidpenky* in the dumplings, but they were so delicious, he ate them quickly. Then he looked hopefully at Parania.

She almost laughed at his puppy-like expression. "Alright then, finish these off," and she put the last couple of dumplings in his bowl.

Sofia glanced at Levko coldly. "You'll get fat."

He refrained from commenting on the irony of this warning from his buxom sister and was surprised to hear Parania defending him. "He's growing. And he works hard. He needs to eat."

Levko was approaching his twelfth birthday and resembled the stem of a germinated bean plant stretching up for the light. He was reed-thin and his winter pallor under his dark hair made him look even more fragile. Parania was beginning to understand what other mothers meant when they complained of their growing boys' appetites. He was quite unlike her daughters in the quantity of food he could eat, while appearing to be on a starvation diet. She silently said a prayer of thanks that their winter stocks of food were bountiful. Ivan had been such a help with their garden.

She turned to Sofia, but her daughter seemed oblivious to the absence of her husband, as she cooed to Antin and bounced him in her lap.

However, Levko was not so diplomatic. "Can I go round to Ivan's later?"

"What do you want to go there for?" demanded Sofia.

"I could sing them some carols."

"They won't want you there."

"They will. Ihor and Lesia both said I can come whenever I want to."

"Yes, you can go," interrupted Parania, nipping the argument in the bud. "But don't stay too long. It might seem rude."

Levko nodded and watched as his mother rose from the table to serve the next course. He wished she would get on with it, as he knew Lesia and Luba had been baking for days and, although he did not articulate the thought to himself, he enjoyed Ihor's gentle joshing. The older man would make up a little for Olha's absence. Despite this being her second winter away from home, Levko still missed her companionship. He often found himself wanting to tell her of his trials and tribulations and he felt the loss of his ally in the household keenly. Again his diplomacy failed him.

"I wonder what Olha's eating?"

Parania sighed. "I hope they're feeding her at that place and not just making her work."

They had received news that Olha had been put to work with several other young Ukrainian women in a canteen, which fed those who drove the trolleybuses in the town of Oberhausen. The work was heavy and twice a day the pace was fierce as they fed the transport staff, but Parania hoped that at least Olha might have easier access to food in this setting.

Sofia dismissed her mother's fears. "I'm sure she's fine. She's a survivor."

Parania hoped her elder daughter was right. She was certainly the best judge of survival skills.

Halia and Nina had set places for the absent girls as well as Petro and they had tried to make the table pretty with its embroidered cloth. The two women had become much closer in the last six months since Petro had left. Nina was no longer the spoilt baby of the family, but her mother's companion and helpmate. They made decisions jointly, like the decision to dispense with the fish course, there being only two of them. So Halia and Nina ate the *varenyky* Petro and the twins loved, allowing themselves both the onions fried in butter and the soured cream to garnish them. As Halia served them up, mother and daughter glanced at one another.

"Petro's last meal with us," murmured Nina.

"Let's hope he has lots more meals with us again."

"He will, Mama. He has plenty to come back for."

Halia nodded. She did not doubt his desire to return, only his opportunity.

Nina stood up, and putting her arm around her mother's neck, kissed her on the cheek. "Don't worry, Mama. They'll all come back and then Natalia and Irina will be telling us what to do from morning till night."

Halia returned Nina's kiss. "Their poor bosses!"

Nina giggled. "They'll have them quaking in their boots."

But as Halia suspected, her daughters were not having an easy time. They had both volunteered for a munitions factory, finding the petty tyranny of housewives unbearable. They worked long, hard hours in regimented rows, but they preferred the superficiality of the order imposed. They could think their own thoughts as they worked. Inevitably, they had discovered that the SS officer responsible for their department was susceptible to pretty smiles and whenever they sought a dispensation, they hunted as a pair. So they endured, keeping each other strong, knowing they could wait out this monotonous and meagre period of their lives.

Petro, too, often suffered meagre rations, but there was no monotony in his life. He had acquired many of the stealthy skills of guerrilla warfare and he had learned to deal with the constancy of the unexpected in his life. His *kurin* had been kept busy protecting Ukrainian citizens from Nazi plunder and each time they defeated the grey-clad troops, the partisans added to their own stores of munitions.

Anna could only hope that he was being careful and lucky. She had not heard from him since August and assumed that he was too busy to write, or that it was impossible to ask couriers of serious military matters to carry love letters. Now, as she served up the *holubchi* to her mother and their old neighbour, Nastunia, her mind touched on him again with love and longing. If her love could keep him safe, there would be nothing to fear. She placed the cabbage parcels with their buckwheat filling on the table and turned to get her mushroom sauce, made with those she had picked and dried in the autumn.

"Anna, I can't remember when I ate so much," said Nastunia. "It was good of you to invite me again."

"You're welcome. We enjoy your company, don't we, Mama?"

Katerina nodded. "We do. It's too sad for all of us women to be alone."

Anna looked at her mother in surprise. It was the first time she had acknowledged the especially painful loneliness of Christmas.

Anna tried not to think of the missing men. She had gritted her teeth three times to cope without Mikola and Yuri at this holy moment in the year, but Petro's absence threatened to tip the balance. She thought of Halia and Nina and wished they had all eaten together, but, wherever possible, women still wanted to cook the sacred meal of Christmas Eve in their own homes. Added to which, Halia had never turned Anna away, but they had tried to be more circumspect in the frequency of their contact. It was safer if Anna was not automatically connected with Petro.

"Where's your *makivnyk*, Anna?" asked Katerina.

Anna fetched her poppy-seed cake and set it on the table. "Perhaps we could have a slice in a little while," she smiled.

Nastunia cackled. "I certainly couldn't eat it yet."

The three women leant back in their chairs and Murchik leapt onto Anna's lap. He kneaded her legs for a moment, turned several times and purring loudly, settled in a happy circle. Anna scratched his ear, taking solace in the warmth and weight of Petro's tom cat.

"He's a very happy cat," commented Nastunia.

"Anna spoils him," said Katerina.

"Of course I do. He's so handsome," said Anna, as Murchik continued to live up to his name with his throaty purring.

Suddenly, the quiet night was disturbed by several pairs of feet on the path outside, a brief knock on the door and then voices raised in a carol: "*Boh predvichni narodivsia…*"

Anna hurried to open the door, delighted that someone had thought to preserve this wonderful ritual. Roman and Vera stood behind a group of youngsters, smiling and singing, as they entered Anna's house, Vera's younger brother, Vasilko, carrying the lighted star. The women joined in the singing as they felt the burden of loneliness being lifted from them.

When they came to the end of the carol, Anna offered them some of her baking before they prepared to move off to the next house.

"Go with them, Anna," said her mother. "They sound as if they need another soprano."

"Are you sure, Mama?"

"I'll stay here till you return," said Nastunia. "If I may."

"Yes, you go, Anna. We two will nod by the stove."

Vera flashed a smile at her friend. "Come with us, Anna. Your mother's right. We do need more voices."

Anna hurried into her coat and scarf, pulling on her boots, delighted to be freed from the long, quiet evening. She followed the carol singers out into the starry night and on to the next house, where doubtless there would be more empty spaces around the table.

Chapter 17

That winter, the Dniester froze as it usually did. Farmers took advantage of the seasonal opportunity to transport loads across to the southern bank, their fully-laden horse-drawn carts crossing the ice, which removed the natural barrier of the river. The thaw came as Easter drew closer. When the approaching Red Army reached Luka, thirty kilometres south-west of the village, they crossed the old bridge to the northern banks of the Dniester. They fought the Germans through the tear-drop of land between the bends in the river, breaking through the border into Halychyna at the shortest point between the Dniester's ribbon-like snaking. From here they pushed west and north, keeping the banks of the river at their backs until the Front stretched for twenty-five kilometres. The Russian soldiers were following the tried and tested routine which they had been using since they defeated the Germans at Stalingrad and Kursk: surround the enemy and cut off his lifelines, then take your time destroying him.

For Anna and her neighbours, the presence of so many olive-green uniforms along the banks of their river was a source of enormous fear. Anna made sure her stores were hidden, knowing that foraging troops would find and steal whatever they could. She feared for her livestock, but tried to be philosophical about what the next days and weeks might bring. The Red Army had not yet made their presence felt in the village, but as Maundy Thursday dawned, the villagers were shaken into a state of alert by the faint ringing of the bells at the shrine followed by the louder pealing from the bell-tower in the village. Reports flew in to Roman Shumenko that the Nazis were massing between Temne and the village. They were mirroring the spread of Red Army troops between Vozovik to the east and Bokova to the north, but the greatest preponderance of German soldiers and tanks, along this twenty-five kilometre Front, was on the north side of the village. Roman saw that their community would inevitably be squeezed between the two forces, neither of whom cared about the civilian population, only about the advance or retreat of their men. But it was too late by the time the Soviets realised the danger of their position. As intelligence reached them of the weight of troops the Germans planned to meet them with, they had to spend all of Thursday withdrawing to the banks of the river.

Anna was hanging out laundry when she heard the bells. She felt her stomach flutter as she hurried in to the house to check if Katerina was dressed yet. "Can you finish dressing quickly, Mama?"

Katerina looked up, eyes huge in her thin face, but she said quite calmly, "I did hear the bells didn't I, Anna?"

"Yes, you did, Mama. We have to go."

Katerina nodded and finished dressing. Anna slipped Petro's Luger from beneath the mattress into her pocket, then she went out to look into the lane. She had an urgent desire to urinate as she saw two men running towards the monument, shouting. Their words were indecipherable, but Anna snapped into action. She walked into the barn calmly, in order not to frighten the cow and, haltering her, led her to the fence where she tethered her loosely. She ran indoors, calling to Katerina, "Mama, we're going!" and scooped up the bundle she had prepared for emergency evacuation. She looked for Murchik, but he was out hunting, so she decided he would have to fend for himself, as would the hens, which she loosened from their pen. Then she took Katerina's hand and they left the cottage, closing the door.

Anna led Katerina across the garden to the fence and slid back all three poles. She sent her mother into the field ahead of her and, unhooking the cow's tether, led her onto the narrow and unaccustomed path. "Go right, Mama." She was relieved to see her mother making good time, so they soon reached the cover of the woods, where Anna came alongside her mother. "Alright, Mama?"

"Yes, Anna. Do you want to lead now?"

Anna nodded mutely, afraid to speak for the traitor tears which threatened to betray her relief at her mother's self-controlled behaviour.

They hurried through the trees, crossed the stream and took a lane between the houses again. Anna had taken a roundabout route for fear of being stopped by soldiers of either stripe, but she wanted to cross the village to make for the deeper woods around Petryn. Many in the village had reasoned it would be difficult to continue any battle in these woods and so would make a safer refuge. The two women zigzagged through gardens, past abandoned houses and finally gained the meadow, which bordered the deep woods. As Anna looked across the open land, she could see others fleeing with their livestock. The villagers were still between the opposing forces, but they would be hidden in the blessed anonymity of the budding woods and they could move if the need arose.

Once inside the wood, Anna saw other families heading towards a small clearing, so she followed. There was safety in numbers. She settled Katerina on a blanket on the ground and went to the stream to fetch water. As she returned, she saw, with enormous relief, Halia and Nina joining her mother. She hugged each of the women in turn. "Thank goodness you're here."

They turned as Ivan's mother and sister approached. Timko's wife was with them.

"Where are the men?" asked Anna, surprised to see only the women and Luba's baby, Stefan.

"They were trying to secure things. The Bolsheviks told them to leave the horses in the yard, but they weren't happy about it. I think they're going to move them to Timko's orchard so they can escape any fire," explained Lesia.

Timko's wife, Palahna, looked resigned. "He really didn't want to leave them. You know how he loves his horses."

The women nodded sympathetically and then made their temporary camps close to one another.

After some time, Ihor, Timko and Nestor appeared and Anna heard Ihor talking about doors. She approached their group hesitantly, not wanting to intrude.

"Come, Anna," called Luba. "*Tato's* just telling us not to expect to find any doors on our houses when we go back."

"Why not?"

Ihor turned to her. "I'm not sure. But as we left, there were Red soldiers everywhere, taking the doors from the houses."

They all looked bemused.

"Were they looting already?" asked Halia, joining the group.

"No. It didn't look like it."

Lesia looked around. "Ihor, where's Pavlo?"

"He'll be up later. He wanted to see what was going on," said her husband.

Lesia blenched. "You should have made him come with you."

"He'll be fine," said Ihor testily. "He's not stupid. He knows to hide himself. We'll see him later." Ihor knew what his wife wanted to say, that their youngest child was only just seventeen and she had already lost her other son to the military. But he understood Pavlo's desire to watch the action unfold… and besides he would bring information to the villagers.

The broken-hearted sobs of an uncomfortable baby broke into their conversation. They looked up to see Sofia and her family trudging towards them. Sofia had Antin strapped to her back with lengths of cotton fabric. Parania was leading the cow and both she and Levko carried bundles containing the items his sister could not live without. Sofia was loth to approach her in-laws, but seeing their camp looking established, she settled for expediency and joined Lesia's group. She embraced her mother-in-law negligently and nodded at Luba's greeting.

"Mama, help me get this screaming child off my back!"

Anna flinched and withdrew, leaving the family to help Sofia manage Ivan's growing baby. As Antin was lifted from his mother, his lusty cries increased and Luba took him in her arms.

"He feels wet, Sofia," she said, touching the sodden cloths around Antin's bottom. "Would you like me to change him, while you get settled?"

"Yes, please. He only has to be wet for a few seconds to make a fuss."

Luba moved to the banks of the stream, taking some cloths from her own bundle and she began to unravel her nephew from his torment. However, when she removed the clothing from his lower half, she drew in her breath at the red soreness of his fleshy buttocks and thighs. He was clearly well-fed and Luba saw that Sofia was happy to sit and feed her baby, but was less enthusiastic about changing his nappy. She lifted him towards the stream and bathed his burning limbs with cool water. Holding him in the crook of her arm, she returned to her own pack and plucked out some salve, which she kept for her own growing Stefan. He was now two years old and, despite his ability to get into mischief, still needed his baby cloths. Luba was ready with an excuse for Sofia, but she did not look up as her sister-in-law bustled about, caring for Antin.

Gradually, the woods filled with many of the villagers, but they had not all taken shelter together. Those who were lucky enough to have relatives in other villages had gone to claim kin, others had chosen different areas of the woodland. They had no idea how long they might need to stay in the shelter of the trees, but for the moment, the sunlight coming through the fine veil of green mist created by the incipient leaf buds had a beguiling effect. The birds seemed unperturbed by the visitors as they chattered and attended to their nest renovations.

Pavlo had seen the doors being taken by the Russian infantrymen. Uncertain about their intentions, he followed discreetly, keeping the last row of houses between himself and the soldiers. He reached the end house and hid behind the barn to watch. The hillside down to the river, and what remained of the plain, was covered with the ant-like figures of the Red Army, although their activities seemed to lack the organisation of an insect colony.

He looked towards the river in its spring flood. At this season, it was often seven or eight metres higher than usual, spreading across the first part of the plain to the steep ten metre high flood bank near the base of the hill, as it was now. The greater breadth of the river did not slow its pace, however. It hurtled along, driving downstream to the tight left-hand bend. Across the water, the trees on the steep bank did not seem very far away to the uninitiated, but Pavlo, along with all of the boys in the village, knew of the treacherous hidden currents which could sweep a man away.

Nearer to him, on the pine-clad hillside he saw a company of infantrymen gather around one of their Commissars. He crept closer to hear what this political representative of Stalin's might have to say. There had been a time when the Comrade Commissars had wielded enormous power, as they countermanded military orders with the weight of their Leader behind them. But by the time the crisis in Stalingrad had called for desperate measures, their power to overturn orders and shoot officers, whose combat decisions did not match theirs, had been curtailed. However, they were still allowed to play a vital role in helping the soldiers to maintain their morale. The Commissar stood surrounded by the men in their soft caps, red stars visible on his sleeves, as he read from a letter from their dear Comrade Father, exhorting them to make every sacrifice to protect the Motherland. He told them of the Nazis gathering to attack them and of their famous ferocity in battle.

"You must not allow yourselves to be captured, Comrades. Our dear Father warns you that these Nazis will torture you. They will cut out your tongues. They will cut off your noses and your ears. They will put out your eyes. They will show you no mercy. So, we must withdraw to the other bank of this river. Those of you who can swim, must do so. Go together in your groups. Help one another. We must try to save the artillery, too. Don't give yourselves up! Don't lose any precious materiel to the enemy!"

The men hurried away and Pavlo noticed how many of them were boys of his own age. There were older men amongst them, too, but so many young faces gave him pause. He began to see what the doors had been taken for; they were being used as makeshift rafts. Several soldiers tried to set off on the uncompromising waters of the Dniester, but the rafts were swirled about like kindling. The craft and their human cargo were soon invisible beneath the brown mass of the river. Pavlo watched as raft after raft disappeared from view and he wondered how the river could accommodate so many bodies. But the men on the banks were not deterred. They tried to pull their cannon onto stolen barn doors. They managed to haul the weapons aboard, but were thwarted in their attempts to float the rafts onto the water. As soon as the doors were halfway over the bank, instead of gliding smoothly away, they simply capsized and, despite their size, disappeared without trace beneath the waters. Some infantrymen decided to put their faith in their ability to swim across the river themselves. Taking the advice of their officers, they stood on the bank in groups of four or six, took hold of one another's hands in a firm grip and jumped into the swirling depths together. They, too, bobbed about briefly, before being dragged beneath the surface.

Pavlo felt sickened as row upon row of young men leaped to their deaths, fearing the near-certainty of drowning in the fast, icy waters less than the voracious monsters from the west, who would tear them to pieces if they laid hands on them. He could not comprehend the quantity of men disappearing beneath the flood. Would the river simply become jammed with corpses? Would the next jumpers be able to walk over a pontoon of dead comrades to the safety of the opposite bank? But, no. The swift currents carried them to the bend and hurled them around the corner, into the unseen lengths of the charging waters, all the way to the Black Sea.

Pavlo rested his forehead against the rough comfort of the barn wall, but looked up again as he heard the thud of hooves in the melee. A cavalry platoon was circling and seemed to be preparing to approach the river. Pavlo could understand the logic that horses were stronger than men, but he also knew the power of the cold river to clamp the heart and lungs on immersion. The horses would be as susceptible as the men. However, since there was no other way, the cavalry approached the bank in single file. Pavlo's heart sank as he saw they were to enter the water by the line of willows. This was the finishing line for the swimmers in their summer competitions and he wanted to cry out to them to take their horses several hundred metres upriver to the starting point of the village race. He knew how fast the current would drive both men and mounts to the bend, where they would be even more at the mercy of fearful currents. But even if he had called out to them, they would not have heard him above the clatter of desperate preparations to escape the Nazi horde. The file of thirty-two horses reached the bank and, like a string of geese flying south, they leapt, one by one, into the rushing waters, the cries of their riders, "For the Motherland! For Stalin!" floating up to Pavlo's ears. The horses tried to swim in the swirling depths and some even reached the middle of the river before submerging, one after another, beneath the water.

Pavlo watched horrified as almost the entire cavalry platoon disappeared without trace, but he was relieved to see half a dozen riders and mounts manage to reach the opposite bank. They might have felt heartened to be almost out of the rushing water, but the river would not loosen its grip on them. They were at the great turn of the Dniester as it vanished from the view of the village above, to plunge left and out of sight. The six riders only had a moment to catch their breath as they paused at the steep bank. They looked up, but there appeared to be nowhere to land at this inhospitable spot. As the water struck again, first two, then a third and a fourth, were swept away as the weight of the water crashed against the bank in a continuous roar, dragging them back into the centre of the river. Finally, the last two horsemen were caught up and then there were no men or horses to be seen above the water. Pavlo thought his heart would burst at the terrible waste of men. It was true, the Ukrainians had no love for their Russian neighbours and had much to fear from them, but the loss of so many lives, thrown so futilely into the spring melt, smote the young man's heart.

As the terrible day came to an end, the sun sank behind the wooded hill on the unreachable opposite bank, its heart bleeding into the earth which had lost so many that day. Dusk came on, the gloom deepened...and then was shattered into vivid brightness as the Germans launched a rocket attack. They fired at the houses which bordered the ridge, their burning thatch providing enough light to see the few Red Army soldiers still defending their position below. The villagers huddled in their temporary woodland shelters, feeling the ground shake with the gunfire and seeing the red sky above the village. They feared for their lives and what they might find on their return to their homes.

Pavlo had rejoined his family before the barrage had begun. He had made his way along the ridge and around the eastern end of the village, flitting between the empty houses, passing Petro's home, which overlooked the deep cleft where the stream ran down to the Dniester. He had paused to watch as the *Panzers* cut a path towards the river plain, knowing that they would be able to outflank the Red Army. He carried his explanation of the noise of the tanks back to his family.

"Pavlo!" called Lesia, as she hurried towards her son, her arms outstretched.

"I'm alright, Mama," he said, embracing her. "Don't worry."

He turned to his father. "There's been a rout, *Tatu*, without the Germans having to do much at all."

"Come and tell us about it," said Ihor, drawing his youngest son into the circle of villagers. There were exclamations of "Fools!" as he described the place where the cavalry had jumped into the river and gasps of horror as he recounted the huge number of drowned men.

"There was a Red Army Division between here and Bokova. More than twelve thousand men. They can't all have gone," said Timko.

"I didn't count, but there were huge numbers trying to swim across the river all afternoon."

"Their officers did too good a job of frightening them," observed Ihor. "They'd have been better to stand and fight than listen to propaganda."

As the villagers tried to settle to some rest, Anna thought, with a pang of sympathy, of the terror the men must have felt, as she remembered her nights on the river in spring flood.

As the sky lightened, the villagers could smell burning, even though they were a couple of kilometres from their homes. They rose in the misty dawn, wraith-like, and washed in the stream. Water was boiled over open fires and Anna made tea for herself and Katerina, Halia and Nina. The women discussed what they should do next.

"I want to go and have a look at how things are," announced Halia.

"I'll come with you," said Anna. "Nina, will you stay here with Mama for me?"

"Anna," said Lesia, joining them. "I don't think you should go to the village yet. Halia and I will go. We're old women. No one will pay any attention to us."

Anna agreed with Lesia's logic, but felt unhappy at letting the older women take the risk.

Ihor joined them. "You take care, Lesia. Don't do anything. Just have a look at what they've done."

Lesia tied her headscarf tightly over her still brown hair. "Don't fuss. Halia and I know what we're doing."

Palahna joined the two women. "I'll come with you. Timko won't rest while his horses are left alone. I'll have to check them for him."

The three older women set off, leaving an apprehensive group to wait, as if blind. They re-entered the village, passing Sofia's house, which like many they now saw, no longer had its roof. The straw had been fired and had burnt through the thick thatch completely. Halia dreaded what she would see at her own house. It was no worse than Sofia's. It stood roofless with all its windows blown out and the door missing. The women turned along the lane towards the centre of the village. House after house was in the same condition. They passed the monument and went towards Lesia's house. The roof and windows were gone but somehow, the thatch on the hay-store remained intact.

"We need to see Anna's house," said Halia and she and Lesia turned back towards the monument.

"I'll catch you up," called Palahna. "I'm going down to our orchard," and she followed the lane past the laundry.

Halia and Lesia walked along the lane towards the church and saw that here, the damage to the houses seemed more serious, standing as they did almost along the ridge above the river. Anna's house was slightly more sheltered, being on the right hand side of the lane, but the houses on the left had been badly scarred.

However, the village was not a ghost-town. Everywhere German soldiers were busy setting up their artillery, officers issuing orders, hordes of infantrymen hurrying to carry them out. And then the smell of frying meat assailed the women's nostrils.

They looked at one another: "The hens!" In fact, there was not a chicken, or a duck, or a goose to be seen.

"I wonder what else they've found to cook," muttered Halia.

A platoon armed with assorted spades hurried past them, on their way to dig the ditches vital to their continued battle.

"Our young men had better stay away. They'll only be roped in to that kind of work," commented Lesia.

The women turned to retrace their steps and had reached the village hall before they were challenged by an officer. "What do you want here?"

"We wanted to return to our homes."

"Just don't get in our way," he began but his voice was drowned by a sudden onslaught of thunderous noise. The ground shook as if an earthquake had erupted and they were deafened by the terrifying roar of *katyushas*, firing from the opposite banks of the river. Halia and Lesia threw themselves to the ground at the first shock, while the soldiers threw themselves behind walls to shelter from the onslaught. In the brief pause which followed, the women rose and, gripping one another's hands, ran towards the northern outskirts of the village, as if fleeing the devil himself.

The mighty Red Army weapon had dealt its punishment. Each *katyusha* fired a salvo of forty-eight shells within several seconds and then withdrew on its ZIS-6 truck to begin the lengthy process of reloading. The Germans dreaded its fearsome reputation. It was not only a weapon which howled hideously, it dealt terrible damage to everything in its path, each missile exploding in a burst of incendiary devices which burned everything – even the surface of water could appear to be ablaze.

The villagers heard and felt the pounding their homes were being subjected to, as they waited anxiously in the woods. Ihor had the almost impossible task of trying to hold Pavlo back.

"Let me go! I must try to find Mama."

"You can't. You have no idea where she is. She's probably sheltering somewhere."

"You don't know that!" shouted Pavlo.

Ihor and Nestor held the youngster firmly between them.

Anna too, was clutching a sobbing Nina. "Mama! Mama!" she wailed, child again.

Anna held her tight. "We'll go and look for her as soon as this barrage ends," she promised.

Timko stood, white-lipped, as he, too, looked in the direction Palahna had taken.

But it did not end quickly as the huge German artillery responded. The explosions continued, almost without pause, in a maddening cacophony, sending up plumes of black smoke and fountains of earth wherever the missiles landed. The houses were ablaze again and could be seen across fields as their flames licked the sky. Even the trees burned brightly, as if their spring blossom had suddenly leapt into the bare branches.

A long hour passed and suddenly there was a cry from the edge of the group. "They're here! They're coming back!"

Pavlo leaped towards his bedraggled mother as she and Halia hurried towards them through the trees.

"Mama!" called Nina, hurtling towards Halia.

The two women were embraced and then they began to describe what they had seen.

"But what we're telling you is already out of date," said Halia. "Heaven knows what damage those Bolsheviks have done."

"Where's Palahna?" asked Timko.

"Isn't she here?" asked Lesia.

"No," said Timko, trying not to shout.

"I'm sorry," said Halia. "She went down to your orchard while we checked Anna's house, and then when the attack came, we just ran."

Halia and Lesia looked at one another shame-faced.

Ihor clapped his old friend on the back and said, "She'll be along soon."

Timko nodded, but his heart misgave him.

Ihor turned back to the women. "What are the Germans doing?"

"They're fighting back," said Lesia. "The village was full of them."

"And they're digging in," added Halia. "We could be here for some time." She did not add that there might be little left to go back to.

There followed a solemn silence as the gathered group tried to absorb the information. Finally, Ihor said, "We'd better get organised." He turned to address the thirty or so neighbours. "Let's make our camp secure. Those of you who settled at a distance need to come in closer. The latrine will be over there, beyond those holly bushes. We'll pasture the cows together. And most important – we'll post lookouts. Pavlo, you and Nestor can take the first couple of hours, while the rest of us organise the rota. Set yourselves up at each end of our encampment and raise the alarm if troops or tanks seem to be coming towards us."

There was a flurry of activity as people re-arranged themselves for a longer stay.

Anna was strengthening the rough shelter she had made for her mother on the previous day, with branches and a tarpaulin.

"Anna, do you think Nastunia is dead?" asked Katerina.

"I'm afraid she might be, Mama."

"If only she had come with us," sighed Katerina.

"But she wouldn't, Mama. There was nothing we could do."

Anna had tried to persuade the old woman to come with them when the subject of the alarm had been raised. Nastunia had refused to consider flight.

"I'm an old woman, Anna. I can't go traipsing about the woods at my time of life. If it's my turn to die now, so be it. You go with your mother and may God go with you."

"Please, Nastunia," Anna had begged.

"No, my dear. Don't waste any more time talking to me about it. When the time comes, you go and, if God is willing, I will see you again."

Anna felt regret, but knew she could not have persuaded her to change her mind. She also understood the philosophical way Nastunia seemed to accept her lot. However, she was not ready to give up and she returned to making her mother as comfortable as possible, before going to see where she could help next.

The villagers remained in their temporary camp for a week before the guns fell silent, but there was no news of Palahna. Once again, Halia and Lesia went ahead to ascertain the safety for all to return and, as expected, found a terrible scene of devastation. Many of the houses were broken shells. Some fortunate families found their walls still standing, but all of the houses were roofless. The church and its bell-tower had both been destroyed and even the stones in the cemetery leaned unsteadily. The community returned like refugees, only to find their belongings burned or scattered. But even before Ihor's family reached the ruins of their house, they suffered another blow.

Lesia was leading both their cow and heifer, Luba carried the baby, Stefan, and the men led the way. But they were no match for a large German cook in a filthy apron and his armed guards. "Take the heifer," he ordered and the hapless creature was snatched from Lesia's hold and led to be slaughtered.

Ihor tried to object, but the soldiers raised their weapons and he decided his life was not worth the animal's, reasoning that if he was shot, they would still take the beast anyway. The family were lucky that they would still have one cow.

Anna and her mother were following behind and, as they witnessed the scene, Anna drew Katerina into the shadow of a ruined house to wait for the moment of danger to pass. Then they hurried home. They found the section of the house nearest the road demolished, but the walls of the second room remained. Anna climbed in to assess the damage and found the floor knee-deep in stale straw, which the Germans had used to sleep on. They had also used this shelter as a latrine and the smell was unbearable. She turned to the ruins of what had been their living room and storeroom. Turning over the rubble with her foot, she saw the icon lying alongside her blue enamel saucepan, both filthy with dust. She inspected the barn whose walls also still stood, but far more precariously.

Anna decided that she could make a temporary shelter in what remained of the house for herself and her mother. "Mama, I'm going to clear this room for us to sleep in," she said, and went to fetch a rake from the barn.

When she returned, Katerina asked, "What about the cow, Anna?"

"We'll have to risk her in the barn."

"No. I mean, what if the Germans take her?"

"Yes, you're right. But I can't do everything."

"I could take her down into the woods below while you're working," offered Katerina.

Anna looked at her mother in surprise. "That's a good idea, Mama. Will you be alright?"

Katerina took the cow's halter. "Of course."

Anna watched the frail figure walk slowly along the path beside the vegetable garden and go out of sight down into the hollow to the woods. She shook her head and turned to begin the filthy task of making a part of their house habitable again.

Timko's home was as devastated as the other houses in the village and there was no sign of Palahna. He felt sure she must have been killed in the attack, but could find no trace of her. He searched what remained of the house and went over the garden and orchard carefully. He persisted in asking his neighbours and the soldiers if they had seen his wife over the following days, and even weeks, but she was never seen again. The gaping shell holes along the lane offered him a little comfort that her death might have been quick.

In his orchard, a few horses remained, but he saw that they had been used by the fuel-starved Germans to haul men and munitions. As he examined the animals, he knew that they had been worked hard and, even as he stood there, soldiers came to harness up the horses to wagons. They brought with them four unarmed Red Army soldiers, who had been taken prisoner, and ordered them to get the carts ready. As the Russians went about their tasks, Timko decided to help them to select the least-worked beasts. At least if he could rotate them, he reasoned with himself, he and Ihor might salvage some animals.

"Take this one," he suggested, "and the bay mare over there."

The Russians fell to their work with Timko's help, harnessing the patient horses. The oldest of the prisoners was more angry and garrulous than the rest and, with little prompting from Timko, began recounting the tale of Maundy Thursday.

"You see what scum our officers were," he said. "They frightened the boys half to death with their terrible stories of what the Fascists would do to us if they caught us. They commanded us – Don't give yourselves up. They'll cut you up! They'll tear your eyes out! And what happened? Here we are," he gestured to the other three infantrymen, "disarmed and put to work. That's all. They even fed us...a bit."

Timko did not know what to say to this explanation of the terrible drownings Pavlo had described. "So they tried to swim the Dniester because they were afraid?" he asked at length.

"Terrified. Our children, our poor boys, gone for nothing."

Both men stood silent, thinking of the row upon row of boys, linking hands and leaping into the flood rather than face the Nazi horde.

The old soldier shook his head. "Ach! They could have given themselves up and survived."

"I don't suppose Stalin would have approved of that," suggested Timko, but he can kill defenceless old women, he thought.

The old man spat, and then remembering himself, glanced around to make sure that none of his fellow-countrymen had seen his treasonous action. "No, he wouldn't," he mumbled and turned to check the horse's harness.

A kind of routine settled upon the village as the Germans held their position, but the young men found themselves deployed to dig trenches in the most fought over positions. The Red Army employed the tactic which had been so successful in the cities where they had taken back strongholds, not only street by street, but house by house; and here, they battled for field after field and wood after wood. However, for Pavlo and Nestor and the other young men, armed only with spades, the enemy often only fifty metres away, digging trenches was a fearsome task. There were many conversations about what options were open to them, when the only real choice was to dig or be shot. But their oppressors provided the solution themselves.

The Germans knew they would have to withdraw from their current position and the same was true for the rest of Halychyna. The Red Army was determined to drive them out, but the Germans would not leave behind such a valuable resource as manpower for their enemies to conscript. So they provided a second opportunity to join the Galician Division. However, this time, the offer was not so clear-cut. All could see that the Fascists were in retreat and their leeching of crops and labourers had disillusioned many. So, the potential conscripts tried to join the Insurgent Army. Here the purpose for fighting would be clearer. They would be fighting for independence. However, the UPA could not arm more men, so it was suggested that this generation of volunteers should join the Germans, take the training and the arms and, at a later stage, put all of that to good use with the insurgents.

So Pavlo and Nestor, who would gladly have taken to the woods, followed Ivan's footsteps into the *Divizia*. They would travel west for training, as he returned east to fight the Red Army...at Brody.

Part Three

Summer 1944 – Winter 1946

Chapter 18

Anna was sifting through the debris of their home, when Vera joined her. The two young women took in each other's altered appearance: greasy hair, dirty faces, slovenly clothes. They grinned and Vera asked, "Do you think it's working?"

"I'm not troubled by the soldiers. Are you?"

"No! They must think we're a filthy lot."

"I don't care as long as they keep their distance."

"And have you managed to salvage much?"

"A few things. And as for the garden, there's not much damage. There are no craters, so once I'd watered everything to wash some of the dust off, it wasn't too bad. The walnut tree's been hit though. I'll just have to wait and see if it'll survive losing a couple of big branches. How about you?"

"We've managed to save some things, but we took a bigger pummelling on our side of the lane."

"We'll have to help each other this winter."

Vera smiled at her friend. "We'll manage, but I'll let you know if the boys threaten to starve! They eat like horses."

"So, did you just come to check my level of attractiveness?"

"Unfortunately not. There's been more bad news."

"What is it now?"

"Let's go and sit on the bench and I'll tell you."

Anna looked at Vera fearfully.

"Don't worry. It's not Petro."

They sat on the bench Anna had replaced beneath the wounded walnut.

"Roman has been receiving bulletins for the last couple of days, about a huge battle at Brody. Apparently the boys who went to the Galicia Division last year were engaged in a big battle with the Red Army. The Russians encircled them and about two thirds of them were killed or captured."

"Ivan?" asked Anna.

"We don't know yet. The Germans still haven't posted lists of the dead."

"How many were involved?"

"They think about three thousand captured and possibly nearer six thousand killed."

"My God!"

"The Germans had losses, too, but they sent our Division in to take the worst of it."

"Those poor men."

"Yes. Apparently, the Germans should have sent in a *Panzer* Division, but for some reason it wasn't there…so the Russians tanks overran them."

"It can't have been as simple as that."

"I'm sure it wasn't, but whatever happened, ours were defeated."

"What's happened to those taken prisoner?"

"Who knows? Roman thinks the Bolsheviks will either have shot them or be planning to deport them to Siberia."

"And what about those who've just left?"

"They'll go into training first, so they'll be safe for a while."

"Do Ivan's family know yet?" asked Anna, thinking of the three young men who had now gone from that household.

"Maybe not. Roman is going to hold a meeting of the men to tell them what he's heard so far."

"Why only the men?"

"He thinks they'll be shocked…but the woman will be hysterical."

"Hmm. He may have a point. He's always very thoughtful in his dealings with people."

Vera blushed.

"And with you?"

"Always kindness itself."

"More than kind I suspect," smiled Anna.

"Yes, he's a lovely man."

The women sat, their minds a jumble of love for their own and incomprehension at the numbers of the dead.

"Poor Sofia," said Anna.

"Perhaps. She'll certainly think she's been hard done by."

Anna glanced at Vera, sitting with her shoulders hunched. She put her arm around her. "What is it?"

"Oh, all those dead soldiers…wherever they come from…and their families waiting for news that doesn't come."

"Have you heard anything of Evhen?"

Vera shook her head. "I'm pretty certain he must be dead. He's been gone since '41 and look at how much has happened since then. Even when the Red Army seems stronger, like now, they still suffer terrible losses."

"He may turn up again."

"Maybe." Vera sighed. "I'm sorry, Anna. I can't talk to Mama about this.

She has enough to worry about with the boys."

"It's alright. You can always bring your troubles to me."

"And where do you take yours?"

Anna shrugged, but Vera waited for an answer.

"I haven't heard from Petro in a while, but there are lots of reasons why a message wouldn't get through." She paused. "I don't know what the UPA will do as the Russians move west either."

"Roman thinks they'll be around here in greater numbers soon. Even though they're pretty stretched both to the north and south."

"We'll see. I suppose it'll depend on whether the Bolsheviks occupy this area or not. That will bring them back. But in the meantime, we have enough work to do."

Every household was working on rebuilding their homes. Anna had received her share of cement from the stores and was making the walls of their remaining room secure, but she would need to rebuild the second room before winter. She had been given permission by Roman to salvage what she could from Nastunia's property. The old woman had perished, as Anna and her mother had feared. Anna turned to her rebuilding. She needed to get a move on if she was to take advantage of the work the remaining men were doing to re-roof as many houses, or parts of houses, as possible, before the cold weather returned.

Sofia received no news of Ivan, and then the Germans withdrew from the village. The Red Army had been edging forwards all along the twenty-five kilometre Front, and now, with a heave, they dislodged the Nazis who had been clinging on for three months since the Easter onslaught. They retreated, leaving behind the semi-derelict village, which they judged would provide scant comfort for the Russian troops behind them. However, they wanted to be certain that the crops in the fields, which were almost ready to be harvested, would not feed the enemy. The wheat had benefitted from the July sunshine and was becoming golden and dry, but there was no petrol to spare for a conflagration. So, the soldiers who had been ordered to burn the crops could not use flame throwers. Instead, they took burning brands and touched them along the edges of the fields and roared away, leaving the fire to destroy the valuable source of food.

The red flames skittered across the rows. The first curls of smoke rose towards the blue sky, but, picking up force from the breeze, whipped about, changing direction on a whim. The smell became acrid and the villagers living nearest the fields mobilised themselves quickly. Several took saucepans and ran towards the centre of the village, beating them and yelling, "Fire! Fire!" while the others took spades and ran for the fields. If they could stem the flow of the fire with a trench, they might save some of the wheat. The fire rattled through the crop and its smoke stung the eyes of those trying to halt its progress. More of the villagers ran towards the fields, beating out the flames with whatever came to hand or helping with the fire-break. The fire did not threaten for long as the determined villagers fought it back and, when they were certain that no spark remained, they tried to assess the damage.

This time, efficiency had abandoned the Nazis and the destruction was patchy. It would be a significant loss, but the villagers could salvage something. They found that only those fields bordering the road from the village to Temne had been fired. Later that night, as people attempted to get some rest, their restless minds began to wonder what would follow the fleeing grey menace.

The pause between occupying forces was brief. Although the Red Army poured west and north driving the Hun before them, by October of that year the olive-clad troops had been followed by the blue caps. The NKVD also wore drab olive jackets and trousers, but the blue piping and epaulettes, and particularly their bright blue head gear, marked them out as Stalin's hammers. He wanted to eradicate nationalism once and for all. He would not allow his State to be threatened again by desires for cultural and individual freedom. So he flooded Western Ukraine with his political troops to stamp out the troublemakers, either by summary execution or by deportation to Siberia. In Anna's village, they announced their arrival with a death.

Anna heard a clamour in the lane and hurried to see what the trouble was. People were hurrying towards the monument from all directions. Both men and women seemed stricken and Anna hurried out of her gate in time to join Vera, who was also striding towards the melee.

"What's going on?" asked Anna.

"I don't know, but whatever it is, people seem upset."

They walked towards their neighbours. As soon as Anna saw the blue caps of the NKVD bobbing among the crowd, her heart lurched. They could only have taken someone for punishment. The women drew closer and Anna caught sight of Roman Shumenko, dressed only in his shirt and trousers, despite the autumn chill. He was being dragged towards the open ground beside the village hall. His face was muddy and marked, his hair dishevelled and he had already been beaten, so whatever was to follow could only be worse. Roman had done too good a job protecting the community, giving them the opportunity to re-establish their self-esteem and their autonomy. There would be no room for his integrity in the Soviet future Stalin had planned for them… and for all of the villages like theirs.

Anna's heart beat wildly in her chest and before she had time to turn to Vera,

Roman looked up, his brown eyes flashing a desperate plea to Anna: Save her!

Anna caught Vera's arm. She pulled her towards her and whispered, "Verochka! Come with me!"

But Vera was pulling away towards Roman.

"Vera! Remember why he didn't marry you," hissed Anna. "Come on!"

She felt Vera hesitate as she tried to understand Anna's message and so Anna was able to begin to draw her friend away from the danger. But once again, Vera seemed to see only her lover being dragged to his death. She tugged herself away from Anna, who nearly lost her grip of Vera's arm. Anna almost despaired of saving Vera quietly before she caught sight of Luba, who had also seen the danger. Anna blessed Ivan's sister for her quick-thinking as she joined them, taking Vera's other arm. The crowd was getting thicker in front of them, so the two women turned their captive away and hurried into Luba's yard. They hastened Vera indoors, despite her protests, and Luba closed the door firmly.

"What is she saying?"

"I don't know. I think she's too shocked to speak properly," replied Anna, rubbing Vera's temples.

The door opened and Lesia hurried in. "Is she alright? I saw you bring her away." Ivan's mother took Vera's chin in her hand and looked into the younger woman's grey eyes. "I'll get her some valerian. Sit her down."

Anna sat with Vera on the makeshift divan and put her arm around her dearest friend. Luba disappeared briefly and returned with a blanket to cover Vera's trembling shoulders. Anna wrapped Vera in its warmth and continued to hold her until Lesia handed Anna a cup. Vera's hands shook so much that she could not take it and Anna fed her sips of soothing tea.

"I have to go," Vera managed to stutter.

"You can't, Vera. Remember why you're not Roman's wife. He wanted to protect you from exactly such a time like this."

"But I am his wife."

"I know you are, my love. But not in any official way which the NKVD can discover."

"Vera, dear," Lesia began, but at that moment a shot rang out and a terrible silence followed.

"No!" howled Vera.

Anna could only hold her as the sobs wracked her body. She held Vera tightly in her arms, trying to pour her own strength into her friend.

The door flew open and Levko ran in. "They shot Roman Shumenko!" he gasped.

Lesia and Luba bundled him away from Vera, shushing him and leading him into the rebuilt storeroom. Anna could hear them whispering, but she was more concerned for Vera, whose sobbing threatened to engulf her and to endanger her rescuers. Anna placed her hand firmly over Vera's mouth and continued to murmur in her ear: "Verochka, you have to be strong. For Roman. He knew this time would come. He loved you so much, he wanted you to survive. You have to be true to his love for you and live." She continued with variations on this litany as she rocked her friend.

As the minutes went by, Anna thought of her mother and how frightened she would be, isolated at home. She turned towards the outer door, but Vera gripped Anna's hand, as if she had read Anna's thoughts. "Don't leave me!"

Levko came back into the room with Lesia and Luba and, although it was a lot to ask, Anna could not help herself.

"I wonder if Levko…" she paused. "I'm worried about Mama."

Levko looked up, his dark eyes troubled.

"Levko, could you slip round to my house the back way, to tell Mama I'm safe. She'll be beside herself with worry."

The boy nodded and Luba asked, "Shall I come with you?"

"No, I can do it."

"Do you know the way?" asked Anna. "Go down beside the stream here and just past the laundry, take the little turning to the left. You could go through the gardens at the top to the back of my house."

"Yes, I know the way. What shall I tell her?"

"Tell her that I'm safe and that I'm here with Vera. You'll also have to tell her who's been shot." Anna looked at Lesia apologetically.

"It's alright, Anna. Levko's a good boy. He often helps us out. He'll reassure your mother."

"Tell her, I'll be home when I can, but I might have to wait until it's dark."

Levko nodded again and then was gone.

The women waited till dusk and then Anna washed Vera's face, retied her headscarf. "Come. I'm going to take you to my house." She thanked Lesia and Luba inadequately for risking their lives to save Vera and she led her friend by the route Levko had taken. They reached Anna's cottage through the hushed and anxious village and, once inside, Anna hurried over to her mother. Katerina was lying curled on her side on the bed. Her eyes were open and she stirred as Anna approached her.

"Mama, are you alright?" She stroked Katerina's cheek and kissed her forehead. "Did Levko come?"

Katerina sat up with Anna's help. "Yes, he came. I sent him on to Vera's."

"Oh Mama, that was thoughtful," and she kissed her mother again. "I'm sorry I couldn't be with you."

"Is it all starting again, Anna?"

Anna could only nod. Her mother had not left the house and yet had understood that the reign of terror, which had taken Mikola and Yuri, was back again.

"Have you eaten, Mama?"

Katerina shook her head. "I couldn't."

"Alright. We'll have some soup. Vera must eat, too."

She looked across at her friend who sat where Anna had left her, her head slumped forward almost onto her chest, her hands in her lap.

"Lie her here," said Katerina, struggling up from the bed. Between them, they laid Vera down and then Anna turned to her cooking. Vera would need to eat before their night's work. She did not allow her own grief to surface as she cooked. She had been here before with a corpse to reclaim and she knew she could do it again. She would have to be strong for Vera.

Anna waited until the night was fully dark. "Verochka, we're going to see if we can take Roman's body and bury him. Do you think you can do this?"

Vera nodded and looked at Anna with blank eyes. Anna's heart ached for her, but they rose, put out the light and left the house. Once again, the women made their way through cold gardens and past darkened houses. As they approached the green, they saw two figures lifting the body onto a hand cart. Ihor and Timko looked up startled, and all four stood still as statues until Ihor gave a sharp signal with his hand to follow them. The men led the way by a darker and longer route, through the woods below Timko's house and up to the back of the graveyard. They paused before passing through the gap in the hedge into the cemetery.

"What do you think you're doing?" demanded Ihor.

"I'm sorry we frightened you. We wanted to bury Roman," replied Anna.

"What…" began Timko.

"I've done it before…and Vera loved him."

The men sighed impatiently.

"Well, just keep quiet," commanded Timko. "No wailing!"

"There won't be," said Anna.

They left the cart behind the hedge and all four carried Roman's inert body to the hole Ihor and Timko had already dug. As they were about to lay him in the ground, Vera bent to kiss Roman's cold face. The men looked anxious, but she withdrew and they were able to lower him into the shallow grave. They covered him with soil and then Ihor and Timko relaid the turves they had cut earlier, to mask the grave. A breeze lifted as they straightened up and Anna whispered to Vera, "He won't be alone."

The men hurried to collect their cart and Ihor said, "Get home quickly!"

Anna led Vera back to her house and once inside, helped her take off her jacket and scarf, and her boots. She laid her down in the bed between herself and Katerina and then she climbed in under the quilt, too. As she lay beside Vera, she felt her begin to tremble again. Vera shuddered from head to foot so Anna took her friend in her arms, laying her head on her breast. She stroked Vera's hair back from her forehead and murmured, "It's alright. That breeze we felt – that was *Tato* and Yuri. They'll look after him. He's safe now. No one can hurt him."

Eventually, Anna felt Vera relax into sleep and she dozed herself, only to be woken with a start as Vera sat bolt upright in bed, gasping for breath.

Anna sat up beside her. "Vera, it's me, Anna. You probably just had a nightmare. Try to lie down again."

Vera lay down and gradually relaxed into a fitful sleep again, while Anna dozed beside her.

When it was fully light, Anna tended to the fire to prepare something warm for her mother and Vera. She set water to boil and picked up Murchik from his seat. The cat had returned cautiously after the commotion of battle and he seemed to have forgiven Anna for abandoning him, although now he always made a swift exit at sudden loud noises. He purred in her arms, enjoying the attention, but was distracted as Vera rose from the bed. Anna put him down and turned to her friend.

"I must go home," said Vera looking around for her things.

"Yes, I'll help you. I was going to make us some breakfast first."

Vera shook her head. "No. Thank you, Anna. I've given my mother enough worry as it is."

"Shall I walk up with you?"

"No. I must learn to do it myself." She looked at Anna bleakly. "I have to..."

Anna watched as she tied her headscarf and struggled into her jacket, her heart bleeding for Vera, who was still numb. The agony of grief had not yet begun to gnaw at her. Vera put her arms around Anna and kissed her cheek, then walked away alone down the path.

Anna spent the morning working on her woodpile and later, finding the anxiety unbearable, announced to Katerina that she was going to take a walk. She took her basket and walked past Vera's house, but when Anna knocked at the door, she was told by Vera's mother that she was in bed, unwell. So Anna walked past the ruined church to the ridge and then followed it east around the edge of the village. There was little to forage, but she gathered some pine cones. Although it was still only mid-afternoon, the grey sky cloaked the landscape in grubby cotton. Not only were sounds deadened, but colour seemed to be muted, too. The bright yellow of the dying willow leaves had paled to dull primrose and up here, the orange of the chestnuts had been bleached to a strange opalescence. She stood among the trees and looked down the valley to the river. The pallid sky rested against the darker water of the river. The water was well up the banks, submerging the grass and lapping around the trunks of the willows. It rippled in its dark autumnal wealth, completely satisfied with itself, while the trees waited in the wings for their moment of glory, little suspecting that it was already fading in a translucent show of bronze and gold. The wounds and scars of Easter's fighting had been masked by summer's blaze of growth and, even as the trees became bare again, Anna saw the land would endure.

History seemed to repeat itself as the villagers were called to a meeting, the blowing of the horn reminding them all of 1940 and '41, when its sound was not an invitation, but a threatening expectation. People hurried toward the hall and sat in quiet rows, looking at the half dozen members of the NKVD on the platform. Among them was a man who could have been Ostapenko's twin. Where do they find them, Anna wondered as she took in his big frame, broad chest and bullet-shaped head; his very stance telling the whole community to expect neither justice nor mercy.

The doors were closed and an NKVD *starshina* began. "Comrades! We have begun the good work in this village by destroying the reactionary, Shumenko. Our work will be continued by our Comrade, Serhiy Zadyrak, who has volunteered for this sacred task of leading the village in the service of Our Dear Father." He drew Zadyrak forward, presenting him to the villagers, not one of whom considered Stalin to be his dear father.

Serhiy Zadyrak stood at the edge of the platform, almost rocking on the balls of his feet. Anna felt a hysterical desire to laugh. If only he would fall from the stage! But she gritted her teeth and made herself focus on Katerina, too frail to attend this meeting, tormented again with the deaths of her husband and son.

Zadyrak was saying, "So we will sow the wheat in the spring as Dear Comrade Stalin has instructed. It will give us a good yield, as it did in 1940, when this village was lucky enough to have the guidance of our Dear Comrade Leader."

Anna did not dare glance at her neighbours. He was right. They had planted the wheat in the spring of 1940 as ordered and the harvest had been reasonable, but all of the farmers knew that the Soviet policy which suited the Urals did not suit the climactic conditions of Halychyna. Here the wheat gave a better yield if planted before the winter. But she knew none of the men would dare to pour scorn on this plan. They would follow instructions and

221

hope to survive, although there was a slight ray of hope this time around. The UPA was stronger than they had been three or four years ago and perhaps they would liberate the country yet. Zadyrak stepped towards the table, ready with the papers which he would need to sign publicly, to formalise his acceptance of the role of *starosta*. The NKVD men stood closer to him and as the sergeant passed him a pen, Zadyrak allowed himself a warning glance.

"Just sign here," said the *starshina*, shielding Serhiy's right hand from the audience.

Zadyrak appeared to scribble a signature and the papers were swept up, the writing hidden. The *starshina* smiled. He had succeeded in placing an illiterate bully in yet another village to control an already apprehensive populace. Stalin's work continued.

Chapter 19

Serhiy Zadyrak began by imposing a curfew on the village. Once it was fully dark, he assumed anyone found out of doors was up to no good and so was treated as a traitor. There seemed to be no concern that people would commit crimes, only that they would commit crimes against the Soviet state.

It had been some time since the insurgents had been present in the woods and forests beyond the village, but one night Anna heard gunfire in the distance. It was not the sound of an all-out battle and besides, the Red Army had moved north and west, leaving the village behind. She lay holding her breath and listening. There was another single shot, but then complete silence. It could only be the partisans returning, she reasoned to herself and she resolved to find out the following night. She felt her stomach flutter with anticipation. It might be Petro's *kurin* returning. It was fourteen months since she had heard from him and she dealt with the twin agonies of uncertainty and separation by clinging fiercely to the belief that he was alive and busy.

From the ruins of her home, she had salvaged every possible thing including her father's old trousers and his cap. The next night, as soon as Katerina slept, Anna got up and put on her disguise, tucking her thick plait under her jacket and jamming the cap down firmly over her brows. She slipped out of the cottage and stood in the corner of the porch, listening intently. There was no sound, so she moved towards the woodpile and stepped between the two poles of her fence, having left the third drawn back earlier in the day. She crouched as she followed the bare hedgerow over the brow of the hill and then trotted down to the woods. She had decided to visit the spot Hrichko had taken her to, not knowing whether it would be inhabited by insurgents once more, but prepared to give it a try. It had taken her no time at all to decide that she would help them again. If her life was now to be controlled by the likes of those who had killed her father and Yuri, then she would fight back. She would not welcome them with bread and salt.

She took the wooden bridge over the Barish and hurried across the open meadow to the deeper woods. Here she was torn with indecision. Should she make a noise, announcing her arrival to the partisans; or should she go as silently as possible, to avoid detection by NKVD patrols. She decided on the latter, but eventually, she was challenged.

"Halt!"

She stood still, her arms wide of her sides. She had not brought Petro's pistol for fear the UPA would think she was the enemy, so she waited while a man armed with his own pistol stepped forward. "What's the password?"

"I don't know. The last time I came here it was "Wolf", but that was about sixteen months ago."

"Stand still," he said and patted her down, finally pulling off her cap. "It's a girl," he announced to someone in the bushes. He pulled a kerchief from around his neck and tied it over Anna's eyes. "Better to be certain," he muttered and taking her arm, led her for a hundred metres or so before halting.

Anna waited several moments before sensing the scrutiny of at least one pair of eyes and then heard a voice say, "It's her."

"Alright, then. Take off the blindfold," said a deeper voice.

As the kerchief was removed Anna turned to look at the source of the voices and recognised Hrichko, now a tall, gangly youth, but still wearing his wide grin. "Hrichko!" She could not help stepping forward to hug him.

He accepted her embrace shyly, acknowledging her right to hug him, despite feeling that he was closer to manhood than boyhood.

"I'm so glad to see you," she said. "Are you well?"

"Alright. Enough of happy families," growled his companion. "What do you want?"

"I heard the shots last night and thought you must be back here, so I came to see what I could do to help."

"Alright. We need food, of course, and some letters taking to Buchach."

"That's fine."

"There should be replies to the letters."

"It's market day tomorrow, so I'll go then. If I can, I'll be back tomorrow night. There's a curfew in the village."

"We know." He disappeared again and Anna assumed he had gone to fetch the letters. She looked at Hrichko. "Are you really alright?"

"Yes. There's never enough food, but we all suffer from that. How're things in the village?" he asked and she noticed the deeper timbre of his voice. He must be almost fifteen, she calculated.

"Battered. Only old men and boys. And the NKVD of course."

"Pretty bad then."

"It could have been worse. The Red Army has been forcibly recruiting in some villages."

"Did they do that at home?"

Anna felt a rush of sympathy for the boy who had no home he could return to, nor had he for almost three years, and yet it still called to him. "No," she replied, "they realised that the Germans had taken as many men as possible into the *Divizia* before they retreated." She paused. "There are a few younger boys still there, but they keep a low profile. The Bolsheviks might not be too fussy about exact ages."

They were quiet again and she knew she should not ask, security did not allow it, but she longed to know whether Petro was back. However, her opportunity to be indiscreet slipped away as the older man reappeared with the letters.

"Take these." And he gave her concise instructions for their destination. "Now go, but quietly," he said, giving her the new password.

"Of course. Good night."

She made her cautious way home, knowing she was being tested by the partisans, but knowing, too, that to be caught by the NKVD would be disastrous. So she moved as quietly as she could among the shadows under the trees, trying not to walk in drifts of susurrating dry leaves. She took her time to reach her cottage undetected. Katerina was still asleep and, as Anna lay down to try to rest for the remaining hours of the night, Murchik curled up on the quilt behind her bent knees, purring happily to have her back.

Early the following morning, as Anna left the cottage, she looked out at the ghostly landscape. The morning mist lay heavily in the river valley and to the west, where the land dropped down to the wood and the Barish below. Every crevice held its white vapour, deadening sound and shortening sight. The trees rose up from their opaque bases, seeming to float weightlessly. Anna shivered a little in the autumn cold and directed her thoughts towards her errand. She carried a basket of walnuts, ostensibly to barter them at market. She set off and once on the busier road beyond the shrine, begged a lift on a passing cart. The farmer was taciturn, as was his son, and Anna was pleased to be left alone with her thoughts.

They passed through Temne and she was surprised to see a bustle of activity about the prison. There were blue caps on guard at the gates of the compound and as they passed the entrance, Anna saw many more uniformed NKVD in the courtyard. The farmer waited until they were clear of the gates and then he hawked and spat. Anna agreed with him, although she did not say so, and she watched the tall walls of the prison disappear from view.

The Germans had made more use of the prisons further afield in Buchach and Ternopil, but the NKVD found the prison at Temne convenient for their purposes. It was a long rectangular brick building, three storeys high and although it boasted six windows along each long side of the structure, Anna assumed correctly that there must be cells without daylight. Despite the smoke curling up from tall chimneys, she guessed that cold, too, would be added to the prisoners' deprivations to discourage resistance. She did not feel afraid as they rode towards Buchach, but felt determined to do what she could to prevent the Bolsheviks' stay becoming permanent.

She delivered her letters first, following the instructions she had been given, which led to an anonymous-looking door not many streets from the market place. Her knock was answered by another young woman and Anna was waved in on repeating the password she had been given. She received the expected reply from the girl and handed over the letters which she carried. Anna could not help noticing the woman's smart white blouse and plain dark skirt. Her dark hair was neatly curled and even her shoes looked tidy. Anna suddenly felt old and plain and, although she told herself that appearances did not matter, she felt as if she had been living in filth and disorder for a long time.

She stood in the bare corridor until the girl returned and said, "You're to wait here," and with a nod, she left Anna alone. It was normal for couriers to know as few personnel as possible and so Anna expected to see no-one else.

About half an hour later, the smart girl returned. "You're to take these back," she said, handing Anna several small packages. She waited until Anna had secreted them about her person and then opened the street door.

In the bustle around the market, Anna bartered her goods for salt and sugar and then returned home. She carried out her chores, cooking for herself and Katerina and resting before her night's excursion. After dark, she returned to the partisan's base, walking the kilometres stoically, fully aware that the letters might contain nothing at all, since it was her integrity which was being tested. She felt no sense of injustice at being sent on a fool's errand. They were fighting a devious and powerful enemy and she was willing to do whatever was required of her.

The missives she carried were accepted without ceremony. "Come back next week and you can take more messages to market."

"I will."

"Oh, and thank you for the *salo*." Anna had brought the belly pork, thinking the high fat content might help stave off the creeping autumn cold.

"You're welcome," said Anna, feeling awkward with this taciturn man. "I'll try to bring more food again next week."

"Good. The boys are always hungry."

"Goodnight," she said and turned away to walk home. She did not let herself feel disappointed at the lack of news of Petro. This group might not know of him or his whereabouts. He would be doing his work, she thought, but could not resist looking up at the moon through the bare trees, hoping its light was shining on him, too.

Over the next few days, Anna re-activated her contributors. Halia was glad to donate food, despite there being no news of Petro. She hoped some other boy's mother was doing the same for her son. Anna hesitated to ask Maria and Andriy, but then decided that for them, too, this might be a kind of insurance for Marusia and Rachel's safety. Anna wished she could bring them good news of the girls, but she had no idea where their fates had taken them. With others, she was as discreet as she had been after her father's death, knowing that the villagers were beginning to polarise into those who remained committed to independence...and those who supported Zadyrak and his protégées.

The following week, Anna returned to the woods at night. It was very windy and while that helped to cover any inadvertent noise she made, it also prevented her from hearing any signs of danger. She struggled with a heavy sack over her back, containing potatoes, loaves of bread and jars of milk. She knew the men would appreciate the latter, although she could not carry enough to satisfy even a few of the group. When at last she was challenged for the password by a disembodied voice, she was relieved to put down her burden. She gave the password and was allowed to make her way nearer the encampment, where she was met by Hrichko.

"Can you wait here till I tell him you've arrived?"

"Yes, I'll wait." She stood easing her shoulders, the bundle at her feet and looked up at the swaying trees, outlined against the flying clouds edged with moonlight. It was exhilarating to be out in the wind and she felt this was a worthwhile deed in a week of quiet routine.

Someone coughed and she looked down to see her contact of the previous week. She was glad of the darkness, that he did not see her blush at her girlish excitement to be out on a windy night.

"What have you brought us?"

She gestured to her sack. "I'd prefer to take this back tonight and I'll need the jars back next time."

He looked at her blankly.

"Many things were destroyed in the village over the last few months," she explained. "Ordinary things have become valuable, because they're so difficult to replace." She made herself stop speaking. Why should she need to explain how straitened their lives had become?

"Alright. I'll see to it." He lifted the bundle and went away for a few moments. When he returned, he looked at her with some appreciation. "That will be really helpful," he said.

"Yes. There are those who'll help."

"Many?"

"Some." She waited. Just as he protected his, she would protect hers.

"Yes, you're right. Don't tell me who. But thank you."

She nodded.

"I have some letters for you to take." He reached into his breast pocket and brought out several packets. "There should be replies."

"I'll come back tomorrow night with those," she said, tucking the letters under her jacket and her blouse, against the warmth of her skin.

"Good."

She turned to go.

"You might also want to add a letter of your own," he said.

She turned to stare at him.

"If you want to… It could be passed on."

Anna continued to stare, her heart pounding, her mouth dry. "I will. Thank you," she managed to say.

"Calm yourself before your journey back," he cautioned.

She nodded. "Yes. Goodnight," and she turned to hurry away, trying not to stumble, or to leap and shout with joy. Why would he offer to receive a letter for Petro, if he was no longer alive? She stopped beneath the spreading branches of a bare beech and made herself take a few calming breaths before continuing. She must concentrate on getting home safely before exploring that thought any further. She resumed walking, focussing hard with her eyes and ears against the darkness and the intoxicating wind.

Later, she was able to lie in the comparative safety of her darkened home and examine the wonderful news that Petro was alive. She tried to sleep, but kept waking with fragments of what she wanted to say to Petro and woke again when it was beginning to lighten.

There was no mist that morning and Anna set off for market, like any other peasant woman, but carrying out her secret errand diligently. She returned via Halia's house, taking her friends some honey she had found at the market.

Halia was pleased to see Anna, especially as she noticed a greater spring in her step as Anna came up the path. "Hello, Anna. You look well. Come on in."

Anna closed the door behind her and smiled at Nina, who was sitting at the table.

"There's news isn't there?" said Nina, rising.

"Yes and no," said Anna. "I've been told I can write a letter and it will be passed on to Petro."

"Then he's alive," said Halia.

"I think he must be," agreed Anna.

"He is," said Nina. "Can we write, too?"

"That's why I'm here. But you have to do it now, I'm afraid."

"That's alright," said Nina, searching out an old school exercise book and a pencil.

"Would you like some tea, Anna, while we write him a note?"

"Yes, please. I've been out all day."

She sipped her tea while Halia and Nina composed their short note. In the end it simply said that they were managing well, that they missed him every day and they sent their love to him.

Anna tucked the letter inside her clothing, agreeing that she could write on the reverse of their sheet of paper. "Please try not to expect a reply soon," she warned. "I'm trying not to feel excited and I'm trying not to show it."

"You're quite right," said Halia. "Those devils might hang us for it." She turned to Nina.

"I know, I know. Tell nobody nothing."

Anna's letter was quickly written. She had spent so long thinking about it that she was able to write without hesitation to her beloved Petro. She kissed the paper before folding it and adding it to the other letters she would carry back to the woods that night.

As Anna hugged the secret of Petro's letter to herself over the coming days, she tried to appear to be the dormant creature she had been since the villagers had re-possessed their houses, busy with the minutiae of survival, with no energy for anything else. On a cold November morning, she decided to clear the last pile of rubble on what had been Nastunia's plot. Sifting through the debris, she found, tucked into what would have been the corner of Nastunia's storeroom, two small jars of dried mushrooms. The jars were filthy with the dust which had protected them, but the *pidpenky* inside were still edible. Anna tucked each of the jars into the two pockets she had sewn inside her coat. She returned home and wiped the jars clean. One she placed in her own store cupboard, the other she took to Vera.

Vera had closed down, too. She was visible doing her work around the village, but she tried to draw a camouflaging cloak over her grief. Whenever it threatened to overwhelm her, she hid herself from view. Anna recognised all of this, so she looked for excuses to visit her friend.

One of Vera's younger brothers answered Anna's knock.

"Is Vera home, Vasilko?"

"No. She's not here."

"Will you tell her I called?"

"I suppose so."

Just then Vera herself drew back the door. "Come in, Anna. I'm sorry, but the boys try to protect me if they can."

Anna looked at her friend's pale face with its shrunken cheeks. "I just called because I made a little find at Nastunia's," and she withdrew the jar from her pocket. "I know you've probably got some mushrooms stored away, but it seemed a pity to waste these."

"You're right. Thank you. But have you got some, too?"

"There were two jars."

Vera's eyes filled with tears and she hugged Anna.

Anna held her friend tightly for a moment. "I've never forgotten the cake on my name-day."

"But that was years ago."

"It was, but sometimes it's like yesterday." Her large grey eyes looked intently at Vera. "And sometimes, it hurts a little less."

Vera nodded and placed her hand over her heart. "Yes, I know it might become easier to breathe."

It was Anna's turn to feel the tears, but she smiled instead. "You're strong, Vera. You'll survive." A clatter made her look across the room to where two pairs of blue eyes watched them intently.

Vera looked at her brothers. "I'm alright. Go and gather some more kindling. You know we're short of it. Anna and I are going to drink tea and talk. I'm alright," she repeated.

The boys put on their jackets and caps and went outdoors.

"They're frightened. I'm never ill and they're not sure what's going on. Even Vasilko."

"I know Vasilko's almost thirteen, but they all need you, Vera."

"You're right. I don't have to tell you how much it hurts, but I'm not going to let myself die of grief. You were right. Roman protected me for a purpose. I won't waste that." Despite her brave words, the tears flowed freely and Anna held her friend as she wept for the man she loved.

Anna's heart had been hardened against Bolshevik bullies many years before, but now she watched as others learned to do the same. The killing of Roman Shumenko had terrified some into submission, but had seared others into rebellion and events continued to teach those who were neutral that there could be no such luxury any longer. In the early dusk of a November afternoon, two men, clad in a rag-bag assortment of military clothing, passed one of the lonely houses in the meadow between the Barish and the deeper woods. The farmer was standing in his garden as they passed.

"Did you see a couple of men go up this way before us?" one of the strangers called.

"Yes, I did. They went up there to the woods," offered the man, pointing further west.

The two men drew closer and the farmer swallowed in fear. Their cold anger was clear in the set of their mouths and their clenched jaws. Before he could move, one held him in a firm grip, while the other delivered clinically precise blows to his kidneys. Just before he lost consciousness, the man holding him hissed, "Never tell anyone anything! You've seen nothing!" and dropped him to the cold ground.

But despite the order, this story became part of the village's mythology. The insurgents' safety was to be protected at all costs. Who was not for them, was against them.

Chapter 20

Anna was turning the wheel on the well, when she was startled by a deep voice behind her.

"Whose house is that?"

She turned to see who had spoken.

Serhiy Zadyrak stood behind her, legs apart, meaty fists on his hips. "That one there," he said, pointing to the Terblenko's house.

"No one has lived there for a while," replied Anna.

"I can see that," he retorted, looking at the dilapidated building. It had been used as an office by the Germans whenever necessary, although it had never been fully employed by them, based as they had been in Temne and Buchach. It had also suffered from the Easter shelling and had lost its thatch, but Hrich Terblenko had built the house to last and, despite the apparent damage, it would be a sturdy dwelling again with a little repair.

"I said whose house was it?" repeated Zadyrak, showing his irritation.

Anna feigned stupidity. "You mean before the Germans?"

"Yes, before the Germans."

"A family who went away," she replied, drawing her full bucket to the surface. She hefted its weight over the lip of the well and unhooked it, replacing the hook in its usual place in the roof over the well.

"Were they deported?"

"Yes, I think so. They disappeared one night."

"Aha." He strode towards the empty house without another word to Anna and she picked up her bucket of water and returned home. She placed the bucket inside the cottage door and checked on Katerina, who sat hunched in a chair by the stove, staring blankly at the tiles which had survived the shelling. Anna sighed and went out to the barn, inside which she was able to stand and peer through a convenient gap in the mortar. She watched Zadyrak striding around the Terblenko house and then step into the shell of the building. Like all of the other houses in the village, it had lost its doors to the Red Army soldiers and its windows to the *katyusha* blasts. Hrich Terblenko's dream for his family had been shattered somewhere on the *taiga* in 1941, but now Zadyrak could re-create an imposing dwelling, suited to his role as village *starosta*. He would never be satisfied with Roman's humble cottage. Anna's heart sank at the thought of the difficulties she would face when leaving her cottage after dark, but at least Zadyrak was not immediately opposite her own house. His was set slightly further back along the lane so that he could not see her door, but she would have to be caution itself.

Before the day was out, Zadyrak was directing operations. He had a team of several volunteers, who had fixed their star to the new *starosta's* chariot. They were soon shouting instructions to one another as they cleared the house of its debris.

"What's all that noise, Anna?" asked Katerina.

"There are some men working on the Terblenko house, Mama. It's nothing to worry about." She glanced at her mother's anxious face. "Shall we have some soup to warm us up?"

Katerina gave a little nod, but her eyes wandered away from Anna's face.

Anna turned her back to her mother and tried not to salt the soup with her tears. Katerina had been doing so well. She had coped with the terrifying days of the shelling of the village and, oddly, she seemed to have benefitted from living in the woods, surrounded as they were by other strong women. She had shown signs of becoming more competent herself…and then Roman Shumenko was shot. It was as if she had been slapped hard in the face. All her confusion and grief after the deaths of Mikola and Yuri had taken control of her again.

Zadyrak could not resist having the horn blown to announce a meeting and watching the peasants scurrying to the village hall. He loved looking down at them from the stage and he had acquired a short, heavy-handled whip, which he carried everywhere. He was unaware of the parody he created of Ostapenko, although the villagers saw it and hoped, secretly, that he might meet the same end as his predecessor. The meetings were often called to announce another detail in his petty tyranny.

"Comrades! There will be a stock-taking of our horses tomorrow. You must bring all of your surviving horses to the green here and we will make a note of our workforce for the spring." He did not add that he would not be the one making the notes, being bent on maintaining the illusion of literacy.

"Comrade Starosta," ventured one brave voice, "will we be leaving them here?"

"Of course not, Comrade." Zadyrak laughed his well-fed laugh. "You'll look after them yourselves over the winter, and we'll be able to make a good start on the ploughing and sowing in the spring."

"Huh," muttered Timko to Ihor as they left the meeting, "we can feed our horses over winter and then he'll work them to death in the spring."

As soon as he had heard the announcement, Timko had decided that he would not include his bay mare in the stock-take. He had had her for fifteen years, from a foal. She was more sensible than most human beings and she was strong. Besides, he loved this horse more than any of his others. She had a broad white blaze down her face, which merged through chestnut until it met the bay of her coat. But he did not love her for her beauty; she was his horse.

The following morning, the men and women began to gather with their horses in a congregation which threatened to become mutinous. Zadyrak stood on the steps of the hall as his men went hither and thither making a note of each family's livestock. He appeared to be quite above any administrative task, but his eyes were everywhere, counting and memorising.

One of his men approached him with a sheaf of papers. "That seems to be all, Comrade Starosta."

Zadyrak nodded. "Good." He turned to the gathering. "Now that we can see all…"

"No! No! Comrade Starosta!" came a loud cry.

Zadyrak was both angry and surprised to be interrupted and, looking towards the voice, saw Danylo approaching him.

"I'm very sorry to interrupt you, Comrade Starosta, but this isn't all."

"What do you mean?" snapped Zadyrak.

"Timko hasn't brought all of his horses."

Zadyrak followed Danylo's pointing finger to a sturdy-looking man in his fifties, who was glaring at his accuser. Zadyrak stepped down from the hall steps and strode over to Timko. "Are these all of the horses you have?"

Timko glared back at him, then shrugged. "There's a bay mare tethered in the woods."

"Fetch her!" ordered Zadyrak and, gesturing to two of his men, "Go with him."

Timko handed his horses' halters to Ihor and the three men strode away.

"The rest of you remain here," commanded Zadyrak.

There was some shuffling, but no one attempted to leave. The *starosta* drew one of his men aside and muttered an instruction in his ear and then they waited until Timko returned with his favourite mare.

Timko, meanwhile, led the way to the place in the woods where he had left her. Palahna would never have allowed him to take such a foolish risk for one of his horses, but the widower had been loath to have yet another part of his life taken from him. Since his wife's disappearance during the battle at Easter, he had been far more reckless in his dealings with those who claimed authority. He unhobbled the mare and led her back towards the village green.

On his return the crowd was larger. Zadyrak had not hindered the swelling of his audience. He wanted as many villagers as possible to see what he would do. Heads turned towards the lane as they heard the clopping of hooves and Timko led his mare onto the centre of the green.

"So," said Zadyrak, circling the mare, noting her strengths, "you thought you would hide this one. Why's that?"

Timko shrugged.

Zadyrak mounted the steps of the hall again to address the crowd. "Comrades! Our neighbour did not want to be a part of this community. He was not prepared to share what he had with the rest of us and granted, this is a fine mare, but she belongs to all of us and not simply to this *kulak*." Zadyrak had selected the final word carefully, harking back to Stalin's fierce destruction of farmers who wanted to remain independent of the state. "But, comrades, our Dear Father in Moscow wants all of us to benefit from our shared wealth, to root out the evil of capitalism and to become the greatest power in the world. We have beaten the Fascists and now we must beat any reactionary forces in our society."

The *starosta* turned towards his man and beckoned him forward. Now all could see what the muttered instruction had been. The man carried a length of rope with a noose at one end. He threw the rope over the biggest branch of the oak tree which stood at the corner of the green, and secured it firmly.

"Mount your mare!" Zadyrak instructed Timko.

Timko looked around and one of Zadyrak's men bent forward with his fingers laced to toss Timko up onto the horse's back. Timko stepped into the hands and sprang onto his mare. She was led to the tree and, being the obedient mare she had been since a foal, she stood quietly while Timko put his head in the noose. He had to stretch up to do so, but as soon as it was done, Zadyrak raised his whip and struck the mare hard on the rump. She sprang forward, leaving Timko dangling. He struggled for a few moments, legs flailing, but then was still, although the rope circled slowly, turning him around for all to see. There was a terrible silence and the women and children on the outer edges of the group began to creep away. At a brusque signal from Zadyrak, they were followed by those still holding their nervous horses.

Ihor was still holding Timko's horses and at another signal from the *starosta*, Danylo took their halters and led them away, ignoring the glare he received from his brother-in-law.

Ihor returned home to find Lesia looking stricken. They were not a demonstrative couple, but they stood in one another's arms.

"I feel so ashamed," said Lesia at last.

"Your brother's actions are his own," said Ihor. "But he'll pay the price for them one day."

South of the Dniester, there ran a main highway from Chernivtsi to Stanyslaviv, along which the NKVD were moving both men and munitions and as winter hardened, it became an irresistible invitation to the UPA. The company Anna helped frequently joined other companies for concerted action, so they crossed the frozen river to swell the numbers for a road ambush. On this occasion, Hrichko, despite his junior position in the company, became the most important member of the group. The river, when frozen in deepest winter, could carry fully-laden carts and horses, but there were *polonky*, thinner parts of the ice which had been disturbed by the movement of the water below the apparently solid surface. They were unpredictable, but, even so, Hrichko had a better idea than most where they might appear, so it was he who led the company across the river. The men crossed the wide expanse cautiously and then trudged through the snowy woods, grateful that the moon was not too bright. They knew that they were far more visible against the bare trees and the white ground. They topped the rise on the Dniester's southern bank and looked down through the woods.

They could see that there was no enemy movement ahead of them as they covered several kilometres of hilly wooded country until they reached the meeting point. The sappers had already mined the road, so the men brushed the snow back over the ground with pine branches and waited for dawn. As the sun rose, it poured its pink light between the trees, the birches' creamy trunks lovely against the rose of snow and sky. It remained quiet, despite the onset of morning, as the birds huddled against the cold.

The calm was broken by the sound of engines toiling uphill. The vehicles came into view, a jeep followed by two trucks full of soldiers. The transport crawled forward along the icy road and as the first passed over a mine, the explosion ripped through the stillness. The jeep and its occupants were lost and the two lorries skidded to a halt, one spinning through a hundred and eighty degrees as the nervous driver applied the brakes too hard.

The *kurin*, waiting in the trees, opened fire with its machineguns, both Russian and German in origin. It was only a matter of minutes before the small convoy was wiped out and the partisans were salvaging arms and ammunition from their victims. They gathered all that they could find, including the NKVD's boots, and then they divided the spoils between the two companies before going their separate ways. Hrichko's company returned to the river, but once close to the Dniester again, they hunkered down till dusk to re-cross the river to their camp. They were satisfied with the success of their attack. There were no losses and their gains had been significant.

However, the enemy was not going to be beaten by such a small opponent. He made them pay heavily for every small victory. The next time a convoy was attacked on the road to Stanyslaviv, the UPA found that its size had increased ten-fold. Stalin had dipped into his bottomless pool of men and the *kurin* was overwhelmed.

The survivors hurried down the snowy bank to the river, hoping to cross it before the shelling reached the ice. They could hear the mortars pounding the woods behind them and, since they could not match the NKVD fire-power, they retreated. But the snow prevented them from melting into the woods, as they often did to the frustration of the enemy. The battered company moved forward, their leader, Ostap, ordering two of the boys in the rear to sweep away any bloody snow with pine branches. It would, at least, make their retreat more difficult to see.

When they reached the river, Ostap maintained discipline. "We mustn't cross the ice chaotically. Hrichko, lead us over. Keep single file! But be quick!"

Hrichko hurried onto the ice and made himself focus only on what lay before his feet. He could not allow himself to wonder if the artillery fire would reach them, nor worry that they might be seen from the banks. He set off, stepping carefully, prodding any suspect ice ahead of him and taking the swiftest, but not the straightest route back across the frozen surface. As soon as the partisans reached the northern bank, they hurried back to their bunkers in small groups, observing the rule of walking two metres apart on previously agreed routes.

They re-assembled at their base and Ostap took a roll call, despite knowing that they had lost six men in the ambush. He also ran a check on the injured. They had carried back two badly wounded men, one of whom had since died, but the other needed urgent treatment. Ostap waited for an assessment from their first-aider, who could competently dress flesh wounds and set a simple limb break, but a bullet lodged in the upper chest was beyond her. Ostap knew the wounded man could be returned to full fighting fitness if properly treated, but for that they would need a doctor.

"There used to be a good one in my village," offered Hrichko.

"Is he still there?"

"I'm not sure. And Anna isn't due for several days."

"Does anyone have any other suggestions?"

"There's a doctor in Temne, but that's further..."

"Let's try Hrichko's first." He turned to the boy. "Make your way over there and remain hidden till it's dark. Then go to Anna. Tell her what's happened and that we need a doctor, the quicker the better. Tell her to get him to come tonight."

"Alright. I'll do what I can. Shall I wait for her?"

"No. She knows the way. And it'll be safer if she comes alone with the doctor. Just wait a moment though," and Ostap went into his bunker. He returned with a revolver.

"She won't need that," said Hrichko. "She's got one."

Ostap raised his eyebrows.

"Petro gave her a Luger before he went north."

"Alright. On your way then."

Hrichko set off towards the village, planning where he would hide until dark. He did not want to wait near the Jewish mass grave in the dusk, but knew he could not risk the open meadow before it was dark. He crossed himself as he passed the site and went to the furthest edge of the woods to wait for darkness. He longed to sit with a tree trunk at his back, but dared not in case he fell asleep. So he stood and occasionally wriggled his toes, singing partisan songs in his head to pass the time and to keep up his spirits.

As soon as it was fully dark, he slipped through the meadow, crossed the Barish and then made his way up through the woods to the back of Anna's home. He approached her house and stood, hidden behind the short wall of her cottage. When he felt certain there was no one in the lane, he stepped forward and scratched at the window with his nails. Then he slipped back behind the house to listen. There was no movement, so Hrichko tried again.

Inside the cottage, Anna had been lying in bed beside Katerina. Since Zadyrak had imposed the curfew, there had been great suspicion against those using a light in their homes after dark. The NKVD assumed that these individuals were involved in helping the insurgents in their counter-revolutionary activities. So Anna had been lying wide-eyed, trying to rest, but her mind awash with the violent images of Zadyrak's executions. When the scratching first came, she had held her breath, waiting for it to be repeated. She crept towards the door and opened it a crack.

"Anna! It's me, Hrichko."

She closed the door and pulled on her boots, coat and scarf before opening the door a fraction again. She waited and listened, then slipped behind the cottage. Hrichko stood hunched against the cold and she gestured to him to follow her. They moved down to the shelter of the trees.

"What is it?" asked Anna.

"We need a doctor," and Hrichko explained the problem. "Is Doctor Koshchur still in the village?"

"Yes, but he won't come."

"How do you know?"

"First because of the curfew and secondly, how do you think he has survived this long?"

"You have to make him come, Anna."

"I'll try, but I'll have to go back to my house first."

"I'm to leave you to make your own way anyway."

"Alright. Tell them I'll be there as soon as I can."

Hrichko was about to turn away when Anna said, "Wait. When did you last eat?"

He shrugged. "I've got a bit of bread in my pocket."

"Wait a few moments," and she hurried away uphill. She collected her Luger and ammunition; filled a jar with tepid *borsch* for Hrichko; and cut him a hunk of bread. She returned to the spot where she had left him and he appeared silently from among the trees a little way off. She could not help smiling at his demonstration of a partisan's craft. "Here, take these, but I want the jar back."

"Thanks, Anna," he grinned and was gone.

Anna stood for a treacherous moment, wishing she did not have to carry out this task, but then she sighed and set off laterally through the trees to circle the village to reach the doctor's house.

She had never asked the doctor for help. Her family had not been wealthy enough to consult him before Mikola's death and since that time, she had medicated herself and Katerina with herbal remedies. She knew she would have to be convincing to get him to open his door to her. The curfew alone was a very good reason for him to refuse to speak to her, but she was determined not to fail. She reached his house and was grateful for the cloudy night sky which obscured the moonlight, and for the large garden which surrounded the doctor's property. Anna approached the front door, looking about her in the gloom, and reached the sheltered porch with no alarm being raised. She swallowed hard, focussed on her story and rapped on the door with her bare knuckles. She waited a few moments and then knocked hard again into the silence. She heard the shuffling of slippered feet and waited. The footsteps had stopped and the silence resumed. Anna waited only a couple of moments before knocking hard again.

"Doctor Koshchur! It's me, Anna. My mother's ill. Please help us!"

When a male voice replied, Anna realised he must be standing close to the other side of the door. "I'll come tomorrow. I can't come now. It's the curfew."

"But she's very ill. She has pains in the middle of her chest."

"Tell her to lie quietly. I'll see her in the morning."

"She might not last till morning and she's very frightened, Doctor. She can't breathe easily and she says she feels sick."

"Even so, I can't come now."

"And the pain has spread through her shoulders and down her arms."

There was a silence on the other side of the door.

Anna let her voice drop to a frightened whisper. "Is she having a heart attack?"

"She may be."

"Will she die?"

"Perhaps."

"Doctor Koshchur! Please give me something for her to take tonight. She's all I have left."

"Alright," she heard him grumble. "Wait a moment."

Anna reached into her pocket and closed her fingers around the rough surface of the gun's handle. She heard the bolts being drawn back and the doctor opened the door far enough to proffer two pills in the palm of his hand. Anna stepped forward, putting her booted foot in the doorway and hefting the door open with her shoulder. The doctor stepped back in surprise as Anna drew the pistol.

"I'm sorry, Doctor, but I need you to come with me. Get your bag."

He stared at her open-mouthed. "Anna, I can't believe..."

"Get your bag. We don't have much time."

He seemed to gather his wits. "No, Anna, I won't do this."

"Your children are in bed, I presume," said Anna, pointing at the doors to the rear of the hall with the barrel of her gun.

"Anna! What's happened to you?"

"Get your bag. I won't tell you again."

She watched him closely as he put on his coat and scarf and then she passed him his boots, having given them a shake first. He reached for his bag of instruments and they prepared to leave the house.

"Don't make any unnecessary noise," warned Anna. "Even if we're both shot, there'll always be others to come after me."

He nodded and they left the house, Anna closing the door behind her. She followed him down the path and then took the lead. She hurried him to the bridge over the Barish, the gun still in her hand. Once across the river, she paused. "I'm going to blindfold you now," she said, drawing a scarf from her pocket.

"Is that necessary?" he asked, his disgust clear in his voice.

"Yes, it is. It'll protect both of us."

"That's nonsense and you know it. If I'm caught by the NKVD, it won't matter how reluctant I was. They'll still kill me for this and they'll deport my family."

"That's too bad. There's no room now for neutrality."

"You silly girl..." he began, but Anna had finished tying his blindfold and she poked him in the ribs with the barrel of her gun.

"Take my hand and save your breath for walking."

She set off at a brisk pace, although keeping a lookout for the doctor's footing. They hurried across the meadow to the woods and then they had to slow down as the path became rougher and narrower.

When Anna approached the bunkers, she saw the guard who had first led her to the encampment. Pylyp nodded to her and Hrichko appeared to lead them to the patient. They led the doctor into a dug-out lit by an oil lamp and then all but the patient withdrew out of sight as Anna removed the doctor's blindfold.

It took a few moments for his eyes to become accustomed to the badly-lit gloom and then he looked about him. "I'll need more light and hot water."

These requests were heard by the first-aider, who had anticipated the doctor's needs. She had had a bitter quarrel with Ostap about assisting the doctor in his operation, but had carried her point. She passed a couple more lamps to Anna and then brought in the hot water herself. The doctor barely glanced at her as he began to examine his patient.

Despite the primitive conditions and the limited resources, Doctor Koshchur removed the bullet and dressed the wound. He gave terse instructions to his assistant on the necessary after-care and then washed his hands and prepared to leave. He waited as Anna re-applied his blindfold and, taking her hand, allowed her to lead him from the camp.

He resented Anna's intrusion into his carefully guarded life, but he recognised that what she and the partisans wanted was legitimate. He would not offer further help, but acknowledged to himself that he had only two choices: to betray Anna to the NKVD, or to become complicit with the insurgents' aims. Neither route would be easy. Both threatened him and, more importantly, his family. He had worked hard to protect them through the mortal fluctuations of recent years and he felt that his period of greatest danger had come. But he would not share his thoughts with his guide: a quiet, serious, young woman who had suffered terrible bereavement herself and whose only aim in life had seemed to be to protect her ailing mother from harm.

As Anna undid his blindfold at the bridge, he could not help asking, "How is she really?"

Anna looked up in grateful surprise. "Oh, she has her good and bad days."

"I'll make my own way from here," he said.

"Thank you, Doctor. Good night."

Chapter 21

The patient was making a good recovery when Anna returned to the woods several days later with the usual sack of supplies, and milk for the injured man. She was met by Hrichko and as he took her into the camp, he asked, "What's happening with our house, Anna?"

She realised he would have been able to see signs of renovation when he had come for her the other evening. "It's being done up."

"Who for?"

There was no point in lying to him. "The *starosta*."

"Oh."

"All the more to fight for."

"Yes, you're right," and he made himself smile.

Her heart ached for him. He did not know if any of his family was still alive, and if so, where they might be. The uncertainty must be more wearing, thought Anna. She turned to look at him and realised that he was now taller than her. He had the thinness of a boy in his mid-teens, but he was growing towards manhood. Anna wondered how much more tragedy he might have to bear before he could have some sort of ordinary life.

Ostap met them and gave Anna the bundle of letters to deliver to Buchach. "And this one's for you," he added as he gave her a separate envelope.

Anna's heart lurched in her chest as she took it and this time Hrichko smiled properly. "There, Anna. That's worth fighting for."

She smiled at Hrichko, but longed to run from the place, to be private, with enough light to read the precious letter.

Ostap, unusually, sympathised. "You can read it in my dug-out before you go."

"Thank you," she managed to say and followed him into his rudimentary shelter. He left her alone and she tried not to tear the letter in her haste to open it.

My dearest Anna,
I have been told that this message will reach you so I am taking advantage
of the rare chance to speak to you. I miss you so much, my love, and have
your dear face before me as I write. Now that I try to write to you, I don't

know where to begin. I talk to you all the time in my head, although I sometimes talk to Mama and Nina, too. It was such a relief to hear from all of you and I hope you are telling me the truth, that you are well and managing. I know all three of you will be making the best of whatever difficulties you are facing.

I have been moved. I am no longer in Volyn. In a big engagement with the NKVD, my kurin *sustained some damage – don't worry, I was not hurt – and afterwards, those of us remaining were allowed to choose which other* kurin *to join. I asked to come to Chorni Lis because I knew men were needed here and it is closer to home. My hope is to return to you all as soon as I can, but I know I must continue to fight here, where there is a great deal to be done. I am always very busy – I'm not allowed to tell you more – but it is a help. I hope that I am doing something to help us achieve independence.*

Whatever you are doing, be safe. Try to be happy – we are, after all, still alive and I pray to God that we can be together soon. Anna, tell Mama and Nina how much I love them and take all the rest of my love for yourself,

Petro.

Anna read the letter twice and swallowing her tears, refolded it and placed it in the warmth between her breast and her blouse. She ducked out of the dug-out to meet Hrichko's sympathetic smile.

"Is he alright?"

Anna could not speak, but nodded.

"Are you ready to go?"

"Yes."

"You will be careful, won't you?"

"I will. Thank you, Hrichko."

Full of love for Petro, she turned to the boy. "Is there anything special you want me to bring you?"

"No. Thank you. Just yourself."

She saw his loneliness and wanted to comfort him, but knew that if she hugged him, they would both weep. "Alright. I'll see you tomorrow night."

She tried to dampen the light-headed happiness she felt as she left the camp and, alone in the dark woods, she stood still for a few moments taking deep breaths to calm herself for the homeward journey. The snow was becoming more difficult to deal with now that the worst of winter was over and the thaw had begun. There would be sudden soft or wet areas and she knew that before long, she would no longer have to worry about her tracks in the snow, but her tracks in the mud.

The following day, she made a detour to Halia's on her way back from Buchach market. As she approached their house, Nina flung the door open, a look of excited expectation on her face. "What have you brought us?"

Anna smiled from ear to ear, her eyes dancing with glee. "Guess!"

Nina tugged her arm. "Come in quick. Where is it?"

Halia hurried forward. "Is it Petro?"

Anna checked the door was closed behind her and drew Petro's letter from inside her blouse. She handed it to Halia, who, despite her excitement, looked at Anna.

"It's alright. Read it."

"Come on, Mama," urged Nina.

Halia unfolded the letter, trying to control the trembling in her hands, and Anna watched as their eyes drank in the message from their beloved Petro. Halia again raised her eyes to meet Anna's, sharing the pleasure Anna must have had in receiving the message from her lover; and when Halia and Nina found themselves mentioned, they turned to each other and smiled, Nina putting her arm around her mother's waist.

"We are, we are coping," murmured Halia.

"Oh, Chorni Lis," said Nina a few moments later.

As they reached the end of the letter, Halia put out her arm to Anna and she joined them as they hugged one another with relief.

"I wanted to come to you last night," said Anna. "I was so excited."

"It is good news," said Halia. "I wonder if they'll let him come home."

"Perhaps," said Anna. "But the fighting seems to be getting fiercer."

"I knew he was alright," said Nina. "I just felt it."

"Yes, but it's good to have it confirmed," said Halia.

And then, they re-read the letter, finding it irresistible.

Later, when Anna had a little time between her excursion to the market and her journey to the woods to deliver the replies, she baked a honey cake.

"Aren't you tired, Anna?" asked her mother.

"Yes, but I got some lovely honey today, so I thought I'd like to use it. We can have a piece with some tea."

Later, as she prepared to leave in the dark, she picked up half of the cake to take with her.

It was a blustery night and Anna was glad of the noisy cover the wind gave her, but was cautious of the branches, which whipped about wildly. However, she reached the encampment safely and was glad to be met again by Hrichko.

"Here," she said, proffering a small parcel.

"What is it?" he asked, beginning to open it. "Is it cake?" he laughed in astonishment.

"It is. I made it for you."

"Oh, my dear sister, thank you!" and he kissed her cheek.

"You'd better take these letters, too," she smiled.

"Oh, yes, of course!" and off he hurried, leaving her waiting in the dark.

As the year turned towards the spring sowing, Serhiy Zadyrak admitted to himself that he must find efficient and tactful help for the administration of the village. Over time, he had developed a powerful visual and aural memory to compensate for his illiteracy, but his position demanded written evidence of the farming life of the village. He could not manage without written records. The authorities in the regional office demanded them, and, whilst some of his men were literate, none of them was interested in keeping assiduous records. A woman was the answer.

"Hnat!" he said one morning to the most sensible of his acolytes, "who would make me a good secretary?"

"A secretary?"

"Yes. A man in my position should not have to bother with the nonsense of writing everything down."

"Of course not, Comrade Starosta."

"So can you suggest someone?"

"Vera did the work for Roman Shumenko."

"No, she won't do. I want someone of my own."

"Yes, you're right." Hnat thought for a moment. "All the girls had four years at school, so any of them could do it."

"Yes, I know, but I want a special one. Someone we can trust."

"Hmm," murmured Hnat. "I'm not sure. Can I think about it?"

"Yes, but don't take too long."

Serhiy Zadyrak was also having trouble with Timko's bay mare. He had taken a fancy to the horse, but was entertained, too, by the figure he cut on this particular animal. It was a regular reminder to the villagers of how far he was prepared to go. He had ridden the horse several times, but each time he had found her, not exactly unco-operative, but skittish and unpredictable. He would not be beaten by a mere beast though, so early one spring morning, he picked up his whip and took her out. They walked along the lane, past the ruined church to the quarry, which was still quiet at that hour, and then he trotted her down the cart track parallel to the river. He was careful here because he knew he was visible to the village above, despite the distance. As they trotted, he felt the slight unevenness of her gait, so he drew her into a walk and then after a few moments trotted her again. Her gait was smoother this time, but she gradually picked up speed and her trot became uncomfortable again. Zadyrak decided to take her up through the trees to canter her where he would be less exposed. They had to walk up the steepest part of the hill and he noticed that if he let the mare choose her own path, she coped well with the rise, but he wanted to bend her to his will so, as they reached the summit, he turned her into the birch woods and, smacking her rump with his whip, they sprang forward into a canter.

However, the sensible mare had never needed a crop and she accelerated into a gallop, less in fear of her rider, but more in indignation. Zadyrak pulled on the reins, trying to slow her down, but she was too strong for him. She galloped faster and he clung onto her mane with one hand, vainly trying to rein her in with the other. Suddenly, she came to an abrupt halt and he somersaulted over her head, landing with a thud and a shout, as the air was expelled from his lungs. Then he lay still.

Anna heard both the cry and the thud as she was attaching another jar to a birch trunk, in her annual collection of sap. She finished securing the jar and stepped away from the tree to look in the direction of the sound. She thought she could discern a horse through the trees, so she hurried towards the animal. She recognised Timko's beloved bay mare as she drew closer. The horse was standing quietly, her reins dangling, nibbling at tender young shoots with her soft lips. Anna looked around and saw Zadyrak's prone figure, so she approached the horse first. She placed herself in the horse's eyeline and walked towards her. "Come on, girl. It's alright now."

The mare allowed Anna to reach her and then sniffed at her proffered hand.

Anna stroked her neck. "There's a good girl," she said as she reached for the reins. She tethered the horse loosely to a sapling and turned to Zadyrak. She wondered if he had broken his neck, but, as she drew nearer, she saw his arms move and a groan issued from his thick lips. She knelt beside him. "Don't move just yet."

He struggled for breath.

"Try to relax. I think you must have been winded in the fall."

He rolled to one side and looked up at Anna. He saw her large grey eyes and full mouth and, despite his shocked state, felt the stirrings of arousal. He tried to sit up and Anna helped him, taking his hand and pulling, while putting her other hand on his back to support him.

"Is your head spinning?"

"Yes, damn it," he growled.

"Then sit still for a few moments. There's no need to worry. I've tethered the horse." Anna deliberately chose not to use the word "your".

"Where did you come from?"

"I was collecting sap."

He looked at her blankly.

"Do you think you can stand now?"

"Yes," he grunted and, as she helped him to his feet, he noticed the strength in her arms which belied the softness of her breasts. Even in her heavy coat, he could see she was full-breasted and he felt the stirrings of desire again. He held onto her warm hand and looked up into her face, seeing her beauty and wanting to possess it.

Anna withdrew her hand and asked, "Can you walk a little?"

He gathered his thoughts and remembered the reason for the position he found himself in. "Where's that blasted horse?" and he bent to pick up his fallen whip.

Anna stayed his hand. "She's fine. You can't be thinking of beating her surely?"

He was about to reply that he would beat her raw. She wouldn't bolt with him again! But as he looked into Anna's mild and disapproving face, he felt unable to continue with the bluster. "No, no, of course not. But she'd better look out. I'm not having her think she can do as she likes."

"Perhaps something frightened her," suggested Anna. "She's a lovely mare and usually so well-behaved."

"Hmm. Maybe."

Anna could see Zadyrak was still attracted to the thought of beating the horse into submission so she said, "I think if you beat her, or try to force her, she'll always fight you." She stepped towards the mare and gave her her hand to smell again. "You might break her, but then she wouldn't be the horse she is now."

"Sometimes it's the only way," he growled as he stepped towards them.

The mare backed away and Anna continued to soothe her by stroking her neck. "There, it's alright, girl. You'll get a lot more from her with kindness. She's too intelligent for the whip."

Again he felt ashamed of his brutishness, but did not know how to proceed.

"Just come and make friends with her," said Anna. "Pat her gently. Talk to her. She's a lovely horse, aren't you, girl?"

He hesitated, still holding the whip in his right hand.

"Perhaps if you put your whip down your boot, she won't be afraid of you."

He did not want to surrender the whip. He wanted to wallop the horse hard, but Anna had embarrassed him. He blew out his breath and put the whip between his leg and the outer side of his right boot. He stepped closer and, despite the mare stepping back again, he held out his hand to her and stood still. She reached her beautiful head forward and sniffed his hand. He glanced at Anna across the horse's head and stroked the mare's silky neck. She was still nervous, but she relaxed a little more as he scratched her withers.

"There, you see. She likes you better already."

He looked up to see if this comely girl was mocking him, but Anna's smile was sweet.

"Hmm. You may be right." He tried not to glare from beneath his dark brows and Anna bit her cheeks to stop herself from laughing aloud at his goblin face.

"Do you want to ride her back?" asked Anna. "I could give you a leg up."

"Yes, I'd better."

They checked the mare's girth and tidied her stirrups. Anna undid the reins and passed them to him over the horse's head. Zadyrak approached the mare on her left and she stood still while Anna bent to make a step for him with her laced palms. He mounted up energetically despite his bulk. He looked down at Anna's honey-coloured hair and her pink cheeks. It almost choked him to say it, but he could not leave without finding out more about her. "I don't know your name."

"I'm Anna. I know who you are."

"Thank you, Anna."

"No need."

He turned the horse's head towards home and she watched him walk the mare through the trees.

Serhiy Zadyrak need not have worried that Anna might betray him and reveal his mortification to the rest of the village. He waited and watched carefully for any sign of a smirk at his horsemanship, but none came. He had restrained himself, with some difficulty, from beating the mare and he found Anna had been correct. He now treated the mare with some respect and she, in turn, was compliant, but distant. He did not care. He did not want the mare to love him; he simply wanted her not to humiliate him in public.

He now knew, too, whom he wanted as a secretary, so taking advantage of the fact that only he and Hnat were in the village office, he returned to their earlier conversation. "Hnat, have you given any thought to who could be my secretary?"

"There are a number," replied Hnat and he proceeded to reel off a list of a dozen names, including Anna's.

"Let's take the oldest," said Zadyrak, rightly placing Anna close to her age of twenty-one, "but I don't want any wives or mothers."

Hnat looked doubtful. "That only leaves Anna."

"Who is she?"

"She lives alone with her mother."

"What happened to her father?"

"He was shot in 1940."

"Shot?"

"Yes. He tried to interfere with the *starosta's* decision. So he was shot. Her brother, too."

"Her brother? Was he a troublemaker, too?"

"No. He was just a boy. I think he just got in the way."

"So is she to be trusted?"

"I think so. She's very quiet. She looks after her mother and she's known to be a good worker."

"So why isn't she married?"

"I don't know."

"No boyfriend?"

"I don't think so." Hnat paused. "There aren't that many left in the village."

"Hmm. Where does she live?"

"Near the house you've chosen. A little further up on the opposite side."

"Oh." Was she the girl at the well? He had paid no attention to her then. She seemed to be like many of the other villagers, old before their time. The woman in the wood had had an undoubted sparkle...

"Fetch her to me."

"Now?"

"Yes," said Serhiy as if it were obvious.

He paced up and down the office as he waited for Hnat to return. Was there any risk in what he was doing? He shrugged. There was a risk in everything these days and he would have her with him in the office. He heard footsteps crossing the hall, so he sat down quickly behind the desk.

Anna appeared in the doorway.

"Come in," he said, too loudly.

She stood before him at the desk.

"I have a proposition for you."

Anna waited. What did this noisy bully want from her?

"I need a secretary. I don't have time for all this keeping of records." He waved at the littered desk. "Are you interested?"

"Yes." She could not refuse without becoming suspect and she could not afford to draw the wrong kind of attention to herself. However, she dreaded being pulled in closer to Zadyrak's orbit. "But I'm not sure that I can do what you want me to do."

"I need someone to keep the accounts...and to do any other writing

I might need. Presumably you can read and write? You can add?"

"Yes, I can," said Anna. "How many days would it be? I have to work for myself and my mother."

"Let's say three days for now. But once we start sowing and harvesting, I might need you more often. You'll be paid for your work here and you can still earn money from any farm work you might do."

"And I would need time to work my garden," said Anna, sensing she should press for advantage now.

"That's fine then. Start tomorrow morning."

"Alright. Thank you," said Anna and she turned to leave.

"Oh and Anna…"

She turned back to face him.

"I expect to be addressed as Comrade Starosta."

"Of course, Comrade Starosta," she said and left the office.

Where would this all lead, she asked herself later. The work would be lighter than field work and she would be well paid in village terms, so she and Katerina would be better off. She would also have much greater access to information which might be useful to the partisans. But on the other hand, she did not relish working closely with Serhiy Zadyrak. She had noticed the way he had looked at her in the wood and she was determined to keep him at arm's length. She knew that might not be as easy as she hoped.

Although she did not want to apologise for having taken the job, Anna felt she should inform those closest to her about her new role. Once Katerina had been reassured that Anna would not find the work onerous, she seemed to put it from her mind. Halia, predictably, took a completely pragmatic approach, but Vera had some advice for Anna.

"You'll be able to help others more than you realise," she told Anna.

"How?"

"Will Zadyrak check your work, do you think?"

"I suspect he won't be able to. I think he's illiterate."

"Can he recognise numbers?"

"I don't know yet. I'll test him as soon as I dare."

"Be careful, Anna. He's a nasty piece of work."

"I know he is. But he won't have things all his own way." Anna looked at Vera's pale, thin face. "Are you planning to work on the sowing?"

"I'll have to. But I'm stronger than I look."

"And the boys?"

"They've been working at the quarry. They're getting so big. Vasilko would eat like a man if we let him."

Neither of the women mentioned Roman, but as Anna turned to leave, Vera said, "I think you must have had some news recently."

Anna blushed a little. "Does it show?"

"Oh yes. You've colour in your cheeks and your eyes are sparkling again. Is he well?"

"Yes, but still far away."

"But there's hope."

"Oh Vera!"

"I'm alright. I'm managing."

"You've been so brave."

Vera barked a rueful laugh. "I learned that from you!"

As the work began on the crops, Anna kept records of the hours worked by the villagers and she wrote down the details of how much land was sown. She found that she could combine the administrative and manual tasks so was not always at Zadyrak's beck and call, a call which was often resented by the adults in the village. He would ride the bay mare right up to their houses in the early morning and, banging on their doors with his whip handle, would shout, "Come on! Let's be having you! There's work to be done."

The women had to work on the heavy ploughing alongside the few remaining old men and boys and so were relieved to reach the lighter task of sowing. Anna found herself beside Sofia in the row of women and girls as they scattered the seed.

"You've found yourself a cosy berth," said Sofia.

"What do you mean?" asked Anna.

"Working for Zadyrak."

"Isn't that what we're all doing?"

"Don't be clever with me, Anna. I don't know how you managed to wangle that job in the office."

"I didn't wangle anything."

"So why did he pick you?"

"I have no idea."

"I wanted that job, but Hnat said Zadyrak didn't want any wives or mothers."

"Well, there you are, then."

"Yes, but there are plenty of girls he could have chosen."

Anna remained silent since she had nothing to add. She changed the subject. "How's Antin coming along?"

"Oh, he's into everything. He wears me out."

Anna wanted to ask if Sofia had heard any news of Ivan, but knowing that this was also a difficult topic, she remained silent, concentrating on her work.

"And I've still not heard from Ivan. At least if he'd been in the Red Army, I'd have got a pension."

Anna looked shocked. "Do you think he's dead then?"

"Probably. You must have heard the numbers who died at Brody."

"But he might have been captured."

"Yes, and sentenced to twenty-five years in Siberia. What use is that to me?"

Anna was glad when they reached the border of the field and had to fetch more grain. She was determined to avoid Sofia in the next line-up. She found herself a place next to Vera and they worked companionably up the field. As they made their way home along the lane in the darkening afternoon, Vera smiled sympathetically at Anna. "Did Sofia give you a hard time?"

"That woman!" Anna tried to stop herself, but burst out, "She was complaining that she gets no pension for Ivan!"

"You can only feel sorry for her. Nothing is ever going to satisfy her."

"She was also angry that I got the job with Zadyrak."

"She would be. What a meal-ticket he would be for her. She could get close to him and then she wouldn't have to work at all."

"I'm afraid you might be right. She once recommended that I find myself a German soldier."

They exchanged glances.

"She would be welcome to Zadyrak though," said Anna.

"If only it worked like that. You take care, Anna. Our people are changing. They've had too much misery and those blue caps are delighted to encourage them to sell each other for a few *karbovanchi*."

For the first few weeks, as Anna kept the books for the village, she did not see any advantage to be gained from her position, but the next time she went to collect letters from the partisans, Ostap took her aside to discuss her progress as Zadyrak's secretary. "So is he illiterate?"

"Oh yes, I'm certain of that. But I still have to be careful what I write. There are a few of his close followers who can read."

"And do you think he trusts you?"

"I don't think he's the type to trust anybody completely, but he seems to trust me to a certain extent."

"Your work will be most helpful when it's time for the harvest. The numbers you record will not need to match the actual amounts of grain. That will give your neighbours a little more for themselves and it'll make them grateful to you."

"You're right, but I'll have to be careful. I can already name some individuals, who would think nothing of betraying their neighbours, even their families."

"Well, be cautious then." There was an awkward pause. "Anna, the last thing I have to say is more delicate. Zadyrak must know about your father, someone will have told him the story. Which makes it all the more odd that he chose you… I suspect he may not simply want you to be his secretary."

Anna met his eyes. "You're right. I've known that all along…but I'm careful. I pretend not to notice that about him and I keep him aware that my duty is to my mother. It'll be fine."

And for the most part it was. Anna kept Zadyrak at a distance by being completely business-like in her work and gently spurning any advances, but she did give him significant help with one particular problem.

The documents for him to sign had begun to pile up on his desk and Anna saw that he had not dealt with a single one. She suspected that his inability to write extended to his name, so, one day, as she prepared to leave work, she pointed to the growing pile of papers and said, "Isn't it a pity I can't sign those for you? Then you wouldn't have the trouble of them and I'd be able to get them delivered to Buchach."

Zadyrak grunted in reply.

She took a piece of paper and a pen and wrote in very clear letters: "Zadyrak Serhiy", enunciating the words aloud. "There! No one would know who had written that," and she left the writing on the corner of his desk. "Anyway, I'd better be going. I need to see how Mama has survived without me. See you tomorrow, Comrade Starosta," she said and left.

Zadyrak waited until he heard her cross the hall and then he got up from his desk to check the outer door was closed. He returned to the office, sat down at the desk and picked up the pen Anna had left on the sheet of paper bearing his name. He pulled the sheet towards him and, holding the pen between his right thumb and his first and second fingers, he attempted to copy the marks Anna had made. He acknowledged the atrocious penmanship of his first attempt by throwing down the pen in disgust, but then he caught sight of the increasingly large pile of documents and he took up the pen again. He knew Anna had written his name out slowly in contrast to the normal speed of her writing and he suspected that she knew his secret. But if she did, she had given him a way out, so he continued to practise. When he reached the bottom of the page, he admitted to himself that his writing still looked idiotic, so he took a second sheet and slowly covered both sides. This time, he felt there was some improvement, but he would not sign the documents tonight. He would not give Anna the satisfaction of thinking she had any control over him. Besides, he needed to practise writing his name when there was no copy of it in front of him.

Anna returned to the woods one lovely spring night, carrying the letters from Buchach and supplies for the insurgents. The breeze through the young leaves had energised her and she walked with a lighter step than usual to the encampment. There was a bright moon smiling down on her and Anna felt too cheerful to regret that the brightness also gifted the enemy. She covered the last half kilometre quickly, and was expecting at any moment to be challenged, when suddenly a man stepped out from among the trees in front of her. She felt a moment's fear because she did not recognise this guard, but then she chided herself that it must be one of the partisans checking she knew the current password. She made herself relax as he continued to approach her.

"Anna," he said in a low voice.

She thought she would faint. He was much thinner than before and his face was gaunt, but his long unruly curls fell over his collar and he was looking at her with such longing in his blue eyes. She tried to speak, but could not and, dropping her bundle, she stumbled forward into his arms. They held onto each other as if they were drowning. At last, she sobbed his name: "Petro! My love!"

He bent his face into the warmth of her neck and she held his head to her; then he lifted his face to hers and they shared their first kiss after almost two years. She wiped the tears from his thin cheeks with her work-roughened fingers and thought her heart would break at the change in him. She looked deep into his eyes, looking for the damage which had been done, but he deflected her with "I'm fine," and a quick smile.

He picked up her bundle and said, "We'd better make our way into camp."

She did as he suggested, but could not let go of his hand as they went to deliver the letters to Ostap. Petro did extract his hand from hers then saying, "I'll take the food to the quartermaster."

She looked bereft.

"But I'll see you again before you go," he smiled.

She turned to Ostap, her head spinning, and tried to be business-like in her replies to his questions, but she wanted, more than anything, to run to Petro again.

The leader of the *kurin* concluded the business quickly and dismissed her. She hurried out of his dug-out to see Petro waiting for her a little way off. She hastened towards him and he led her away from the encampment through the trees, a blanket over his shoulder.

Chapter 22

Over the following weeks as spring burgeoned into summer, Anna tried to maintain a composed demeanour, as did Halia and Nina. Petro had risked a visit to them one night and they, too, were relieved that he was nearby. Anna tried to take him greater quantities of food, but he would only share it scrupulously with his colleagues.

"Let me bring you extra milk," she pleaded.

"There's no need. I'm not an invalid."

"But you're too thin. Let me feed you up."

"No, my love. I'll soon be stronger now I'm near you."

She stroked the clear planes of his face, looking anxiously into his eyes, whose expression was playful as he sought to reassure her, but she could see he was changed. He was no longer the kind, helpful boy who had brought her a kitten; he was harder, and at the same time more troubled. As he drew her closer to him, she gave herself up to the love he offered.

"Is the fighting easier now?" she asked later.

"Not really. The Fascists were more organised and fought well to the bitter end, but the Bolsheviks…their forces get bigger and bigger. We've hit them hard a few times when there were only companies, but then they've hit us back with battalions and divisions. They don't fight harder, but Stalin can throw in the weight of numbers. We're better armed now than when I first joined, but we still don't have American tanks and planes."

"So what do you think will happen here? Will they pour in more men?"

"They might. You've seen how many NKVD there are. That's why our commanders sent my *kurin* up here. What's it like in the village?"

She told him of the fear which had leeched out from the executions. "And people are tired, Petro. They've borne so much. I know we haven't seen as many battles as those of you who are fighting, but they've been ground down by the loss of so many. There are very few men left in the village and we women manage as best we can."

She had told him of her work for Zadyrak and he returned to it now. "Be careful, Anna. Men like him don't like to be refused."

"He knows I'm not available. I keep Mama well in front of him."

Anna could not know that Zadyrak was torn between his desire for her body and his reluctant awe of the young woman who had so many skills which he lacked. He had ample evidence of her discretion and was grateful for it. He could now sign documents and he did not fail to notice how often she offered to read new communication aloud to him. She enunciated slowly and clearly, giving him time to think and to memorise the information. He no longer simply wanted to throw her across his desk, he wanted her in his home. So he played a longer game and the advice she had given him on handling the bay mare, he applied to her. He protected her from hard labour, giving her lighter tasks whenever he could, but such tender treatment could not go unnoticed in a village where women now did their own work and that of the men.

Anna had never thought to take advantage of Zadyrak's protection, but as the summer weeks passed, she realised with greater certainty that her physical condition would become increasingly vulnerable over the coming months. She had suspected that she was pregnant for some weeks, after missing first one, and then two periods. She had told no one, but she was filled with excitement as she became more convinced of her condition. She had no fear of bearing this child or explaining its origins. She only wanted Petro's baby. She had debated with herself whether to tell Petro or not, but had decided to wait until she was absolutely certain and in the meantime, she kept her secret from everyone else. However, some women were more observant than others.

Anna had been gathering linden flowers with Nina and had stopped to drink tea with Halia, glad of the chance to rest and to talk with Petro's mother. They sat in the shade of the garden, but when Anna tried to sip her tea, she found the taste made her feel nauseous. She put down her cup and watched as Halia and Nina seemed to enjoy theirs. She lifted the cup to taste it again and found even the smell repugnant. Nina's chatter was interrupted by Marusia's younger sisters, Oksana and Odarka, calling to see if Nina wanted to join them in a trip down to the river. The girls set off down the steep hillside, their voices rising to Halia and Anna like the cries of swallows.

Halia turned to Anna as she tried a third time to sip her tea. "Leave it, Anna, if it isn't to your taste."

Anna looked troubled. "I don't know why I suddenly don't like it."

"Some women find they can't drink tea when certain changes have taken place in their bodies."

Anna looked up startled and then blushed.

Halia waited.

Anna did not speak for a few moments and then she said, "I've missed my period twice."

"Have you told Petro?"

"Not yet."

"So you could be between eight and twelve weeks' pregnant."

Anna nodded and then said, "I want this baby. I've wanted it from the first moment I suspected I was pregnant."

"Of course you do," said Halia. "Have you thought about how you might explain it in the village?"

"No, but I don't have to tell anyone anything."

"You might have to eventually." Halia leaned forward, placing her square, work-worn hand on Anna's knee. "I'm not judging you, Anna, but you need to be careful that you don't compromise your safety and the baby's."

"I know."

They both sat on through the birdsong of the afternoon and then Halia glanced almost shyly at Anna. "It will be lovely to have a grandchild." And although Halia smiled and patted Anna's hand, she feared for both the mother and her unborn infant.

As harvest time came around, Zadyrak's knocking on doors with his whip in the early morning, became tyrannical to some.

"Mama, I don't feel well," complained Sofia. "You and Levko will have to go without me today."

She pulled her shawl tightly around herself and sat down at the table, her shoulders hunched. Antin tottered over to her, grizzling, wanting his morning milk. He stood beside her knees and patted them, his little hands only serving as a nuisance to his mother. "Stop fussing, Antin! Levko, give him some milk will you? He's driving me crazy."

But a thirteen-year-old Levko, who now had to do a man's work, was not the easy target of his sister's bullying that he had been. "What are you going to do today, Sofia?" he demanded. "You don't want to work for your bread and you don't want to look after your child either."

"Mama!" she began to wail.

"He's right, Sofia. Either go to the field or do my work here," said Parania, picking up the unhappy child, as she so often did, unable to bear his discomfort.

Sofia shot an evil look at Levko and then deliberately included her mother. "Alright then, I'll go. But I'm not putting up with this for much longer."

*

257

Zadyrak sat astride the bay mare directing operations, ordering the women to their tasks. As they dispersed to the fields, he saw Anna moving off with her sickle. "Anna!" he called.

She stopped and returned to stand at his stirrup.

"There's no need for you to do this," he said in an undertone.

"I must," she said. "I won't be a parasite, Comrade Starosta." And she turned to join the harvesters, despite wishing that she could be excused this hard labour. But at the same time, she comforted herself with the thought that most of the women around her had carried their babies through the harvest period.

It was perfect weather, hot and dry. The villagers could expect a high yield, although they still did not know how much of the wheat would be theirs and how much would be siphoned off by Moscow now that there was no Roman Shumenko to protect them. As Zadyrak rode, shoulders back, chin high, along the edges of the broad fields, there was anxiety under the bent backs below him. When he called a halt around midday, the sweating workers made their way to sit in the shade of the trees. Anna returned to the top of the field with Vera, both women perspiring. Anna had tied her blue headscarf over her hair, little realising how its colour enhanced her eyes. But Zadyrak absorbed it all as he watched the women form an orderly queue for water. He rode over to Anna, unable to resist looking down at the opened neck of her blouse, not knowing that the fullness of her breasts spoke of her love for another man. He was about to tell her to go to the head of the queue, when Sofia pre-empted him in loud tones.

"Anna, here's your champion, come to tell you that you needn't wait with the rest of us peasants."

Several women turned to look at Anna, who was annoyed with herself for blushing, but she forced herself to speak coolly to Sofia. "Not at all, Sofia. I'm happy to wait my turn, as I'm sure you are."

Sofia looked furious, but then turned the full beam of her smile up at Zadyrak. "You look so fine up there, Comrade Starosta. You make all of us girls lose our heads."

Serhiy looked down at the hussy who had begged him for Anna's job and saw again how she offered her full breasts in her deeply cut blouse.

She removed her white headscarf, tossing her black curls over her shoulder. "It's so hot, I'd like to strip off," she sighed. Had she looked about her, she would have seen that her neighbours had created some distance around her, but Zadyrak had seen enough to know that this one could be easily had.

The women sat in the shade to eat and Anna was pleased to be flanked by Halia and Nina, who sat beside her, talking of inconsequential things until the break was over. But in her present mood, nothing was going to be missed by

Sofia. She took in the little group and understood. Finished with him after our wedding, did she? Well, let's see…

The following day dawned with the blessed coolness which belied scorching sunshine later on. The work began early and Anna took her place in the rows. They worked across the seemingly endless fields, this time raking the previous day's fallen stalks into long ribbons to dry. Anna worked with the rhythm of her long-toothed rake and swung through her arms and shoulders, conscious only of the sun on her back and the stalks at her feet.

At mid-morning they saw a cart rumbling down the track towards them, laden with water barrels.

"What on earth?" cried one.

"It's not midday yet, is it?" cried another.

"Water? For us?" said yet another.

Vera spoke quietly to Anna. "Was this your idea?"

"Yes," Anna replied, just as quietly.

"Let's hope Sofia doesn't find out."

Anna rolled her eyes and the two took their place in the queue.

Zadyrak could not resist riding up to see the labourers enjoying his bounty. Sofia saw him out of the corner of her eye and, taking the ladle from the water barrel, threw back her head and poured the water over her face in an extravagant gesture. The droplets sparkled on her black curly hair, but much of it coursed across her cheeks and down her exposed throat to soak into her cotton blouse over her breasts. Without a word, she looked him full in the face, challenging him. He was watching her and, as she had intended, felt a stirring in his loins. The bay mare sensed the disturbance in her rider and took a step or two back. Sofia turned away, managing both to flounce and sway her hips at the same time. Vera and Anna dared not look at one another for fear they might burst out laughing.

Towards the end of the day, Zadyrak rode up to the edge of the field and Anna looked up, knowing he wanted her to record the workers present that day. She excused herself to her neighbours in the row and made her way over to the *starosta*. He handed her the notebook and pen from his saddlebag and she placed herself at the top of the lane, where each worker would pass her to be noted for their wages.

As Sofia drew level with Anna, she said, "It's so good of you to do this for us, Anna. We're all so grateful, you know."

"You're welcome," replied Anna, as she continued to make a scrupulous note of each worker.

Vera was the last worker to be noted by Anna and the friends set off back to the village together, much to Zadyrak's chagrin at being denied the opportunity of a tête-à-tête with Anna. As they put some distance between them, they linked arms and Anna said, "Thanks for that!"

"I have an ulterior motive, too," said Vera apologetically.

"What is it?"

"It's Vasilko."

"What about him?"

"I'm afraid for him. He keeps talking about Petro."

"Petro?"

"Yes. He says Petro went off to fight the partisans, so why shouldn't he?"

"But he's only…"

"Fourteen, I know. I don't know what to tell him, Anna. I fear for him if he stays and I dread the thought of him going."

Anna thought of Hrichko, who had not only survived in the woods, but seemed to have thrived on the rough protection he had received. But the UPA were so much more professional and driven now. She doubted that they would welcome a raw boy. "I don't know either, Vera, but I'll talk to Petro the next time I see him. I can't make any promises though."

"Well, at least I'll have some kind of answer for him," sighed Vera.

"Answers would be helpful," murmured Anna.

Vera looked at Anna quickly, wondering if she had upset her friend with her talk of her younger brother, but then something in the curve of Anna's cheek made her pause and ask, "Is everything alright, Anna?"

Anna turned to Vera, unable to hide the trouble in her eyes. "Yes and no."

"Come on, then. You can tell me."

Anna glanced down at herself and Vera's eyes followed Anna's. "Oh," she breathed. "How long?"

"I've missed three periods now."

"Have you told Petro?"

Anna shook her head.

"Have you told anyone?"

"Halia guessed."

"How did she react?"

"She's happy to be a grandmother."

"And your mother?"

"I haven't told her. I think it might worry her, so I'm going to wait for a while yet."

"Why haven't you told Petro?"

"I think he'll make a fuss and not want me to come to the woods. I couldn't bear not to see him and it's far too risky for him to come into the village."

"Yes, but it's risky for you, going to the woods. Not only the danger of being caught, but the danger to the baby."

"Oh, we're alright," said Anna, drawing her hand across her abdomen. "We will be alright, Vera," she said with absolute conviction.

"Yes, but you must still look after yourself. What can I do to help?"

"Nothing for now. Except to keep my secret."

"Of course, I will," and the two made their way home, heads bent close together.

Anna kept her promise and spoke to Petro about Vasilko, but it was as she expected.

"We can't take children, Anna. It's far too dangerous."

"I thought that's what you'd say, but Vera is so worried."

"We might be able to use him as a messenger. If you think that will satisfy him for now, tell him that."

"I will. It'll be better than nothing and might keep him safe for the time being."

As the harvest came in, Anna was required to supervise the weighing of the grain and to keep careful records of how much wheat was yielded by each field. Zadyrak could not be everywhere and he lacked the eye of an experienced farmer. He could not judge at a glance how much an area might yield. So when Ihor came to Anna with his produce, they both noted, with only a flicker of a glance between them, how the numbers Anna wrote were smaller than those they had both seen on the scales. She continued to do the same for all those she trusted, knowing they would have the sense to conceal the surplus she had wordlessly allotted them. There was a sigh of relief from many as she eased their burdens and, occasionally, Ihor or Andriy would accompany someone Anna knew less well, so that here, too, Anna's accounting eased an anxious farmer.

As the collecting and counting came to a close, Anna went through the totals with Zadyrak.

"We seem to have done well," he said.

"Yes, I think the harvest has been good."

He pretended to look over her shoulder at the figures, so Anna leaned away from him while pushing the ledger towards him.

"Anna, there's no need to be stand-offish with me."

"Of course not, Comrade Starosta. I hope we work well together."

"But there's no need for you to work so hard. I find you very helpful here. You don't have to work in the fields anymore."

"I must work. I have my mother to keep."

"Anna, you know I would look after you and your mother." He drew closer to her and Anna regretted not getting up from her seat sooner.

He stroked her hair with a clumsy paw. "Anna…"

She pushed back her chair and stood away from him. "I'm sorry, Comrade Starosta…"

"Don't be hasty, Anna. There's no need to be afraid. I want to help you."

"Thank you. You have helped me. But the rest…it's not possible."

"Everything's possible, Anna. I'm in a position to give you and your mother a comfortable life."

"Thank you again, but Mama's not well. She needs to have peace and quiet."

"She could have it. You could both come and live with me. It's a big house."

"I couldn't move her. She couldn't cope with a move."

"Anna, please re-consider," he said gruffly and she was painfully aware of what this conversation was costing him.

"I can't leave her, Comrade Starosta. She's experienced some terrible things and she deserves to be looked after now she's old."

He looked at her determined face and watched her stepping back from him, so he forced himself to go no further now. She must see the advantages he could offer her.

However, Anna had begun to feel more uneasy. She began to fear his inevitable discovery of her pregnancy. He would be furious. She decided it was time to tell Petro. She needed his strength as well as her own.

As she set off for the camp the next time, she noticed the autumnal changes. It was getting dark earlier, but she was also aware of the dangerous beauty of the thinning foliage and dry, whispering forest floor. She thought ahead to a time when she would be able to bring the child here and teach him, or her, about the wonders of nature…but first she had to tell Petro. She hurried on. Before long there was a brief hooting and Anna looked between the trees for her beloved. He was standing between the birches, a hand raised to his lips in caution. She reached him and smiled happily into his bright blue eyes. He looked almost triumphant, so happy was he to see her. They gripped hands and turned towards the camp. Anna delivered the food and collected the post for Buchach; and then she and Petro withdrew into his part of the dug-out. It was becoming too cold to be outdoor lovers any longer. He dropped the canvas curtain, lit a candle and turned to look at Anna whose face seemed even more beautiful to him in the flickering light. He stroked her cheek.

She smiled at him, her eyes full of delight. "Wait a moment." She took his hand and opening her coat, she placed it on her belly.

"Anna?" he asked, not wanting to understand.

"I'm pregnant."

"Are you sure?"

"Yes. I've missed three months now. It's never happened before."

There was a silence as he tried to absorb the news, but his mind was full of the problems this pregnancy could only bring.

"Aren't you glad?" she asked and then said, "I am. When you were away, I longed for your baby. I want this baby, Petro."

"I understand that..."

"No, you don't. You were away for so long and I wanted so much to have something of yours. I couldn't help but think of you dying and me having nothing left of you."

"Anna, things are so difficult at the moment. How will you manage? I can't come back to the village with the way things are."

"I don't expect you to. Anyway, other women have managed with their babies. I'm sure I can, too."

"But if you tell them I'm the father, you'll put yourself in terrible danger. They might deport you... They could even have you shot."

"I don't have to tell anybody anything."

"Anna, that's too naïve. What about your Zadyrak?"

"He's not my Zadyrak. And I think I might be able to manage him."

"You know there's much more danger to come, don't you? The Bolsheviks are nowhere near finished with us."

"I know that, my love, but life's been dangerous for the last five years. If we waited for the world to be safe for our baby, we'd wait forever."

He took her in his arms then, and she rested her head against his chest. She leaned back and looked up at him. "You know I'm strong. You said it was what made you love me."

"I know, I know. But there's no need for you to make things so much harder for yourself."

"Stop. We can go around in circles. I know I'll have so much help. There's your mother and Nina, Vera, and even my mother might revive with a baby in the house."

"Very well. We'll try to make the best of it."

"Don't you want our baby?"

"Of course I do," and his eyes filled with quick tears. He tried to ignore the sudden image of a little Anna, or a son to teach all he knew. It was too tantalising...and impossible. A wanted man in the woods was no kind of father for a child. But he smiled at Anna in response to her delighted grin.

The work in the fields ended and even harder tasks were allotted. Zadyrak decided that the main lane of the village needed repair, leading as it did from the outside world to his office and thence to his newly renovated home. The villagers were given little choice but to carry out his orders and many had to swallow their anger and do his bidding…but Sofia had never been good at doing anyone's bidding. After a day of moving stone from the quarry to supply the setters on the lane, she rebelled. That evening, despite her exhaustion, she took a bath and washed the dust from her hair, rinsing it with rosemary. She put on her most revealing blouse and her best skirt; and, raiding her mother's pantry for the damson vodka they had made, set off for Zadyrak's house.

He was not surprised to see her and sent away his cronies, who were gathered in his Spartan living room, with a wink and a leer. "So, Sofia, what can I do for you?" he asked, once they were alone.

"Oh no, Serhiy – I may call you Serhiy, mayn't I? – it's what I can do for you," and she smiled sweetly, presenting him with the bottle of dark liquid.

"What's this? A woman's drink!" he said with disgust.

"Not at all. I think you'll find it has some strength to it. Let me pour you a glass." She looked about her and failing to find anything resembling a glass, half-filled an enamel mug. She passed it to him with a giggle. "We might have to share. I can only find one."

They drank in a business-like way, passing the cup between them, barely bothering to pretend that the purpose of her visit was anything other than a clumsy attempt at seduction.

When they had drunk most of the bottle, Sofia drew Serhiy to the old sofa in the corner of the room. "Come, Serhiy, let's be comfortable," and she pulled him down beside her. She put her arm around his shoulders and drew herself up into his lap, feeling the satisfying bulge in his trousers. She loosened his belt and inserted her warm hand into his warmer groin and covered his wet mouth with her own.

Sofia did not hurry, but made sure Serhiy became fully acquainted with the pleasures he might have regularly with her. Her only difficulty was in slowing him down so that he could make the most of the opportunities she was giving him.

However, when he had had his fill, he stood up, re-belted his trousers and said, "So. What's the price?"

Sofia decided she would be as frank as he was. "I don't want to shift stone."

"Alright. I'll find you another job."

"I could do a good job here," she gestured around the almost bare room. "I could make you very comfortable."

"There's no job for you here."

"But I could make one. You work hard and I could make your evenings and your nights very pleasurable. As you have seen."

He looked at her stonily and for a moment she felt a flicker of fear, but she suppressed it. "Come on, Serhiy, you know I could make you very happy," and she moved towards him to stroke his thigh.

He pushed her away. "Enough. I've told you, you can have an easier job. Now be satisfied."

"But..."

"Be quiet. You think I'm going to let a whore take over my life? Go home!" and he took her arm and began to lead her to the door.

Sofia played her final card. "So you think Anna will do this for you, do you?" She saw that she had struck him most accurately. "You think Anna will let you anywhere near her?"

He began to push Sofia again. "Out!"

"I bet you've already tried and been turned down, haven't you?" She looked at the anger in his face. "You have! You've asked her and she won't have anything to do with you!"

He managed to manoeuvre her almost to the door.

"Of course she won't. What would she want with a Bolshevik beast like you when she can have her handsome partisan!"

Serhiy stopped. "What?"

Sofia smiled triumphantly. "You didn't know, did you? Not only would she not let you touch a hair of her head, but you've been harbouring a traitor in your own office!"

Serhiy looked as if she had struck him.

Sofia laughed. "You fool! They've been lovers for years!"

"Who have?"

"Anna and Petro. She claimed it was all over when he went to join the partisans, but she's looked too happy recently. He's in the woods around here somewhere, I'm certain of it."

"How do you know?"

"Everyone knows. There's a group nearby." She stopped, realising it for the first time, "Anna collects food for them."

"Who from?"

Sofia paused. The realisations which were tumbling in her head were far too valuable to be poured into Zadyrak's lap for nothing. "I'm not certain. I'd need to look into it."

Despite the shock he was experiencing, he recognised another opportunist in Sofia, so he nodded. "You do that. You wanted another job."

She drew herself up straighter. "I'll keep you informed. But you need to keep your eyes open, too."

He barely nodded.

"Goodnight, Serhiy. See you soon," and with that she opened the door and walked out into the night.

As soon as she had gone, Zadyrak began to take an inventory of Anna. He admitted to himself that he could not judge the changes Sofia claimed to have seen in her. He did not know her well enough. She always seemed quiet and polite, even cheerful; and she had helped him. He knew she had taught him to sign his own name and neither that, nor being thrown from his horse, had been revealed…to his knowledge. But she had turned him down. Perhaps there was more to it than an ailing mother. He wanted to rush into her cottage across the lane and demand answers, but he made himself wait. He would have to watch and see…

For the next week, Serhiy did watch Anna closely from beneath his heavy brows. She came and went as she had always done, but on one of the days she was not in his office, he called at her cottage. Her mother answered his knock.

"Good day, missus. I'm looking for Anna. I have some work for her."

"She's not here."

"Where is she?"

"She's gone to Buchach, to the market."

"Tell her I called."

The old woman closed the door and Zadyrak went away, wondering about Anna visiting the more distant market at Buchach.

He called again the next day and this time, it was Anna who answered the door. He saw that she had been sleeping, although it was the middle of the morning. "Are you alright? You don't look well."

"I have a very bad headache, so I was trying to sleep it off."

"Then I won't bother you."

"But did you want me to help you? My mother said you called yesterday."

"No, it can wait. Get yourself better," and with that he strode away.

Anna returned to her bed, feeling irritated with his persistence.

Zadyrak, for his part, went away wondering whether she was usually so tired on a Friday and, if so, why.

The following week he asked Anna if she were going to Buchach to the market. "I need some papers delivering to the *raion* office."

"I can do that for you," replied Anna.

"Do you always go to the market in Buchach?"

"Yes, it's a good place to trade home produce."

"But isn't it a bit far?"

"I often manage to get a lift."

Apart from these questions, Zadyrak appeared to be working in his usual way with Anna, although there were moments when she felt his small brown eyes upon her. She worked on, trying to ignore the disturbance she felt and forcing herself not to look up at him. For his part, Zadyrak continued to be tormented by the softness of her lines, the pink cheeks, the sleek hair, the roundness of her breasts. Had Sofia told him of anyone else, he would have arrested them and torn the truth from them, but, despite knowing everyone had the capacity for betrayal, he did not want Anna to be one of their number. He was not sure yet that her trips to Buchach had any significance, but the tiredness he had witnessed in her had suggested far more than a long day at market. So he formed the simple plan of watching her the following Thursday night. He would watch alone. He did not want to reveal his suspicions to any of his subordinates until he could be more sure of her. Once she had been accused, even he would be powerless to help her. He had to be certain of the nature of her betrayal.

So on the following Thursday, after dusk, he walked into his garden and along the backs of two more until he could enter the garden opposite Anna's cottage. He concealed himself in the tall hedge corner and watched her cottage door. He settled down to wait. An hour or so after full dark, he saw the cottage door open. There was no movement for a few moments and then Anna slipped out, her hair covered, not by her usual headscarf, but by a man's cap. He watched her go around the back of her house, a full sack in her hands. He strained to see which way she would go, but he dared not follow her, knowing the noise of his movement over dry autumn foliage would alert her, so he decided he would wait for her return. His patience was rewarded when several cold hours later, he saw her climb through her fence and hurry back into her house, an empty sack in her hands.

He took action the next day. Alone in the office with Hnat, he asked: "If I needed a poacher, would there be a good one in the village?"

Hnat looked afraid.

"It's alright. I want someone with a poacher's skills to do a job for me."

Hnat still hesitated.

"He would be well rewarded...as would you, if you could help me."

"Well," said Hnat, "there's Danylo. He prefers hunting and trapping to farming."

"Danylo...Is he the one who told me about Timko's horse?"

"Yes, that's the one."

"Good. Fetch him please."

They returned a short time later and Hnat made himself scarce. Danylo stood before Zadyrak trying not to fiddle with the cap he held in his grubby hands.

Zadyrak watched him for a moment. "You helped me once."

"Yes, Comrade Starosta."

"Why was that?"

"Well, as you said – we should all share what we have."

"And do you share what you have?"

"Of course, Comrade Starosta," replied Danylo, sounding less certain.

"Including the animals you poach?" asked Zadyrak.

Danylo reddened and mumbled, "It's only rabbits."

"Only rabbits. That doesn't sound like much to me. I would have thought a man like you might go for bigger game."

Danylo looked at the *starosta* slyly. "The Nazis didn't leave us much."

"But enough surely? For a good hunter like you."

Danylo licked his lips. "Well, you can find things if you know where to look."

"What if you don't know where to look?"

"Comrade Starosta?"

"How are your tracking skills? Could you track a deer, for instance?"

Danylo shrugged. "Yes, as long as you're quiet and keep downwind of it. It helps if you know the terrain too."

"And do you know the terrain?"

"I'd say so. As well as anybody."

Zadyrak examined Danylo closely. "I need you to do a tracking job for me."

"Of course, Comrade Starosta."

"Where are you living?"

Danylo looked surprised. "Where I've always lived. The cottage at the end of the lane, past the laundry."

Zadyrak nodded. He knew the hovel. "Timko's house is still empty," he said.

Danylo flushed again and looked at Zadyrak like a dog. "I'd be very happy to help you, Comrade Starosta."

"With no word to anyone?"

"With no word to anyone."

"Very well." And he proceeded to outline the task of following Anna wherever she might go on Thursday night. "Don't interfere with her or anyone else. I only want you to observe everything she does and report back to me."

"I will, and gladly, Comrade Starosta."

Danylo waited motionless in the corner of Anna's garden behind her barn. His silhouette was masked by her walnut tree and he knew well enough that it was movement which alerted prey. She came out of her house as cautiously as usual and tried to listen for movement beyond the slight breeze which was coming from the north. But Danylo stood, still as a post, south of her and so her senses failed her. She set off with her bundle down to the woods. Danylo did not need to crowd her. He kept well back and listened for her footfall crossing the wooden bridge over the Barish and then he, in turn, stepped across silently in his felt boots. He kept closer to her until he saw she was making for the deeper woods and once, when she turned around suddenly, he stood stock still, one foot in the air. But there was nothing for her to see. Danylo was dressed in dark colours from head to foot. He noticed how Anna moved confidently and knew she must have used this unmarked route often. He followed her more cautiously when she entered the darker woods, being both alert to her movements and to any insurgent challenge. When the challenge did come, he stopped, perfectly still. He listened to the exchange between Anna and the guard and then saw her move further on alone. He contemplated circling round to try to enter what he imagined must be an encampment, but decided not to risk it on a first visit. He would return to do more reconnaissance when he did not have to wait for Anna. He realised he would not fulfil Zadyrak's brief, but secrecy was the priority. If he was discovered now, nothing would be learned. The partisans would kill him.

Within half an hour, Anna had returned, no longer carrying the bulging sack. So she must be helping to feed them, he thought. He followed her, rightly assuming that she was returning home. Anna set a quick pace now that she was no longer hampered by her heavy bundle and, besides, she was cold and disappointed. Petro had not been at the camp. It had been very quiet with most of the *kurin* engaged in action elsewhere, so she hurried home.

Zadyrak eagerly awaited Danylo's arrival. He had told the poacher to report to him as soon as Anna returned. "So you think she's feeding them?"

"I'm pretty certain, Comrade Starosta. She took a heavy sack and came back empty-handed."

"And she was only with them for about half an hour?"

"Yes, Comrade Starosta."

"But you don't know who she spoke to?"

"No. I couldn't follow her into the camp. I had no idea how many men might be there." He looked at Zadyrak pulling at his lip. "I'll go and look again when I don't need to follow Anna."

"Yes, alright. You do that. Keep watching her at night. If she goes out, I want her followed and report back to me immediately."

"I will, Comrade Starosta."

Alone, Zadyrak paced the floor. If she had a lover, if Sofia had told the truth, Anna would not have returned so quickly, he reasoned. So perhaps she had had a lover before and now continued to show her allegiance to the partisans. If she was only feeding them – and he recognised that this would mean a death sentence for anyone else – he could draw her away from that. He mused again. She had been so concerned for her mother. What if there was no mother...just as there was no lover...then she could be his and once he had her, he could squeeze her. He would make her his, and woe betide her if she slipped off again at night! He clenched his fist as he thought his plan through and continued to pace up and down the echoing room, picking up his whip as he did so and slapping it against his boot.

Over the next few days, little changed except the weather. It became much colder and the first snow fell. It was not the heavy fall of deepest winter, but enough to show the inexorable turning of the year. On Wednesday night, Anna leaned over to kiss her mother's soft, warm cheek goodnight and was relieved that Katerina already seemed to be dozing. She pulled the eiderdown up to her mother's chin and made sure she would be warm enough in her absence. She checked the fire in the stove and put on another log, knowing it would last until she returned. She turned off the lamp and then she put on her coat and her father's cap, pulled on her boots at the door and slipped out.

She glanced around. The moonlight reflected off the snow and there was a deep quiet. She listened and then went around the back of the woodpile for the sack of supplies she had stowed earlier that day. She slung the heavy weight over her shoulder and set off in the shadow of the hazel hedge to the woods beyond. She was as cautious as ever, but could do little to quieten the crunch of snow underfoot. Danylo, too, was wary of the snow. Not only could its sound betray him, but the hunter knew how visible predator and prey became against its empty backcloth. So he set off, keeping a careful distance between them...little knowing that Zadyrak was watching both of them. In his hiding place, he had to stop himself from rubbing his hands with gnomish glee, but he could not resist a peek at the future. Anna would be more than glad of his protection when she knew the danger she was in. She would have no mother to hide behind. She would be entirely his...

He shook his head. This was no time for fantasies. He needed to get on with the task in hand first. He crossed the lane swiftly for a man of his bulk, and stepped up the path to the door, lifting the latch cautiously. He peered into the dim room and reached across to lift the sacking from the window. The moonlight would give him enough illumination to work by.

Katerina lay in bed in the corner of the room. He had taken two steps over to the bed, when the old woman turned to face him. "Did you forget something, Anna?" she asked and then her eyes widened as she saw Zadyrak's form looming over her.

In a flash, he picked up the empty pillow beside her and bore down on her, adding his considerable weight to the density of the pillow. But Katerina had more strength left in her than he could have predicted and she thrashed vigorously for a few moments, while he struggled to hold her down. Then he threw all of his weight onto her again and she became limp. He waited a few moments more and removed the pillow to look at her. She appeared to be dead, but he needed to be sure of her. He lifted her shoulders and holding her in one arm, thrust her head back, snapping her neck. Then he arranged her inert body in the bed, fluffing up the spare pillow, straightening the quilt. He stepped back from the bed and turned to go, only to leap in fear as a hissing creature turned on him. Only a cat! He shook himself and left the house as carefully as he had entered. Then he disappeared along the garden hedge, returning to his own home to wait for Danylo's report.

Anna stepped down the path in the hushed woods and allowed her spirits to lift as she reached their shelter. The snow was no threat to a woman going to see her lover, while carrying the precious cargo of their first child… When Anna reached the Barish, she saw the gluey texture of the ice at its edges, but it was not yet cold enough for the river to have frozen fully. She stepped carefully onto the frosty bridge and made herself slow down and walk along gingerly, despite being aware of her visibility. As she left the bridge behind her, she hurried through the snow, lifting her feet higher, aware both of her tracks and her dark clothing sharply etched against the whiteness. She reached the trees and leaned for a moment against a trunk, her breath coming in cold clouds. She had to admit to herself that these night time excursions were becoming too taxing and she knew that she would soon have to acquiesce to Petro's wish that they cease altogether until the baby was born. But for tonight, she made the journey slowly and carefully, glad to be able to share some precious moments with Petro. He seemed to be as mesmerised as she was by the rounding firmness of her belly.

Her return journey seemed to pass as quickly as ever in the habitual cloud of joy at having seen Petro. She came to the bridge over the Barish again and continued to hurry back to her warm bed, but as she stepped down from the bridge, her foot slipped on the treacherous surface and she slid a metre or so down the bank. Her left foot broke through the ice and entered the water as she tried to gain some purchase with her right hand. She found the edge of the plank bridge and clung on, gasping for breath. She was desperately afraid she might fall into the freezing waters, but she half-turned and hauled herself up, scrabbling and scrambling her boots against the smooth surface until she lay on the bank panting. She knew she must get home and attend to her soaked foot. Even this early in the winter no risk could be taken. She must get out of her wet things and warm herself.

She struggled to her feet and trotted painfully towards the trees, her left boot full of icy water and her trousers clinging to her legs. She limped and hobbled as quickly as she could into the house, latching and locking the door, before turning to check that her mother was still asleep. Katerina lay still, so Anna took off her coat and her outer clothing. She removed her boots, trousers and wet socks and climbed into bed. She threw caution to the wind as she curled around her mother's body for warmth, whispering, "Help me, Mama. Help me!"

But her mother's body had no warmth to offer Anna. Even the bed felt cold. Anna pushed her hands down and on her right side, next to her mother, she felt a damp patch. Her caution was now tinged with fear as she reached out to stroke her mother's arm. But it was cold and unresponsive. Anna cried out, "Mama?" and shook her mother's lifeless body. There was no answer. She leapt out of bed and lit the lamp. She turned the flame up full and shone it on her mother's face. Katerina's jaw was hanging slack and, although her eyes were open, there was no evidence of any sense in them.

"Mama!" Anna cried again, ripping back the quilt to see her mother had evacuated her bladder and bowels on death. Knowing it was in vain, she placed her ear on her mother's chest, but there was no heartbeat. She felt for the pulse at her throat but again there was no response.

"No!" cried Anna, "no, Mama, please!" She was sobbing as she took her mother's inert body into her arms. Katerina's corpse did not respond to her child's outpouring of love and grief. Her head sagged back and Anna tried to hold it up as she wept for the mother who had suffered so much.

Chapter 23

When the sky finally began to lighten, Anna put on her coat and boots and made her way to the doctor's house once more. Her knock was answered by a girl of eight or so, her dishevelled plaits swinging as she turned to fetch her father. Anna waited, her eyes on the ground. When she heard the doctor approaching, she looked up into his cold gaze.

"Good morning, doctor."

"Good morning," he replied tersely.

"Could you come to my house, please, to certify my mother dead? She died in the night."

He did not need to question Anna's veracity, her demeanour told him she was telling the truth. The doctor collected his bag and accompanied Anna to her house.

As he examined Katerina, he glanced once at Anna and then completed his examination. "Describe to me how she died."

Anna looked at him bleakly. "I can't. I wasn't here."

He looked as if he had suspected as much. "How was she before you left?"

"The same as usual. She wasn't ill, only low in spirits and often tired." Anna stroked her mother's hair back from her forehead. "She was in bed for the night and asleep when I left."

"How long were you gone?"

"About three hours."

"And when you came back?"

"I was cold. I'd got my feet wet coming back so I jumped into bed with her. That was when I knew."

"How did you know?"

"She was cold. And the bed was wet."

He looked at Anna kindly for the first time. "That must have been a shock for you."

Tears filled her eyes.

"Then what?"

"I waited till I could fetch you."

"Do you think anyone else had been in the house during your absence?"

She looked surprised. "I don't know. I didn't lock the door." She was thoughtful for a moment. "But I left the cat indoors with Mama and when I came home, he wasn't here. Why?"

The doctor hesitated before replying. Should he tell her that her mother had probably been suffocated, as the corpse's blue lips and fingertips suggested, or should he simply give her the one incontrovertible fact... "Anna, your mother's neck has been broken."

Anna was speechless. Her heart pounded in her chest and she felt a band tighten around her head.

"I'm sorry, Anna, but I'm certain she was killed."

"No!" she sobbed but her mind raced. Who could have done this? She realised the doctor was speaking again.

"Who else knows you leave the house at night?"

Who could have betrayed her? Her mind darted through her list of contributors. Surely none of them would do such a thing? Who would have been cruel enough to kill an innocent old woman? Who would have dared?

As the doctor began to speak, Anna shook her head at him and mouthed one name, "Zadyrak."

He nodded, thinking desperately of his own dilemma. He had to be very careful what he wrote on the death certificate. He could not be found to be complicit with Anna, but to cry murder? That would unleash all kinds of furies. He decided he would rather be judged incompetent. "Anna, you're in great danger. It's highly probable that people know more about you than you think. I'll say that I didn't examine your mother. An old woman dying in her bed isn't remarkable. But you need to take great care how you proceed. Your enemies will be watching your reaction."

"Yes." Anna's grief was raw and this might give her some temporary protection from whatever her adversary had planned.

The doctor filled in the death certificate. "You shouldn't be alone. Who can I fetch to help you?"

"Vera. My friend, Vera."

"I'll fetch her on my way home."

"Thank you, doctor."

"And, Anna, are you taking proper care of yourself...and the baby?"

She looked startled.

"I'm a doctor, Anna," he said kindly. "How far gone are you?"

"About five months."

"Good. Then the dangerous time has passed and the foetus should be secure. But you still need to take care. A shock like this could affect the baby."

Anna crossed her hands over her belly and looked stricken.

"Don't upset yourself. Make sure you rest, and tell your closest friends. You'll need their support. Now, I'd better go and get Vera."

"Thank you," she murmured.

Not many minutes later, Vera hurried into the cottage. "Anna, I'm so sorry."

The women embraced through their tears, Anna still thinking of the betrayal. She knew she could trust Vera, yet she feared burdening her with another of Zadyrak's executions. But who else could she confide in? So she related the doctor's findings.

"That bastard!"

"But if he knows I'm helping the boys in the woods, why kill Mama? Why not kill me? Or at least, arrest me?"

"Because he wants to trap you and keep you for himself. How many times did you turn him down? And each time, your mother was the reason."

"You're right." Anna turned to her mother's body. "I can't bear the thought of her being hurt because of me."

Vera put her arm around Anna's shoulders. "If he broke her neck, at least it would have been quick. Let's wash her body now. Doing something will ease you."

So they prepared Katerina's body for burial. There would be no priest, but Vera sent Vasilko around the village with the news of the death and soon, Anna's little house was busy with women coming to pay their respects to Katerina and to give their condolences to Anna.

The person Anna most wanted to see was Petro. She decided to risk leaving the cottage that night, but Vera again saved her. She drew Anna aside during a lull and asked, "Where will I find him?"

"No, Vera. We're all in danger now. I couldn't let you go for him."

"You must. You need him now. This can't go unpunished. But you can't go yourself."

"What about Vasilko?" asked Anna tentatively.

"He'd be thrilled that we trust him," said Vera. "I'll talk to him."

There was a stamping of boots outside Anna's door and Zadyrak entered the small room, seeming to loom over the women. He looked towards Anna. "I heard your mother died. I came to express my condolences. Is there anything I can do to help?" He shifted his eyes uncomfortably.

Anna held Vera's hand tightly. "Thank you, Comrade Starosta, but no. As you see, I have lots of help." She reached for a piece of paper on the table. "The doctor has written the certificate. Perhaps you could read it in the office," and she handed it to him and went to sit at her mother's head. Katerina's corpse was dressed in her embroidered blouse, a flowered kerchief on her head, her hands crossed on her chest.

Zadyrak glanced away quickly and took the piece of paper, saying too loudly, "I'll send a couple of my men to dig the grave."

"Please tell them to come here first. I'll show them where I want it," said Anna, gambling on the fact that he would be willing to make this concession to assuage any guilt he might feel. She was determined her mother would be buried beside Mikola and Yuri.

Anna kept the overnight vigil with Halia and Nina, whose presence comforted her. As the hours passed, Halia insisted that Anna take some rest.

"You must. You haven't only yourself to think of anymore," and she helped Anna to lie down.

Nina eyes widened as she absorbed her mother's words and saw the rounding of Anna's belly as she lay on her back.

Halia turned to her. "Not a word to anyone, Nina."

Nina moved towards Anna and shyly took the proffered hand. "Are you…"

Anna smiled, "You'll be an aunty, Nina."

Nina leaned forward to hug her.

"Gently now," said Halia. She still felt anxious for Anna. She knew how the girl had longed for Petro's baby and she knew that Anna was resilient and resourceful…but how would she explain its father?

Vasilko tapped on Anna's window at dawn and she left the house to meet Petro. She walked to the woods where they had first become lovers. Petro was waiting for her, his soft cap with its *tryzub* pulled forward over his brows. As she told him what had happened to Katerina, she wept in his arms, for her mother and the last traces of her girlhood.

A late owl hooted overhead as Petro asked, "So it was Zadyrak?"

"I can't be sure, but it seems so."

"Well, we'll be sure of him before he dies."

"How will you catch him?"

"Are you able to find out where he plans to be today?"

Anna lifted her chin. "Yes, I'll do it. How will I let you know?"

"Send Vasilko back to me." He looked into her grey eyes. "Are you sure you want to do this, Anna?"

"I'm sure. He killed Mama."

"Alright then. When will you have the funeral?"

"This afternoon. There's no priest, but we'll say some prayers for her."

"I'm sorry I won't be there."

"Don't be sorry. You're here now. And you'll have work to do."

They embraced again, holding one another tightly and Anna found herself memorising Petro, drawing in the scent of him and feeling the hardness of his chest against her. She noticed the shirt he wore and remembered stitching it when he had first gone away. She felt full of loss, as if he had left her again. "Take care, my love."

"I will. I doubt I'll be able to come to you tonight..."

"No, you mustn't," she interrupted him. "I'll come to you, as soon as it's safe."

He kissed her and they parted reluctantly, each to deal with the terrible demands of their day, but as Anna reached the top of the rise, she turned to see Petro disappearing among the trees below. She wanted to call him back, but shook herself and returned to the business in hand.

She went straight to the Terblenko house, but, finding Zadyrak was not there, went on to the village office. He was seated behind his desk, Hnat at his elbow. "Anna! I wasn't expecting to see you here."

"I just wanted to tell you when the funeral would be. It's this afternoon."

Zadyrak adopted what he hoped was a suitable expression. "I'm sorry, Anna, I won't be able to be there. I have urgent business in Temne."

"Never mind," said Anna. "I just wanted you to know," and she turned away.

"Goodbye, Anna. I'll look in on you tomorrow."

Anna left the office, her head bowed and Zadyrak shuffled uncomfortably on his seat. "She seems badly hit," he muttered.

"Well, she's all alone now," replied Hnat.

Petro received the message, through Vasilko, that Zadyrak intended to go to Temne that afternoon, so he and two of his colleagues hid among the cherry trees, which bordered the lane to the shrine. They waited patiently, despite the cold, well-hidden against the snow in their white camouflage suits. Eventually, Vasilko came running up the lane from the village, whistling the signal that Zadyrak was approaching. The lookout checked and saw the *starosta* was alone on Timko's bay mare. The men tightened the wire they had previously slung between the trees and signalled to Vasilko, who trotted back towards his victim.

"Hey, Mr Starosta," he shouted, "what were you doing in Anna's house the other night?" and he made an obscene gesture.

Zadyrak looked thunderstruck. "Come here, you little bastard. I'll give you something for your cheek!" He pushed the mare into a quick trot and called to Vasilko, "Why weren't you obeying the curfew?"

Vasilko laughed derisively. "Did you get into bed with the old woman as well?"

Zadyrak dug his heels into the mare's flanks and whipped her forward. They cantered towards the boy, who was still laughing and running backwards towards the shrine. Zadyrak was determined to catch him and whip his hide to shut him up. He glared down at the boy just in front of the horse's head. As he closed in on Vasilko, he raised his whip hand to strike out at him, so did not see the wire until it was too late. It struck him across the neck, unseating him and he fell heavily from the saddle, his back slamming onto the compacted snow. He was badly winded and Petro and the other two partisans were on him in a flash, pinning his considerable bulk to the ground. Petro knelt at his head, a sharp blade to Zadyrak's throat.

"So you did kill a defenceless woman."

Zadyrak gasped for air and then spluttered, "She was old. She'd have died anyway…"

As the two men continued to hold Zadyrak down, Petro pulled the *starosta's* head back and drew the knife across his thick throat with a fierce downward thrust, cutting through the muscle to the carotid artery. The blood pumped violently from his body as Zadyrak's heart beat fiercely in the last seconds, staining the snow bright crimson. The desperate plea in Zadyrak's eyes faded and the three men stood up from their work.

Petro turned to Vasilko. "Good lad. But not a word to anyone, understand?"

"Yes," said Vasilko. "When can I come and join you?"

"Soon, but for now, send this mare back to the village. Don't lead her yourself." He turned to the others, "We'd better make ourselves scarce," and he was through the hedge and sprinting across the field to the woods beyond.

Vasilko approached the mare, who was standing a few metres away. He gathered her reins over her head and weighted them with one of the stirrups. He led her past the bloody corpse toward the village, then trotted a short way with her before slapping her on the rump and leaving her to make her way home, taking himself off by a circular route.

The snowflakes swirled around the villagers as they made the short walk from Anna's cottage to the cemetery. Katerina's body had been sewn into a linen binding and her body was carried by Ihor, Andriy and Levko. Anna followed the body, flanked by Vera on one side and Halia and Nina on the other. Despite the lack of a priest and the strictures of the Bolsheviks, the women raised their voices in hymns. The sound of the quavering notes on the cold breeze brought the tears to Anna's eyes again. She could not help remembering the dark silent night when she and her mother had buried Mikola and Yuri. Anna wondered why she and Katerina had survived if this was all it had led to…but then she thought of her own baby, curled warmly in her womb and understood that there was no choice. They gathered around the open grave and Anna knew she would be comforted later when she remembered how many people had come to pay their respects to Katerina. But it was also an unspoken gesture of support for Anna herself. There were many who had cause to be grateful to her and as they sang "Eternal memory" together in the mournful snow, the kindness and sorrow united them…and provided them with a useful alibi in the days to come.

Sofia, though, would have no such alibi.

"Are you ready, Sofia?" Parania asked, adjusting her dark shawl over her greying hair.

"For what?"

"The funeral."

"I'm not going."

Parania stopped what she was doing. "But Anna's been such a good friend to you."

"So what? I haven't seen her in ages."

"Sofia, this won't do. She was your bridesmaid and she's helped you more than once with Antin."

"I don't care," replied Sofia stubbornly.

Parania looked sorrowfully at Sofia's firm cheeks and her down-turned mouth. She left the cottage without another word and as she walked towards the cemetery, she tried not to weep for the loss of both of her daughters.

Anna returned to her empty house with only Halia and Nina for company. She had not had the heart to arrange a wake. Halia warmed some soup at Anna's stove, while Nina helped Anna to change the bed. They were quiet as they worked and so heard the shouts in the lane as soon as they began. They hurried out to the gate to see several of Zadyrak's cronies gathering around the riderless bay mare. Anna returned indoors, caring little about the fate of the *starosta*. Halia and Nina continued to watch as a couple of Zadyrak's lieutenants mounted their own horses and rode towards Temne. Then they, too, went indoors to try to encourage Anna to eat something.

It was only a short time later that the trumpet sounded, calling everyone to the village hall. Anna and her companions joined the throng of women and a few old men and boys to see the stage taken by several blue-capped NKVD soldiers, the most senior of whom ordered everyone to sit down. They did not wait for long before hearing a vehicle draw up and an NKVD captain entered the hall and took the stage. He, too, wore the hated blue cap, but his bright blue jodhpurs and dark green jacket distinguished him from his men. He looked out at his audience seeming to scrutinise each individual separately.

"You will all give your names to one of my comrades and tell him your whereabouts this afternoon and then you will return to your seats."

The villagers filed up and repeatedly gave Katerina's funeral as the place they had spent the afternoon. The papers were passed to the captain, who had been watching the proceedings through his glinting spectacles, trying to separate the guilty from the merely fearful. He glanced through the pages. "Hmm. A funeral. How convenient." He looked up at his anxious audience. "Where's your *starosta*?"

The villagers looked back at him blankly.

"I'll tell you where he is," said the captain coldly. "He's lying in a pool of his own blood on the road to Temne. His throat was cut." He appeared to be glaring at his audience, but in fact he was examining their expressions closely.

"Who was being buried?" he asked.

Anna stood up. "My mother, Comrade Captain."

"And how did she die?"

"In her sleep."

"Then she was lucky."

He glanced at the list again, but before he could speak, Hnat approached him and whispered in his ear. The captain looked at Anna sharply and then said, "These people stay behind," reading the names of those with no alibis. "The rest of you return to your homes. But you," he pointed at Anna, "can come with me."

He strode through the hall and Anna followed him out to the car with the initials NKVD on its sides. He opened the back door for her and she got in. He sat beside her and his driver took them towards Temne.

Anna sat still, her hands in her lap, but her heart pounding, as they drove past the bloody spot where Zadyrak had died. His body had already been removed, but there were blue caps still checking the scene of the murder. Anna knew she must rely on the fact that she knew nothing of how Zadyrak had died, nor who had taken his life.

The car slowed down at the high walls of Temne prison and turned under the archway into the courtyard. It drew to a halt and the captain ordered Anna out. "Follow me."

She walked behind him as he strode into the building, and along a grey corridor to an office on the ground floor. An orderly followed them into the room and Lukyanov waited as he seated himself at a side table with notebook and pen. Anna waited, too, reminding herself that she was a simple young woman who had buried her mother that afternoon.

Which was where Lukyanov began...

"So, you were at your mother's funeral this afternoon?"

"Yes, Comrade Captain."

"And where was Comrade Zadyrak?"

"I don't know, Comrade Captain."

"I think you do."

Anna looked blank. "He wasn't at the funeral."

"But you knew where he was?"

"No, Comrade Captain."

"Didn't he tell you where he was going?"

"Yes. He said he was going to Temne, but I didn't know when he was going to go."

"Didn't he tell you?"

"Only that it was in the afternoon."

"So you knew where he was..."

"No, Comrade Captain. Comrade Zadyrak only mentioned his intention to go to Temne."

Captain Lukyanov looked at Anna more closely. "He 'only mentioned his intention'?"

"Yes, Comrade Captain."

"How's that?"

"He told me he couldn't attend Mama's funeral because he was going to Temne."

"Nevertheless. Whether he went or not, you, and only you, beyond Comrade Zadyrak's close staff, knew that he was going to Temne."

"I can't say, Comrade Captain."

He glanced at his army issue wristwatch. "Well, I'd like to give you some time to think this matter over. Perhaps then you will have something you can say." He opened the office door and beckoned in two NKVD guards. "Escort the prisoner to cell 9."

His gesture dismissed Anna and she turned to follow one of the guards, while the other stepped up behind her. She was led up a flight of stairs to a cell on the first floor. The door was unlocked and she entered the cell to hear the door clang behind her. A key turned in the lock.

So I'm a prisoner, thought Anna. She looked around the cell. The walls and floor were grey and bare although a wooden plank lined one wall. She went to look out of the barred window which faced the road home. Home... She wondered how long they might keep her here. She had done nothing wrong, she told herself. She had been nowhere near the murder spot, nor had she known anything about it. They could not hold her for long...and she forced herself to breathe evenly and deeply.

*

Amongst the small number of villagers who had not attended Katerina's funeral, two made special requests of the officer questioning them. The first was Sofia. "I'd like to speak to your Captain privately," she simpered. "I have some interesting information for him."

"He won't be interested in that sort of information."

Sofia pretended to be offended. "I don't know what you mean, but I have very useful information regarding Comrade Zadyrak which may throw some light on his murder. And if you don't pass me up the chain, I'll make sure the Captain gets to know that you ignored me."

So Sofia found herself standing before Lukyanov in Temne. She had read his character immediately and knew she would gain nothing here except by frankness.

"What is your 'interesting information'?" he asked impatiently, looking up from the papers on his desk.

"I had recently warned Comrade Zadyrak that Anna, his secretary, was a traitor. She has a lover in the UPA."

"And how do you know this?"

"They were lovers when I got married in '42 and then he joined the rebels in the woods."

"How do you know they're still lovers? A lot has happened since 1942."

Sofia could not tell the truth, that Anna looked too happy, but she had no real evidence…and this man would definitely recognise a lie.

He watched her debating with herself. "Well?"

She shrugged. "Anna was like the rest of us for a while – quiet, unhappy… and then she looked happy again." Even to Sofia, this sounded foolish and she blushed.

"Good. That is exactly the sort of observation which destroys the traitors in our midst."

Sofia looked at him hopefully.

"And you warned Comrade Zadyrak?"

"Yes, I did. I went to his house one night…" she stopped.

"Didn't he take you seriously?"

She blushed again, furious with herself. Why wasn't this interview going as she'd intended?

"Where's your husband?"

Sofia started. Dear God… "I don't know."

"Where was he when you last heard of him?"

"At Brody."

"Fighting on which side?" Lukyanov asked, knowing the answer already.

"The Germans," she muttered.

"An Enemy of the People." He made a steeple of his fingers and said in a satisfied tone, "So, you dislike this Anna and try to suggest she is a traitor and your husband fought against the Red Army at Brody. Why might I believe you?"

Sofia's eyes filled with angry tears at the injustice of life. She had tried to stop Ivan from joining the *Divizia*; she had tried to give herself to Zadyrak; and now this cold fish was suggesting she was a liar. "I'm trying to help our Motherland!" she burst out.

Lukyanov laughed. "I believe you would stamp your foot if you dared. Take her away and put her in a cell," he rapped out to the orderly.

Sofia's shoulders sagged and she felt her heart beating painfully in her chest. As she sat in her cell, her mind darted hither and thither, trying to find a way out of the trap she had created for herself.

The second petitioner was Danylo and he, too, found himself in front of Lukyanov before the day was out. Danylo knew that his work for Zadyrak might come to the Captain's attention and so he hoped to curry favour by offering his information sooner rather than later. Besides, he had argued with himself, the nationalist dream was over. No one would mount a rescue from the Russians, so they might as well get used to the return of the old enemy.

"What was so private that you could only tell me?"

"I was working for Comrade Zadyrak," began Danylo. "He asked me to follow Anna. He was suspicious of her."

"Where did she go?"

"To the woods. At night. I told Comrade Starosta that she was taking food to the partisans."

"Did you see her do that?"

"Yes, Comrade Captain."

"And do you know where their camp is?"

"Yes, Comrade Captain."

Lukyanov looked at Danylo with interest. "And you could find it in the dark?"

"Of course. I followed Anna at night."

"How many rebels do you estimate are camped there?"

"About thirty. But I can't be sure." Danylo hesitated to say that he had been back to the encampment alone as he feared incriminating himself. The NKVD Captain might think he was working for both sides.

"Show me on this map," Lukyanov said, rising from his seat.

Danylo approached the map and tapped the centre of a green area in an ox-bow of Dniester. There was no road nearby.

"Are there tracks wide enough for vehicles to get through?"

"Some cart tracks, yes. But the last part has to be on foot."

Danylo was left standing in the middle of the room as Lukyanov gave a flurry of orders and several officers began to assemble around the map.

"Tell us everything you know about this camp," Lukyanov ordered Danylo.

He told of the places where he knew the guards were usually stationed, of passwords overheard and the general layout of the camp, including the positions of the dug-outs. He drew a diagram of these and the officers memorised their configuration.

Lukyanov turned to his officers. "We'll strike them tonight. They might expect reprisals, but they won't think we have any information yet. I want to hit them hard." He turned to Danylo, "And you will show us the place."

Danylo swallowed.

"Should anything go wrong," Lukyanov continued, "I will, of course, shoot you."

Anna had remained standing at the window of the cell. She watched the beauty of the wintry light changing as the pink of the sky bled into the snow, and even when it darkened, she stood, calming herself by looking out blindly towards home. The light was on in her cell and would remain on all night. The less the prisoners slept, the more malleable they were. She did not allow herself to become flustered by the questions crowding the edges of her consciousness. She pushed them back and stood, breathing slowly and deeply, letting nature soothe her.

She could not know that Petro stood in the outer darkness, hidden behind the houses across the lane, peering towards the louring walls of the prison. As soon as he could, Vasilko had fled from the village, running towards the camp to tell Petro of Anna's arrest. The *kurin* was placed on alert and Petro, irrationally, hurried towards Temne. He knew the place was too well guarded for his company to mount a rescue of Anna, and he knew he could not barge in alone…but he wanted to be close to her. So he stood helplessly in the dark, seeing figures at lit windows, but unable to be sure if any of them was Anna. He tried to send her his strength and chose not to imagine what might be being done to her within those walls.

They were both startled when, in full darkness, an armoured car and several lorries loaded with NKVD personnel, roared out of the prison compound. Anna's heart pounded once again as she saw them turn towards the village. They could only be going to smash and destroy…but who was to be the victim this time? Anna held her hand to her throat and tried to control her fear. She told herself she was powerless to help and her agitation could only harm her baby so she made herself lie down on the narrow bench to rest. Come what may, she would not endanger her unborn child.

Petro, though, was able to react. He set off across country towards the encampment. Like Anna, he did not know what the NKVD planned, but he knew he must alert the *kurin* that they were on the move. He circled fields of snow, clinging to the limited cover of the bare hedgerows, and then he made his way through the deep woods towards his colleagues.

But his progress was slower than the vehicles which halted a couple of kilometres from the camp, the soldiers jumping down in their camouflage gear. They followed Danylo for a kilometre or so along barely discernible tracks and then spread out to encircle the camp. There was a hiatus while the furthest soldiers got themselves into position and then the circle of white suited men drew their stranglehold ever tighter before the alarm was raised. The NKVD infantry knew they had only themselves to rely on since none of their artillery or support vehicles had been able to penetrate the dense wood and so, armed with their Maxim machineguns and hand grenades, they approached the UPA camp cautiously. They allowed themselves to be a little comforted by their weight of numbers, but those soldiers who had encountered the insurgents before knew they fought with fearless tenacity.

An alert guard heard and then saw the NKVD's cautious approach and whistled a warning to the other insurgents. All who heard it, repeated the blast and the partisans leapt into action, grabbing their weapons and taking the defensive stance which had been so well-rehearsed. They were seasoned fighters, determined to achieve their goal of an independent state, but they were only thirty men surrounded by two companies of infantrymen. The three hundred or so NKVD soldiers drowned the camp with the clattering of machinegun and rifle fire and advanced, tightening the garrotte, killing all in their path. When every partisan above ground lay dead, the soldiers moved forward, throwing grenades into the dug-outs. The blue caps strangled the camp, making certain of every body with another bullet to the head.

When the slaughter was complete, Lukyanov reviewed the corpses with Danylo. "I'm told the girl, Anna, had a partisan lover. Is he here?"

Danylo shook his head. "I can't see him."

"But you'd know him?"

"Yes, Comrade Captain."

"Then, look again."

Danylo repeated the grisly task of looking into the faces of the dead, but finally shook his head at Lukyanov. "He's not here."

"Alright. I want you to hide nearby with a small group of my men. If he returns, I want him caught and brought back for questioning." He motioned to a group of soldiers and they followed Danylo to set up their look-out positions. The rest of the men were ordered back to their vehicles, leaving the dead where they had fallen.

Petro had taken the most direct route back to the camp, but even so, he arrived to find complete silence. He circled the camp, finding the careless tracks of many men. He stopped to listen to the silence. He could smell cordite on the air and his heart misgave as he anticipated what he would find. He crept forward, gun in hand, and lay hidden observing the camp clearing. He could see fallen bodies and blackened earth where dug-outs had been blown by grenades. He edged forward again and listened, but heard nothing. In the murky light of the winter dawn, he entered the clearing. At his feet lay the body of a tall, thin teenager and tears sprang to Petro's eyes as he looked down into Hrichko's still face. The boy might be sleeping peacefully…but for the bloody hole in his forehead.

Petro dropped to his knees. He knew as he did so that his grief was useless, but he felt the agony of the waste of this boy's life and he thought of the futile risks Anna had taken to rescue him. She would be grieved by his death… As he knelt, he felt the cold steel of a muzzle prodding the back of his neck. He spun around and fired into the face of the soldier, who had thought to apprehend him. A volley of shots rang out as the other soldiers fired at Petro and he fell to the ground, his chest pierced by several bullet holes.

There was a moment's quiet and then one of the soldiers said, "Was that the one Captain Lukyanov wanted alive?"

"Yes," replied Danylo.

The others shrugged. "We had no choice. He'd have killed us. We'll take his body back though."

They searched between the dug-outs and found a workable sledge. Petro's body was thrown onto it and they set off for the village, Danylo bringing up the rear.

Anna had dozed a little during the night. There had been the disturbances of slamming doors and shrieks. She had woken with a start, her stomach churning, groping to understand where she was. When the sky outside her cell lightened, she heard the roar of the vehicles returning from their foray and she stood to look out of the window, but was unable to see whether the NKVD had taken any prisoners. She had a sudden vivid memory of Petro smiling broadly, his blue eyes sparkling, the sun on his long curls…and then the image of him faded away. She put her hands over her abdomen and prayed that he was safe. The door of her cell slammed open and one of the guards ordered her out, while the other led her down to the basement, to an almost bare windowless room.

The walls consisted of unadorned brick. There was a table, at which Lukyanov was already seated, and a chair for the prisoner. Anna stood before Lukyanov, holding her shoulders back, keeping her breathing even. The location suggested a more serious interrogation, but Anna reminded herself that she was only a village woman who had been orphaned two days ago.

"How often did you take food to the partisans?" was Lukyanov's opening gambit.

"I don't understand your question, Comrade Captain."

Lukyanov merely gestured with his right forefinger to one of the guards, who approached Anna with a blade glinting in the light of the naked bulb. He placed the point under the ties of Anna's blouse and flicked the knife upwards towards her throat.

"I did not take food to the partisans, Comrade Captain."

"I have witnesses who say you did."

"Then they're liars."

Lukyanov did look up at her then. "Exactly. That is what I am here to find out... Who is the liar?"

Anna waited, making herself return his look, keeping her wide grey eyes on his.

"So where were you going when you went out at night?"

"There was a curfew, Comrade Captain, which I obeyed."

"How many people live in your cottage?"

"Just me now. My mother lived with me, but she died two days ago."

"No man?"

"No, Comrade Captain. My father and brother were killed in 1940."

"Then you have a lover who comes and goes at night?"

"No, Comrade Captain."

"So who was it? Who was seen leaving your house on more than one occasion, dressed in cap and trousers? Who picked up a full sack and set off for the woods?"

Anna stiffened herself not to react to the proof that she had been seen leaving the house more than once. Her mother's murderer had not been an opportunist.

Lukyanov saw her reaction. "You're surprised that I know about your activities. There are loyal people in your village after all."

"No. I'm shocked that someone thought they had seen a man at my house at night. Do you have the right house?"

"Oh yes. You live opposite Comrade Zadyrak, do you not?"

"Yes, but a little further up the lane."

"And the house immediately opposite his is empty. The old woman died."

Anna nodded. Nastunia's house had not yet been taken over by anyone else. "Then I have the right house."

Anna waited.

"What was in the sack?"

"Which sack?"

Anna gasped as the bright blade flicked across her right breast, leaving a clean rent in the white linen and the pale skin beneath. She looked down and saw the blood begin to gather in the shallow wound, followed by the sting of pain. She looked up in shock.

Lukyanov was watching her closely. "You're very lucky. Comrade Valkov usually takes off the whole breast with one slice."

Anna gathered up the cloth of her blouse and pressed it to the open wound, trying to stem the flow of blood.

Lukyanov waited, watching her. After several moments, he asked again: "What was in the sack?"

"I don't know, Comrade Captain. I did not take food to the partisans. That is all I can tell you."

"No, that is not all you can tell me and I can assure you that you will, sooner or later, tell me everything."

He nodded to the guard and Anna was marched back to her cell. She sank onto the bench with some relief, glad to be locked in alone, and turned her attention to her wound once more. It's alright, she told herself, it's a deliberately shallow cut. They just want to scare me. It's alright...and she subdued her desire to sob. She leaned back against the wall, closed her eyes and searched for Petro's bright face among her memories. But she could not see him. She tried to relax, thinking the memory would come sooner it if was not forced, and was more shocked, than by anything which had happened in recent days, to feel a flutter...of something...in her abdomen. She listened again. It must be the baby moving, she thought. She was filled with wonder and wanted to laugh aloud at the joy of it. Despite everything, her baby was alive and moving!

A messenger had gone on ahead to alert Lukyanov that Petro had been found. He had called for a car and they had sped up the road from Temne to the village, where the NKVD soldiers would have to emerge from the forest with Petro's body. They met on the lane at the edge of the woods, as the blue caps pulled the sledge onto the road. Petro's corpse lay on its back, his hair across his face.

Lukyanov pulled back the long curls with his gloved hand. "I thought I said I wanted this one kept alive?"

"He fired at us, Comrade Captain. We had to fire back."

"It didn't occur to you that you could have wounded him?"

The soldiers hung their heads, not only in shame at failing to follow the captain's orders, but also in genuine fear of his retribution.

"Well, we'll see how his death is received, shall we?" He turned to Danylo, skulking behind the small group. "Does he have any family living?"

"Yes, Comrade Captain. His mother and youngest sister."

"Where do they live?"

"On the other side of the village, Comrade Captain."

"Good. Then all is not lost." He turned to the anxious soldiers. "Pull this sledge slowly through the village. Make sure he's seen." And to Danylo, "Show us the way to his mother's house."

The convoy set off, Lukyanov's driver following and sounding the car horn loudly.

There was no care shown to the shattered cargo of the sled. It bumped and bounced its way over the snow-covered road and began to pass between the first houses. People appeared at their cottage doors, at garden ends and on the lane, all having been tormented by the sound of the distant gunfire. By the time the convoy reached the monument, a crowd had begun to gather. Lukyanov halted.

"See this man," he called, "he is the last of a nest of traitors found in the woods. They have all been executed. You have no more to fear from their banditry." He looked around the circle of faces, pale with cold. "If anyone has anything they can tell me about this band of criminals, you will be well-rewarded." He paused and turned to Danylo. "Is his mother here?"

Danylo shook his head. He had already scanned the faces of the crowd for Halia. But neither he, nor the soldiers, had seen a teenage boy slip away through the garden of the house opposite. Vasilko ran through his neighbours' gardens, hurdling fences, running as fast as the snow would allow, until he reached Halia's house. He tore up to her door and pounded hard.

Halia opened the door, but before she could speak, Vasilko blurted out: "The blue caps are coming here. They have Petro's body."

She stared at him wide-eyed and then said, more loudly than she had intended, "Go! Hide yourself!" and she hurried indoors to Nina, her heart thumping in her chest and reverberating in her throat. She, too, had heard the gunfire earlier and had hoped, against hope, that Petro would survive whatever was taking place in the depths of the wood. She turned to Nina, who was lying in bed with a heavy cold. She had been unwell since Katerina's funeral and Halia had been trying to nurse her back to health.

"Nina, listen to me carefully," said Halia. "Petro has been killed and the soldiers are bringing his body here." She placed her hand over Nina's mouth as the girl took a breath to scream. "No, Nina! You can't do that. We can't show we know him. At all. Or they will kill us, too. Do you understand?"

Nina nodded, her eyes wide.

"I'll try to keep them outside," continued Halia. "But if they come in, or call you out, you must not react with any emotion. Do you hear me?"

Nina nodded again, her eyes full of tears.

"And wipe your eyes. You can't do that now either."

At that moment there was a loud banging at the door. Halia got up from Nina's bedside and went to open the door. She let in the cold air and the wintry daylight and kept her eyes on the face of the blue-capped soldier in front of her.

"Yes?"

"The Captain wants you out here," he said with a jerk of the head.

Halia stepped out of the door to the group waiting outside in her snow-filled garden, deliberately failing to see the sledge and its bloody burden. She looked at the Captain, her hands folded beneath her apron.

"So mother," began the Captain, "where's your son?"

"I don't know," she replied.

"Well, come and look here." He drew her towards the sledge and Halia looked down at the broken body of her child. Petro lay on his back, one arm outstretched, where it had been shaken free of the sledge. His head was tilted towards Halia and his eyes were staring. His face looked taut and cold, the mouth hanging slightly open, his curls haloing his forehead. She noted the blood on his chest and belly and saw he must have died quickly, but she looked up again at Lukyanov impassively.

"Don't you know him, mother?"

"No. I never saw this before in my life."

"Look again. Be sure."

"I am sure."

"Is this your son, woman?"

"No, it is not." Halia held his eyes briefly and then took a step back as if this affair had nothing more to do with her.

Lukyanov looked at the matron before him. She had been a strong, healthy woman, but he could see the lines of strain which must have appeared over recent years. The hair beneath her headscarf was greying and she had begun to stoop. However, he knew the protective power of a mother's love.

"Where's his sister?" he demanded suddenly.

Halia looked surprised. "Whose..." but before she could continue, Lukyanov gestured to his men.

Two soldiers hurried into the cottage and moments later, Nina was dragged out of its door.

"Wait a minute!" she was shouting. "Are you crazy? I have nothing on my feet!"

But the soldiers manhandled the struggling girl towards the sledge. She looked at Lukyanov in indignation. "I'm surprised at you, Comrade Captain, allowing your men to behave like this. I need my boots!"

Lukyanov remained unmoved. "The only thing you need, young lady, is to identify this corpse as your brother's."

Nina glanced briefly at the sledge. "That's not my brother. Now can I get my boots before my cold becomes pneumonia?"

"Look again."

"I already have," said Nina, but then appeared to look more carefully at the body on the sledge. "I'm sorry, Comrade Captain, but I've never seen this man in my life before," and she looked into Lukyanov's bespectacled face with clear blue eyes.

He held her gaze for a long moment. "Take this body back to the monument and leave it for all to see." He strode away up the path. In the lane, he got into his car and was driven away towards Temne, while the soldiers roughly pulled the sledge behind them, back towards the centre of the village.

Halia bustled Nina indoors. "Your feet! Let's get them warmed up!"

But once they had closed the door behind them, the women clung to one another, trying to control the harsh, dry sobs which threatened to tear out their hearts.

Chapter 24

Sofia stood before Lukyanov as he outlined her task. "So you'll tell Anna that her lover is dead. I'll be watching."

"And when I've helped you?" she dared to ask.

"You may go home."

She bowed her head and tried not to let herself be swamped by relief. Don't relax yet, she told herself. He might be lying.

She was led to Anna's cell, Lukyanov following. She did not feel nervous: Anna had it coming. She's always thought herself cleverer than other people so let's see where her cleverness gets her now, thought Sofia. Besides she's brought her troubles on herself.

The door to Anna's cell was unlocked and opened by the guard. Sofia walked into the cell to face Anna, who had turned towards the door. She was standing with the grey daylight falling through the window behind her. Her impulse was to greet Sofia, but she held herself back, for what could Sofia be doing in this dreadful place.

"Hello, Anna."

Anna simply nodded…and waited, her hands folded over her abdomen.

"Petro is dead. He was shot for the traitor he was," Sofia said, a little too loudly.

Anna held herself stiffly as she looked into Sofia's eyes, trying to determine whether she was telling the truth. Anna let out her breath and continued to stand, still as a statue, as the girl she had grown up with searched her face for signs of pain.

"Did you hear what I said? Petro, your Petro, has been killed."

"Yes, I heard you. But he was not my Petro."

"Oh come on, Anna. Of course he was."

"No. I told you before. We split up after your wedding," said Anna flatly.

Lukyanov stepped into the doorway. "Enough. Get out," he gestured to Sofia.

She turned and hurried past him and decided to take the only opportunity she might get to leave. She strode along the corridor and made herself maintain a brisk pace down the stairs and out of the building. She walked to the gate and turned along the lane to go home. Only when she was out of sight of the prison, did she allow herself to run.

But Anna had nowhere to run to. She stood before Lukyanov, looking into his face with persistent innocence.

"Nothing to say?" he asked.

"No," she replied.

"Well, we'll see. Bring her to my office," he ordered the guard as he turned away.

As Anna followed the guard to Lukyanov's office, she laid aside all thoughts of the man she loved and focussed only on her role as a single woman who had looked after her aged mother. That was the only role she would show to her interrogator. The kernel of her secret lay hidden, curled in Anna's womb.

She entered Lukyanov's office and stood before his desk, her grey eyes upon him as he settled himself in his chair, Stalin's portrait overseeing the Captain's work.

"So, your lover is dead. You have no one to protect now," he announced.

Anna said nothing.

"The whole lot of them were shot," Lukyanov continued. "All those whom you've been feeding. How many corpses were counted, Comrade Corporal?"

"Thirty-two, Comrade Captain."

Lukyanov gave Anna a slow stare. He had not decided yet whether she was stupid or stubborn and he needed to find out. "Take a seat, Anna," he said, trying another tack.

She sat on the hard, straight-backed chair opposite him and waited.

"Petro's body was identified by his mother and sister," he began.

Anna did not speak.

"We dragged his body to their house and they identified him there."

Anna remained silent.

"He was shot several times in the chest. There was a lot of blood on his clothes, on his shirt." He thought he detected the faintest flicker in her eyes at that moment, so he pressed on. "If there's a lot of blood on a corpse, it means that person died slowly."

Anna refused to be drawn.

"Have you nothing to say?"

"I don't know what you want me to say."

"Let's start with Petro."

"An old boyfriend. He left the village in the summer of '42. I haven't seen him since then."

"And you feel no sorrow for his death?"

"He made his choice."

"But to die so young…"

"So many have died so young."

"That's true. Some of the partisans were only boys."

Anna did not react.

"How many of them were there when you were taking food to them?"

"I told you, I did not take food to them."

"Anna, I know you did. You recognised yourself when I described you leaving your house in disguise. You know you were seen." He waited.

Anna sat, her hands in her lap, haloed by the light from the window above the interrogator's head. She concentrated on Lukyanov and held all other thoughts in abeyance.

"You won't hurt anyone by telling me now. They're all dead." He looked at her beautiful face and wondered if she were vain. But they could try that method later, if necessary. "I would like to close the file on Comrade Zadyrak's death," he added. "With your testimony, I could do that."

"I can't help you. I was at my mother's funeral."

He sighed. "Anna, look around you. I am speaking to you in my office, not downstairs. This could be sorted out very quickly and you would be free to go."

Anna's large grey eyes met his. "I haven't done anything wrong. I buried my mother yesterday."

"Yes, you did. But someone killed Comrade Zadyrak and witnesses have linked you with the partisans. You have nothing more to lose by telling me the whole story."

Anna sat, implacable.

"Well, we shall see," said Lukyanov, sighing. "Take her back to her cell for now."

Anna followed the guard back to her cell and then stood looking out over the courtyard to the road beyond. She believed that the NKVD had killed Petro and as many of the others as they had found, including Hrichko, but she did not believe that Halia and Nina had identified him. They would have been shot themselves, in that case, and Lukyanov would have made capital of it. She did not allow herself to think of Petro or the manner of his death – it would undo her now and she had to be strong. She could mourn when she was free of this prison cell, she told herself. She stroked her abdomen and thought of the baby who must be protected and suddenly thought of Katerina, shocked again that it was only three days since she had found her dead. But, Anna reflected, she had been mourning her mother since Mikola and Yuri were murdered. Her thoughts turned to her father. Mikola had always been cautious and counselled saying the least possible to those in authority. She felt comforted by the image of him seated at the table, "Trust nobody, only your own family." She would hold on to that precept. Besides, her father had taught her to be strong, both by his life and by his death. She had had to cope with terrible loss before and had had to maintain a calm exterior. She could do it again, she told herself, despite whatever the "witnesses" had said. She wondered who, beyond the venal Sofia, had betrayed her.

Sofia had arrived home, hot and dishevelled despite the winter cold. She burst into the cottage to see her mother at the stove with Antin tugging at her skirt. "*Baba*! *Baba*!" he was crying.

Parania turned to Sofia. "Thank God!" she said and lifting the heavy two-year-old, she hurried forward to hug her daughter.

Sofia allowed herself to be hugged and then took Antin, who was now calling for "Mama! Mama!", from her mother's arms.

"They let you go then?" asked Parania, stroking Sofia's curls from her face.

"Yes. That Captain said I could go, so I did."

"Did they keep you in a cell last night?"

"Yes. But they let me go today when they realised I knew nothing."

"Thank God," repeated Parania. "But why they thought you knew anything I can't imagine."

"Where's Levko?" asked Sofia quickly.

"I don't know. Probably at Ihor's again." Parania turned back to her saucepans. "Let's eat something. You must be hungry after your ordeal."

Sofia sat at the table with Antin in her lap, after unsuccessfully trying to put him down. She ate a good helping of her mother's *kasha*, her mind racing, but she gave no clue of this to Parania, who fussed over her as if she were a child again. Parania sat down to eat and automatically took Antin into her lap. Sofia sat across the table from them, watching her aging mother feed small spoonfuls to Antin, who opened his mouth like a baby bird. The scene should have made her smile, the circle of love surrounding the two who were closest to her. But instead she felt only relief. Antin's large blue eyes travelled from his grandmother's hand to her face, in complete trust, as he ate whatever she gave him. Parania smiled at the child and murmured encouragement as he ate from her bowl, while she lifted a spoonful to her own mouth from time to time.

After they had eaten, Parania handed Antin to Sofia saying, "I'll just go and close everything up outside."

Sofia waited until her mother had gone from the room and then ensured that her coat and boots were tidily to hand by the door. She hurried into her bedroom and gathered some of her clothes into a bundle, which she tied and stuffed under the bed. She took a handkerchief and went to the kitchen cupboard, where she tipped out her mother's pot of notes and coins, tying most of them into the handkerchief. She took the handkerchief back into the bedroom and pushed it deep inside her bundle. Then she hurried into the kitchen again and began to wash Antin's hands and face for bed.

Parania bustled back indoors. "It's getting really cold out there."

"When will Levko be back?"

"Who knows? You know he pleases himself nowadays."

"Aren't you worried?"

"Yes, but that won't change anything."

Sofia finished wiping Antin's hands.

"No, Mama," he cried, snatching them away.

"I think he's tired, Mama, and I'm worn out too. I didn't get a wink of sleep last night. I think I'll go to bed now."

"You're right. There's nothing to sit up for. Levko will manage for himself when he comes home."

So the little household settled down for the night.

Sofia lay on her back in her marriage bed, Antin protected in the other half of the bed by bolsters and pillows. She looked out of the window at the stars. She had made up her mind. There was no future for her here. The men of the NKVD were of no use to her, since she would not sell herself for a few grammes of vodka and there would be no protector amongst them. She would not wait until Lukyanov called her in again. She refused to become embroiled in Anna's mess. She thought of her sister and wondered how she had fared in Germany and whether she still lived, but there would be no point in hunting for Olha. No, she had to go alone, as far west as she could, and hope to find someone who would care for her. She would not wait here to be worked to death in the fields, or to be sent to the frozen wastes of Siberia for some imagined crime. She told herself she was strong. She could undertake this journey alone.

Once again, Ihor found himself stealing a corpse, but this time it was not his childhood friend but a boy of the village. Andriy was his willing partner, and as they carried Petro's body to the cemetery, he thought of his daughter, Marusia, and prayed that she was alive and safe somewhere. It was a long time since he and his wife had heard from her or Rachel. They did not know where the girls might be, or if they were still together. He only hoped they were still alive. When they reached the apparently empty part of the cemetery, they found Levko and Vasilko digging furiously at the cold ground. The men set to and the four living quickly prepared a hole deep enough for the dead man. Petro was laid approximately beside Roman Shumenko and Ihor's mind flickered to an image of Vera and Anna mourning their beloved men, side by side. Levko had no idea what part his sister had played in this most recent death. He had come to help Ihor, who had once had three young men in his household, but now had none…except the lonely boy who had adopted him.

They covered Petro's body and stamped down the ground. Then the boys took the pine branches they had brought and brushed the snow over Petro's grave. The men hurried away, having hidden the corpse from further dishonour, knowing that, as ever, the women would howl in silence.

In the same darkness, Sofia rose and dressed quickly. She took her bundle from under the bed and, taking her coat and boots, stepped into the wintry night. She walked through the garden where Anna and Vera had made her wedding crown and out of the gate into the lane. She turned left to follow the road away from the village, hurrying away in a westerly direction. Levko had heard her footsteps as he approached home, but he had hidden, not knowing who else was out in the secret night. He had peered from his hiding place and had seen his sister stealing away, bundle in hand. Good riddance, was his first thought, but as he approached the cottage door, he knew of two who would suffer at her stealthy departure.

Anna scratched a third mark with her nail into the peeling paint on the wall of her cell. She had no idea when she might be released and she was determined to keep track of these days, when one horror seemed to follow another. She had been taken on Friday so it must be Sunday and she looked out of the cell window at the grey sky, knowing she was lucky to be able to see whether it was night or day. There would be no way of knowing from anything else. Doors banged, footsteps pounded and voices shrieked, it seemed, without any reference to the customs of night or day. Anna had been fed thin soup and a hunk of bread. She had eaten every scrap for the baby.

It was still daylight when she was taken down to the cellar again. It was colder than her cell and smelled dank. There was an underlying smell which Anna associated with barns, but she did not have time to analyse why before she was told to kneel. She looked up at Volkov and saw the gleam in his eye. He would need no excuse to slash at her again with his knife. One glance at his tight face, glossy with self-righteousness, told Anna he would be merciless towards her, and she feared the fullness of his lower lip which spoke of a sensuality in his nature, quite contradicted by his impeccable uniform. He would enjoy hurting her. So she knelt on the damp floor. Volkov strode from the room after ordering the guard to shoot Anna if she tried to rise from the position she was in.

The pain began almost immediately in her knees and, as she tried to hold herself straight, there was pain in her lower back, too. She wondered how long she might have to stay like this, but then put that treacherous fear aside. She would take a walk in her mind, she told herself, she would ignore where she was. So she chose a spring day when the woods were full of a green fluidity. The leaves swayed in a warm breeze. The sun shone green and gold on nettles and buttercups, just as it did on pink campion and white cow parsley. She gazed at the green waterfalls of light as she waded through the waist-high undergrowth. She listened to the birdsong pouring forth and looked up into the canopy to watch for blackbirds and jays. In a brief shower, she took shelter under a friendly sycamore as warm rain pattered on the leaves. She looked down at the horseshoe-shaped seeds scattered on the ground like bright confetti…as the bones of her knees broke through this vision with their cries of agony. She shuffled a little to try to ease the pain.

"Keep still, bitch. I don't mind shooting you," said a deep voice behind her.

She looked at the desk before her. It was empty, as was the chair behind it. She found herself longing for someone to fill that chair, someone who would tell her she could rise from her knees…but still no one came. She searched her mind again for solace and a picture of Petro arose, but she reluctantly put it aside, fearing that her longing for him might undo her. She took herself back to the lanes, this time in summer and smelt the dill overwhelming the verges, the air thick with floating dandelion seed. In her mind's eye, she saw the lines of ducks waddling down to the stream to drink together in a gaggle of busy chatter, only pausing in their noisy quacking to stretch their necks to the water. Water… Was every thought going to betray her, she wondered, as she turned her mind away from the sudden thirst she felt.

The cellar door clanged open and Anna swayed as Lukyanov strode past her to the empty chair. He put down his papers on the desk and settled himself before her. He looked at her for a moment and then gestured to the guard. "Help her up. Sit her there."

Anna tried to stand, but her legs would not hold her. She was pulled to the seat of the chair and left to fend for herself. She remained slumped for a few moments and then, as Lukyanov began to speak, she made herself sit up. The pins and needles in her legs were agonising, but she tried to listen to what he had to say. She heard only part of it.

"…Buchach…"

"I didn't hear you. Could you repeat that?" she asked.

"I asked you: why did you go regularly to Buchach market?"

"To trade goods."

"Don't treat me like a fool, Anna. I have plenty to do. I could easily give you another hour on your knees."

Anna wanted to swallow, but tried hard not to.

"So why Buchach market?"

"It was a good place to trade what I had grown. The people in town did not have the space to grow what I grew, so I could get good prices."

"I'm told you went every week."

"I did."

"And I'm told you thought nothing of the distance."

How did he know that, Anna wondered and then heard herself saying it to Zadyrak in the office… Hnat. Hnat must have been questioned, too.

Lukyanov watched her patiently. "Yes, you see, I have spoken to many people who knew you and your habits. I admit they did not know it all, but each person gives me a piece of the puzzle, Anna, and I end up with a picture of a young woman acting as a courier for the UPA."

"You're mistaken. I was trading vegetables and butter."

Lukyanov looked sorrowful. "You mustn't persist with this fiction. You'll make me hurt you."

"I'm sorry. I can't help you."

"Oh yes, you can. I have a *starosta* murdered in broad daylight, probably by partisans. You have been identified by several of your neighbours as having links with those partisans, and I will get to the bottom of this." He gathered his papers together, pushed back his chair and ordered Anna to her knees once more. "Make sure she stays there," he said to the guard as he left the cell.

Anna found that if she leaned back slightly, the pain lessened, but she knew it would take a shorter time than before to become unbearable. It's only kneeling, she admonished herself. I can manage that…but the pain would keep demanding her attention. She tried to take an inventory of her situation. Had Zadyrak asked Hnat to spy on her? Even if he hadn't, it was clear that other people had known some of her secrets. She had been careful, but not careful enough. And the spies… She had feared Sofia, and if Sofia could betray her, so could others. Nevertheless, she had to keep faith with those who had helped her feed the insurgents. They were all scarred by their experiences. Halia would never betray her son; Andriy would never betray his daughter. She would never reveal their names… And the boys in the woods? All dead according to Lukyanov. She thought of Hrichko and instantly closed the door to that memory. She would mourn them all later, but she could not betray them now… And what of the contacts in Buchach? Fortunately, she could only reveal a location and a visual description of a young woman. She knew nothing else. UPA security had never seemed so sensible to Anna. She felt calmer. She knew so little. There was indeed nothing to tell.

And what of those who had told the NKVD about Anna? Sofia travelled by night and hid by day, continuing her journey beyond the sight of any blue caps. Hnat continued to work for another Bolshevik *starosta*, ensuring that his behaviour could not be interpreted in any way other than showing complete loyalty to Moscow. And Danylo...

For a day or two, he went about his business as usual, sleeping till late and waking in the stale sweat of his crumbling hut, wondering when he might claim his reward of Timko's house. After a bowl of *kasha*, he prepared his traps and around dusk set off to lay them in the twilight, his pointed face scenting the breeze as he remained downwind of his prey. He had not returned to the deeper wood of the camp, a primitive superstition gripping him. He made for the birch woods instead. He listened for any sound, but the snow deadened all noise except the crunch of his footsteps. He paused now and then like a fox, to stretch his eyes and ears for any sign of life. But all was quiet.

He knelt to lay a snare and, as he concentrated on the delicate trap, his head was jerked back, a garrotte around his neck. He almost fell sideways into the snow, but the man who held the wire around Danylo's throat, also held him upright. Danylo looked up in helpless entreaty and saw a second man leaning over him. The two wore a muddle of greenish uniforms, but as Danylo saw the *tryzub* on their lapels and buckles, his guts turned to water and he felt a hot rush of fluid in his trousers.

"Did you think there was only one *kurin* in the UPA, you snake? Did you think wiping out that one camp would destroy us?"

The strangler began to tighten the wire, but his colleague stayed his hand. "Wait. I want to hear him speak."

Danylo felt relief flood him as the tension in the wire relaxed. He swallowed and moved his tongue around in his mouth to flex it.

"Get up, you vermin."

They walked Danylo towards the edge of the wood and his hopes soared. Perhaps this was just going to be a warning.

It was indeed a warning. The insurgents planned to kill Danylo and leave his body to be found. It would remind any waverers that there would be repercussions from this quarter, too. Danylo was forced to his knees again, his neck still bound by the wire. He could hear his strangler's calm breathing behind him.

"So, you traitor! Who were you working for?"

"Zadyrak. Zadyrak made me do it," he babbled. "He wanted me to follow the woman, Anna."

"Where to?"

"The camp. At night."

"When?"

Danylo's eyes narrowed a little. "Only once or twice."

"How often did you go to the camp alone?"

"Oh, not at all."

His questioner looked at him contemptuously. "Enough," he said. "You have betrayed your neighbours and your country." He nodded at his colleague and the strangler twisted the wooden handles of the garrotte, tightening the wire around Danylo's neck. The traitor kicked and struggled, but age told. The younger man braced himself and continued to tighten the wire until Danylo stopped struggling and then his executioner allowed the body to drop to the ground. The questioner checked for a pulse and the two men dragged the corpse to the edge of the wood and slung it on the verge beside the lane. Then they melted back among the trees.

The orderly knocked on Lukyanov's door. "There's a visitor for the prisoner in cell 9, Comrade Captain." The statement was in fact a question and Lukyanov looked up with interest.

"What sort of visitor?"

"A young woman, Comrade Captain."

"Bring the prisoner down to the outer office to see her visitor. Stay with them and I'll expect you to report back every word to me."

The orderly saluted and turned away to fetch Anna. As she followed him along the corridor and down the stairs, she wondered what tactics the NKVD were trying now. She took her time to prepare herself for the next onslaught, so she was surprised to be taken into an office containing a nervous Vera.

"Vera!" she cried and then clamped her lips together to prevent herself from saying anything further.

"Hello, Anna," said Vera, coming forward. She embraced Anna, but the orderly reminded them, "No physical contact. Stand there."

They stood several feet apart and Vera was able to take in Anna's appearance. She was still wearing the clothes she had worn to her mother's funeral, her dark winter coat, her best headscarf, her boots and her dark winter skirt... Vera's eyes travelled up to Anna's embroidered blouse and noticed the rip and the brown stain around it. Her fearful eyes met Anna's who smiled gently.

"I'm alright, Verochka. Are you?"

Vera nodded and cursed the tears which threatened to undo them both. She swallowed hard. "I thought you might be hungry," she blurted out and thrust a bundle towards Anna.

The guard ordered her to stop. "You can't give that to the prisoner. Let me see it."

Vera handed him the bundle for inspection. "It's only food, some clothes and a spoon."

He examined the contents of the bundle and passed it over to Anna.

"Thank you for thinking of me," said Anna.

"You need to look after yourself," said Vera.

"I am managing," replied Anna, trying to convey all that she was "managing" in that simple statement.

Vera turned to the guard. "Can I give her my sweater?"

He shrugged.

Vera removed her coat and then her thick woollen cardigan. "Take this. It's getting colder."

Anna nodded, almost blind with tears.

To give her friend a moment to collect herself, Vera announced: "We're taking care of your livestock. I'm feeding the chickens. Halia and Nina are milking the cow and looking after Murchik."

"That's good. Please kiss them for me."

Vera hesitated and then said, "Roman has a new neighbour..." She paused and stared at Anna, willing her to understand the message.

Anna blinked slowly in acknowledgement. "They'll be company for one another."

The two women exchanged a long look and both were startled as the door was slammed back against the wall. Lukyanov stormed into the room.

"Out!" he ordered Vera, who hurried away from the office and the prison before anyone might think to stop her.

"Take the prisoner out to the van and secure her in it," he shouted to the guards who had followed him.

Anna was hurried out into the courtyard and pushed into the windowless black van. The doors were slammed and locked on her, as she waited in the cold dark, full of misgivings, still clutching Vera's gifts. Lukyanov had been hard and resolved, but she had not yet seen him angry and she wondered what further revelations there had been. She felt her way over to one of the side benches and sat down. The van shifted as its front doors were opened. The engine was started and they lurched forward. Anna almost fell from her seat, so she tried to brace herself against the corner of the van. She had no idea where she was being taken, but she feared the worst. They were not returning her home.

Chapter 25

As Anna's blind journey continued, she wondered if she had been taken to Ternopil. She, like many others before her, would be passed up the chain of command. Questioning which began in or near a village would continue in Ternopil, and even in Lviv, if the prisoner warranted it. She wondered what she would be accused of and felt her heart begin to thump harder as she anticipated what the NKVD might do to her, but her panic was arrested by a tiny flutter of movement. She spoke silently to her baby, You're right. We'll manage. I will keep you alive for your father's sake. We'll get through this...

But the brave words flew away as Anna felt the van come to a halt. She heard the doors being unlocked and then she was dragged, blinking and stumbling, into the dusk of a winter afternoon. She was in a courtyard, surrounded on all four sides by walls twenty metres high. The outer wall to the street was bare, but those to her left and right were interrupted by windows covered with iron grilles. At each corner of the courtyard, there was a watchtower, roughly constructed of pine with a ladder leading up to the viewing platform, which was roofed to give the guard some protection from the snow which lay everywhere. Anna was dragged indoors, along a bleak corridor to a crowded cell, whose inmates stood closely packed and apparently silent. However, once the guards had withdrawn, there was a susurration among the women as they elicited from Anna where she had come from. But before they could share their advice with her, the door was flung open again and Anna was marched along another corridor and down some stairs to a basement.

The room she found herself in was tiny. If she stretched out her arms, she could touch both walls in each direction. It not only smelled damp, but she could see moisture clinging to the walls. There were no windows and the only light came from a bare bulb. She hunkered down against one of the walls and tried to slow her heart beat. She had never suffered from claustrophobia, but now she found that she had to take firm control of her breathing to hold the threatening panic at bay. She breathed in loudly through her nose and expelled her breath through her mouth, counting as she did so. She continued until she was sure that the lurking beast of overwhelming fear had been repulsed and then she turned to a more logical examination of her situation. She tried to understand why she had been moved from Temne and could only assume that something unexpected had happened for her transfer to have been so abrupt. She squatted until her legs began to cramp and shifted her position, but there was not enough room to lie down. She curled up on her side and was glad of Vera's cardigan, the scent of her friend comforting Anna in her isolation. She must have dozed for a while and then the lock rattled. A guard entered, ordering her to her feet and out onto the corridor.

"Leave that there!" barked the guard, referring to Vera's bundle.

Anna placed the bundle on the floor and stepped out into the silent corridor. As she followed a second guard, she was ordered to put her hands behind her back.

She was led down another flight of stairs, the air growing colder as they descended. The stairs turned at intervals so Anna could not see how far below ground she was being taken and her apprehension threatened to turn her bowels to water. They entered a low wide room with chains attached to the walls. Anna was hustled towards them. She was spread-eagled against the wet wall and her wrists were clamped in irons.

Anna felt terribly exposed. Her womb stood unprotected and she was acutely conscious that she could not cross her arms to cover it. However, as time passed, the pain in her shoulders demanded her attention. The ache spread from the ends of her fingers, up her arms, across her shoulders to meet at the base of her skull. She tried to rest her weight against the wall so that she did not sag against the manacles, but knew that it would be only a matter of time before her wrists had to take the entire strain. Suddenly an image of her father flashed upon her memory. He was grinning across the kitchen table, telling them a story of his youth; of how he had been sent out to pasture the *Pan's* horses and how he had ridden them bareback for the sheer pleasure of it. She could see the boy Mikola had been in her mind's eye, leaping on the back of a strong farm horse and letting it gallop at speed, holding onto its mane. Mikola had laughed at the trouble he would have been in had he been caught and Anna felt her spirits lift. She wondered if he was watching over her now, when she needed him most.

An NKVD officer strode into the cell, removed his blue cap and handed it to one of the guards as he approached Anna, cane in hand. This was not a Lukyanov, an interrogator who might use a variety of tactics to elicit information; nor even a Volkov, who might take sensual pleasure in hurting the helpless. This man was a professional. He was not tall, but Anna was not misled by his lack of stature, nor by the dark hair framing a pleasantly handsome round face. She saw only the blank wells of his eyes and knew he would not stop until he had got what he was searching for. He took a long slow look at Anna as she tried to convince herself that he could not look into her soul. It was just a trick he used. But he gave her no time to marshal her thoughts.

"If you're only a simple peasant woman who lives with her mother, why was the man who informed on you murdered?"

Anna looked at her interrogator in shock. "Who…"

"Danylo Malenkiv was found murdered this morning."

"Danylo?" Anna tried to understand how Ivan's uncle could have informed on her and who might have killed him. "I don't know anything about this." There was nothing to hide here. She knew nothing.

Her interrogator changed tack. "Who contributed food for the bandits?"

"I don't know. They left the food outside my house at night."

"But you took it to the rebels?"

"Yes," Anna conceded, hoping that this admission would satisfy him.

"How often?"

"Every week."

"That is enough to condemn you to death."

Anna bowed her head waiting for the next blow.

"We know that you made weekly visits to Buchach. What was that for?"

"To go to market."

He raised his cane and Anna saw his eyes target her exposed abdomen. "Wait!" she cried. "Unchain me and I'll tell you."

He paused and then ordered the guard to release her wrists.

She clasped her hands together and then lowered them to cover her belly.

"So…" he prompted.

"I took letters."

"From whom?"

"My contact at the camp."

"What was his name?"

"He's dead. You killed them all."

"Nevertheless…" He waited.

"Ostap," she breathed at last.

"Ostap who?"

"That's all I knew."

"And who did you take them to?"

"I left them behind a wall."

He raised an eyebrow. "Which wall?"

Anna described a narrow street leading from the square, which she had frequently passed. There had been a derelict house with a tumbledown wall and by using this location, she hoped that she was not implicating anyone living.

305

Her inquisitor gave her a long look. "And the replies?"

"I would collect them after I had finished at the market. In the same place."

"So you never had a contact in Buchach?"

Anna lifted her grey eyes to his darker ones and, holding his look, said, "No."

He stepped towards her and took her left hand lightly in his. He drew her towards the cell door as if leading her in a dance. In a moment, he had placed her fingers between the door and the jamb and, holding her left wrist securely, he reached for the door handle and slammed the door closed.

Anna cried out, blackness overwhelming her, and as he opened the door to release her fingers, she fell against him. He took a step back and let her fall to the floor. She could not breathe and the blood pounded in her ears. Her head was spinning as she tried to keep her broken hand still.

"Take her to cell 5."

Everything swirled about her as the guard ordered her to stand, but she could not obey him. She was in a whirlpool of pain and could neither see nor hear anything else. The guard called to his colleague on the corridor and together they lifted Anna to her feet. They took her under each arm and dragged her to her appointed cell. The heavy wooden door was unlocked and she was thrust in, the door relocked behind her.

Anna remained where she had fallen, still reeling from the pain. She tried to get to her knees; her face, wet with sweat, tears and saliva, almost touching the floor. Then Anna felt rough hands lifting her and moving her to sit on the edge of what served as a bed.

"What have they done to you, girl?" asked a voice, as her hair was smoothed back from her face.

"It's her hand," said another, gingerly touching Anna's left arm.

There was a muttering among the women and the sound of cloth ripping; then Anna's smashed and bleeding fingers were tightly bound in strips of cloth. She almost fainted again, but was held in someone's arms, and she heard, as if from another room, the comforting sounds of the woman who was binding her fingers. "There, there. This will hold them tight. They won't hurt so much then. You must keep them straight to heal. There. Almost done."

Anna fought the wave of nausea which threatened to overwhelm her and tried to keep still as the ripples of pain receded. She felt her face being wiped and then a bottle was lifted to her lips. The burn of vodka in her throat almost made her retch, but someone was stroking her back. "Yes, it tastes vile, but it will help the pain. Let's lie you down."

Anna felt herself being lowered onto a hard surface and then she let herself sink into blessed unconsciousness.

*

When she woke, she could not understand where she was. She had dreamt of Katerina and in her confusion, she looked around for her mother. "Mama?"

But no answer came. Anna blinked in the bright light from the ceiling bulb and looked about her. She was in a small cell, measuring roughly three metres square with a breathing mass of bodies between herself and a barred window at the far end. There was a terrible smell of excrement and stale urine and she turned her head to see a large lidded bucket by the door, not far from where she lay. She tried to move, but it was almost impossible in the press of bodies. Anna touched the surface she lay on with her right hand and felt wooden boards. She had no idea what time it was, but the sky beyond the window was dark.

The throbbing in her left hand told her where she had been and she began to explore her hand. The fingers of her right hand felt the smooth skin around her left wrist. Its wholeness comforted her so she flexed it tentatively. Her left hand moved back and forth and she was reassured that her wrist had not been broken. Her hand was covered in the makeshift bandages her cellmates had provided, but Anna pressed her right thumb into her left palm, delicately at first, but then feeling no pain, she explored the length and breadth of her palm. There was no injury to the bones or the knuckles. So the pain and the fractures were in her fingers then. She thought fearfully of what might happen to them and she wondered if she would be crippled forever. But just as her mind touched this thought, she whisked it away to find an even greater anxiety. As she stroked her abdomen with her right hand and searched for a flutter of movement to tell her all was well, she found none. Babies must sleep in the womb, she reassured herself. She's just resting. And then wondered at herself ascribing a gender to her unborn baby. It doesn't matter who you are, she told the baby, as long as you get here safely.

She closed her eyes and saw an image of Danylo, swaying, drink in hand, at Ivan's wedding. What could he have known about her to tell anyone, she wondered. She searched her memory for reasons why Danylo might have hated her enough to betray her, but gave up trying to explain the inexplicable. Who might have killed him was easier to answer. She knew the UPA would have left his body to be found, as a warning to others who might want to collaborate with the NKVD. She made herself relax in the cramped space.

When she next opened her eyes, it was to shouts of "Prepare for the toilets!"

She looked across at her neighbour who muttered, "It'll be our turn in a moment. Make sure you use the facilities. You won't be able to go again till tomorrow morning."

The sleeping mass broke up into seven separate figures. The women lumbered to their feet and one pair prepared to take the stinking bucket to be emptied. Anna struggled to the edge of the boards trying to put her weight only on her right hand. Her neighbour helped her up. "I'm Nadia. Follow me."

The women were led to the bath house and given fifteen minutes to bathe and use the toilet. Anna was guided through the routine by Nadia and she managed to wash her face in the cold water provided. There was no talking allowed so when they had been returned to their cell, Nadia said to Anna, "We must change the dressing on your hand tomorrow and try to bathe it."

"Will I be able to see a doctor?"

Nadia looked doubtful. "There's a prison doctor, but she's not usually available to us."

"She's there to pronounce prisoners dead after their torture has gone too far," said a gloomy voice from deeper in the cell.

Anna placed her hand almost automatically over her abdomen. So they might not be finished with her yet. She raised her troubled grey eyes to Nadia's face and the older woman saw both Anna's fear and the protective gesture she had made.

"Are you pregnant?"

"Yes."

"Then you know you must try to be as calm as possible, for the baby's sake. How far along are you?"

"Just over five months."

"Then the most dangerous period has passed, but you must still be careful."

Nadia's kind words were interrupted by the arrival of breakfast. A thin gruel was thrust through the waist-high rectangular gap in the door and Anna made herself eat every drop of her portion.

Nadia looked on with approval. "Good. You must try to keep your strength up."

Anna looked into the eyes of her self-appointed guardian. "Thank you for your kindness."

"Try to get some rest now."

Anna lay on the boards and closed her eyes, trying not to worry about being called out for questioning. Instead, she tried to listen for the flutter of the baby's limbs. She felt a far greater dread of the baby's silence and hot tears gathered in the corners of her eyes... Just as she thought she would be unable to hold off from sobbing, there was a tiny tremor. Anna let out a long sigh. There you are! She stroked her abdomen and let her hand lie over the site of the movement. Her baby was still with her.

Sometime later there was the click of the plate being slid away from the spyhole in the door and then a loud rattling as a guard entered, holding the bundle Vera had brought for Anna. It was thrust at her along with needle, thread and three pieces of canvas bearing large numbers stencilled onto them. "Sew these on your clothing. I'll be back for the needle in a few minutes," barked the guard and withdrew.

Anna put the bundle to one side and picked up the needle.

Nadia leaned across and took it from her. "I'll do it for you." She stitched the prisoner number to Anna's coat, skirt and headscarf, so that she resembled the other inmates of her cell.

It seemed to Anna that this ordinary action secured her irrevocably on a road she had not chosen and she wondered if she would ever see her home again. She had not been tried and sentenced, but she knew that others had taken this route before her, disappearing into a Bolshevik limbo.

After the guard had collected the needle, Anna opened Vera's bundle. She found a change of underwear wrapped around a wooden spoon. She blessed her friend as she found a bag of sugar, a small block of butter wrapped in muslin and a whole salami. Anna looked across at Nadia: "I'd like to share these things."

"That's kind of you, but you have your baby to think of."

"I know. But for whatever reason, we're all in this cell together."

"Then keep your food till mealtimes and it'll help to make our rations bearable."

Anna looked round at her companions and they nodded in agreement. Their faces all told similar stories, of shock and grief at being torn from their lives. Anna had gone from her mother's funeral to the meeting in the village hall, not knowing that she might never see her home again.

"Don't do their work for them," Nadia counselled her. "Try to relax and get through each day. If you try to anticipate their next move, you'll drive yourself crazy."

She heeded Nadia's advice, relaxing her jaw and loosening her shoulders whenever she felt them tense up. Her hand continued to throb, but the swelling had gone down as she bathed her fingers in cold water each morning during the toilet visit. She was glad when one of the other women would tell a story to distract them all from their anxieties, but her neighbours in the cell seemed to come and go with no warning. She asked Nadia why this might be.

"They're often moved on to Lviv prison."

"And then?"

Nadia shrugged. "They're sentenced."

Anna looked her question at Nadia who continued, "And they're either shot or sent to Siberia."

"Doesn't anyone ever go home?"

"Not that I've heard about."

Anna lay examining her fate. So she would not be allowed to go home. She tried to reason with herself that there was no one left there. But the pull of her little house and its garden, the life she had led there made the tears sting her nose. Her grief seemed to be composed of the great and the small, from the losses of Katerina and Petro, to Murchik's confusion. She thought of her hidden stores of food and regretted not having had the foresight to tell Halia or Vera where they might be found. Grief struck her again as she contemplated a life without the women she had loved.

"Are you sleeping?" Nadia interrupted her thoughts.

Anna kept her eyes closed, but shook her head.

"You have your baby with you," said Nadia.

Anna nodded and swallowed her tears, but it was hard to do lying down. She sat up and blew her nose, dried her eyes.

Nadia nodded her approval. "Most of us in here have had to leave our children behind. Count your blessings."

And Anna did count her blessings as each new day passed in a reassuring repetition of the previous one. But it could not last forever. As one of her cellmates was taken away for questioning, Anna could not help but shudder. She looked across at Nadia. "I know I shouldn't do their work for them. But he looked so ordinary."

"Which one was it?" asked Nadia.

"I don't know. How many interrogators are there?"

"Several. They take it in shifts if they want to keep you under questioning for several days."

Anna looked horrified. "Days?"

Nadia looked grim. "They obviously went for violence and quick results with you."

"He looked almost normal," Anna said again. "You might even say he was handsome, but his eyes... He looked dead."

"That's Kaposnik."

Anna stopped herself from asking whether he was the worst the prison had to offer. It did not matter. He had broken her hand. She did not want to contemplate further torture. If it was to come, then it would. She turned away from her own troubles.

"Did you meet Kaposnik?" she asked, knowing the euphemism seemed foolish.

"Yes, but I didn't have much to tell. When you only wash shirts for the boys in the woods, you're hardly a threat to the state," Nadia said, smiling a little at the irony.

"I took them food."

"That, too."

"Was your husband…"

"He went in '42 with the *Divizia*. But I had to leave my children."

Anna did not know what to say.

"Three of them. They're only little." She sighed. "The youngest is five, then there's Ivash who's eight and the oldest is ten." She stopped again and swallowed. "They're with my mother."

Anna reached forward and placed her right hand on Nadia's arm. "That's good. That they're with their grandmother."

Nadia turned away to lie on the boards of their beds, her face to the wall.

As darkness fell outside the cell, one of the women saw the moon sailing in the fast clouds of an indigo sky. She began to sing:

"The moon is in the sky, the stars are shining.
Quietly across the sea, a boat is sailing."

The others took up the song, but Anna's throat was full of tears as they sang about the girl in the boat and the Cossack dying of love for her. She closed her eyes and let herself see Petro's smiling face, his bright blue eyes, his generous mouth and those long curls. She enfolded the vision of him in her heart and allowed it to comfort her. Eventually she slept, its balm healing some of her pain.

There was a loud rattling of a key in the lock and the cell door was slammed back against the wall. The women were startled awake, but kept their eyes closed, hoping not to hear their own number. However, it was Anna's number which was called. She raised herself heavily from the wooden boards and stood waiting for further instructions, trying to still the pounding in her chest.

She was marched along the grey corridors and down flights of stairs into an interrogation room, knowing that she had to hold on to her own life and that of her unborn child. She cupped her hands over her belly, but heard the shouted order, "Hands behind your back!"

She waited to be told what to do next and heard other footsteps entering the cell. Kaposnik appeared before her and seated himself on the only chair. It was a straight-backed chair, but he seemed to lounge in it as he leaned back and crossed his legs in an almost feminine gesture. He took a packet of cigarettes from his pocket, shook one out and lit it in a relaxed fashion, keeping his blank eyes on Anna's face.

She waited and tried to remain detached as she made herself meet his gaze.

"We searched for your wall," he said at last. "Beside a derelict house." He watched her. "Very convenient…for you. But no use whatsoever to us."

There was silence.

"What do you have to say?"

"I can't tell you anymore than I already have."

"I think you can. No one else we've questioned left letters to be found. They all passed them on to one other human being, so you must have, too."

"I can't say…"

"Not yet, perhaps," Kaposnik replied, as he blew out smoke and watched it dissipate in the air. He turned to the guard. "Shackle her to the wall."

"Oh no," cried Anna. "Oh no, please don't."

"Why not?" asked Kaposnik.

"I'm pregnant," she blurted out.

He inhaled as he looked at her, a glint in his blank eyes. "That's very interesting."

She stood watching him, torn between a futile hope that he might be gentler with her and terrified that he would not, that she had put her baby in jeopardy for nothing.

"And presumably you want to keep your baby?"

"Yes. Yes, I do."

He looked across at the wall with its chains hanging slack and empty and then he stood up and approached her. He passed the palm of his hand over her abdomen and murmured, "The spawn of an antisocial parasite. Why should I care?"

"Oh please," sobbed Anna, tears flowing down her face. "Please."

"Come," he said gently and took her right hand in his.

She balked, but he tugged her softly. "Come."

She followed him as he led her to the door, but as she realised his intention, she tried to pull her right arm back. He jerked his head to the guard, who gripped Anna from behind and half-lifted her closer to the doorway.

Kaposnik realised he would not be able to make Anna straighten her fingers as before, so he pulled her towards the open doorway. He turned to the second guard who stood in the corridor: "Take her hand!" and then, with one guard on each side of the door, Anna's arm was stretched through the doorway. Kaposnik slammed the cell door with all his strength, snapping Anna's arm above the wrist. Anna howled as Kaposnik reopened the door.

"Shackle her against the wall."

Anna began to scream in agony as first her left wrist was manacled, her broken fingers pounding with pain, then her smashed right arm was slung into the second manacle. Her head swam, but she knew she had to stay upright to save her arm. She leaned her head forward and vomited, retching again and again against the waves of agony which assailed her.

Kaposnik called for water. When the guard brought in a jug, the interrogator threw the water in Anna's face. Her head reeled back in shock and she struck it against the wall.

"Now perhaps you'll tell me," was all she heard. She tried to focus, but her sight was blurred by tears and the water dripping from her hair.

"Who did you take the letters to?"

"I don't know."

"You do."

"I don't know," she pleaded.

"Let me remind you: you're still pregnant," announced Kaposnik calmly.

Anna groaned. "I don't know her name. I was never told."

"But you know where she was."

Anna bowed her head, sobbing.

"Where did you take the letters?"

Anna continued to sob like a child, giving full vent to her sense of injustice.

"Go ahead," she heard him say and looked up to see the guard raising Kaposnik's cane over his shoulder, his eyes on her belly.

"No!" she screamed. "Zarvinskiy Street."

"What number?"

"Twenty-eight," and she let her head fall forward again as she wept inconsolably.

"And..."

Anna shook her head to and fro. "That's all I know. I never saw anyone else."

"Describe her."

Anna hiccupped and tried to swallow her tears. "Young...dark hair..." And then like a photograph in her mind: "White blouse, smart skirt." As if realising her betrayal anew, she began to cry again, weeping for the loss of her honour. They had been right not to trust her.

"Take her back to her cell," said Kaposnik in disgust.

She screamed again as her broken arm and fingers were roughly released from the manacles and she was half-carried, half-dragged by the guards back to her cell.

She was thrust into the group of anxious women and Nadia led her to the side of the bed. She helped Anna down and saw the bloody mess of Anna's right arm. Anna groaned and one of the women passed Nadia a cloth, which she had moistened from their precious daily ration of water. Nadia wiped her face and crooned to her as Anna dipped in and out of consciousness.

When the orderly brought their thin porridge, Nadia said, "This prisoner needs to see a doctor. She's pregnant and she has a broken hand and a broken arm."

The orderly glanced at Anna's pale face glistening with a sheen of sweat and nodded. However, several hours passed before she was collected again by the guards. As they called her number, she sobbed, "No! Not again, please!"

One of the guards snapped at her, "We're taking you to see the doctor. Stand up."

Nadia helped her to her feet and Anna stumbled out of the cell after the guards.

She was led to a bright clean surgery where she stood swaying in the centre of the room. The doctor was a short, stocky woman with an uncompromising haircut and eyes, which, had Anna been able to look, would have told her that this woman had seen much, but despite her brusque manner, she recognised a patient who was about to faint. She ordered the nurse to help Anna onto an examination couch.

The doctor examined Anna's right arm first, her fingers feeling along the bones for the break. The arm was swollen below the elbow and the skin had been broken by the slamming of the door. The doctor announced that she thought both the radius and the ulna were broken. "This will need to be cleaned and set," she said to the nurse at her side. Then she lifted Anna's left hand. "Remove these rags and let's have a proper look." She made a note on a chart while the nurse cut away the cloth from Anna's fingers. When Anna's hand was clear of its bindings, the doctor took her left wrist and began to search for breaks and immobility. "The metacarpals all seem intact," she murmured and then moved on to the fingers. "The thumb is intact, but the four fingers all have breaks in the phalanges." She looked at Anna. "When were these fingers broken?"

"I'm not sure. A few days ago," replied Anna.

"They need to be cleaned and set, too," the doctor informed her subordinate. She turned to Anna. "And I'm told you're pregnant."

"I think so."

"What do you mean, you think so?"

Anna eyes filled with tears. "Sometimes I can't feel my baby move."

"How many weeks do you think you are?" persisted the doctor.

"About twenty-two, twenty-three…"

"Alright," said the doctor. "Let's lie you down and I'll examine you."

Anna's clothing was loosened and her skirt lifted to her waist. The doctor approached her patient calmly, but Anna's heart pounded with fear and apprehension, both of which evaporated like mist as soon as the warm dry hands of the doctor were laid on her abdomen. The doctor's expert hands explored the swelling area gently but firmly; then she turned to pick up a wooden implement about fifteen centimetres long. Anna regarded it fearfully, but the doctor said, "Nothing to be afraid of. I'm just going to listen for your baby's heartbeat."

Anna raised her head to watch the doctor place the open end of something which resembled a fluted wine glass against her skin. The instrument rose to a thin stem and ended in a flat disc, which was also open. The doctor placed her ear against the disc and listened. Anna wanted to hold her breath as she watched the doctor choose another location for her instrument and then listened again. She raised herself up and glancing at Anna, announced, "Your baby has a regular heartbeat. That and your size suggest that, as you say, you are about twenty-three to twenty-four weeks' pregnant."

Anna let out a great sigh of relief. Her baby was still with her. She was told to sit up and the nurse helped her to dress herself again. She sat obediently while her arm and fingers were splinted and dressed, although she could not always control her cries of pain. The nurse was not especially cruel, simply detached, as she helped repair another broken body.

When the dressings were complete, the doctor turned to the nurse. "Give her a sling for the arm. Try to keep both limbs elevated if you can," she said to Anna with the ghost of an ironic smile. "And try to keep them clean. If you remain here, I'll recall you in a week's time." She let the uncertainty hang in the air for a moment and then added, "I can't give you either antibiotics or painkillers as you're pregnant, but I can ask that your ration be increased. If they move you, make sure you tell them that you're pregnant. You're entitled to a larger ration until the baby's born. And once those fingers have healed, exercise them to regain strength and function."

Anna tried to absorb the information she was being given, but the pain had made her too light-headed to do more than give a feeble nod.

One morning, after breakfast, her number and Nadia's were called.

"Get your things!" they were told and Nadia quickly bundled up her own few possessions, and Anna's, and the two women shuffled out onto the corridor. They were taken down to the courtyard and, after a moment's pause in which they were able to smell the fresh cold air, they were loaded into the back of a truck with separate compartments for each prisoner.

Nadia placed Anna's bundle at her feet, "Just in case," and was locked into the cubicle next to her. Anna leaned back in the darkness and tried to still her heart yet again. She told herself that this seemed a more organised movement of a group of prisoners and that, reduced as she was to a number, there was no longer a spotlight on her in particular. Besides, she had no more to tell.

Chapter 26

The journey seemed to take several hours, but Anna knew nothing of her surroundings until she heard the motor of the vehicle being cut after they had come to a halt. She heard the banging of the doors at the back of the van and then keys rattling in locks as the prisoners were turned out of their coffin-like spaces. They were hustled out of the van by women in NKVD uniforms and lined up in the enormous snow-filled yard. Anna looked around, almost in wonder, at the barracks surrounded on all sides by brick walls, higher even than those in Ternopil. There were sentry boxes on all sides of the courtyard and guards walked the perimeter with their German Shepherd dogs tightly leashed. The snow swirled in the floodlights of the dark November day. She blinked against the flakes and was nudged into line by one of the guards. She seemed to surface, as if from a deep sleep, and stood hunching her shoulders against the cold as Nadia took her place beside her. The prisoners were marched between numerous brick buildings towards the barracks, where they paused.

"First four in here," barked a guard after consulting her clipboard.

Four women entered their appointed barrack.

"March on!" came the order and Anna led the women to the next barrack.

"Next two in here," snapped the same guard.

Anna and Nadia tried not to glance at one another in relief and they entered the barrack to a sea of faces. The long room was lined with iron bunks on each side with a stove in the central section.

A tall haggard woman strode towards them. "I'm Lidia and I'm in charge here. You can have the bunk by the door."

Anna had begun to turn towards the bunk when Nadia said, "My friend's pregnant. She'll need to be warmer than that."

Lidia looked at Anna's figure. "I can't move people from their beds, but as soon as some of these go, I'll put you somewhere warmer. I'll see if I can get you an extra blanket though."

"Thank you," said Anna.

Anna and Nadia moved towards their allotted bunks.

"It might be warmer on top..." began Nadia.

"I know, but I won't be able to get up there," said Anna dropping her bundle onto the bottom bunk as Lidia approached with an extra blanket. She held it out to Anna.

"Here. This'll have to do for now."

Anna tried to grasp the blanket between her left forearm and her right hand, but it slipped between the two women. Nadia picked it up.

"What's wrong with your arms?"

"Broken," said Anna.

"What? Both of them?"

"My left hand and my right arm," she replied, lifting the affected limbs.

"How…"

"Tortured," said Nadia.

Lidia looked at Anna's pale face again and said, "Get yourselves sorted out here then. I'll tell the others. They're not a bad lot. They're all politicals."

Anna looked confused.

"There are no criminals in this barrack at the moment. We're all here because of what we believe."

Lidia left them and when Nadia had prepared Anna's bed, she lay down gratefully. "Thank you, Nadia. I feel so tired."

"Of course you do. We've had a long journey and you need to rest. Try to get some sleep."

Anna lay with her eyes closed and stopped herself from wondering if this was to be her life now, a series of unannounced and unexplained moves from one prison to another. She made herself unclench her jaw and relax. She dozed, her aching arm resting on her belly, her left hand across her thighs to ease her throbbing fingers.

Nadia woke Anna when the prisoners' supper arrived. The thin broth was accompanied by a hunk of bread and Anna tried to feed herself with her right hand, leaning well over her bowl, but it was a slow process as she spooned the greasy fluid, with its shreds of cabbage, into her mouth. Lidia watched her from across the room, but Anna did not notice as she tried to garner all the goodness she could for her growing baby.

She slept fitfully that night, colder than she had been in the prison cell where the press of bodies had kept her warm. She woke from time to time as she tried to change position to make herself more comfortable, but the combination of the baby and her own tormented limbs made it almost impossible. Despite this, she felt torn from sleep by the abrupt reveille just after dawn.

The morning routine of ablutions, roll call and breakfast passed in a confusing blur for the newcomers. At least the prisoners were not required to work. It would be some months before their Soviet masters created employment for the tens of thousands who would pass through this transit camp. So as the

317

women returned to sit in groups in their barrack, Lidia approached Anna and Nadia.

"I won't ask if you were warm enough last night. I'm sure you weren't."

Anna shook her head. "No, I wasn't."

"Some prisoners might be moved on soon," continued Lidia. "They seem to hold us here for anything from a few days to a few months, so we could have changes in this barrack at any time." She did not add that it might be Anna or Nadia who was relocated.

Anna nodded. "I understand."

"There seem to be a lot of barracks." Nadia's statement was actually a question.

"Yes. More than twenty."

"But what do they do with all these prisoners?" asked Nadia.

"All sent to Siberia," replied Lidia. "They gather us here and put us on trains at the station behind us and then send us north and east."

"I thought I'd heard trains," said Anna. "Siberia..."

Lidia glanced down at Anna's hands. "I'm concerned about your injuries. I can see they're bandaged so presumably you've seen a doctor?"

"Yes, about a week ago."

"Then I'll see if I can get you in to see the doctor here. We've missed this morning's opportunity, but I'll take you tomorrow after roll call."

Lidia was as good as her word. The following morning when reporting the forty occupants of her barrack present, she requested the doctor for one of them. She accompanied Anna to the hospital, a grand name for a crumbling brick building, where Anna was briefly examined, her dressings roughly changed and an order for an extra three hundred grammes of bread and half a litre of milk a day was given for her. Lidia seemed satisfied, but Anna was conscious of the uncaring distance the medical staff in Lviv managed to add to the professional coolness she had experienced in Ternopil. However, she was glad of the extra rations, not only because the thin gruel of the morning had left her hungry, but she knew her baby would not develop fully on such poor fare. She still had some of the precious food brought to her by a prescient Vera, but it would not last much longer and Anna was conscious of her body's more demanding appetite as her pregnancy progressed.

The weeks which took Anna to the end of 1945 passed uneventfully except for one crucial moment when she was called to the offices in the administrative building. Before two officials and an NKVD officer, she was sentenced to twenty-five years of exile and hard labour for anti-Soviet activities under Article 58, which branded her an Enemy of the People. The stentorian tones of the acting judge reverberated within Anna's frame as she tried to absorb the shock. To be sent away from her country to an unknown land for longer than she had already lived; to live among strangers who would have control over every detail of her daily life; and to deal with all of this while being worked to death in some utterly inhospitable place... Anna simply could not comprehend it. The hearing took no more than five minutes.

Nadia received the same sentence. They were not alone. Two of their cellmates were handed the same punishments for religious beliefs which they would not renounce for Comrade Stalin. They were both nuns.

As the New Year approached, there was no sense of anticipation and not even the holy festival of Christ's birth could lift the spirits of the prisoners. On Christmas Eve, the nuns led the carols in Anna's barracks and the women raised their voices together trying to hold back the flood of images of home, as they sang, "*Nova radist stala*":

> "*A new joy came, which had never been experienced before,*
> *The star above the manger lit up the whole world...*"

Anna saw her father leading the Christmas prayers, Katerina placing the plaited bread before them and Yuri's excitement at being allowed to go out with the carol singers after supper. She thought of Petro calling for her in the cold snow and the warmth of his kisses. Her heart ached with the weight of her beloved dead. She tried to join in the carols, thinking of the living, and she sent her love and prayers to Halia and Nina alone in their house, to Vera with her growing brothers, and to Ivan's family, shrunk, like so many others, to half its former size. She could not help wondering if she would ever see any of them again. Twenty-five years was a long time to survive the horrors of Siberia. She would be an old woman and her unborn child, an adult.

It was in the middle of January when the morning's roll call changed the course of Anna's life again. A list of names was read out of those who were to be transported that day to Kazakhstan or Vorkuta or to some other point, thousands of kilometres east and north of Halychyna. There were several prisoners from Anna's barracks travelling to unknown and terrifying destinations, including Anna and Nadia.

They gathered their few belongings quickly, Anna's healed hand and arm allowing her to fend for herself until they reached the railway platform among a column of equally apprehensive women. Here they had to climb up into the cattle trucks which would take them to the frozen camps. There were no steps up into the trucks and the women had to haul themselves up, using the handrails on either side of the doorway.

Anna hesitated and a rough voice shouted, "Come on! We're freezing to death here!"

"We're trying," replied Nadia.

"Not hard enough, love. We can't wait to get to Siberia!"

Anna glanced across at the three women, cackling with laughter. They looked middle aged, but Anna guessed they were probably in their twenties, too.

"I thought it was too good to last," muttered Nadia.

"What was?"

"Being incarcerated without the criminal element."

"Oh," said Anna, looking over at the trio again.

"What is it, love?" called one of them. "Fancy me, do you? I'll do women as well as men."

"Take no notice, Anna. Whores and thieves!"

Nadia and a couple of women nearby helped Anna to hoist herself onto the floor of the truck on her bottom and then she swung her legs up and round, coming up onto her knees. She saw there were some bunks and a couple of very small windows high up in the walls of the truck. Nadia hurried Anna towards the bunks, claiming a lower one for Anna and the one above it for herself. As Anna seated herself on the straw-filled mattress, one of the trio barged towards her.

"Move over, darling. You're far too pretty to be in a bunk on your own."

Anna wanted to laugh, so ridiculous did this overture seem. "I'm pregnant. Hadn't you noticed?"

Her two companions jeered at their friend and the tallest pulled her away. She winked at Anna. "I'm Raisa. Don't worry. You'll be alright with us."

Anna smiled and was not sure whether she was supposed to thank this Amazon or not, for despite their coarse exterior, she did not feel intimidated by the three women. It might even be useful to have them in the wagon. They certainly looked as if they knew how to look after themselves. The prisoners' conditions were Spartan, with only a small stove in the centre of the truck to take the edge off the cold. Besides the inadequate bunks, their only other facilities were a hole in the floor to be used as a toilet at one end of the truck. Raisa's forceful nature might prove to be more of a help than a hindrance.

The bustle and commotion of boarding the train and finding a space to travel among so many prisoners had distracted Anna temporarily, but as the train lurched from its siding, her heart lurched with it. She felt the fizz of fear in her stomach and being unable to peer out of the window, listened to the voice of their fellow prisoners saying farewell to the landmarks of Lviv. Then there was quiet as each woman tried to stifle her sobs.

They travelled east all morning and into the next day too, crossing the breadth of Dnipro, moving inexorably towards the *taiga*, which waited for them with its fearsome reputation. Anna tried to allow the rhythmic clatter of the train to calm her fears and its changes of rhythm formed a soothing cadence as she dreamed away the cold hours of the journey, trying not to think of the hollow distance opening up between herself and home, her little house with its garden, the woods and the river. Her loved ones were all locked in her memory, she told herself, so they would always be with her, wherever her exile took her.

Anna awoke in the thin light of dawn on the second day with a groaning pain in her lower back. She tried to shift her sleeping position, but the band of pain encompassed her lower abdomen, too. She also felt damp, so she struggled up to use the toilet. It was difficult enough for anyone to use, but for Anna, with the bulk of her pregnancy, it was extremely difficult. She found traces of blood and for a moment, felt the clench of fear. She struggled back to her bunk holding on to the wooden uprights as the train swayed.

Nadia lay awake, watching Anna. "Alright?" she whispered, her breath freezing on the cold air.

Anna shook her head. She leaned forward and whispered back, "No. I have pains in my back and I'm bleeding."

"Let's see," said Nadia getting up.

Anna lay down on her bunk and raised her skirt up around her knees. Nadia's only expertise lay in the three births she had experienced herself. She placed her hand on Anna's abdomen and, as she did so, Anna felt the first contraction grip her. Nadia felt it, too, and counted the seconds it lasted, then she set herself to try to count the time until the next contraction, holding Anna's hand firmly and smiling into her wide eyes. When the second contraction came, Nadia gripped Anna's hand again while the pain wracked her. As it subsided, she told Anna, "You've gone into labour, but there's no need to be frightened. You'll be alright. I've had three and survived."

"But it's too early," said Anna, her lips beginning to tremble.

"You're past seven months," Nadia reassured her. "The baby is old enough to survive without you now. It'll be fine. The contractions will gradually come more often. When they come, don't fight them. Just let them have their way. They're bringing your baby to you." She stroked Anna's hand. "Try to relax and save your strength. This won't happen quickly."

"How long?" asked Anna.

"I don't know, but it's likely to take several hours. If you need to get up and move about, you should. It can help you and the baby."

"I don't want to wake the others," began Anna, but Raisa called out, "Too late for that. We're awake."

Anna looked around to see several faces peering at her, nodding encouragement.

"Give her some water," came Raisa's voice again.

Nadia fetched half a cup of water from the barrel, cracking the ice on top first.

"Just take a couple of sips."

Anna did as she was told and the strange day continued in the half-light of the cold wagon as she was subjected to a quickening rhythm of respite between the fierce periods of pain. She tried to walk to ease it, but found it difficult with the swaying of the train, so she knelt beside her bunk, the change of position helping her a little. Anna tried to think of her baby arriving, but could only suppress the terrifying thought that they would not be able to get the baby out of her, so hard did the labour seem.

As another wave of pain rose within her, Nadia rubbed her lower back, trying to soothe her. "Don't fight it."

Anna let herself rise up with it as it flowed over her. She thought she heard her own voice cry, "Mama!", but was swept away by the flood. When she found herself beached behind the agony again, she realised she could hear the gentle singing of a hymn. Several of her fellow travellers were singing to the Virgin Mary and Anna had a vivid memory of the lit candles in the church of her childhood, the smell of incense and the firm grip of her mother's hand.

She lay down on her bunk and let the next wave take her and then she heard Nadia cry, "I can see the head. Next time, Anna, you must push as hard as you can."

Anna lay back on her bunk in the brief lull and tried to follow the instructions being given to her through the drift of pain. As the next wave approached, she prepared to push. In the agonising moments when she was engulfed by pain, she tried to force the baby forward, gritting her teeth, the veins in her neck pulsating. She shrieked aloud as she felt she was being torn in two. That wave passed and as she panted between contractions, someone wiped the sweat from her forehead and stroked back her hair.

Anna felt worn out, but Nadia was still exhorting her to greater efforts.

"One more push might do it, Anna. This time..." and the wave galloped towards Anna and drove her forward. She felt she was pushing with all her might, when there was a sudden easing and a cry of, "There's the head!"

Nadia spoke to Anna. "Your baby's head is out. You should be able to push the baby's body out next time."

Again Anna propelled herself forward in the maelstrom of darkness and was rewarded with a cry.

"It's here! Your baby's here!"

She tried to raise her head to see the tiny sliver of humanity having its mouth emptied of mucus and being slapped for the pain it had caused. There was a shrill cry as the baby was passed into Anna's arms.

"It's a girl," said Anna as Nadia nodded and tucked a piece of linen around her small form. Anna drew the baby to herself, overawed by the miraculous appearance of Petro's daughter. "Hello, baby," she said as she kissed the wrinkled red face and reached for the delicate fingers which curled around her mother's misshapen one. Anna's heart filled with an overwhelming love for this little stranger.

Nadia came back to Anna with some string and tied off the umbilical cord before cutting it with an illicit blade offered by Raisa.

"You need to feed her," came the advice from another bunk and Anna opened her blouse and encouraged the baby's searching mouth to find her nipple. She marvelled at the fact that such a small creature knew what to do to survive, as the baby's sucking caused Anna's breasts to tingle.

Once again it was Nadia who took Anna through the next stage of birth as the placenta was delivered and the contractions gradually slowed and eased as Anna's womb closed down. Mother and baby dozed as the sky darkened. They were woken by the train lurching to a noisy halt and a ration of bread was delivered to each truck. Nadia made sure of Anna's share, although she need not have worried about Anna getting her fair portion of the paltry meal. Their equally hungry fellow-travellers had all been touched by the birth and felt protective towards mother and child.

"What are you going to call her?" asked Raisa.

Anna smiled down at her tiny baby and touched the silky hair. "Zoya. Yes, Zoya."

"That's a good name," commented one of the nuns. "It means "life". That's a good choice."

There was much admiration of Zoya, although those who were already mothers exchanged subtle glances at the baby's size. Their eyes said it all. Not only was this an early baby, but a very small one. Anna did not need to be told that her dainty daughter was susceptible to cold, so she kept her wrapped in the linen cloth, and tucked her inside her own clothing to share her mother's meagre warmth. Anna's thoughts turned to Katerina, dead less than four months and yet that life was now a world away. How she would have loved her grand-daughter...as would Halia. Anna wondered if she would ever be able to let Halia and Nina know that Petro had a daughter. But she hugged her baby to herself. She would have to love her for the father she no longer had and for the family who were either dead or lost to them.

Anna arranged herself for sleep by placing as much padding as she could between herself and the outer wall of the cattle truck. There was no spare bedding, so she pulled up the straw-filled mattress and leaned back against it. She made sure Zoya was upright against her bare breasts and then wrapped as much clothing as she could around the pair of them. She dozed, but was woken by Zoya's cries so she helped her baby find the nipple and Zoya sucked vigorously.

The night crawled by in a bitterly cold procession and Anna felt like the only person left alive with her baby as her fellow prisoners slept through the freezing temperatures. The train rattled along and, despite the soothing rhythm being broken by the occasional deeper note of metal clanking, Anna dozed through the hours of dawn. When she woke again she was surprised by Zoya's lack of warmth. The baby's feet were cold, but more worrying, so was her torso.

Nadia leaned over the side of the bunk. "How are you doing, Mama?"

"Nadia, she feels cold. The baby's cold," whispered Anna.

Nadia climbed down from her bunk. "Let me see," and she slid her hands inside Anna's blouse to feel the baby. "Has she been feeding?"

"Yes, but not for a while."

"Did she feed well?"

"The first couple of times, yes." Anna thought back. "But she didn't suck as hard last time."

"Let's try her now," suggested Nadia and she pulled the blanket off her own bed and put the extra covering around Anna.

Zoya showed little interest in being fed. Anna tried to stimulate her sucking by passing her nipple over the baby's mouth, but Zoya did not respond. She lay quietly in Anna's arms.

Nadia did not want to communicate her fear to Anna, but she knew that the low birth-weight of the premature baby and the sub-zero temperatures they were travelling in were a worrying combination. She glanced around and caught the anxious eye of Sister Laurentia. Nadia nodded to the nun and went to fetch some water from the barrel, hoping it would not all be frozen. She brought it back to Anna and the nun joined them.

"Anna, I'd like to baptise your baby for you," she said.

Anna lifted horrified eyes to the two women. "Why?"

"Just to be sure God will keep her safe. May I?"

Anna barely nodded and the nun touched her water-moistened fingers to the baby's brow and made the sign of the cross, saying, "I baptise you, Zoya, in the name of the Father, the Son and the Holy Ghost. Amen."

As soon as the nun had finished, Anna covered Zoya's head with her clothing and hugging her baby to her, she made herself ask Nadia, "You don't think she's going to survive, do you?"

Nadia felt stricken for her friend. "It's very cold, Anna, and she's so small."

"You think I can't feed her, don't you?"

"No, it's not that. You're still making milk for her, aren't you?"

As Anna nodded, she gulped and tears splashed down her face. "I can't bear it if she doesn't live."

"I know. I know. It's hard," said Nadia hugging Anna to her and stroking her hair. "You've done so well to keep her this long on what we've been eating."

There was a stirring in the wagon and Anna whispered to Nadia, "Don't tell them."

"Of course not. You try and get some rest. I'll get you something warm just as soon as the guards bring our food."

Anna sat back against her pallet and rocked herself and Zoya. She stroked her baby's head with its fine down and kissed her. She did not want the others to overhear her conversation with Zoya, so she whispered into the baby's ear.

"Your daddy would be so proud of you, being a good girl like this. He would. He has a lovely smile, your daddy. I bet you will have, too. And curly hair like his." She crooned to her baby and closed her eyes. She was so tired, she would just rest for a moment.

As the other women observed Anna sleeping, they jerked their heads to Nadia and several of them gathered at the further end of the compartment.

"How's her baby doing?" asked Raisa.

"Not well," admitted Nadia. "She's not feeding and she's very cold."

"Dead?"

"Not yet."

They looked at one another.

"But soon will be," commented Raisa.

"What can we do?" asked another of the women.

Nadia shrugged. "I've given her one of my blankets, but it won't be enough. They both need to be warmer."

Anna stirred and the women separated to their bunks, their hearts heavy for the mother and her tiny scrap of hope.

By evening, Anna had eaten with the other prisoners when the train had stopped from a pot of lukewarm, greasy soup... But Zoya had not fed. Anna knew a newborn baby suckled frequently and she hid Zoya's lack of activity even from Nadia. She pretended to place the completely cold baby against her breast and rocked and hummed as if feeding her new baby. Anna had travelled a little way into Katerina's kingdom. She could not acknowledge to herself that her final reason for living had left her. She would not allow herself to compare all the gurgling babies she had ever seen with her own silent darling. So she rocked and hummed as the women tried to keep warm through the long winter night.

As the light filtered through the two tiny windows high up in the wagon walls, the women stirred and hoped that soon the train would come to a halt and that they would be fed, however poor the rations. Anna appeared to be dozing in an upright position. She was stiff and cold, but when Nadia nudged her urgently, she opened her eyes. Nadia could not help recoiling from the depths of despair which she saw in their dark wells.

"Oh Anna," she cried, leaning forward to embrace the younger woman.

Tears poured down Anna's cheeks as she accepted her friend's comfort, but it could not touch the stone of her heart, nor could it revive the lifeless form Anna still held to her breast.

"Anna, let me take her. I'll wrap her up for burial."

There was a hush in the wagon as the women wept for another lost child.

Anna could not speak. She simply shook her head. She felt as if she would crumble in on herself if her baby was taken from her.

Nadia looked around beseechingly and the unlikely pairing of Raisa and Sister Laurentia came forward.

As Nadia stroked Anna's forehead, the nun said, "Dearest Anna, your baby is so lucky. She is in God's safe hands. She is with her father and her grandparents, who will guide her. You have a little angel, who will never suffer any harm. Nothing can hurt her now."

As she spoke, Raisa lifted the little corpse from Anna's chest with unexpected gentleness. She wrapped her tenderly in the piece of linen Anna had kept for her daughter. Nadia closed up Anna's clothing and tried to bring some warmth to her cold hands while Sister Laurentia led the women in prayer. They prayed aloud in the rhythms they were all familiar with from childhood and went through "Our Father, who art in heaven" and "Hail Mary, full of grace". When they had finished, it was Raisa who began the mournful strains of "Eternal memory", through which the voices broke and returned to the grieving melody as they wept, not only for Anna's lost baby, but for all their losses and loved ones, and perhaps, too, for the loss of home and hope.

As the notes died away, the train clanked and screeched the announcement of a halt and Nadia glanced nervously at Anna and then at Raisa, who made the slightest sign in return. The door of the truck slid back with a bang and two guards struggled forward in their padded greatcoats to lift the urn of thin gruel into the wagon. They lifted it up and pushed it across the wooden planks of the floor as one of them leaned in and called, "Any dead?"

Quick as a flash, Raisa lifted the wrapped corpse, but Anna surprised them all. She leapt forward with a snarl. "No! She's mine!" and tore the baby from Raisa's arms.

"Pass her over here," barked the guard.

Anna backed into a corner like a wild animal at bay, looking from one to another of the faces around her.

Sister Laurentia approached her. "Dear Anna, your baby is with God. She has left her body behind because she has no need of it. So now the body must be buried." The nun held her arms out for the bundle as Anna looked quickly from left to right. Nadia approached her from the side and put her arm around Anna's shoulders.

"You must give her up, my love. She's not with us anymore."

As Anna hesitated, Raisa took the baby and in a couple of swift strides had handed the corpse to the guards. "Take it quickly," she muttered and one of them had the wit and the vestiges of humanity to take the tiny bundle and turn away from Anna, while the other slammed the door closed. As they heard the lock rattle, Anna leapt out of Nadia's arms towards the door, howling: "No!" She thumped her fists against the unyielding door, ignoring the pain in her left hand. "No!" she screamed again as the train couplings clanked and they began to move forward.

"Zoya!" she called. "Zoya!" as she collapsed on her knees in the cold wagon.

"They're taking her for burial," said the woman at the window, but she shook her head at the onlookers, for Zoya's body had simply been placed on the snow beside the track, as the train pulled away into the wastes of Siberia...

Part Four

1987

Chapter 27

The faded blue bus stopped at the mound where the road divided and an old woman stepped down into the dusty road. She was wearing men's brown leather shoes and grey woollen socks folded over at the ankle. Her skirt had once been black, but was faded to a dark grey. She wore a moss-green cardigan over a brown jumper and, though her clothing was unseasonably hot, she did not look warm. Her grey hair was covered with a plain headscarf and she pushed it back from her forehead before reaching into the bus for her luggage, a cloth sack. She hefted her bundle over her shoulder and, thanking the driver, took the quieter fork in the road.

She walked at an even pace, knowing that she had a couple of kilometres to cover before she reached her destination. She drank in the sight of a field of sunflowers, at that point in the afternoon smiling towards the road. Their bright faces gave her a moment's hope, but she had long schooled herself against disappointment. As she passed beneath the cherry trees shading the lane, she glanced up to see how well the trees were fruiting and then paused to look at the ground. It was an unremarkable mixture of dust and stones, rutted where the heavy carts, and cars she assumed, wore it down in wet weather. She gave a little shrug. She supposed every ordinary place in the whole world had, at some time, been momentous for someone. She walked on, reaching houses before she had expected to and saw that some new building was taking place. The newer houses were a stark contrast to some of the older dwellings, which had not received their spring coat of whitewash in many years. She looked into gardens as she passed and saw cucumbers and tomatoes ready for picking. A screech of calls made her look up at a group of swallows diving above the long grass where the green had been. The village hall still stood, its windows boarded up, but there was the sound of someone sawing wood beyond its open door. When she reached the monument to the end of serfdom, it was completely overgrown with ivy and dog roses, busy with bees.

The woman moved her bundle to her other shoulder as she maintained her pace, meeting no one's eyes, despite the oblique glances she received as she passed kitchen doors and garden gates. She walked on to the spot where the lane divided again and looked at the well with its battered roof and worn wheel.

Her stomach churned as she made herself turn to the right, to examine the plot before her. There was little visible of the tumbledown house, overgrown as it was with weeds. The gate had gone and the fence was broken. She stepped into the long grass of the garden and looked to her left. There were the ruins of a barn and beyond that a spreading walnut tree, thick with green fruit. The land beyond the house and garden was a wilderness alive with butterflies.

The woman approached what had once been a house, but, putting her bundle at the spot where the front door would have been, she tried to clamber among the rubble to see what remained.

"Anna! Anna, is that you?" called a woman's voice.

Anna turned from examining the dereliction of her home and squinted in the sunlight at an old woman standing in her gateway. She stepped down from the rubble and peered at the figure approaching her, similarly dressed in a faded blouse and an old skirt with broken shoes, but her headscarf glinted with shiny decorative threads.

"Vera?"

From their weather-beaten, wrinkled faces, the two women broke into smiles and tears, revealing the gaps in their teeth, like aged babies. They lurched towards one another, their tears flowing freely, and fell into each other's arms.

It was many moments before they could speak. They seemed, each, to have held her tears for decades and, now that the seal on that vessel of grief had been broken, their sorrow poured forth. They held onto one another as if they were drowning and sobbed out their anguish into the summer air. But at length, they were spent and mopping up their own and each other's faces, began to smile again as they nodded encouragement to one another.

"Come," said Vera, taking Anna's arm, "there's nowhere to sit here. Let me make you some tea at my house."

Anna glanced at her former home. "I want to rebuild. Do you think they'll let me?"

"Maybe now, yes." Vera took her friend's arm. "Things are changing and the young *starosta* is encouraging new building. But you'll have to get permission."

Anna nodded. "I will." She picked up her bundle and followed Vera out into the lane, where the women linked arms and made their slow way to Vera's house, through her garden, bright with phlox and rudbeckia.

"Do you live here alone?" asked Anna as Vera seated her at the small kitchen table.

"Yes. We lost Mama…and Vasilko…the two younger boys are married."

Anna stroked the plastic cloth on the table. "You've got it very nice," she said, thinking of the decades she had spent without her own hearth.

"Well, you're welcome to share it with me until you have your own house again. Now drink your tea. You've had a long journey."

They did not hurry to tell all that had happened. Both women knew they would have a lot of time to talk. After they had drunk their tea, Anna stood up. "I'd like to go to the cemetery now."

"I'll come with you."

They went back out into the sunshine and crossed the lane, where the sound of hammering told Anna that the church was being restored. It looked a sad affair, but the vigorous calls of the workmen promised renewal. The women entered the cemetery and walked past the older rows of budded Byzantine crosses where hens foraged happily, past the rectangular Soviet headstones to a grassy expanse which had recently been mowed. Anna looked surprised.

"My brothers keep up the mowing," explained Vera.

Anna looked about her. "They're all here?"

"Yes. This part has never been disturbed. And I don't think it ever will be now."

"Good," said Anna. "So...they're all here."

They stood, communing with their dead, while the sparrows flew in noisy gangs from the guelder roses, bright already with their crimson berries.

Anna looked out past the unmarked graves, across the wooded valley to the blue sky beyond and gave thanks to whatever spirit it was which had brought her back to Mikola and Yuri, Katerina...and Petro; and sighed deeply that not all of her dead were there. That somewhere, in an unmarked spot on the vast *taiga*, lay the bones of her tiny daughter. She bowed her head over the memory of Zoya. Not long now, she thought. We'll soon be together, my loves.

There was a shout behind them and Anna turned to see a sprightly old woman, white curly hair flying from her headscarf, bowling down towards her.

"Who..."

"Anna! Anna!" the woman yelled.

"Nina? Is that you?"

The woman was almost upon them, her eyes shining, grinning widely. "I knew you'd come back!"

Acknowledgements

I would like to thank Nastia Shkatuliak, whose tale first inspired me, and my father, Ivan Semak, for telling me some of the stories and showing me some of the places. I would also like to thank Stefan Sianchuk and Maria Korolewycz for generously sharing their memories and Mary Wilson for her medical expertise.

I am very grateful to my helpful and supportive readers: Larissa Dziedzan, Alex Dziedzan, Sonia Iwanczuk, Steve Taylor, Dr Joy Sullivan and especially Zig Dziedzan, who went beyond the call of a husband's duty and read every draft.